GOU

Gould, Judith
The Parisian affair

DUE DATE		K481	23.95
NO 27 04			
DE 11 04			
JA 03 05			
JA 13 05			
FE 23 05			
MR 12 05			
AP 01 05			
JY 03 05			
MY 10 05			
JE 16 05			
AP 16 09			

❧ *The* ❧
PARISIAN AFFAIR

JUDITH GOULD

The
PARISIAN AFFAIR

NEW AMERICAN LIBRARY

NEW AMERICAN LIBRARY
Published by New American Library, a division of
Penguin Group (USA) Inc., 375 Hudson Street, New York, New York 10014, U.S.A.
Penguin Books Ltd, 80 Strand, London WC2R 0RL, England
Penguin Books Australia Ltd, 250 Camberwell Road, Camberwell, Victoria 3124, Australia
Penguin Books Canada Ltd, 10 Alcorn Avenue, Toronto, Ontario, Canada M4V 3B2
Penguin Books (NZ), cnr Airborne and Rosedale Roads,
Albany, Auckland 1310, New Zealand

Penguin Books Ltd, Registered Offices:
80 Strand, London WC2R 0RL, England

First published by New American Library,
a division of Penguin Group (USA) Inc.

First Printing, October 2004
1   3   5   7   9   10   8   6   4   2

(NAL) REGISTERED TRADEMARK—MARCA REGISTRADA

Library of Congress Cataloging-in-Publication Data:

Gould, Judith.
The Parisian affair / Judith Gould.
p. cm.
ISBN 0-451-21274-6 (hardcover)
1. Americans—France—Fiction. 2. Jewelry—Design—Fiction. 3. Jewelry auctions—Fiction.
4. Paris (France)—Fiction. 5. Conspiracies—Fiction. I. Title.
PS3557.O867P37 2004
813'.54—dc22   2004006689

Set in Sabon

Printed in the United States of America

This novel is dedicated to the memory of Lucy Gaston, my own extraordinary Auntie Mame, who showed me the world through her eyes. Without her faith, trust, and unconditional love I would never have become a writer, much less the person that I am today. And in loving memory of others who have touched my life in wondrous ways: Patricia Carpenter, a fragile beauty of great courage; Cassandra "Mrs. Greenthumbs" Danz, an inspiring comedic spirit who made the nation laugh on the *Live with Regis and Kathie Lee* show and without whom Thanksgiving and Christmas dinners will never be the same; Richard Bernstein, a wonderful artist and man whose *Interview* magazine covers were an inspiration for many years; Alberto Silviero, an old friend and accomplished artist; Samuel Wheeler, a loving uncle; and Mark Wheeler, a truly golden boy. All of you will be missed but lovingly remembered.

PROLOGUE

PARIS, 1970

She went to him just as dawn broke on a mist-shrouded Sunday morning when most of Paris was still asleep. Her driver let her out on a deserted side street, and she walked quickly, her high heels creating a staccato click-clack on the damp pavement. In the unlikely event that someone should see her, she wore dark tortoiseshell sunglasses to conceal her well-known violet eyes, and a tan Burberry raincoat over her Mainbocher couture dress. Leaving nothing to chance, she'd covered her hair with a large black hat of sheared beaver, its decorative veil pulled down over the brim to cover her famous face.

She reached the rear entrance of Jules Levant Joaillier, the most exclusive jeweler in the city, passing a faded photograph of Colette taped up in a small window just before his door. A frisson of disgust made her shiver. The famous writer had lived upstairs in the building for years, holding court. *The fat shrew,* she thought uncharitably, putting the image of the heavily made-up, frizzy-haired writer out of her mind.

She pursed her lips into a thin carmine line, and raised her custom-made black calfskin–gloved hand to press the tarnished brass doorbell. In no way did it resemble the highly polished one that mirrored customers at the front entrance in the courtyard of the old Palais Royal.

The door swung open immediately, and Levant himself, a short, plump, immaculately dressed gentleman of sixty-five, ushered her inside with a sweep of his hand. She saw that the hair at his temples had become streaked with a silvery gray and matched the Charvet silk tie he had carefully tied into a Windsor knot. He wore a handsomely tailored dark blue, chalk-striped suit. Savile Row, from the looks of it. His shoes, which gleamed with black polish, were no doubt custom-made by Lobb. These details were of utmost importance to her, for whom appearances were everything. And not for the first time, it reassured her that she was dealing with a man of quality and discretion.   •

His business, as exclusive as it was, was riddled with unsavory types, particularly those who loaned money against jewelry or purchased it outright. Some paid pennies on the dollar, then boasted of their feats to talkative colleagues and customers. A few of these woeful tales had reached her own receptive ears over the years, most frequently when they involved a down-at-the-heels friend who was the object of derision.

That explained why she had come to Jules Levant. Her lawyer, Maître Blum, as notoriously irascible and tough a legal brain as there was in all of Paris, had recommended him to her several years before. She might despise Blum and find her ugliness repellent, but she always took her advice. And, as usual, she had been right. Levant's reputation for discretion was legendary, and his fairness in negotiation—a quality for which the French were not renowned—had made this aspect of his business a well-guarded secret among the plutocrats who sought him out. His name was passed along in sepulchral whispers, and more often than not these hushed confidences were shared among the same clients who had once come to Levant and lavished a king's ransom on the most sought-after jewelry in the world.

A good number of his clientele were trust fund recipients who simply needed a small infusion of cash to tide them over until the next check came in, their lavish spending habits having exceeded their monthly stipends. They left their precious trinkets with Monsieur Levant in exchange for cash, then repaid him for their recovery with a generous but fair amount of interest. Others, like his current client, needed a much more serious injection of capital to replenish their dwindling resources.

In her mind there was no question that the all-important appearances must be maintained to ensure the generous handouts she and her aging, ailing husband received from friends and rich hangers-on. She and her husband were accustomed to living in royal style, and she was determined that would never change.

She would always be grateful—as much as was possible for a woman of her limited emotional capacities—to Maître Blum for sending her to the jeweler. Jules Levant had become a lifeline.

They walked down the short, thickly carpeted hallway. Her head was held high as he indicated a door on the right. He opened it, and she stepped into a small room. There was a magnificent ormolu-mounted, inlaid *bureau plat* in the center of the room. On each of its long sides stood two Louis XV gilt-wood chairs, upholstered in pale beige pink suede. The walls were covered in the same material and completely unadorned with the exception of a large baroque, gilt-framed mirror. The floors were carpeted in identical color. She knew that the pinkish beige color, along with the pale pink lightbulbs in the carefully concealed indirect lighting, was important. It flattered the skin tone and made the jewelry stand out.

Levant pulled a chair out for her, and she sat down. *"Merci,"* she said in her tight, clipped voice. Stationed at one end of the *bureau plat* was the familiar two-sided, revolving mirror, one side for magnification and the other for a normal perspective. Directly opposite it was a large rock crystal vase filled with dozens of long-stemmed red roses, a jarring note in this largely monochromatic space. *How wrong these ridiculous hothouse roses are in this room,* she thought. *But then, most people never get it right.*

He took a seat opposite her and folded his hands on the table. His fingernails were perfectly manicured and painted with a clear, nongloss varnish, and on one plump pinkie, he wore a gold signet ring. His discreet Patek Philippe wristwatch was barely visible inside his French-cuffed shirt, with its gold and enameled cuff links made to resemble a globe. *Fulco di Verdura's design,* she thought. *Levant either shops at the competition or makes clever copies for himself.* She made a mental note to tell the Sicilian count about this the next time she visited his shop in New York City or saw him in Palm Beach.

"How may I help you, madame?" Levant asked, careful to maintain the pretense of not knowing her exalted name.

She lifted the stiff short veil and gently pushed it up onto the brim of her hat. "I have a few pieces of jewelry to sell," she said decisively. She took off her gloves and placed them on the *bureau plat,* then opened the black calfskin Hermès pocketbook that she held in her lap. She extracted a large red leather pouch lined in the softest suede. Placing it on the *bureau plat,* she looked over at Levant with steely eyes.

"These pieces *must* be reset," she stated emphatically. "Otherwise I cannot leave them. They must also be sold separately, broken up in some way, rather than as a matching set." She watched him for a reaction.

"But of course, madame," he replied without hesitation. He opened a drawer on his side of the desk and withdrew a large piece of pinkish beige suede, which he placed on the desk and straightened. "I understand perfectly."

He realized that the jewelry—no matter what she'd brought him this time—might very well be recognized by many of his clientele, or even by the occasional fashionista or celebrity hound who decided to have a look around his premises. The lady might have been photographed wearing them, or a few of his customers might have actually seen the pieces on her at a party or dinner.

Pulling open the drawstring pouch, she began removing its treasures and placing them with careful precision on the suede. She handled them delicately, her red-varnished nails glistening in the light. Levant observed her with a carefully cultivated neutral expression, the merest shadow of a smile on his lips. As she continued to position the jewels, however, he was unable to contain the gleam that came into his eyes. At first it was a spark of mounting curiosity, but then it became a gleam of awestruck wonder. He felt an unfamiliar tremor in his hands and had to refrain from gasping aloud.

Before him lay a magnificent emerald necklace, its setting of ornately wrought yellow gold, its enormous stones of the same size, color, and cut. In and of itself, the necklace was extraordinarily beautiful, but she placed a matching bracelet, earrings, and finally a brooch next to it. Seldom, if ever, had he seen emeralds more closely matched by size and, in this case, the most desirable and valuable dark green color. Yet their magnificence alone, rare though it was, was not what took his breath away. It was their provenance that stunned him into speechlessness.

So it's true, he thought excitedly. *What they've been saying for decades is true. This is proof of it at last!*

If his assumption was correct, he was looking at jewels that, until this moment, he had been uncertain even existed. They had sparked vicious rumors and whispered debates the world over, elicited discreet and disparaging comments from members of royal families in all of Europe, caused quarrels and rifts among the cognoscenti of international high society.

"Oh," she said, training her heartless gaze on him, "I forgot to mention one other detail. The emerald pendant on the necklace must be sold separately. It mustn't be reset with any of the other stones." Although her statement was delivered in a flat monotone, there was no mistaking that she was giving an order.

"Of course, madame," he said again. "We'll be glad to oblige your wishes as always."

He never wore his jeweler's loupe around his neck, thinking the practice common and beneath a professional of his status, but now he wished he did. He would like nothing more than to immediately snatch it up to begin a quick examination of the emeralds, particularly the pendant on the necklace. Instead, he took a deep breath and calmly slid open the desk drawer and slowly took out the loupe as if performing a rite.

She was watching him, seemingly serene and composed, her head held high, as if these were nothing more than ordinary jewels that she'd brought in. *She's a very good actress,* he thought. *Frightfully good. I would hate to be her enemy.*

"Lovely," he said at last, looking down at the emeralds.

She nodded slightly. "Yes."

Still betraying no excitement, he carefully picked up the necklace and began examining its stones one by one, deliberately beginning at the clasp rather than with the pendant. He knew that if his suspicions about the jewelry's provenance were correct, then it was the pendant where he would find his answer. He took his time, looking at each of the stones through the loupe, amazed by their perfection. There were no inclusions, cracks, or other flaws, a rarity in emeralds, and the stones had not been treated with oil, or otherwise, to enhance their color.

"Colombian," he muttered as if to himself, then looked up at her. "The finest."

She nodded again, a tight hint of a smile on her darkly painted lips.

He focused on the necklace again, patiently looking at the next stone. "Important emeralds," he said casually, peering through the loupe, "those of any historical importance, I should say, came from Cleopatra's mines in Egypt." He looked up at her again and smiled. "But of course you knew that."

She nodded again, her expression unchanged. *Why doesn't the fool get on with it?* she thought. *Why must he drag out this tedious process with his inane comments?* But it was part of the game, of course, and she knew that, too.

At last he moved the loupe to the pendant. When he saw the one imperfection in the stone, his hands began to quiver involuntarily, and he laid the loupe and the necklace down on the desk hastily, hoping she hadn't seen his reaction. Tiny beads of perspiration broke out on his forehead, and he dabbed at them with a crisp white linen handkerchief from the breast pocket of his suit.

It is true, he thought, almost faint with expectation. *They do exist, and here they are. With their one defining stone. In my possession.*

Levant was tempted to negotiate the purchase price immediately. He knew without looking that the rest of the emeralds would be flawless like these, but he also knew that he should examine them regardless. The charade must be carried on till the finish. Picking up his loupe, he forced himself to methodically examine the bracelet, then each of the earrings, and finally the brooch before setting it down on the *bureau plat* once more and looking over at the woman.

Her large violet eyes returned his gaze unflinchingly, as flinty a regard as he'd ever seen. *Perhaps they were once beautiful,* he thought, *but living has made them hard.*

"The stones are beautiful," he said, smiling. "Of that there is no doubt." He cleared his throat. "Did you have a figure in mind?"

"Yes," she replied. She opened the pocketbook in her lap and drew out a folded piece of heavy ecru paper and handed it to him.

Levant unfolded the piece of paper and looked down at the figure. *She must have a mind like a calculator,* he thought, *and she also knows her stones. She's even taken into account the fact that they will be sold with no provenance whatsoever. But then,* he reminded himself, *this is not her first trip to me.* He looked back up at her. "I think this is acceptable," he said. "Shall we proceed as in the past?"

"That would be fine," she said.

"Good," he replied. "I'll see to it first thing in the morning. You should have the cash tomorrow afternoon at the latest."

"Very well," she said. She closed her pocketbook and shifted in her chair as she put her gloves back on.

Levant quickly got up and went around to her side of the *bureau plat,* then slid her chair out for her. She rose to her feet and turned to him. "*Merci,* Monsieur Levant," she said, extending a gloved hand.

He took her fingertips in his, and in the continental manner leaned over and made as if to kiss her hand, careful not to touch it with his lips. "It was a pleasure," he said. "Anytime I can be of service."

She withdrew her hand. "I appreciate that," she said. "Now I must go."

She turned to the door, and he hurriedly opened it for her. Then they walked down the hallway to the rear exit.

"Au revoir," he said, opening the steel door for her.

She put her dark glasses on and pulled the stiff little veil down over her face. "Au revoir, Monsieur Levant," she responded, for she knew, as did he, that they were saying their good-byes only for the present. They would meet again. The world-famous lady went through the doorway and, heels click-clacking on the cobbles once again, walked quickly away from the shop.

Levant locked the door and for a moment stood staring down the hallway without seeing anything. *If only I could sell the emeralds as they are,* he thought sadly, *and if only I could provide the provenance. They would be worth millions of dollars.*

Ram hurried from the basement room where the video monitors were housed, and closed and locked the door behind him. Forgoing the elevator— Levant must not know he'd been down there—Ram headed up the staircase to the ground floor. Leaping up the steps two at a time, he rushed up the next flight to his workroom. He sat down on the high stool at his worktable and tried to look relaxed despite his excitement and wildly beating heart. He took a few deep breaths to calm himself.

I can't believe it! he thought. He had heard the gossip about the jewels— everybody had, hadn't they?—but he hadn't known what to believe. So many rumors swirled around the departed woman that it was hard to separate truth from fiction. But from what Ram had seen through the monitors, he was certain that these were indeed the emeralds of legend.

He soon heard the whir of the elevator, then the doors sliding open and Levant's footsteps in the hallway outside his workroom. He bent over the intricate platinum setting he'd been working on, waiting for his boss and mentor to appear.

"Ram," Levant said, coming into the room, the red leather pouch in hand. He smiled at his twenty-year-old protégé, appreciative of his honey-toned Algerian handsomeness and his dark eyes that flashed with vitality.

"Yes, sir," Ram said, looking up at him.

"This is the reason I asked you to come in today," Levant said. He placed the pouch on Ram's worktable. "I have some important work for you to do immediately, so drop whatever it is you're doing. I want the emeralds in this pouch"—he tapped it lightly with his fingers—"taken out of their settings. The settings must be cut up and melted down at once. They're too ornate and old-fashioned to use nowadays. Put the emeralds in the vault. All of them together."

He paused momentarily, a thoughtful expression on his face, then cleared his voice. "On second thought, keep the necklace pendant separate from the others. I think that perhaps it will make a nice ring. We'll decide on new settings for them this week. You can help me choose."

"Yes, sir," Ram said. "I have some drawings of new designs. Maybe you could have a look at them?"

Levant nodded. "Yes, yes," he said. "Of course, my boy. Tomorrow afternoon sometime. I have a little business to take care of tomorrow morning and have to be gone."

"Okay," Ram said. "I'll get started on the settings right away."

Levant went to the door, where he turned and stopped. "And Ram," he said, "don't mention your work today to Solomon. I'd rather he didn't know anything about it." He was referring to his longtime assistant, an excellent repairer and gem cutter and polisher.

"Of course not, sir," Ram said.

Ram watched as Levant left. When he heard the elevator doors slide shut, he opened the pouch and took the emeralds out, then picked up his loupe and looked first at the necklace pendant.

Exactly as I thought.

He slid off his stool and went over to the cabinet where he kept his camera. He got it out, then carefully arranged the pieces of jewelry, adjusted the lighting, and began to photograph them, both together and separately, from various angles, and with various lenses, making certain that the gold settings were clearly visible. When he was finally satisfied that he had the shots he needed, he took the film out of the camera and put it in his briefcase. After he removed the stones he would also photograph the empty settings and the loose emeralds.

From another cabinet he took out one of the shop's signature aubergine quilted suede pouches. When he was finished with his work, he would place the intact gold settings in the pouch, put it in his briefcase, and take it home with him. There, in the tiny fourth-floor walk-up apartment that Levant provided for him, he would secret away the pouch. If Levant ever asked to see the melted-down settings, Ram had an appropriately sized lump of gold to show him. It was only one of many that he'd made from the accumulation of gold that came from the shop's daily vacuuming of the worktables. He'd taken a minuscule portion from the tiny vacuum every day, squirreling it away for just this sort of purpose.

Sitting at his stool again, he adjusted the powerful lights and began removing the emeralds from their settings, a simple but tedious task. *Levant will never know the difference,* he thought. *No one will. And if I bide my time . . .*

As he worked, his mind swirled with possibilities. Thanks to Hannah Levant, the jeweler's wife, gone two years now from breast cancer, he had started working at the shop when he was only fifteen years old. Like her husband, she'd been seduced by his dark handsomeness, his thirst for knowledge, and his polite manners—all this after an initial confrontation that held little promise for friendship, much less their virtual adoption of him.

It had been late at night, and he had been with Ahmed, a friend from the projects, when he first encountered Hannah. He and Ahmed had been wielding cans of spray paint in the quiet lane behind the jewelry shop, defacing the wall with lurid red swastikas. When Hannah Levant stepped out of the door and fearlessly faced him down, Ramtane Tadjer stood glued to the cobbles, his legs unwilling to move, while Ahmed threw down his can and ran away.

Hannah grabbed his forearm with a claw of a hand and pulled him into the shop, where she sat him down and lectured him at length about what he had so mindlessly done. He had no idea what swastikas represented, he confessed. He'd only been following Ahmed's lead. Touched by the seemingly genuine tears of remorse that fell from his huge dark eyes, she had fallen for him that evening. Eventually she and her husband had taken him in, treating him as if he were the son they'd never had.

Five years had gone by since they'd rescued him from the bleak, soulless high-rise housing project on the outskirts of Paris known as les Bosquets. Inappropriately named, the Copses was where many Algerian immigrants like his own impoverished family lived. After he'd lived for weeks in a basement room at the shop—a room he'd gladly made his own—they'd taken him to a tiny apartment in the Marais district on the rue des Rosiers, the heart of the old Jewish quarter. They had showered him with clothing he'd only dreamed of, paid him well, and begun educating him in the business from the ground up. They saw that he had time to finish his secondary education.

At only twenty years of age, he had a formidable knowledge of gemology, jewelry making and design, and the business of buying and selling top-quality merchandise. Whether working on the selling floor or in the workrooms, he had quickly become an expert, absorbing everything they'd passed along, easing into their world. He seemed born to it.

After Hannah's death, Levant promised him a share in the business someday, but for Ram that someday couldn't come soon enough. He had a ravenous craving for a magnificent *hôtel particulier* like Levant's. It was very close to his tiny fourth-floor walk-up in the Marais but might as well have been a million miles away. He coveted the chauffeured Bentley that carried Levant to and from the shop while he had to peddle a secondhand bicycle. But more than anything else, he wanted to have the power and status that were Levant's because of his position at the pinnacle of the world of rarefied jewelry.

He knew that he himself was regarded by some of the customers and many of the elegant citizens of Paris as the Other—an Algerian, from the projects, with no breeding, no money, and no prospects. Ram felt his otherness acutely and had sworn to change that. He was going to be richer and more powerful than Levant someday.

These jewels are going to help me get that and a lot more, he thought as he worked, *and the famous lady's bad luck is my good fortune.*

He began removing the necklace's pendant from its setting, but stopped and looked at it with his loupe once more. A smile spread across his sensual lips.

My road to true riches, he thought, *beyond anything even this shop could ever provide.*

Chapter One

New York, 2004

Allegra Sheridan sat at her desk, bent over a drawing pad that was perfectly centered on its expansive surface. She was lightly sketching in the details of a new design for a pendant. With a barely audible groan of exasperation, she upended the pencil and began furiously erasing the delicate lines she'd just roughed in. *Hopeless,* she thought with a grimace. *Completely hopeless.*

As hard as she tried, she found it impossible to concentrate. She just couldn't put on paper the beautiful pendant that loomed in her imagination. She brushed an errant strand of her lush strawberry blond hair from her eyes and sat staring at the drawing pad, as if to magically conjure the design.

Is there anything worse than a blank page? she wondered.

It was unusual for her to feel as defeated and anxious as she did, but she knew why. The telephone on her desk seemed accusatory and intimidating in its silence. She'd told herself time and again that there was nothing to fear, that when the call eventually came the news would be exactly what she wanted to hear. It *had* to be.

Nevertheless, she couldn't remember when she'd been this distracted. But, she reminded herself, it wasn't every day that her immediate future, and that of her business, hung on the news that would come sometime that day.

The telephone rang, and Allegra nearly leaped out of her chair. She grabbed the receiver but hesitated before picking it up. *Don't appear to be too anxious,* she told herself. Two rings. Three.

She lifted the receiver. "Atelier Sheridan," she said in the most cheerful voice she could muster. She took a deep, calming breath.

Jason Clarke, her assistant, knew that she was overwrought about the telephone call—he was no less so—but he couldn't resist looking over at her, knowing that doing so could make her more nervous. Before she frowned and pointedly turned away from him, he saw Allegra's expression cloud over and a distinct clenching of her jaw.

Uh-oh, he thought. *If I'm not wrong, that's Fiona Bennett, and there's definitely trouble in the air.* He glanced out of the corner of his eye and saw Allegra's shoulders slump. *Oh, jeez. It must be really bad news.* He tried to refocus on the jeweler's loupe and examine the pigeon blood ruby he held with tweezers. To no avail. Like Allegra's, his immediate future hinged on the news, and as he sat gazing at the cabochon ruby's low luster, he realized that he was actually seeing nothing at all. If there were inclusions or other imperfections beneath the ruby's surface, he would surely miss them. He put the ruby down on the worktable's wooden bench pin and let the loupe fall against his chest, where it dangled on its chain. His attention was now fully devoted to Allegra's end of the conversation, and he attempted to divine what Fiona Bennett was saying on the other.

Allegra, her back still to him, listened raptly. When she spoke, it was in a firm voice that belied the nervous anxiety she'd felt all day. She didn't want Fiona to hear the terrible vulnerability she felt, nor did she want her to be privy to Allegra's crushing disappointment or the tears that threatened her eyes.

"Oh, of course, Fiona," she heard herself say steadily. "I know you did the best you could, but—" She emitted a short, nervous laugh. "I guess that's that, isn't it?"

She listened a few moments longer, said an upbeat good-bye that was summoned out of long practice at putting a good face on a bad situation, then slowly and quietly replaced the receiver in its cradle. She stared off into space, her beautiful blue eyes lackluster.

Jason wiped his hands on the apron he wore, then took a sip of the mineral water on his worktable. "You want to talk about it?" he asked softly, looking over at her.

Allegra shook her head. "There's really nothing to talk about, Jason," she replied in a small voice, gazing blankly toward the windows. "That was Fiona. They've decided to pass on the jewelry."

"Damn." Jason exhaled a noisy stream of air. "Did she give you a reason, Ally?" he asked. He was one of the few people who used this diminutive form of her name.

She sat back down at her desk and picked up the wheatgrass juice that she'd bought earlier in the day. After taking a long sip, she held the glass in her hand, unconsciously swirling the liquid around in it. "Yes and no," she said, her eyes still faraway and unfocused.

"So what did she say?" Jason asked, growing impatient. "What kind of excuse did she come up with?"

She shook her head as if to rid it of the oppressive effects of rejection. "It's the same old stupid nonsense. Except that Fiona's come up with a little variation on the theme this time."

She set her glass of juice on the desk with a loud bang, straightened her spine, and tossed her head back regally. " 'Oh, Allegra, dahling,' " she mimicked, assuming a haughtily drawling English accent, " 'we adore your work. Naturally. Doesn't absolutely everyone? But we've decided we can't carry your beautiful line. It's simply *too* interesting for us.' "

"Je-*sus!*" Jason laughed loudly, then quickly put a hand over his mouth. "Oh, I'm sorry," he said, "but I can't help it. What a lame fucking excuse!"

Allegra's big eyes had lost their dullness and focused on him with a glittering fire. "Have you ever heard such crap in your life?" she spat. " 'Too interesting'?" She hit the desk with a fist. "I mean, how do you even respond to something like that?"

"You can't," Jason said. "Why couldn't the bitch just say, 'No, we're not buying at the present time'? It's like they have to say something to soften the blow."

"Well, Fiona's way of softening the blow doesn't make it any easier to accept the reality," Allegra said. She emitted a sigh. "And the reality is . . . well—" She hesitated a moment before continuing. "The cruel reality, Jason, my dear, is that we're going bust fast."

"Is it really that bad?" he asked, looking at her questioningly.

She nodded. "Yes, Jason. At this point I've got nearly everything tied up in inventory. Gemstones and gold and platinum and silver." She took another sip of her juice and set the glass back down. "What the hell am I going to do?"

She looked at him beseechingly, knowing that he didn't have the answer. "What are *we* going to do? I don't even know how much longer I'll be able to pay your salary." She slammed a fist against the desk again. "Damn it all. First, we lose our biggest account when Ponte Vecchio shuts down, and now we lose this."

Jason leaned back in his chair and propped one leg atop the knee of the other, careful not to disturb the small cabochon rubies that were sprinkled over the worktable's small bench pin. He ran his hands through his disheveled dark blond hair, then looked over at her, his gentle brown eyes full of concern.

"Listen, Ally," he said. "Something's going to work out. It always does, doesn't it? We've made it through tough times before. We have a guardian angel, remember?"

"Yes," she agreed, "but this time I really don't know, Jason. This time it's going to take a miracle to bail us out." She drummed her fingers against the desktop nervously. "I feel like we're back where we started." She propped her elbows on the desk and slumped forward, putting her chin in her hands.

"But we're not," he said emphatically. "We've come a long way."

She ignored what he said, her eyes taking on a faraway look. "A few lean years," she said, her voice wistful, "and then along came some recognition for our work. A few profitable years, and all that wonderful dot-com money that people had to spend. Now Silicon Alley's gone up in smoke. Poof!" She flung her hands up into the air in an extravagant gesture, then let them fall onto the desk.

She turned and looked at him with sad eyes. "And along with it the best of our business. I'm beginning to feel like my luck is definitely running out."

"No, Ally," he said loyally. "I don't believe that. Your work is beautiful; everybody thinks so. It's just getting it to the right market, the right way. You've already made something of a name for yourself. You've even got a cult following, and it's only going to get better with a little more time."

"Well," Allegra said with unerring logic, "time is something I don't have too much of right now. The landlord's not about to let the rent slide because I need time. You know what a shit he is." Her voice rose in pitch as she became more anxious. "And the gemstone dealers aren't going to wait on their money, are they? Or the metals dealers. Can you picture that?" Tears suddenly threatened again, and her voice broke.

Jason resisted the impulse to go over to her and put his arms around her comfortingly. He expelled a sigh of frustration. Every instinct he had told him that she needed a helping hand, but there was little he could do, financially or otherwise. As he'd learned from years of working with her, she had a streak of hardheaded independence that made it impossible for her to either ask for or receive help. He didn't think he'd ever met anyone who was as determined to do everything for herself as Allegra.

And now, he thought, *I might be victimized by her stubborn independence. Because if her ship goes down, I'm going to go with it. Then what do I do?* He propped his elbows on the worktable and rested his chin on interlaced fingers, considering his alternatives. Slowly his lips spread into a smile as he remembered an encounter with Cameron Cummings the other day. The well-known jewelry designer had asked him if he'd ever considered leaving Allegra and told him to get in touch with him if he was interested in a job. *Well, I might be doing just that, and a lot sooner than I would've ever thought. Especially if Allegra goes bankrupt.*

He watched as she got up from her desk and quietly, thoughtfully walked toward the windows, a somber but elegant figure. *Funny,* Jason thought. *"Elegant" was the word Cameron had used.* Cummings had told him how crazy he was about Allegra's designs. "They're as elegant as she is," he'd said, "and she's the best designer in the business. I wish I had her talent." Then Cameron had laughed. "Or her designs." It occurred to Jason that maybe . . . just maybe . . . there was a way to save Atelier Sheridan after all.

"Ally?" he softly called over to her.

She turned and looked at him. "Hmm?"

"I saw Cameron Cummings the other day."

"And?" She looked at him with raised eyebrows.

"He said he's crazy about your designs," Jason told her.

"Good for him," she replied in a voice tinged with sarcasm.

"What I was thinking," Jason went on, "is that maybe . . . uh, you know, you could offer to sell him some of your designs. Maybe—"

"Stop right there," Allegra snapped. "No way am I going to sell my designs to Cameron Cummings. Or anybody else for that matter. So don't mention it again, Jason. Don't even think about it."

"Sorry," he said sheepishly. "I didn't mean to offend—"

"Forget it," Allegra said. She turned back to the big window and stared out over the rooftops of Soho to the Hudson River and the setting sun in the distance. It was a wintry sun, almost concealed by the gray haze, only the faintest hint of pink coloring the cloud cover.

Slowly turning back to Jason, she said, "Why don't you go on home? I think I'd like to be alone for a while."

"Are you sure?" he asked. "I can stick around for—"

Allegra shook her head. "No, Jason," she said, "go on home. I really want to be alone now. There's nothing to stick around for. Maybe we'll talk later. Okay?"

"Whatever you say, Ally," he replied with a sigh. He reluctantly rose to his feet and took his apron off, shaking it over the large suede catchall suspended beneath his work area, then draped it neatly over the back of his chair. At the door he took his jacket off the coat hook and put it on, then shouldered the backpack that hung on a hook next to it.

Opening the door, he turned to Allegra. "See you tomorrow," he said.

" 'Night, Jason," she said. "And I'm sorry to be so gloomy."

"Ally," he replied, "I just know it's going to get better. Some—"

"Later, Jason," she said in a determined voice.

"Okay," he said, finally acceding to her wishes. He quietly closed the door behind him as he left.

When he was gone, Allegra turned her gaze back to the window, but all of her attention was focused inward, on the storm of emotions that the telephone call had stirred up. She realized that she had reached a point in her career where she had to make a tough decision.

Should she try somehow to weather yet another financial crisis and continue to work? Or should she admit defeat and find a nine-to-five job to support herself, working on her jewelry in her spare time?

The thought almost made her physically ill, as it had so often in the past. *Why do I have this need to prove myself?* she wondered. *Why is it I can't be content with a job designing for a brand-name jewelry house? Why is it I can't be happy designing jewelry that can easily be mass-produced?*

Over the past few years she'd had several opportunities to sign on with one major jewelry manufacturer or another, but she had always turned down these offers, regardless of how lucrative they were or how desperately she needed the money. She preferred being able to control the production of her own designs and was protective of her independence.

In the past, she'd also been told by more than a few cooing department store buyers who loved her designs—buyers like Fiona Bennett—that they would order huge quantities of her work. But Allegra had long since re-signed herself to the impossibility of filling such orders; her designs were virtually impossible to reproduce inexpensively. And damned if she was going to let factories in China or elsewhere make cheap facsimiles of her jewelry, substituting inexpensive metal for gold or platinum and man-made stones for real gems. She'd seen other jewelry designers do it, and their work had become unrecognizable.

Ideally, she had hoped to land at a big-name jeweler like Buccellati or Bulgari or Verdura with her own label, much as Elsa Peretti and Paloma Picasso had done at Tiffany. She had envisioned ads in fashion magazines and newspapers many times: *Allegra Sheridan for Verdura.* Or Bulgari. Or whatever. But that simply hadn't happened. She had come to New York with a lot of talent and ambition, but she didn't have a grand family name or the kind of connections that might make her a shoo-in at a topflight jeweler. That was not to denigrate the work of Paloma Picasso or Elsa Peretti. She appreciated their designs and applauded their success, but she wondered if they would've been able to succeed on the level they had without their names and who they knew.

So here I am, she thought as her gaze shifted northward, toward the West Village, *a victim of my own standards. Going broke so nobody can see or wear my jewelry.*

What she needed was a retail outlet, a very expensive proposition in New York City. When people saw her jewelry used in magazine fashion spreads, they should be able to hop in a taxi and go to the shop where the jewels came from. In her case that was impossible. They had to call a tele-phone number and make an appointment—a practice, she had long since discovered, that eliminated a vast majority of the buying public. Forget those who made impulse purchases. There was no shop to feed their habit. But she had spent a small fortune on assembling the necessary tools of her trade, and the first few years paying off those purchases. Opening a shop had been an impossibility.

She was so lost in thought that when Todd quietly crept up behind her and put his hands on her shoulders, she was startled. "Oh, jeez, Todd," she said, jerking out of her reverie. Without turning around, she instantly recognized the feel of those big hands on her shoulders and the distinctly masculine aroma. "I didn't hear you come in. You scared the daylights out of me."

"Sorry," he said. "I didn't mean to." He gently massaged her shoulders and planted a kiss atop her head. "I have an idea," he said, looking out at the lights of the city twinkling in the quickly descending winter darkness.

"What's that?" she asked, enjoying his attentions to her weary shoulders and back.

"Let me treat you to an extravagant dinner," he said, his voice a seductive whisper. "Just the two of us. Hell, Ally, that'll make us both feel a whole lot better."

Allegra's ears perked up, and she turned to him and looked up into his lively green eyes. "You saw Jason on your way up, didn't you?"

He nodded. "Yep," he said. "Told me the news. I'm sorry."

"I don't want to talk about it now," she replied.

He shrugged and smiled. "Fine. You won't hear another word about it from me if that's what you want."

"Good," she said. "Anyway, you can't afford to take us to an extravagant dinner, and you know it. But it was sweet of you to offer."

"I'll put it on my card," he offered.

"You mean it's not maxed out?"

"Not yet," he said.

"No, Todd," she said, shaking her head. "I won't let you do this. I don't want to feel guilty about using up the last little bit of credit you've got left. You might need it."

Todd grinned mischievously. "Aw, so what? Come on, Ally," he cajoled, holding her arms in his big hands. "Where's that daredevil I used to know, huh? Where's that beautiful girl who was never afraid to take chances?"

"She's a woman now," Allegra said. "Nearly a spinster, in fact. With hardly a sou to her name."

"More the reason to go out and paint the town," he said. "With the straits we're in, what difference is a few dollars on a credit card going to make? Besides, I've got some money coming in soon."

Allegra laughed helplessly. "That's great logic, Todd," she said, reaching up and ruffling his raven black hair.

"Then you'll do it," he said, the smile widening on his face, exposing perfect white teeth.

She nodded. "I shouldn't, but . . . I will."

"That's my girl," he said, tapping her playfully on the butt. "We'll have a blast. We'll both forget about work tonight. No worries. No cares. Just the night and the food and the drinks and the dancing."

"Oh, dancing, too?"

"Why not?" he asked. "What say we dance all night long? We'll club hop."

She laughed again. "You're crazy, Todd Hall, and I guess that's why I love you so much." She reached up and kissed the tip of his nose. "Sometimes, anyway."

His radiant smile didn't change, but Todd felt his heart leap into his throat. As long as he'd loved her, it still gave him a thrill to hear her say those words. He wrapped his arms around her and drew her against him. They kissed long and deeply, his hands stroking her back tenderly.

"I love you, too, Ally," he said when their lips parted. "And not just sometimes."

Their relationship had been long and fraught with trouble—battles, separations, and dramatic reconciliations—principally because of his wandering eye. But he was trying to convince her that he had that under control now. His insatiable sexual appetite was all in the past, he'd sworn. He wanted her more than ever.

Allegra was a creative designer, gemologist, jewelry maker, and salesperson all rolled up into one strikingly beautiful and very sexy package. Todd, on the other hand, had no interest in gemology as such, and none whatsoever in the rarefied world of custom jewelry making that she thrived in. He found most of her customers unbearable, as he did many of his father's architecture clients and his mother's painting aficionados.

After doing time in army intelligence, he had taken a job as an investigative reporter. While he excelled at his work, he quickly grew weary of the newspaper bureaucracy and politics. He found that he had stories "killed" on a political basis or, on the other hand, given unmerited feature space because his subject happened to be a pet target of a high-echelon editor at the paper.

Finally, he had settled into something he loved. He had become a developer in downtown New York, turning old industrial buildings into luxurious loft apartments. He'd fallen into it almost by accident. When he'd discovered that rents in the downtown neighborhoods like Soho and the East Village were skyrocketing to astronomical proportions, he'd borrowed the money from his parents to buy a small, derelict building. Then, armed with architectural plans drawn up by his father, he'd overseen the conversion of the building into loft apartments. As money began to come in, he invested it in others, repeating the process until he'd acquired a considerable fortune in downtown real estate. While he had to some degree rejected the elite environment of his parents' world, the exposure to arts and crafts that he had grown up with served him well now. He had developed an eye for quality and that which intrigued. He was happy overseeing the rebuilding of the properties, although the work was all-consuming and had its headaches. There were times when he had cash flow problems, as he did right now, because of the heavy commitments, but he knew that in the long run his efforts would pay off handsomely.

Over the years, he'd made quite a reputation for himself as a hip, young developer with devastatingly handsome looks, and his work garnered its share of publicity in the newspapers and magazines. While he'd always been sought after by the opposite sex, he quickly became a major babe magnet in New York City, attracting beautiful, sexy, and sometimes rich young women who threw themselves at him as if they were offerings to some pagan god. And Todd had succumbed. More than once or twice. He'd sown wild oats far and wide.

These meaningless flirtations, one-night stands, and brief affairs had taken a toll on his relationship with Allegra. Besides which, he freely admitted, he'd been commitment-phobic. He had no ambition or desire to harness himself to the kind of tempestuous relationship he'd seen in his parents' marriage. However, as the years rolled by, he had grown weary of brief, meaningless affairs.

"What do you say I go home and shower and change, then meet you back here?" he said.

"Good plan, my man," she replied, poking his chest with a fingertip.

"Be back in, say, an hour. Hour and a half. Okay?"

"I'll be ready."

"Okay," Todd said. He took the gloves out of the pockets of his old, worn leather jacket and put them on. "Ciao," he said. "Be back *tout de suite*." He kissed her again.

"Ciao."

Allegra watched as he left the workroom and disappeared down the hallway to the front door. She locked the door behind him, then turned and stood glancing around the workroom. Its floor-to-ceiling shelves were stacked chockablock with see-through plastic boxes containing lengths of gold, silver, and platinum wire; sheets of platinum, silver, and gold; casting grain; semiprecious beads and stones; handmade molds; rubber and plaster for molding; and countless tools—all the trappings of a highly organized jewelry maker. And near the German-made worktable, there were many different kinds of pliers, hammers, and measuring rings. The various machines and tools used in the work drew her attention: rolling mills, flex shaft drills with foot pedals to polish and grind, gravers with different blades, stone-setting burrs, beading tools, a vulcanizer, wax injection equipment, and polishing lathes. It amounted to quite an inventory and an expensive one.

On bookshelves, there were catalogues from the various purveyors of metals and gemstones she dealt with, as well as those from the machinery manufacturers and toolmakers. Her treasured drawing books, many of them expensively hardbound, made a neat row along the shelves in their own bookcase. They contained the countless detailed drawings she'd made of the jewelry she had designed and wanted to see brought to life. In some cases the drawings had become reality.

On the walls hung the drawings of a few of her favorite pieces of jewelry, alongside photographs of the finished products. Over the years several customers had thought her drawings were works of art in and of themselves and had wanted to purchase them, but Allegra had always refused, preferring that no one else saw what she considered rudimentary work in the process of producing an exquisite final product.

What hubris, she thought now as she looked around. *But I never imagined then that I would need money as much as I do now.*

Jason's worktable caught her eye, and she frowned, then crossed to it quickly. "Damn it," she swore aloud, before realizing that it was her fault that he'd left his work area in such a mess. Had she not ordered him to leave, she would be very angry with him and justifiably so. Shimmering atop the wooden bench pin of his worktable was a small fortune in cabochon rubies, thousands of dollars' worth of small stones that could easily vanish.

She peered down closer at the pin to see if she could detect any metal shavings or stone chips, but there were none. She scooped the rubies up and put them in a suede pouch, which she placed in the ugly old safe that sat in a corner in plain view.

She kept a store of her most valuable semiprecious and precious stones in it, knowing that with its old combination lock it was no more than a deterrent to an enterprising thief. The rubies tucked away, she shut the safe's heavy door, then twirled the brass lock around several times.

Rising from her crouch and stretching her arms ceilingward, she decided that tomorrow she would have to remind Jason about their rules, despite her having caused today's distraction. Rule number one in the atelier was that at the end of the day each of them had to stow any valuable gemstones in the safe, then vacuum up any precious-metal shavings from his or her worktable. The contents of the vacuum were regularly emptied into containers for each of the metals. The metals, whether gold, platinum, or even relatively inexpensive silver, were eventually returned to the refineries from which they'd come. The refineries bought them by weight. It might seem a miserly practice, but it wasn't: at hundreds of dollars an ounce for platinum and gold, this waste had added up to a substantial amount of money over the years. Behind the polishing lathe, there were even fans that sucked up the dust and metals produced by polishing. This so-called waste was sent to the refinery.

She took a final glance around and caught sight of a catalogue from Dufour, the auction house in Paris, that she'd placed atop a stack of magazines and catalogues to go through. *Magnificent Jewels,* the catalogue was titled. She picked it up, deciding that she would flip through it while having a bath. Taking a final glance about the workroom, she was satisfied that everything was in order. She turned off the lights and went through the doorway into her living quarters. In the tiny kitchen, she stopped at the 1950s vintage refrigerator and took a bottle of Stolichnaya vodka out of the freezer. She poured three fingers into a glass and took it to the small bedroom with her.

She put the vodka on a bedside table, then went to the closet, where she began riffling through her dresses, sliding hanger after hanger back across the rod, slamming one against the other, hoping that she would see something—anything—that would be appropriate for tonight and lift her spirits at the same time. *Black, black, black,* she thought. *My closet is awash in black.* Like so many of New York's most fashionable wardrobes, hers had an elegant, if somewhat funereal, air about it.

Then she saw it. *The* dress. She'd forgotten she had it, but it was perfect for tonight. A long-sleeved, Empire-waisted baby-doll dress by Gucci, with a see-through panel at the bodice and cut up to *there.* So right with her long, slender legs. And black.

Oh, well, she thought. *Nobody's seen me in it yet, and it's sexy and looks great on me . . . and with my jewelry.*

She took it out of the closet and hung it on the door, then reached up to the shelf and took down the box that held her Christian Louboutin stiletto-heeled shoes in black velvet with wide satin ribbons that tied in a big bow at the ankle. From one of the jewelry boxes on her dresser, she took out black diamond earrings and their matching necklace and bracelet. She'd chosen the stones herself and designed the pieces; then Jason had made them. They weren't her favorite stones, by any means, but they were enjoying popularity right now, and she reasoned that they were a good advertisement for her work.

She held the necklace against her chest and looked in the dresser mirror. *Perfect,* she thought. It had a pear-shaped pendant that she would let rest *behind,* rather than atop, the sheer panel of her bodice, rendering it mysterious and hopefully capturing attention. The combination of the stone's dark glitter and her own ample cleavage should do the trick.

After a hot soak in Kiehl's foaming muscle relaxant—one of her favorite indulgences—she toweled off, carefully applied makeup, then brushed out her long hair before dressing and putting on her jewelry. Twirling in front of the full-length mirror on the bedroom door, she decided that she looked great in the outfit, and she felt refreshed after the bath. She had about fifteen minutes before Todd was due, so she stretched out on the bed and sipped the vodka.

Glancing around the room, she knew that, despite the bad news today, she was lucky to have this wonderful, if eccentric, apartment, with its small high-ceilinged rooms. She'd furnished it primarily with her somewhat wacky flea market finds and castoffs from friends, with a few choice pieces Todd found in buildings he bought. It offered a refuge from the noise and breakneck pace of New York City and her workroom next door.

The only problem with her cozy retreat was that there was no one to share it with. Well, actually there was, she reminded herself, but she still had mixed feelings about Todd.

If only I knew that he's really ready to grow up and pass up the constant temptations that are being thrown at him.

She took another sip of the vodka. She knew that her problems weren't exclusive to Todd's philandering. Over the years, both before and after she'd met Todd, there had been quite a few men in her life. She'd always had a boyfriend; then when she'd found out about Todd's affairs, she'd extracted her revenge by rushing headlong into short-lived and sometimes self-destructive relationships with other men.

Some of them had been more meaningful relationships than others, and a couple had actually held promise. There had been Anthony, the charm-

ing, unbelievably handsome, and alcoholic ex-model turned party pro-
moter and club owner. Louis had succeeded him. He was an ultrahip-
looking but misogynist up-and-coming painter who, like Anthony, was so
self-absorbed that she ultimately decided she was better off alone than
being his neglected chattel. Dickie, the darling, rich, and talented British
cartoonist who dabbled in body piercings and tattoos—and heroin, she'd
discovered to her chagrin—had followed Louis.

When she'd all but given up on the idea of ever meeting a stable and
mature man with whom she thought she could settle down, she'd met
Allen Bancroft, a preppy investment banker. All pin-striped suits, sedate
ties, shiny wing tips, neatly clipped hair, and impeccably good manners
to go with his impeccably good schools, good family, and good friends,
he seemed to be the answer to her prayers. But she'd soon learned that
beneath his polished veneer, Allen was probably the kinkiest man she'd
ever met. His needs, when revealed, had revolted her.

She groaned aloud and slid off the bed. She picked up her little black
beaded evening bag, wishing now that Todd were early. *Anything—or
anybody!—to take my mind off my dreary love life.* Then she amended the
thought: *Make that lack of a love life. I'll soon be thirty-three years old,
without any prospects except the unreliable Mr. Todd Hall.*

As if on cue, the intercom buzzed, signaling that Todd was in the lobby.
She started for the hallway to buzz him in, when the telephone rang. She
went over to pick up the receiver, then thought, *To hell with it. I'll let the
machine answer it. I've had enough of the telephone for one day.*

CHAPTER TWO

"What did you find out, Sylvie?" Hilton Whitehead asked his chestnut-haired assistant as he looked at her from the doorway. Her office was located on the first floor of his penthouse triplex on the Upper East Side. Through the glass wall behind her, he could see the city lights reflecting off the East River, and beyond the river the gleaming lights of Queens.

Sylvie looked over at him from behind the highly polished burl amboyna and macassar ebony Ruhlmann desk at which she worked. "I got the machine, so I left a message." Her English held the merest trace of a French accent. "But don't worry," she added, seeing his look of concern. "I know Allegra, and she'll get back to me very soon. She has my cell number and my number at home, so if she doesn't get me here before I leave, she'll get me on one of those. Okay?"

"All right," he said, relieved. Although he was anxious, he knew there was no reason to fret about this matter, not if it was in Sylvie's hands. Sylvie Javelle was efficient, trustworthy, and dependable to a fault, in addition to which she was hip and chic. All angles, without an ounce of fat, she was not what most Americans would call a beauty, with her flat chest, prominent nose, huge eyes, and sharp jaw. But she compensated for her physical imperfections with superb haircuts and makeup, and a small but expensive and well-chosen wardrobe. She possessed a certain élan, Hilton thought, that was unique to Frenchwomen.

"Are you leaving now?" he asked.

"In about two minutes," she responded. She looked over at him quizzically as she pulled a desk drawer open and took out her Hermès Birken handbag, a major investment in French craftsmanship.

"Why?" she asked in a flat voice. "Has something come up that you need me for?" The urge to ask the question was irresistible, and she had to force herself to contain the smile she felt. She knew there would be no more business to take care of today, at least not in the office. Kitty the Magnificent had swept in earlier on her stiletto heels and was ensconced in the master suite.

"No," he said, shaking his head, "that's it. I'll see you tomorrow."

"Good night, Mr. Whitehead," she said.

"Ciao, Sylvie," he replied, closing the office door behind him as he left. He bypassed the private elevator and headed for the stairs up to his third-floor aerie.

When he was gone, Sylvie spritzed herself liberally with JAR's Ferme Tes Yeux perfume, then picked up the telephone and tapped the REDIAL button. One ring. Two. Three. Four. Allegra's machine kicked in again, so Sylvie hung up. *Merde,* she cursed silently. *I hope I get hold of her soon. I don't know if she's going to love me or hate me, but I can't wait to tell her what's going on.*

"Boring!" Kitty complained aloud. She flipped the auction catalogue shut and tossed it onto the floor. She couldn't imagine anybody in the twenty-first century who would be interested in the ugly, expensive bric-a-brac pictured in the Sotheby's catalogue.

She lay back against a pile of pillows on Hilton's big bed, with its heavily padded leather headboard, waiting for him to finish his business. Clicking her long, manicured fingernails together, she sighed with impatience. She reached for the crystal flute of champagne at the bedside and caught the glint of the recently applied lacquer on her fingernails. Pausing to admire the Bitter Chocolate polish, she twisted her hand this way and that. She decided she'd made an excellent choice. With its matching lipstick, it was not only the latest shade from Dior, but it looked beautiful and sexy against her pale honey skin. Satisfied, she took a sip of the champagne. As she set the flute back down, she noticed another auction catalogue on the table. This one was from the Galerie Dufour in Paris. *Magnificent Jewels,* it said on the cover.

"Now, that's more like it," she said. She picked up the catalogue and began leafing idly through it, scanning the jewels and their estimates. Most of them, she thought, were ugly. Grotesque even. Definitely too old-lady for her sensuous thirty-four-year-old body. She could think of nothing she detested more than old-fashioned jewelry. The kind that looked like it belonged on the hideous, powder-faced old dowagers who populated posh playgrounds for the rich and nearly dead like Monte Carlo. She was about to toss the catalogue aside when her attention was suddenly drawn to an emerald ring.

She spread the catalogue out on the bed and studied the ring closely. "Oh, my," she whispered reverently. "Now, this is *my* kind of jewelry."

In the photograph the enormous stone appeared to be a rich, dark green, and its yellow gold setting looked very modern, as if it had been created yesterday. It had been designed not to bring attention to itself, but to show off the stone. And while the ring itself was more than enough to make her body quiver with avarice, it was the ring's provenance that made her begin to hyperventilate with excitement.

Property of Her Royal Highness Princess Karima, the catalogue announced.

It need have said no more to whet Kitty's ravenous appetite. She had followed the extraordinary life of the princess—had idolized her even—since Kitty had been a child. She knew that the legendary Arab beauty was the former companion of one of the richest industrialists in Italy. She knew that the princess had houses all over the world where she entertained royalty, the richest international society, and a choice few of the merely famous in a style so lavish that it was unequaled.

What Kitty hadn't known until this moment was that the princess had decided to sell her jewelry collection. According to the catalogue copy, Princess Karima had recently embarked on a spiritual journey and wanted to devote the rest of her life to charitable work. Thus, the proceeds of the sale were going to her favorite charity.

Jesus Christ! Kitty thought. *Spiritual journey! She must've gone completely over the top on drugs. That's the only thing that could account for such a crazy and dramatic change in the woman's life.*

She bit a Bitter Chocolate lip in concentration as she gazed at the accompanying photograph of Princess Karima. She still looked very . . . attractive, Kitty had to admit, but it was easy to see that she would no longer capture the attention of the rich men who could afford her, unless one of them happened to be fixated on screwing his mother.

Oh, my God. Serious wrinkles and sags, she thought with disgust as she studied the photograph more closely. *Why doesn't the crazy bitch do something about them? She really has gone totally nuts.*

Kitty had no respect for a woman who didn't take advantage of every cosmetic and surgical wonder available to stave off the ravages of time. Didn't she herself already have a daily regimen devoted to conserving and enhancing the beauty that God in his generosity had seen fit to give her? Of course she did, and it occupied a major portion of her time. It was work, but work for which she was born and which bore a great return.

Her gaze was drawn back to the emerald ring, a shimmering dark green even in the photograph. The stone was a step cut, the emerald cut used to minimize loss of material. No surprise there. And it was not flawless. Nothing remarkable about that, either, since emeralds were rarely found without some sort of flaw. What was unusual was that the catalogue mentioned an "interesting" inclusion. Normally a fault in a stone was minimized by the seller, and it certainly wasn't trumpeted as was the case here.

What the hell was that all about? Kitty wondered. Particularly since the estimated price was enormous. She guessed that it was simply because Princess Karima owned the piece. Even though it had a fault, there were a lot of women who would kill to own a ring that had once graced the long, elegant finger of the princess. She'd met more than a few rich women who obsessed on anything that had belonged to Marie Antoinette and would spend whatever asked—no matter how outrageous—to possess a jewel-encrusted hair comb.

Hilton strode into his huge makore wood and glass-walled bedroom. It was a room that would dwarf ordinary men, but it suited him. His presence was such that he seemed to fill any room he walked into. He was unbuttoning his shirt and unhooking his belt when he saw that her luscious honey-toned body was naked and that she was completely absorbed in something. "What's that?" he asked, tossing his shirt onto a chair.

"A jewelry catalogue," she said, still not looking up at the lean, well-defined muscularity of his body.

"Which one?" he asked, stepping out of his trousers and tossing them atop the shirt.

"Galerie Dufour," she replied, her eyes glued to the pictures. "In Paris."

"See something you like?" His voice was casual, even disinterested.

Finally she looked up at him and nodded. "Yes," she said, "as a matter of fact I do."

"What?"

"An emerald ring," she said, "but not just any emerald ring."

"Let me see." He stepped closer to the bed and looked down at the catalogue.

Kitty held it out for him. "Princess Karima's," she said.

He let out a low whistle. "Through-the-roof estimate."

"I know," Kitty said, pouting. "And I can't afford it."

"Very few people in the world can," Hilton pointed out as he took off his Jockey shorts and then his socks. The black marble floor felt cool on his bare feet.

"When I was growing up," Kitty said wistfully, "she was my idol. I always dreamed of being just like Princess Karima."

"You and a million other little girls your age," he said.

"She was the most beautiful woman in the world," Kitty went on, "and one of the richest. And a princess to boot."

Hilton, his well-tanned body finally naked, sat down on the bed beside her. He placed a finger on Kitty's lips, and she kissed it, looking into his vibrant dark brown eyes. He ran his hand down her neck, gently brushing it against her flesh, and on down to her breasts, where he caressed each one in turn.

Kitty shuddered with pleasure and let the catalogue slide out of her hands and off the bed. She reached over and placed her arms around Hilton's neck, drawing him to her. Their lips met, and he kissed her tenderly as he repositioned himself on the bed. His powerful arms went around her, and his sensuous lips began kissing her in earnest. His tongue explored her mouth forcefully before it traveled to her ears and neck, where it darted and flicked. Its every stroke sent shivers of excitement through her.

Moving to her breasts, he licked and kissed them, their perfection filling him with desire. They were large with rosy nipples, which he felt harden against his tongue. Kitty moaned aloud, and her hands, which until now had been stroking his back and shoulders, sought out his manhood. She could feel him against her, already hard and powerful, and when she gently grasped his cock in her hand, she loved the gasp that escaped his lips. He arched back slightly, and she licked and kissed his nipples before slowly tracing a path down to his navel, circling it lazily with her tongue, then licked her way on down to the thatch between his thighs.

Hilton held his breath as she repositioned herself between his legs, then descended upon him with wanton desire, as if she had been made simply to give him pleasure. He leaned back against the headboard, gritting his even white teeth as she moved up and down, slowly, then more rapidly, then slowly again, teasing him mercilessly.

Oh, God, he thought. *Nobody . . . nobody on earth can give head like Kitty Fleischman.* He looked down at the tangled mass of jet-black hair at his groin and smiled with a mixture of sheer pleasure and wonder.

"Whoa," he gasped, grabbing her eager head between his hands and holding it in place. "You're going to get me off, baby. Got to watch out. We want to make this last a long time."

Kitty looked up at him with huge, hurt-looking almond-shaped eyes. "Oh, Hilton, I was having so much fun," she said in a little-girl voice. Then she smiled, her collagen-injected lips a taunting, sensuous, and messy chocolate, before drawing herself up to her knees, fully exposing her large, cosmetically enhanced breasts.

Hilton's eyes were immediately drawn to their blushing, pert nipples, so like overripe strawberries begging to be plucked. He knew they weren't entirely a gift from Mother Nature. In fact, he knew Reid Thornton, the plastic surgeon who'd done the work. But he didn't care. They were a turn-on for him. Maybe even more so, he thought, knowing that Kitty had gone under the knife for him, something she had refused to do for her ex-husband.

She slithered over the sheets up next to him, and laid her head on his well-muscled shoulder. Hilton put an arm around her, cradling her head against him possessively. Kitty stuck a long finger in her mouth, then brushed its wetness around his nipples, making circles around them, one at a time, barely touching his lusty flesh.

"That feels so good," Hilton said in a near whisper. Then he reciprocated, thrumming her succulent nipples between his fingers, fascinated with their growing hardness, amazed anew at the power that even his fingers held over the most beautiful and desirable woman he'd ever seen. He never failed to be astonished that his body responded to hers like it never had to anyone else's. Maybe it was something chemical, he mused. He didn't know, but whatever it was, sex with Kitty was the best sex he'd ever had—and he'd long since lost count of the parade of beauties whom he'd bedded over the years.

He was a vigorous thirty-eight years old, and hardly a night had gone by since he'd been sixteen in which he hadn't enjoyed the company of a woman. He loved women, and he had to have them. When he wasn't working—and he worked very hard—women and hunting occupied nearly all of his spare time. Not for him were the golf courses, tennis courts, or yachts of his male friends. Women and hunting were his passion. When he wasn't actively pursuing wild game in some part of the world, he was chasing down unsampled female flesh. It was the hunt that intrigued him above all, and once the animal, or the woman in question, was in the bag, he invariably became bored and began to hunt anew.

He slid a hand down between Kitty's firm thighs and rubbed her engorged clitoris, a testament to her body's desire, then slipped a finger inside her. He expelled a heavy stream of air. She was soaking wet. She wanted him, all right. Her wetness, and her little catlike mewls, said so.

He pulled her closer to him then, relishing the feel of those big breasts against his chest, and began kissing her bee-stung lips, gently and tenderly. With mounting excitement, he began exploring the depths of her mouth more passionately, more hungrily, as if he wanted to devour her beautiful body.

With featherlight fingertips, Kitty brushed against his throbbing manhood and encircled it with her hand once again. She delighted in hearing him suck in his breath as she began working up and down its formidable length. She felt empowered by knowing that she could excite him so easily, and it was this sense of empowerment from which she derived one of her greatest pleasures. For Kitty reveled in being the master puppeteer, manipulating the strings of the people in her life to get what she wanted. Sex with Hilton was certainly enjoyable for her, more so than with most of the men she'd known intimately. But the sex act itself was, and had always been, nothing more than a prelude to securing favors.

Hilton moaned as she moved her hand from his cock to his balls, which she stroked, then gently squeezed. She knew that it wouldn't be long before he was deep inside her.

She was right, only it happened with an alacrity that was startling, being as Hilton, unlike most men in her experience, normally savored lengthy foreplay, teasing and tantalizing them both into a state of excruciating, animallike hunger before sating their lusty desire. Now he mounted and entered her in one swift motion, unable to hold off an instant longer, eliciting a gasp from Kitty as he plunged in to the hilt of his cock. She grasped his back, holding on to him as tightly as she could, thrusting herself up at him, anxious to give him the ride of his life.

Hilton licked her nipples as he began thrusting inside her, half mad with desire, but his mouth moved to hers when she began moaning aloud, his lips over hers, stifling the cries of pleasure that she was unable to control. Faster and faster they moved together, in a wanton rhythm of carnal lust, until neither of them could wait another second. Kitty began thrashing from side to side, her raven hair whipping the sheets as she was swept up into the ecstasy of orgasm, and Hilton, urged on by the flood tide that engulfed him, plunged still deeper inside her, then suddenly jerked his head back and bellowed as his body went taut, quivering over hers, his seed bursting forth in a torrent that sated them both. For the time being at least.

Gasping for air, he eased down atop her, his muscles sweat-slick against her breasts, his chest heaving against hers, his lips kissing her neck, her ears, and her face, his arms hugging her to him tightly, as if in gratitude for the gift of her voluptuous body. She relaxed her ferocious grasp of his back and began caressing him possessively, elated that once again she had satisfied this most remarkable of men.

Hilton slowly eased over onto his side, and Kitty, knowing that he liked being inside her, moved with him, clamping her thighs together to keep his cock firmly implanted where it was.

"That was so great," he said, stroking the length of her arm.

Her black eyes glittered. "It . . . it always is . . . with you," she rasped, her breath still short. "Never has a man . . . made me as happy as you do . . . Hilton. Never."

He smiled and kissed her, wondering at the same time if what she said had as much as an ounce of truth in it. He had no doubts about his sexual prowess, but in his experience most of the women he had known for more than a few weeks had wanted a lot more from him than sex. A hell of a lot more.

Kitty was an enigma to him, however, impossible to read thus far. That she enjoyed their sex, he had no doubts. But did she want more from him? It had been six months—a long time for him to date the same woman—and he still hadn't made up his mind. She had asked for nothing during those months. Nothing.

At times she seemed like a spoiled, spaced-out hedonist, lavishing attention on her body, clothes, makeup, diet, and shopping. She was sharp, but if she had any interest in intellectual pursuits, he wasn't aware of it.

Hilton knew that she didn't really need his money, although that wasn't necessarily a criterion for judgment. After all, there were women—and men—who couldn't have enough, no matter how much they had. Kitty, who'd grown up like him, in relative poverty, was comfortably fixed now. She had a few million conservatively invested and a luxuriously decorated apartment in a modern high-rise building nearby, thanks to a very short marriage and quick divorce from a much older film producer she'd met at the annual film festival in Cannes.

Hilton wanted to believe what Kitty had told him because he liked her, admired her even. She was what the French call a *tordue,* a woman who's had to fight for everything. He supposed that was one of the reasons he was drawn to her . . . aside from her magnificent body, of course.

He hugged her, and she responded with a sweet kiss. "Are you getting hungry?" he asked.

She nodded. "Ravenous," she said. "You know that sex always makes me hungry."

"Just like me," he said. "Willie and Boyce are on vacation, and I didn't get anybody to come in while they're gone. Should we go out and get something really good? Or we could stay piled up in bed and order in?"

She looked thoughtful for a moment. "Let's go to Swifty's," she said at last. "The food's okay, not great, but it'll be fun to make all those society snobs drool over us."

He grinned. "I'm game," he said. He knew how much she loved showing off her body, her clothes, and him. While he kept a fairly low profile and cared nothing for being a part of New York or international high society—a factor that made him all the more mysterious and alluring to those social titans he avoided—he was enormously rich, handsome, and available, and thus couldn't entirely avoid the scrutiny of the gossip columnists or the glaring flashbulbs of the paparazzi.

"I'm going to shower off," he said. "You want to join me?"

"I'd better use the other bathroom," she said, poking his chest with a pointed finger, "or we'll never get to the restaurant."

He grinned again. "I'll only be a minute."

He kissed her and slid out of bed, heading into the big black marble and mirrored bathroom with its gold fittings.

When she heard the blast of the shower, Kitty retrieved the jewelry catalogue from the floor and flipped through it until she found the emerald ring again. She studied it closely, her black eyes darting from the ring to the estimate. When she'd had her fill, she placed the catalogue on the bedside table and heaved a sigh.

She looked toward the bathroom that Hilton was using. *Maybe,* she thought, *I can get Hilton to spring for it.* He could certainly afford it. But would he do it? She wasn't sure. She was reluctant to risk whatever future she might have with him by making what he might consider unnecessarily expensive demands on him now. And an emerald ring—Princess Karima's or not—was nothing compared with what she could have if she succeeded in landing Hilton Whitehead as husband number two.

Over the last few months, she'd asked for nothing. Nada. Zilch. Zero. And she'd reaped a king's ransom in gifts from him. So far, so good. Her patience was paying off. But now she was faced with a real dilemma. She wanted Princess Karima's ring. She had to have that ring.

Kitty got out of bed and went across the expanse of black marble floor to the closet where she kept a few things for occasions like tonight. She wouldn't have to go back to her apartment and change. Opening the makore wood door, she flipped through the few dresses available and made up her mind in a flash. The Roberto Cavalli with the shredded hem. The wild one in various animal prints that had a neckline that plunged down to *there.* And was slit up the sides to *there.* That and her big sable coat. The floor-length one with the hood. Very dramatic on a cold New York evening.

Oh, she thought with delight, *will those stuck-up heads turn tonight! All the men will be drooling, and the bitches will crane their awful turkey necks with their horrible lifted faces to see the only woman who'll ever succeed in corralling New York's most eligible bachelor into marriage. Kitty Nguen Fleischman. The future Mrs. Hilton Whitehead.*

She didn't care if the marriage lasted ten minutes or ten years, but pronouncing the vows was definitely on her menu. She was determined that he was going to be hers. Long enough to soak him for a few hundred million and garner a scrapbook full of publicity.

I'm going to become the Princess Karima of my day, she told herself with pride. *The envy of women the world over. It takes a lot of hard work to become that kind of legend, but I can do it.*

She slipped on the twenty-five-carat D-flawless white pear-shaped diamond that Fleischman had presented to her as an engagement ring and looked at it in the mirror, puckering her collagen-injected lips. *There's a lot more where this little bauble came from,* she told her reflection, *and I'm going to have my pick of them.*

CHAPTER THREE

R am took one last look at the familiar emerald ring, then closed the glossy catalogue from Dufour. In a loving gesture he brushed his fingertips across its slick cover before putting it atop the high stack of auction catalogues on the Napoleonic Empire desk at which he sat. Unnecessarily, he placed a heavy malachite paperweight carved in the shape of a tortoise on top of the catalogue, and positioned it square in the middle.

At long last, he thought joyously, restraining the urge to shout with glee, *I can complete my work. Work that started over thirty years ago.* His entire body was tense, his jaw ached from clenching his teeth, and in an attempt to relax, he lounged against the ancient leather-upholstered back of the Louis XV chair in which he sat. He could feel his pulse racing, and his heart seemed to pump in double time against his chest. Taking a deep breath of the room's scented air, he took off his gold-rimmed half-glasses, slipped them into their alligator case, and rubbed his eyes.

He was too excited to sit still, and he abruptly stood up and crossed the priceless eighteenth-century Aubusson rug to one of the four pairs of French doors in his library. They offered a view out over the gray and chilly, but elegant, rue Elzevir on which he lived. Brushing aside a faded bottle green silk drapery that was heavy with elaborate passementerie, he peered out with satisfaction.

I will have all of Paris at my feet, he thought, surveying the distinguished eighteenth-century *hôtel particulier* opposite. Its ancient oak gates were ajar, and beyond them he could see the formally clipped garden, now barren, in the center of the limestone-paved motor court, and the old Comte de Sabin's highly polished black Bentley. *The haut monde will be begging for invitations to my soirees. Even the arrogant and snobbish old comte and his viper-tongued comtesse across the street.* Neighbors for many years, they had yet to acknowledge his presence with so much as a nod.

Turning from the window, he surveyed the library in which he stood. The carved, polished boiserie on the walls and the matching shelves with their thousands of leather-bound and gilt-decorated volumes glowed luxuriously beneath the twin antique wooden chandeliers suspended from the coffered ceiling high above. Heavily carved gilt frames surrounded early Impressionist paintings that bespoke not only great wealth but an appreciation of high culture and a discerning taste. There were even two very good Jacquelines by Picasso, purchases that he'd made in the last decade. Otherwise, the room had changed little since he had inherited the house from Jules Levant so many years ago.

Like the rest of the seventeenth-century *hôtel particulier,* the library had seen its share of the rich and famous come and go, and, more important to Ram, a number of the truly aristocratic.

It had been 1980 when the old man had finally had the good sense to die—not without a helpful nudge in that direction—and leave all of his earthly possessions to Ram. In the ensuing years that he'd owned the magnificent house and the venerable jewelry firm of Jules Levant, however, Ram had discovered that despite his dark, handsome looks, his exquisite taste, his sizable wallet, and his respectable position, he was still considered something of a servant to the blue-blooded aristocrats who were his principal clients.

He provided them with the world's most magnificent jewelry, with stones that were unobtainable elsewhere and settings that were unmatched in design and execution. They wore his merchandise at balls and parties in their own *hôtels particuliers* or palaces, their luxurious seaside or mountaintop summer homes, their ski chalets and yachts, and the few resorts worthy of their presence. They provided him with little more than their money in return. And while the monetary rewards were considerable, Ram had an insatiable hunger for more.

He was almost never asked to one of their soirees. Many was the Rothschild, the Bourbon, the d'Orlean, Savoie, or Hapsburg who'd crossed his threshold to partake of his hospitality without once reciprocating. Not to mention the less exalted, even if far richer, habitués of international society who had frequented his emporium and had enjoyed his home without a backward glance. No matter that he had a great fortune, this magnificent mansion here in Paris, the villa on the Côte d'Azur, a string of servants, the chauffeured Rolls-Royce, the Ferrari, and all the other accoutrements of an aristocratic lifestyle, he was still not considered one of them.

Like Levant, he had continued the discreet practice of buying jewelry from down-at-the-heel clients, offering them fair prices for their treasures, and he loaned cash to the temporarily strapped, keeping their valuables safe until they could repay him. Initially, he had thought that these practices would endear him to his clientele, but he quickly discovered that the reverse was often true. Many customers harbored resentments against him because he was privy to the shame of their impoverishment.

That would change now. For the final piece of the puzzle he'd long needed was within his grasp at last, as were the hundreds of millions of dollars that would be his. He would be far richer than most of the blue bloods who had disdained him. The objects of his obsession would no longer be able to ignore him. He would suddenly be one of them, propelled into their world by the one thing more important than bloodlines nowadays. Money.

For the other bidders at the auction, he knew that the emerald would be nothing more than a trinket. An expensive trinket, to be sure, but its intrinsic value to anyone else was nothing in comparison with what he could extract from owning it.

That ring will be mine, he told himself. *No matter what it costs. No matter the competition. Nobody else is going to have it. Nobody.*

He strode over to his desk and picked up the catalogue again. Flipping to her picture, he stood and gazed down at it.

Thank you, Princess Karima, he thought, a smile on his lips. *And thanks be to your precious Allah that I didn't have to murder you to get the emerald. Allah akbar!* He emitted a derisive snort. *Allah akbar indeed.*

He replaced the catalogue atop the stack, then put the malachite tortoise on it. He sat down at his desk and stared off into space. He remembered the day that Princess Karima and the famous Italian industrialist Stefano Donati had come into Jules Levant Joaillier and purchased the ring. The memory was vivid.

It had been in early spring while the couture collections were being shown, and her picture had appeared in the papers on a daily basis. She was always seated front row at the shows—as was the industrialist's long-suffering wife—since the princess was one of the handful of women in the world who could still afford couture and spent hundreds of thousands of dollars annually on her wardrobe. Donati was obviously madly in love with her and had recently presented her with a magnificent *hôtel partic-ulier* decorated by Renzo Mongiardino, the world's greatest interior de-signer. *Tout* Paris had talked of nothing else.

When the lovebirds had swept into the shop, Ram had sent an assistant to the vault, while he pulled out the book of photographs he kept of jew-elry reserved for his very special clients. He didn't show the pictures to everyone, let alone the jewels themselves. In fact, very few people ever got to see his most magnificent pieces. With the emeralds, the list of clients al-lowed to view them was narrowed down even further. He wanted to know—*had* to know—the potential buyers and make certain the jewelry would be easily traceable in the future. When he had shown the only emerald remaining from his special cache, the ring, to Princess Karima and Donati, they had been stunned by its dark green beauty, despite its small inclusion.

After the sell was completed, the princess had invited him to her new home for cocktails, a social triumph. He had gone, hoping to ingratiate himself with the couple and gain entrée into their rarefied world. He and the princess shared an Arab heritage after all, even if she was of royal blood, so he reasoned that he stood a good chance of becoming an inti-mate of the most talked-about couple in Europe. Little did he know that she would take the opportunity while having cocktails to query him about his Algerian roots, and then belittle him in front of Donati as she might the lowliest of servants. Aside from her great beauty, she was possessed of a great intelligence and quick wit, and being the object of her ridicule was one of the most embarrassing and shameful experiences of Ram's life.

The memory was as fresh in his mind as a recently inflicted wound, but he couldn't help smiling. A poetic irony lay in the fact that he should be able to get the emerald because the legendary whore of Islam—for that is the way most of Islam viewed the infidel-marrying princess—had decided to devote her life to spiritual matters. What was more, he would make cer-tain that word ultimately reached the princess as to exactly who had pur-chased the ring. He knew that her fury would be that of a woman scorned.

Ram got to his feet. At a marble-topped Louis XIV gilt console that served as a bar, he poured himself an Armagnac, then lit a thin Dutch cigarillo. In the Louis XVI mirror over the console, he looked at his reflection. His black hair was tinged with the slightest silvery gray at the temples, but he thought it only made him more distinguished. His honey skin was barely marked with the signs of age. His dark eyes flashed youthfully, and the musculature of his gym-toned body was evident, even under the custom-made suit he wore. He finally tore himself away from this picture of polished perfection and sat back down at his desk. His mind swirled with the changes about to take place in his life, then inevitably went back in time to the other transactions involving the emeralds and his subsequent recovery of the stones.

The brooch had been the first piece to find a buyer. Costas Stephanides, a Greek of immense wealth, was a regular customer of the shop. When he summoned Levant to Athens or one of his Aegean Island retreats, the old man would board one of the Greek's private jets and take a hoard of his most exquisite pieces to Greece for the magnate's personal inspection. On one such occasion, Jules had been ill and had sent Ram, who took with him all of the reset emeralds. After the jet had landed in Mykonos, a Land Rover had met him and taken him directly to the Greek's hilltop mansion near Aghios Stephanos. From this perch overlooking nearly all of Mykonos and five other surrounding islands, Costas Stephanides and his . mistress, the actress Marina Koutsoukou, had selected three pieces of jewelry, among them the emerald brooch.

"To wear on my turbans, darling," the actress had cooed seductively as her large dark eyes blatantly swept over Ram's handsome body, despite her lover's watchful proximity.

When Stephanides died a short three years later, a bitter battle over his estate ensued, and the brooch had gone on the auction block as "property of a lady" at Christie's. The tempestuous actress desperately needed cash to help pay her legal fees, but didn't want anyone to know how dire her situation really was. Thus, the brooch was auctioned anonymously. Ram had been the high bidder, of course, and put the brooch in the vault, where it still remained.

The bracelet had been bought by an Argentinian general for his beautiful wife, Dorisita. "It's the same green as in my new Givenchy dinner suit," his flame-haired wife had pronounced. Sadly, Dorisita was to have it in her possession for less than two years. The dictatorship in which her husband served an important role was overthrown by another junta, and the general and Dorisita barely managed to escape to their high-rise penthouse on Brickell Avenue in Miami. The luxurious apartment was a considerable comedown from their baroque mansion in Buenos Aires and the 180,000-acre estancia where they'd raised cattle and bred polo ponies in the country. But they had their lives at least, unlike the thousands of the general's victims whose blood he had shed in his native country. Cash was in relatively short supply, however, and the general contacted Sotheby's and sent the bracelet to auction. Secrecy was essential in this case, too, and the bracelet was sold as "property of a lady," as the brooch had been at Christie's. The ever watchful Ram recognized the bracelet immediately and was the high bidder at auction. Thus, the bracelet was stowed away in the vault, where it shared a small compartment with the brooch.

Snapping out of his reverie, Ram stubbed out his cigarillo in the malachite ashtray on his desk and took a sip of the Armagnac. He relished its warmth on his palate and the fiery trail it made to his stomach. Within moments, its warmth seemed to spread throughout his body, suffusing him with the glow of well-being.

I must celebrate, he told himself. *Yes, I must mark this day in a very special way.*

Setting down the crystal snifter of Armagnac, he picked up the alligator-bound Hermès address book on the desk and flipped to the Gs. There it was, her name and number. Denise Girard. He would call her and arrange to get together this evening. Perhaps they would have a light dinner first. Then he would take her to the tiny fourth-floor walk-up on the rue des Rosiers that he'd retained possession of all these years. The same apartment in the old Jewish quarter that the Levants had given him so many years ago.

He could bring her here or take her anywhere, for that matter. After all, she was beautiful, sophisticated, and well-mannered. But he preferred taking her here tonight. With the right drugs, he could get her to do almost anything, and for that, the little apartment was perfect. The neighbors, primarily gays who'd invaded and begun to gentrify the neighborhood, asked no questions, being the misfits they were. He picked up the telephone and dialed her number.

Although a magnet to women, he'd managed to stay unattached. No matter how beautiful or rich the various women in his life had been, he'd always ended their affairs quickly and with minimum fuss. He didn't want the unnecessary complications that inevitably arose from relationships with women, and had always found it more expedient to hire one when he felt like it.

Denise picked up at the other end of the line. *"Bonjour,"* she said in a breathy voice.

"I want to see you tonight," Ram said.

"Oh, it's you," Denise replied. "I . . . I . . . of course. What time?"

He heard the initial hesitancy in her voice, and he smiled slightly at her obvious change of mind. Money always talks. "Eight o'clock," he said. "We'll have a little dinner."

"Where?" she asked. "How shall I dress?"

"Nothing too fancy," Ram replied. "I'm in the mood for simple bistro fare."

"Okay," Denise said, disappointment in her voice.

"See you then."

"Ciao."

He replaced the receiver in its cradle, leaned back in his chair, and smiled with satisfaction. He would have a good time with the whore tonight, and although she wouldn't want to see him for a while, she would inevitably be drawn back by the money and the drugs. And once again she would let him do whatever he pleased. He felt a familiar hardening in his trousers and finished off the Armagnac, setting the empty snifter down with deliberation. *Anything,* he thought. *Anything I want.*

CHAPTER FOUR

Allegra sank back onto the plush banquette and, panting hard, untied the satin bows at her ankles and slipped out of her high-heeled shoes. Wiggling her toes and massaging her feet against the thick carpeting, she took a sip of the champagne in her glass. *Ah, that's better,* she thought, setting the glass back down. She glanced at the black Louboutins that lay on their sides at her feet, like fallen monuments. Beautiful as they were, they weren't made for dancing. *At least not the relentless way Todd goes at it,* she thought with amusement. She'd almost forgotten that he was an indefatigable dancer, and tonight he was absolutely a dancing fool, refusing to sit out a single number. Allegra finally had to take a break.

The DJ was spinning a spectacular dance mix, and they'd been on the dance floor for at least thirty or forty minutes. She wasn't sure because she'd lost all track of time, but her feet had started killing her. Dehydrated, she wanted nothing so much as a long, cold drink of water. She looked toward where she'd left Todd wildly gyrating with Candie Gundersen, but didn't see them.

Thank God she was out tonight, Allegra thought. The young blond beauty, a giantess of about six feet three inches in height, was a fixture on the downtown art and club scene whom they both knew slightly.

She took the last sip of her champagne, then put back on the uncomfortable shoes. Standing up, she took her beaded bag and started weaving through the crowd that stood between her and the bar. They were watching the action on the dance floor or gathered into little clumps engrossed in conversation. *How they can hear one another I'll never know,* she thought. She loved the music, but it was deafening. A space opened up, and turning sideways, she slipped through it. In the distance she could see the bar. As enormous as it was, it was jammed with people four and five deep.

Allegra didn't find the scene off-putting as she sometimes did. Tonight, on the contrary, she was enjoying being out among the trendy revelry and away from her workshop.

"Scusi," an extremely tall young man said in a heavily accented voice as he bumped her side. His deep, resonant voice was raised so she could hear him over the music.

Allegra turned and looked up at him. He was very handsome, deeply tanned with longish dark hair combed straight back, dark eyes full of mischief, and a square jaw. "It's okay," she said with a smile, raising her voice as he had.

His high forehead creased in a frown. "Don't I know you?" he asked. Then his lips spread in a smile, exposing gleaming white teeth. "Yes, I'm sure I do. It was Positano last summer, wasn't it?"

Allegra shook her head. How many times had she heard this or a similar pickup line? "No," she replied good-naturedly. "In fact, I've never set foot in Positano."

"Saint Moritz, then," he said, unwilling to end the game. "Last winter. Yes. At the Corviglia Club."

"I hate to disappoint you, but I haven't been there, either," Allegra said. "Now, if you'll excuse me, I want to get some water."

His handsome features collapsed into a mask of mock disappointment. "No, no," he said. "You must allow me to get it for you."

"That's really not necessary," Allegra replied.

"I insist," he said. "Look." He gestured to the crowded bar. "I'm a regular here. They know me well, so I can save you time." He looked at her with a theatrical plea.

Why not? she asked herself. She had to admit that he was extraordinarily good-looking, and his manners were impeccable. "Okay," Allegra said at last. "Why not?"

"Come with me," he said, gently placing a hand on her arm. "I'm Carlo, by the way. Carlo d'Annunzio."

"Allegra," she said, following him into the crush of bar patrons.

He turned and smiled down at her. "Ah. You're Italian, also?"

Allegra shook her head. "No," she said. "I hate to disappoint you again, but my mother just happened to like the name."

"I see," he said. "So you are Allegra. And that's it?"

She looked at him with puzzlement.

"No last name?" he said, his eyes twinkling. "That's okay. I understand. After all, I could be a serial killer."

"Sheridan," she said obligingly.

"Stay right here on this spot, Allegra Sheridan," he said, pointing a finger downward, "and I'll have your water in a flash." He turned and elbowed his way into the crowd, politely excusing himself as he went, one arm held high in the air, gesturing toward the nearest bartender.

Allegra turned and looked back toward the dance floor, but still saw no sign of Todd or Candie. She felt a hand on her shoulder and turned back. Carlo, already.

"Mademoiselle," he said, smiling as he handed her a tall glass of ice water. "Or is it madame?"

"Mademoiselle," she replied, "and you really were fast. Thank you very much."

"It's nothing," Carlo replied with a shrug. "I told you. They know me. Well, cheers." He lifted a glass of pinkish liquid and waited for Allegra to follow suit. They touched glasses and took sips of their drinks.

"What is that you're having?" she asked.

"It's champagne," he said, "with a shot of Campari. Would you like a taste?"

Allegra shook her head. "No, thanks," she said. "Water's perfect. I'm so dehydrated from dancing."

"Of course," he said, "you would be. I'm sure every single man in this place has asked you."

"That's nice of you to say, but actually, no one's had the chance," she responded. "I've been dancing with my friend since we got here."

"And where is this friend of yours now?" he asked.

"Dancing with someone else," Allegra said.

"You've been deserted?" His eyebrows went up, feigning surprise. "I can't believe a man would desert a woman as beautiful as you in a club like this, where nearly every man is on the make."

Allegra laughed. "You're too much."

"What do you mean?" he asked, pretending innocence.

"You know very well what I mean," she replied. "You—" There was a light tap on her shoulder, and she turned around expecting to see Todd. "Sylvie!" she exclaimed.

Sylvie Javelle air-kissed her on both cheeks in the continental manner, then stood back. "Don't believe a word that Carlo says because he is a terrible womanizer," she said. Allegra noticed that she was wearing what appeared to be Chanel couture.

"Ah, Sylvie, *chérie,* how could you?" Carlo began, holding his arms out to her. She quieted him with kisses and returned his hug.

"You know I'm only making a little joke," she said with a laugh. "I'm so glad to see you both."

"So you two know one another," Allegra said.

Sylvie arched a thinly plucked brow. "You might say that."

"A little bit," Carlo said, shrugging.

"Allegra, I've been trying to get you on the phone. Did you get my message?"

"No," she said. "But I haven't listened to the machine."

"We've got to talk," Sylvie said.

"What's up?"

"Hmmm, not now," Sylvie said, looking from side to side as if expecting spies to be eavesdropping. "Later. In private."

"You don't have a drink," Carlo said. "What would you like, Sylvie? Or have you had plenty of medication?"

"Oh, Carlo, aren't you funny?" she said, looking at him mischievously. "But you're a darling. I'll have a cosmopolitan."

"I'll be back in a minute," he said.

"Thank you, Carlo," she said, watching him leave. She turned back to Allegra. "Isn't he a hunk?"

"He's very good-looking," Allegra agreed, "and he knows it."

"Oh, yes," Sylvie said, nodding her head. "You're right about that, but still . . . he's not unbearable about it."

"Who is he?" Allegra asked.

"He's with an investment company downtown," Sylvie said. "From a very good family in Turin."

"You know everybody," Allegra said with a laugh.

"If I don't, you do," Sylvie said. "Where's Todd, or is he out of town?"

"He's dancing with Candie Gundersen," Allegra said. "Or at least he was the last time I saw him."

"Aha, the giantess," Sylvie said. "How are things between you two?"

"Oh, God, Sylvie, who knows?" Allegra replied. "What about you? Who're you with?"

"Ahhh, Jean-Pierre," she said with a Gallic shrug of her shoulders, as if the subject bored her.

"So is it serious with you two?"

"God, no!" Sylvie exclaimed. "It is impossible. Jean-Pierre can't be serious for five minutes. Not with anybody. He's probably screwing somebody in the loo right now."

Allegra laughed, nearly choking on her water. "How do you put up with it?" she asked.

"How could I bear him otherwise?" Sylvie retorted. She saw Carlo returning with her drink.

"Here you are," Carlo said. "A cosmopolitan." He handed it to Sylvie.

"*Merci,* Carlo," she said. "You're a lifesaver."

"And another glass of water for you, mademoiselle," he said to Allegra.

"You didn't have to do that," she said, "but thanks."

"My pleasure." He turned to Sylvie. "Is Jean-Pierre here?"

She nodded. "Somewhere."

"I think I'll have a quick look for him," Carlo said, "but don't worry, I'll be back soon." He winked and headed off.

Sylvie and Allegra laughed. "He's so crazy," Sylvie said, "but so amusing." She took a sip of the cosmopolitan.

"So he and Jean-Pierre are friends, I take it?"

"Yes," Sylvie nodded. "They've known each other for years. They went to school together in Switzerland."

"Oh," Allegra replied. "I must be practically the only person in New York City who didn't go to school in Switzerland."

Sylvie flapped a hand breezily. "Who cares about things like that, *chérie*? It's meaningless now." She looked around them, then leaned in toward Allegra. "Anyway, can you talk now? If so, let's go somewhere we don't have to yell to be heard."

Allegra nodded. "Sure, why not?" She was curious as to what Sylvie wanted to discuss. They had met several years ago when a mutual friend had introduced them. Sylvie had bought a piece of jewelry from her—the first of several choice pieces—and they had been friendly ever since. But they had never really been confidants, sharing secrets like best girlfriends.

"Good," Sylvie said. "Let's go upstairs, then."

She led the way and Allegra followed until they reached the expansive staircase. When they were seated in a darkly lit, uninhabited corner, Allegra was the first to speak. "Okay," she said, "what's this all about?"

Sylvie leaned in close to her again. "You swear you will not discuss this with anyone? Not Jason? Not even Todd?"

Allegra looked at her with surprise, but nodded. "I promise," she replied, putting her hand on her heart and laughing.

Sylvie did not return her laughter. "This is very serious," she said solemnly, "and really must be kept secret, Allegra." Her voice dropped to a whisper. "It has to do with my boss, Hilton Whitehead."

"Hilton . . . Whitehead," Allegra said slowly, as if testing the name on her lips. Her curiosity was more aroused than ever. She knew, of course, that Sylvie worked for the somewhat elusive software billionaire, but she also knew that Sylvie never discussed him, his business, or his private life with anyone. Allegra remembered that he'd made her sign a ten-page confidentiality agreement before giving her the job.

Sylvie leaned in closer and put her hand to Allegra's ear. "He has a proposition for you," she whispered, "and he wants to meet with you tomorrow morning."

"A proposition?" Allegra said. "For me?" She pointed her fingers at her chest. "I don't even know the man, Sylvie."

"Yes," she said, "but he knows all about *you*. He's asked me more than once about one of the brooches you made for me. You know, the one that looks like a dollop of caviar?"

"Yes," Allegra nodded, remembering with fondness the brooch made of hundreds of little gray pearls. "But what about it?"

"I told him that you know all about jewelry," Sylvie said. "How you are an actual gemologist and all that. Not just a designer."

"So?"

"So, he wants to talk to you about something," Sylvie said.

"But what?" Allegra asked, beginning to become exasperated with Sylvie's vague answers. "If he wants a piece of jewelry designed and made, then why doesn't he simply come down to the atelier and place the order?"

"I'm not permitted to discuss that," Sylvie said mysteriously. "You must come to the office to discuss it with him."

Allegra emitted a short, nervous laugh. "But why? I just don't get it. Even rich people come to the atelier."

Sylvie shook her head. "No, no, *chérie*," she whispered. "He can't do that. It's far too confidential a matter for that. Come to the apartment tomorrow morning about eleven o'clock. He will explain everything then."

Allegra looked at her, but she finally nodded. "Okay," she said. "I'll be there, but I don't know why."

Sylvie hugged her, then drew back and cried merrily, "*Merveilleux.* I'll see you at eleven." She opened her gem-studded minaudière and took out a thick vellum business card. "Here's the address," she said.

Allegra took the card and slipped it inside her beaded bag. "Okay."

"Remember. Not a word of this to anyone," Sylvie said. She air-kissed Allegra on both cheeks, then stood up. "Now I will try to find Jean-Pierre. Are you coming downstairs to have some fun?"

"Yes," Allegra replied, getting to her feet. "And I should probably hunt down Todd." But she wondered if she could have fun until her curiosity was satisfied regarding the billionaire Hilton Whitehead.

"How about a nightcap, baby?" Todd asked, nuzzling the nape of her neck.

"Don't you think we've both already had too much?" Allegra asked with a helpless giggle. She finally managed to unlock the lobby door and pushed it open.

"Oh, come on," he said. "You know me better than that." He followed her into the lobby and encircled her with his arms from behind, hugging her to him and kissing the back of her neck. "The night is young, Ally."

"It's almost three o'clock, Todd," Allegra pointed out, "and I've got an appointment on the Upper East Side at eleven o'clock in the morning." But even as she said the words, she could hear the unmistakable sound of surrender in her voice.

"That's never stopped you," he said, squeezing her tightly. "Besides, eleven o'clock's a lifetime away."

Allegra pushed the elevator button. "Okay," she said, turning to face him, "but just one little drink." She held up a finger.

He kissed her finger and looked into her eyes. "I promise," he said. "Just one."

Allegra was spread out on the couch in the living room, her head in Todd's lap. He'd lit the candles on the coffee table and put a soothing trance mix on the CD player. They were nursing the second of the straight Stolis on ice that he'd poured.

"Did you have a good time tonight?" he asked, running his fingers through her hair.

"Uh-huh," she said. "I had a good time. And I know you did. You and Candie. She's just like you. She can't stop dancing once she starts."

"Jealous?" he asked.

"Of you and Candie? Ha! Why would I be jealous?"

"Well, you shouldn't be if you are," he said. "I saw you spending some time with the Italian Stallion."

"Who?"

"Don't give me that," he said. "You know exactly who I mean. Carlo d'Annunzio. I saw you talking to him."

"You did?"

"I sure did," he said, "and everybody knows what a cocksman he is."

She laughed. "Well, the only thing he did for me was get me a drink of water," she replied. "I didn't spend half the night with him on the dance floor like you did with Candie."

"Oh, yeah," he said mischievously, "we had a real good time. Especially slow dancing. Getting up real close and personal, you know?"

"Well, if you're trying to make me jealous, it isn't going to work," Allegra said. "Besides, isn't she a lipstick lesbian or something?"

"Yeah, but I think she's falling for me," Todd teased.

She grabbed his hand and bit it playfully. "You think you're really God's gift to womankind, don't you?"

"I don't know about that," he said, "but there's one woman I sure would like to make happy." He leaned over and kissed her forehead. When she didn't protest, he kissed her cheeks and nose and lips and ran his hands down her arms, gently and tenderly. "I love you, Ally," he said softly. "I really do."

His voice sounded earnest and his words heartfelt, and in the warm glow from the drinks and the gentle caress of his lips and hands, Allegra felt herself respond to him. Despite her mixed feelings about his intentions, she knew that she wanted him.

Her lips sought out his, and her hand went up to run her fingers through his raven hair. Todd sighed happily and let his hands wander to her breasts, where he brushed against them gently. "Why don't we get comfortable?" he said.

"Hmmm." She slowly sat up, then got to her feet, drink in hand. He picked up his drink and the candles and followed her into the bedroom. He placed the candles and his drink on a bedside table, then took her in his arms, kissing her passionately.

Allegra slid her arms around him and returned his kisses, losing herself in the comfortable strength of his embrace. His mouth moved to her ears and neck, his lips kissing, his tongue licking her, and she shivered ever so slightly as she felt an electric-like pulse run through her body.

"Let's get out of these clothes," he said when he felt her response.

She nodded silently and held up her hair so that he could unzip her dress. He did so slowly, his lips and tongue tracing a trail down her back as he pulled the zipper down. When he'd finished, he helped her pull the dress off her shoulders and watched as she let it drop to the floor. His gaze swept over her lacy black bra and slip. She started to take off her bra, but he protested.

"Here," he said, "let me." He unhooked the bra, his dark eyes riveted to her ample breasts as they sprang free of it. He tossed the bra onto the chair, then began to pull her slip over her slim hips and on down to the floor. Allegra lifted her feet, one at a time, and he leaned down and picked up the lacy black silk and tossed it onto the chair with the bra.

As she stood in nothing but her black panty hose and the black diamond jewelry, the candlelight flickered off the pale beauty of her skin, and the diamonds glinted at him seductively. Todd went down on one knee and, with both hands, drew her panty hose slowly toward the floor. His tongue circled her navel, then made a path down to the mound between her thighs, where he nuzzled against it lustily before licking it.

Allegra gasped aloud as she felt bolts of electricity shoot through her body, and her legs trembled. "Oh, Todd. Oh, my God, that feels so good."

He began licking her with heightened passion when he heard her reaction, and she placed her hands on his head, steadying herself. Then he reached up and took a firm round cheek in each of his hands, pushing her against his face. His tongue licked her engorged clitoris before delving inside her.

"Ahhhhh," Allegra moaned with pleasure. "You're going to make me . . . you're . . ."

Todd abruptly stopped and rose to his feet. He stroked her hair lovingly and kissed her lips. "Let me get undressed."

As he quickly took off his clothes, she watched, enjoying the sight of his lean, defined musculature and the little ripple of those muscles with his every movement. His was a classically proportioned body with a long torso, a small waist and obvious abs, slim hips, and long legs, and every time she saw it she was thrilled anew. He was like a magnificent Greek statue brought to life.

He left his clothes in a pile on the floor, and when he was finally naked, his gaze traveled the length of her lovely softness, his already engorged manhood a testament to his desire for her.

Extending both of his hands toward her, he began stroking her breasts reverently as if they were objects of worship, then gently thrummed her nipples between a thumb and finger. He loved hearing Allegra's sharp intake of breath as her body responded to his ministrations. She reached out and encircled his manhood with a hand, and Todd gasped at her touch, featherlight as it was. She stroked it, and he moaned with unbridled desire, then pulled her naked body against his, unable to resist the sensual, almost magnetic pull between them.

They kissed with a ravenous hunger for one another that demanded gratification. Allegra reveled in the feel of his muscular hardness against her soft, yielding flesh, and was enthralled with his distinctly masculine odor, an aroma that, whatever its components, was unique to him and never failed to arouse her. She'd forgotten how wondrous these sensations were, and asked herself why she had denied herself such pleasure.

He led her to the bed, where she spread out lengthwise, her legs apart, her body anxious to receive him. Todd mounted her, and though he was in a rush to satisfy his carnal urges, he was gentle and loving. He wanted Allegra to savor these moments they were having together, to remember this night as the one that finally convinced her of his devotion.

When he entered her, Allegra emitted a mewl of delight and put her arms around his back, holding him to her tightly, as if she never wanted to let him go. The wonder of his being inside her, the desire that he obviously felt for her, and the sense of womanliness that he made her feel, along with the powerful erotic pleasure she felt, engulfed her in a state of otherworldliness. She and Todd were suspended apart, as if on another plane altogether, in a state of bliss that they created together.

He began moving inside her slowly, kissing her lips, her ears and neck, and her breasts, breathing heavily as he began to stroke faster and more deeply. She moved with him, his desire inflaming her own, until she thrust herself up to meet him, her body anxious to sate itself.

Suddenly she was overcome by the powerful intermingling of love and lust that consumed her, and her body began contracting as never before. Her floodgates opened and wave after wave of orgasm engulfed her in an ecstasy such as she'd never known. She cried out, unable to control the potent senations and emotions that possessed her. Todd, his desire fueled by her animallike cries, released his seed in a final lunge, exploding in a torrent. His body tensed into a rigid line as he expended himself in one body-wracking spasm after another until he was completely drained and spent.

He lay atop her, gasping for breath as he clutched her to him, aware of her labored breathing and slick flesh, as sweat-soaked as his own. When he finally caught his breath enough to speak, he said, "I love you, Ally. I love you, love you, love you." He peppered her face, her ears, her neck with tender little kisses, still gasping for breath.

"Hmmm," she breathed at last, "you make me feel so wonderful, Todd." She hugged him tightly, then loosened her grip and let her arms linger on his back. She couldn't bring herself to say more, not yet. No one else had ever made her feel like Todd, but she still couldn't completely trust the love he professed for her.

When he rolled off her, they snuggled close together. Then Allegra kissed him. "I've got to go to sleep," she said, "because of that appointment I have in the morning."

"I know," he said softly. " 'Night, Ally."

" 'Night, Todd." She kissed the tip of his nose, then turned to her side, her back to him. Todd put his arms around her, holding her lightly but possessively.

He kissed her neck once; then she heard his breathing change as he fell into a deep sleep.

What will tomorrow bring? she wondered. *Why does Hilton Whitehead want to see me?* But she fell asleep before she could speculate any further.

CHAPTER FIVE

Princess Karima, her floor-length ecru silk dressing gown swishing about her, paced the pale ivory Savonnerie rug in her bedroom, a cigarette in one hand and a cut-crystal old-fashioned glass of straight Jack Daniel's on ice in the other. The heavy velvet draperies with their intricately embroidered satin trim were pulled shut against the morning sun of Paris, and only a small bronze *dorée bouillotte* lamp on her desk cast a diminutive pool of light in the vast, dark room. Its walls, painstakingly hand-painted to resemble lace years ago, were virtually invisible.

The princess took a long draw on her cigarette and stubbed it out in a large onyx ashtray on the desk. She held her drink up and eyed it curiously. She was a great lover of this distinctive whiskey from that obscure place in America called Tennessee, and international society the world over knew to keep an ample supply on hand when she was expected as a houseguest. She drank down the remainder of the fiery liquid, then set the crystal glass down, deciding that she would wait a bit to have another. She didn't normally drink in the morning unless she'd been up all night partying, but today was different.

Circling around the desk, she sat down in the embossed velvet *Régence* throne that served as a desk chair. Before her, on the desk's surface, was the catalogue that Dufour had sent her, and next to it, in a small pinkish beige box, reposed the emerald ring that Stefano Donati had given her years ago. Today, a security detail from Dufour would arrive to take it to the venerable auction house.

She opened the box with long ruby-lacquered fingernails. The dark green emerald glimmered up at her from its heavy gold setting. She took the ring out and put it on her finger, twisting her hand this way and that, her eyes glued to the magnificent gemstone. *It is beautiful,* she thought.

She slipped it off her finger and replaced it in its suede niche. It had been a symbol of an undying love, she'd thought at the time. A love affair with one of the richest, most powerful, and best-looking men in the world. For years she had been convinced that he would leave his wife for her. But she had been wrong. She eventually learned that Stefano would never leave the beautiful Bettina, a princess of ancient lineage, not for an arriviste Arab princess.

Princess Karima slammed the box shut, but not before noticing the gilt-stamped name inside the lid: JULES LEVANT JOAILLIER. And below that: PARIS. Suddenly, she threw back her head and laughed aloud. She would never forget the day Stefano bought the emerald. They had invited the handsome young Arab who had handled the purchase to come to her newly decorated *hôtel particulier*—another gift from Stefano—for a drink. In the salon, she had belittled the Algerian from the housing projects in front of Stefano, who had taken great pleasure in watching the young Arab's humiliation. It had all been a show put on for Stefano's amusement.

He must hate me still, she thought with a feeling akin to merriment. *But so what? Most of the Arab world hates me. They despise me as they would the most odious infidel.*

She had hardly mingled in the Middle Eastern world. She'd been sent off to boarding school in England when she was young, then finished in Switzerland. Her life since had primarily revolved around European society and the aristocracy. After her first marriage, to a French pharmaceuticals heir who was also a *vicomte,* her position in society was assured. Her title and enormous wealth had helped, of course, but hadn't made her an automatic member of the "club." Her subsequent divorce and high-profile affairs with the most sought-after men in Europe had done nothing to diminish her star in this celestial firmament.

She had become a legend in her own time. Rich and beautiful, she was also a seductress without peer. But all of the attention and acceptance she felt did nothing to salve the wounds caused by her breakup with Stefano. She would never be like his wife, descended from an ancient European royal house, and thus would never be completely accepted by the uppermost level of the social order. Princess Karima still felt that despite her status she was an outsider, and she knew that would never change.

Her youth and beauty on the wane, she still attracted men, but she found herself increasingly relying on gay "walkers" to squire her around the world in her endless search for diversion. They were rich and handsome men, many of whom would willingly marry her, but she did not relish growing old in such a relationship.

Then an idea had come to her only a few months ago, during a sleepless night when she'd nursed a bottle of her much beloved Jack Daniel's and chain-smoked till past dawn. She would announce her "enlightenment," and the establishment of a charitable foundation in her name, the endowment of which would begin with the proceeds from the disposal of her worldly goods. In her quest to see that only the most deserving would enjoy the largesse of her foundation, she would single-handedly control the foundation and handpick its recipients.

Fueled by whiskey and cigarettes, she had written the press release before she finally slept that fateful dawn. She included her intention to sell her luxurious residences and move to a charming little millhouse on the outskirts of Paris, where she could meditate and make decisions without the intrusions of society. She concluded with the announcement that she would appear once a year—and only once a year—at a grand ball in Paris that would serve as a fund-raiser for her foundation.

Lighting a cigarette, she rose to her feet and walked to the liquor cabinet and minibar that were concealed behind a jib door in the wall's handpainted lace. She poured Jack Daniel's into a clean glass and tossed in some ice cubes. Swirling the drink around, she turned and strode over to her vanity table, where she sat down and looked at her reflection in the baroque Venetian mirror over it.

Her gaze studied her carefully dyed black hair pinned back in a loose chignon; her perfectly arched and dyed brows; her subtly made-up eyes, face, and lips. She shrugged out of her silk dressing gown, and her eyes surveyed her flesh. A web of wrinkles traversed her neck and the cleavage between her once lovely, firm breasts, which now hung like useless appendages. Soft, dimpled skin exhibited itself from between her arms and chest. Simply lifting an arm exposed the loose, aging flap of a woman far beyond her prime.

She was still a beauty—a mature beauty—but the ravages of time were taking their inevitable toll, and no amount of cosmetic surgery and makeup could conceal her loss of youth. But no matter. Now that these physical assets had deserted her, she had others to put to use.

She raised her glass in a toast. *You're brilliant,* she said to her reflection. *As your legend grows in the eyes of the entire world, as it's burnished beyond the brightness of mere stars, no one will know who you really are and what you are really doing. No one will know the vengeance you're extracting until it's far too late.*

There was a soft knock, and the princess shifted her gaze from her mirror image to the door. It would be Mimi, her devoted housekeeper of many years. Slipping back into her silk dressing gown, she called out to her. "Come in, Mimi," she said, placing her drink on the vanity.

The door opened quietly, and the ancient, wrinkle-faced woman hobbled into the room, her small, close-set eyes focused on her mistress. Despite her advanced age and slow movements, she was still sharp-witted and strong, with the stamina of the peasant stock from which she came. "The men from Dufour are here, madame," she said.

"Already?" the princess asked, turning to face Mimi. "I had no idea it was so late."

"Shall I have them wait for you to dress, madame?" Mimi asked.

"No," Princess Karima replied. "You can show them in. They'll only be a minute."

The old woman nodded, then turned and left the room, closing the door behind her. Princess Karima had a sip of her drink and lit another cigarette. Taking one last lingering glance in the mirror, she rose to her feet and crossed to her desk. She picked up the box that held the emerald ring and started to open it again, but decided against it. Putting the box back on the desk, she went around to her chair and sat down, flicked ash off her cigarette into the ashtray, and waited for the Dufour security detail. Her fingernail lacquer shone in the small pool of light cast by the desk lamp, but she was in the shadows; her features were barely visible, though her dark eyes glittered.

There was another soft knock at the door. *"Entrez,"* the princess commanded imperiously.

Mimi opened the door, then stood aside to let two men enter. They stood silently in the triangle of light emitted from the hallway. One of them appeared to be no more than twenty and was a tall, strong-looking specimen with short-cropped blond hair. The other was middle-aged, his muscular body covered with layers of fat. Both of them wore dark blue livery, somewhat like police uniforms, and there were holstered guns on their belts. They held their caps in their hands.

"Please, gentlemen," she said. "Come forward. I assume you brought the paperwork I have to sign?"

"Yes, *madame la princesse*," the older one said, nodding and stepping forward slightly.

The younger man lifted his gaze from the floor and looked toward Princess Karima. She saw his cap quiver slightly in his big, powerful-looking hands. She rose to her feet and came from behind the desk. "The ring is there," she said, indicating the box with a hand.

"I have the paperwork here, *madame la princesse*," the older man said, holding out a folder in one hand. His head was nodding rapidly, and he was smiling widely. "With your permission, *madame la princesse*, I have to fill out the time of pickup and the exact location, things like that, then get your signature."

"Of course," she replied. "There. Use the desk. There is a pen if you need it."

"*Merci, merci*," the older one said, his head still nodding. "So sorry to disturb you, *madame la princesse*. It will only take a minute." He stepped forward to the desk, gingerly placed the folder on it, withdrew a triplicate form, looked at his watch, then began filling in the appropriate blanks.

Princess Karima ignored him and kept her gaze on the young man, whose face reddened before he averted his eyes from her. She stepped toward him boldly and loosened her dressing gown, letting it slip off her shoulders, revealing ample cleavage. "You must be new at Dufour," she said as she provocatively thrust a leg in his direction.

Without looking at her, he replied. "*Oui, madame la princesse.*"

She lifted a hand and, with one finger, traced a line down the side of his face. "I didn't think I'd seen you before," she said, barely able to contain her amusement at his embarrassment.

He didn't know how to respond. He'd never met anyone like her before, had never been in such a palatial house, had never smelled such an intoxicating perfume nor seen such a lavish dressing gown.

"I hope you will guard my ring with your life," Princess Karima said to him, her finger trailing down his uniformed chest.

The nod of his head was barely visible. "*Oui, madame la princesse,*" he replied. "I . . . we will." Still, he would not meet her brazen glance, but his face reddened as the bulge in his pants became apparent.

The older man turned from the desk. "I only require your signature, *madame la princesse,*" he said, "and we will take the ring and leave you in peace."

"Of course," Princess Karima said. She turned from the young man, deliberately brushing against him, then leaned down and signed the form on the desk. She stubbed out her cigarette in the ashtray, then looked at the older man. "There you are," she said to him. She picked up the box. "And here is the ring. I suppose you should check to make certain that it is there."

"Oh, no, *madame la princesse,*" the man said, his obsequious smile still in place. "That certainly won't be necessary in this case. We'll be going now, and you can rest assured that your ring is in good hands. There are two more armed guards outside, and we're traveling in an armored truck." He held his hand out for the box.

"Very good," Princess Karima said. "One can't be too cautious in Paris these days, can one?"

"*Ah, non, madame la princesse,*" the older man replied. "You're absolutely right. Paris can be very dangerous, especially for someone like yourself."

Princess Karima turned back to the young man. "Here," she said, proffering the box in his direction. "Since you're new, I think you should have the pleasure of taking my ring to Dufour."

The young man cleared his throat. "*Merci, madame la princesse,*" he said, unable to look at her again. "It would give me the greatest pleasure and honor."

Princess Karima took one of his large hands in hers and could feel the barely perceptible tremor. She almost laughed aloud as she placed the box in his sweaty palm and closed his big fingers over it, then placed her free hand atop his. "There," she said, holding his fist tightly before patting it several times. "I can trust you, can't I?"

"With your life, *madame la princesse,*" the older man said.

"And you?" she asked, shaking the younger man's hand. "You will guard it with your life?"

He nodded. "*Oui, madame la princesse.*"

"Ah, very well," she said gaily. "Good-bye, gentlemen." She released her grip on the young man.

The men began backing out of the room toward the hallway as Karima watched them, reveling in their subservience. When they reached the hallway, the older one bowed toward her, and the younger one followed suit. Princess Karima nodded, and they started down the hallway.

When they were gone, Princess Karima finally laughed aloud.

CHAPTER SIX

The taxi lurched to a stop in front of the new high-rise building in the East Seventies, and Allegra handed the driver a wad of singles. "Keep the change," she said, already swinging the door open and sliding across the slick vinyl seat. The instant her heels hit the pavement, she righted herself and made a dash for the building's entryway.

Normally for an appointment like this, she would have taken great care with grooming and dressing and would have allowed plenty of time to take the trip uptown. This morning, however, it had been a mad race to shower, put on her makeup, and dress, and now she felt thrown together. Last night—close to four a.m.—she'd forgotten to set her alarm after she and Todd had made love, and she didn't wake up until around nine thirty. When she'd dashed out the apartment door, Todd was still fast asleep, snoring away without a care in the world. For a moment, she'd felt like giving him a violent shake to wake him up. But as her gaze lingered on his tousled black hair and his handsome slumbering body, her hard feelings had softened. He looked so adorable, so defenseless, and so . . . sexy.

The smartly uniformed doorman swung the mirrorlike chrome and glass door open, greeting her starchily. "Good morning, miss. How may I help you?"

"I have an appointment with Mr. Whitehead," Allegra replied.

"Please see the concierge, miss," he said, indicating the desk where she would have to be announced before going up to Hilton Whitehead's.

Allegra crossed what seemed like an acre of gleaming black granite before reaching the identically uniformed concierge, who stood behind a high reception desk of highly polished steel and more black granite. A massive bodybuilder with bleached blond hair, he gave her a big smile.

"How may I help you?" he asked.

"Mr. Whitehead," Allegra replied. "I have an appointment."

The concierge nodded, then stared at her with appreciative blue eyes as he phoned the apartment. Allegra, who pretended not to notice his attention, gazed about the ultramodern lobby. It was all glass, steel, and granite, with leather-upholstered couches and chairs in seating areas on thick, plush rugs. Huge floral arrangements, primarily composed of brightly colored tropical flowers in crystal vases, decorated coffee tables and commodes.

"Go right on up," the concierge said. "It's a private elevator in the vestibule to your right. The penthouse."

"Thank you," she said to the still-staring concierge. She strode to the vestibule and found the appropriate elevator. As she pushed the button, she caught her reflection in the mirrored walls. *Well, not too bad,* she thought, *considering that I got ready in record time.* The doors slid open instantly, and she stepped in. Ascending to the sixtieth floor, she began to feel the fluttering of butterflies in her stomach.

Now that the moment had come, she began to wonder anew what Hilton Whitehead could possibly want to see her about unless it was to order a piece of jewelry. It would have to be something very special, she thought. After all, he was one of the country's richest men, and rather than taking a ride downtown, he had seen to it that she came to him. It was the only thing that made sense.

She was just beginning to do a mental inventory of the largest and most precious gemstones she had in stock when the elevator came to a stop and its doors slid open with hardly a sound. She stepped out into a large vestibule in which there was a magnificent commode covered in shagreen. A mirror above it was covered in the same sharkskin and reflected a huge orchid plant with its dozens of ivory blooms. At either end of the vestibule, huge modern paintings hung on walls that appeared to be covered with parchment. Before she got more than a glance at them, one of the tall, ebonized double doors to the right of the commode opened.

"Miss Sheridan?" A tall African-American man with a black patch over one eye stood at attention in the doorway. His hair was snow-white, and he appeared to be at least seventy-five. He was wearing an immaculate black uniform.

"Yes," Allegra said, holding her hand out to be shaken.

Momentarily nonplussed—obviously few visitors ever offered to shake his hand—the butler took it in his and shook it. "I'm Boyce, ma'am," he said. "I'll take your coat."

"Thank you, Boyce," she said, turning to let him help her out of the knee-length black cashmere cape that served as her wintertime coat for uptown business.

"If you'll follow me, please," he said.

Allegra trailed just behind the elderly gentleman, her eyes feasting on the large circular entrance hall. Its walls were entirely covered in an exotic wood, and the floors were marble. Suspended from the center of the room's high ceiling was a large Calder mobile that hung nearly to the floor, each element in a different bright color. All around the room, the walls were hung with modern paintings in gilt frames. She glimpsed two Picassos, a Léger, a Braque, and two or three others that she couldn't see long enough to identify. Boyce opened one of a pair of double doors, and they turned right and went down a hallway. After walking a short distance, Boyce stopped at yet another pair of tall double doors and knocked lightly.

"Come in," someone called.

It's Sylvie, Allegra thought, hearing the unmistakable French-accented voice.

Boyce opened the door and stepped aside for Allegra to enter. "Thank you, Boyce," she said.

He nodded. "You're welcome, ma'am."

Sylvie stood up and came around her desk to greet Allegra. *"Bonjour, chérie,"* she chirped. "I'm so glad you could come this morning." She air-kissed each of Allegra's cheeks.

"Bonjour to you, too," Allegra replied. "This is really some place you work at."

"It is nice, isn't it?" Sylvie said. "I'll tell Mr. Whitehead you're here."

Allegra noticed the wall of glass that faced her, and immediately went over to it. "My God," she said, looking out at the view. "It's like being on top of the world up here. You can see for miles."

"Yes," Sylvie said. "Isn't it fabulous? All the way past the tip of Manhattan to Staten Island, and over to Queens and Brooklyn and Long Island. And New Jersey, of course, on the other side." She sat back down at her desk, where she picked up a telephone.

"Mr. Whitehead," Allegra, still taking in the view, heard her say. "Miss Sheridan is here." After a moment, she said, "Okay."

Allegra tore her eyes away from the skyline and sat down in one of the chairs. "I hope I'm on time," she said. "I overslept."

"Oh, so you and Todd had a bit of a long night, did you?" Sylvie said with a sly smile.

"You might say that," Allegra replied.

"Good. Anyway, you're precisely on time." She looked over at Allegra. "And you look stunning, *chérie*. No one would ever believe you were up half the night. I adore your necklace. Your design, unmistakably."

"Thanks, it is," Allegra said, her fingers going to the necklace and adjusting it slightly. She'd worn a simple black cashmere long-sleeved T-shirt with a matching skirt, but the austere look was offset by the drama provided by the necklace. It was gold, set with hundreds of tiny garnets, that wrapped loosely about her neck and dangled like a long apple peel.

"Did you and Jean-Pierre have a good time? I didn't see you again after we had our talk."

Sylvie shrugged. "With Jean-Pierre it's always the same. He's like a bunny, you know? But I get the feeling that I could be an old teddy bear and it wouldn't matter. He just goes at it like a maniac and that's that."

They both laughed.

"Sensitive type, I see," Allegra said.

"Ha!" Sylvie snorted derisively. "He can be amusing at least. And after a day of work, sometimes that is enough."

"Well, at least you get to work in a beautiful place," Allegra said, looking around. "Does Mr. Whitehead work here all the time?"

Sylvie shook her head. "Oh, no," she replied. "This is just a little home office. The company is headquartered in San Jose. He has another office here in New York, but he keeps this one as a place to get things done without any distractions."

The office door opened, and a handsome man over six feet tall entered. He had brown hair that was just beginning to gray and alert brown eyes. He was tan and lean, fit for a man approaching middle age, and dressed casually in slacks and a sweater. He smiled winningly. "You must be Allegra," he said, reaching her chair in a couple of long strides.

"Yes," she said, as she started to rise. "I am."

"Don't get up," he said, taking her hand in his and shaking it. "I'm Hilton Whitehead."

"It's a pleasure to meet you, Mr. Whitehead," she said. Somehow he wasn't what she'd expected. Perhaps it was his easy manner that surprised her, added to his casual dress and obvious charm. But then, why shouldn't a billionaire look and act like him? she asked herself. Nowadays, there were a lot of rich men of the Bill Gates ilk, almost never seen dressed up, and less than formal in manner.

"Hilton, please," he said. He admired her lively eyes and shiny strawberry blond hair, her pale skin and shapely figure. She had a touch of the bohemian artist about her, something indefinable that made her all the more desirable to him.

Allegra nodded. She didn't fail to notice his interest.

He eased down in a chair next to hers and scooted around slightly so he could face her. "You must be wondering what I wanted to talk to you about."

"Yes," Allegra said. "I have to say that I'm very curious."

"Well, I apologize for the secrecy," he said. "I'm not usually so mysterious, but in this case it seemed like the best way to go about it."

"Exactly what is 'it'?" Allegra asked.

"It's like this," he said, looking her in the eye. "I've always thought that the jewelry pieces Sylvie's bought from you were beautiful. Different from the stuff you usually see in the stores. Even the best ones. They're . . . unique. Like the necklace you're wearing right now. It's like art, I guess you'd say."

"Thank you," Allegra replied. "I'll take that as a compliment."

"You should," he replied. "Anyway, Sylvie told me all about how you're a gemologist. Says you really know your stones."

Allegra nodded. "I like to think so."

He looked at her with a serious expression. "I need someone like you to do a job for me," he said.

"What kind of job?" Allegra asked.

"There's an auction coming up at Dufour in Paris. One of their Magnificent Jewels auctions."

"I know," she said. "I have the catalogue at home, but I haven't looked at it yet."

"So you've bought there?" he asked.

"Oh, no," she said with a laugh. "I'm afraid it's a little out of my league. I get the catalogues just to look at the jewelry. To see if any of it inspires me. I also like to see the exceptional stones when they come up. Just because they can be so beautiful."

He nodded thoughtfully, then looked over at Sylvie. "I think we've found the perfect person," he said.

Sylvie smiled. "I know it."

Hilton took a deep breath and steepled his hands together. "Allegra, Dufour has an emerald ring coming up for auction, and I want that ring. It is exceptionally beautiful. A huge emerald. But it's the provenance that's really important in this case."

"That's often true," Allegra said.

"Well, it is with this ring," he said, "because it's Princess Karima who's selling it."

"Oh, I see," Allegra said. "That would automatically make it worth a lot, considering who she is."

"The point is," Hilton said, "I have to have it. It's going to be a surprise for a lady friend of mine."

Allegra knew it was irrational of her to feel disappointment, but she did. Maybe it was because a ring of such provenance was going to end up as a gift for just another rich woman. But maybe, she told herself, it was actually jealousy because she wasn't going to be the recipient of his largesse.

"The thing is," he went on, "if I bid on the ring personally, the price will go through the roof. All they have to do is hear my name, and dealers and fat cats all over the world will start trying to outbid me." He gazed into her eyes. "You understand what I'm talking about, of course."

"Oh, yes," Allegra said. "So you're looking for somebody to bid for you," she said.

"That's right," he said, "and I think you're the perfect person."

"But why not Sylvie?" she asked. She looked over but saw that Sylvie had quietly disappeared from her position behind the desk.

"Sylvie's known in the auction houses," he said. "She's bid for me before. Plus, I don't want to send just anybody into that auction."

"Why's that?"

"I want somebody who really knows stones," he said. "I want you to go to the preview and study the ring to make certain you're getting the right one."

"Don't you trust Dufour to deliver the goods? My God, you're talking about one of the world's most respected auction houses. They're over two hundred years old."

"I know," he said. "I know. But we both know that so-called experts goof up all the time."

"That's for sure."

"Anyway, you know your stones, so you can make sure that the ring you get is the ring that Princess Karima is selling."

"Yes," she said with certainty, "I'm sure I could do that."

"Then would you be willing to do this for me?" he asked, looking at her hopefully.

"I . . . I think so," she said. "I have to give it some thought."

"I'm willing to pay you handsomely," he said, smiling.

"It's not just a matter of money," she said. "There's my business to consider, and quite frankly I'm having a really tough time right now." She looked him in the eye. "I'm close to going under," she admitted, "so it's not a good time for me to leave."

"I'm sorry to hear that," he said. She heard the genuine concern in his voice. "But this wouldn't take long. You would have my personal jet, to take you to Paris, see the preview, bid the next day, and fly straight back with the ring. What've you got to lose? A couple of days at the most. Plus, an extra paycheck might help you save your business."

"How much did you have in mind?" she asked.

"I'm willing to pay you twenty-five thousand dollars and expenses," he said.

Allegra kept her face devoid of expression, though her heart leaped at his figure.

"My Gulfstream V, a suite at the Ritz or wherever you prefer to stay, and all your meals with a credit card I'll give you. You'll have permission to sign on it. What do you say? Fair?" He was staring into her eyes questioningly.

She managed to retain her composure while returning his gaze, but she was performing mental calculations at the same time. The rent. The gemstone dealer. The gold and silver and platinum dealers. Jason's salary. Also, she had to figure in what Whitehead was going to get out of her services. She knew that he needed her.

"What do you say?" he repeated.

"I can't do it for twenty-five thousand dollars."

"You can't?"

"I'll need fifty," she said, her voice unwavering and her eye contact unbroken. "In advance. I've got to pay some bills, and that'll do it."

"Fifty thousand dollars for a couple of days' work?" he said with a laugh. "In advance?"

"Take it or leave it," Allegra said. She made movements in her chair as if she were going to get up.

"No, no," he said, waving her down with his hand. "Wait just a minute there. Just a minute."

"Okay," she said. "I'll wait. But just a minute. I've got a business to run, you know. It may not be a multibillion-dollar multinational, but it's my life."

"You're something else, Allegra Sheridan," he said. He sat staring at her, his lips spread in a smile. Finally, he offered her his hand. "You've got yourself a deal."

Allegra shook his hand, trying to slow the wildly beating heart within her chest.

Sylvie, who had quietly reentered the office, began clapping her hands together lightly. "Hooray!" she exclaimed. "Now we must celebrate." On the desk, she had placed a tray that held a bottle of champagne in a silver ice bucket and three crystal flutes. "Shall I do the honors?" she asked, looking toward Hilton Whitehead.

"Certainly," he said. "You will stay and have a glass of champagne with us, Allegra?"

Her stomach did a turn. After last night's drinking and the excitement of the moment, a drink was the last thing she really wanted. "Sure," she said. "I'd love a glass of champagne. But just one quick one. I really do need to get back downtown to the atelier."

"Good," Hilton said as Sylvie popped the cork.

Sylvie filled the three flutes and handed Allegra and Hilton theirs.

Hilton raised his in a toast. "To a successful venture together," he said.

"*Bonne chance,*" Sylvie chimed in.

"Give her the schedule," Hilton said, looking over at Sylvie as they sipped the champagne.

From a desk drawer, Sylvie took out a single sheet of paper and handed it to Allegra. "This is the proposed schedule," she said.

Allegra glanced down at it. The auction was a week away. *That'll give me plenty of time to get things straightened out here before I leave. Like paying bills,* she thought. "This will work for me," she said, folding it and putting it in her pocketbook.

"Is your passport current?" Hilton asked.

She nodded. "Yes."

"Good. One less thing to take care of. Sylvie will handle all of the reservations for you and take care of the details."

"That's fine," Allegra said. "Is Sylvie also going to write my check?"

Hilton laughed. "You're too much," he said, "but I like that. You're one of the more straightforward people I've met lately. You don't meet many." He looked at Sylvie. "Get a check ready for me to sign," he said, "and Allegra can take it home with her."

"Thank you," Allegra said, then took a sip of the champagne. "There is one thing we didn't discuss," she added.

"What's that?" Hilton asked.

"What if I don't place a successful bid, and end up not getting the ring for you?"

"That's not going to happen," he said. In the background they could hear Sylvie typing.

"But how can you be certain of that?" she asked. "There're going to be a lot of rich men like you trying to get that ring. Princess Karima's name alone is going to make it a very hot auction. Remember the sale in Geneva a few years ago with the Duchess of Windsor's jewels?"

"I certainly do," he said. "Everything went through the roof."

"Exactly," Allegra said. "Some things went for twenty or thirty times their estimates. The same thing could happen in Paris."

"I'm sure that the same thing *will* happen in Paris," he said. "It's bound to. Princess Karima's name has the same kind of cachet that the Duchess of Windsor's had."

"That's what I mean," Allegra said. "I could lose out to somebody who's a fanatic devotee of hers. And has the money to back it up."

He shook his head. "I don't think so," he said. "I'm going to give you a letter of credit with the funds deposited and immediately available in the Citibank in Paris."

"Yes, but—"

"For a hundred million dollars," he added.

"A hundred million dollars," she repeated. She looked down into the flute of champagne, then back up at him. "That should do it, I think."

"I think so, too," he said. "The estimate is eight to ten million."

"How many carats?"

"Thirty-four and a half, I think. I can get the catalogue if you want to see it."

"No," Allegra said. "I can take a look when I get home. I was just curious."

Sylvie rose from behind the desk and went around to Hilton. "Here's the check," she said. "It only needs your signature." She handed him a pen and winked at Allegra.

He set his champagne flute on the desk, then placed the check alongside it and signed his name. "Here you go," he said, handing it to Allegra with a smile.

She wanted nothing more than to kiss the check, but she took it and slipped it inside her pocketbook. She would deposit it in her bank account as soon as she left. "Thanks, Mr. . . . Hilton."

"You're welcome," he said. "I'm sure everything's going to work out fine. I'll see you before you leave for Paris. Sylvie will let you know about that. Now, I'd better get back upstairs. I've got some things to do." He got to his feet and offered his hand again.

Allegra took it and shook firmly. "It was nice to meet you, Hilton," she said. "And thanks for this opportunity."

"Thank you, Allegra," he said. "We'll get together again soon." He turned and went to the door, thinking, *And not soon enough for me.*

When he had gone, Sylvie leaned down and air-kissed Allegra's cheeks. *"Merveilleuse, chérie. Merveilleuse."*

"I can hardly believe this," Allegra said. "When you told me I'd be glad I came up here today, I didn't dream it would be anything like this."

"I'm glad you're pleased," Sylvie said. "I hoped you wouldn't be insulted by his proposition."

"Insulted?" Allegra said. "I'm thrilled, Sylvie."

"Well, I was worried that you might think he was being rude. You know, by not buying a piece from you but asking you to do him this favor."

"Well," Allegra said with a laugh, "we can work on the piece of jewelry when I've come back from Paris with the ring." She looked thoughtful for a moment. "*If* I come back with it."

"Oh," Sylvie said with a shrug, "don't be silly, *chérie.* Of course, you'll come back with it. I'm sure there'll be no problem there. What in the world could happen?"

CHAPTER SEVEN

Jason looked across the breakfast table at Cameron Cummings and didn't think he'd ever seen a more handsome man. Cameron was just out of the shower and wore nothing but a towel around his waist. He was somewhere on the north side of forty, but his body was magnificent, a real gym bunny's, hard, buff, and sleek.

"So you think Allegra's really going down the tubes?" Cameron asked him, biting into a piece of toast.

"Yes," he replied. "She doesn't even think she can pay my salary or the rent, and yesterday she said she owed all of the wholesalers. You know, the gemstone and precious-metals dealers."

"Ouch," Cameron said, lifting a brow. "Those aren't the kind of people you want to get behind with. The landlord may give her an inch because she's been there for a long time, but the wholesalers? I don't think so. They'll take their money out of her flesh if they have to."

"I know that," Jason said. "That's one reason I'm really worried. She may have a good reputation with them, but that only counts for so much."

"Listen," Cameron said, "in this business reputation is everything, and if she gets the least little bit behind, the word will get around so fast her head'll be spinning like Linda Blair's in *The Exorcist*. She won't be able to find a wholesaler anywhere that'll give her two cents' worth of credit. And you're talking to somebody who knows. I've been around the block a few times in this business."

"That's why I wanted to talk to you. You're the most successful independent jewelry designer I know." Jason sighed. "I'm afraid that Ally will be ruined."

"You don't want to be associated with a sinking ship, do you?" Cameron said, taking a sip of coffee.

"Of course not," Jason said. "It's just that . . . well, I've been with her since the beginning, and I hate to jump ship."

"Then you're a fool," Cameron said. "What do you owe her?"

"I . . . well, nothing," Jason said. "It's just that we've worked together a long time."

"You're a bigger idiot than I thought," Cameron said, pointing a finger at him. "She's been using you all these years. Sure, she's the designer, but you're the one who's been doing all the dirty work for her. You're the one who makes those designs reality. And believe you me, if she hit it big, she'd be the one taking all the credit. She'd leave you behind in the dust."

"But she's always promised me a percentage if she hits it big," Jason said defensively. "You know, if she gets a contract with somebody like Tiffany or something."

"Keep dreaming," Cameron said cynically.

"She says that if she gets backing for her own shop, she'll give me a percentage of the business."

Cameron set his coffee cup down with a bang. "Shut up, Jason," he snapped. "You're making me ill. Allegra Sheridan is a lying bitch, and what's worse, she's a nobody. And my bet is, she'll stay a nobody. She operates in some kind of ivory tower, tinkering away at her precious jewelry, treating each piece like it's the fucking Sistine Chapel ceiling, refusing to do mass-market. If you're smart, you'll get your feet on the ground."

His harsh words stung Jason. He'd always believed that Allegra had it in her to make it big. He knew without a doubt that she had the talent, but he also knew what Cameron said was at least partially true. Allegra had refused several good offers in the past, and Jason didn't think that would ever change. She was too strong-willed to work for anybody else, and she refused to compromise the quality of her work. But would she lie to him about giving him a percentage? He didn't think so, but he couldn't be sure.

Cameron sat staring at him, waiting for a response. When one didn't come, he realized that he'd hurt the young man. The trouble with guys like Jason was that they were so masculine in appearance and manner that you forgot they could be hypersensitive. Cameron had the feeling that if he took Jason under his wing, he could inspire the kind of deep devotion that Allegra Sheridan obviously had done. For Jason, like most people he knew, needed to be led.

He looked over at Jason with a contrite expression. "I've hurt your feelings," he said, oozing sincerity. "I'm so sorry, Jason. I didn't mean to. I just hate . . . well, I just hate to see you taken advantage of. You could be making a much better living for yourself if you left Allegra's atelier and went someplace else."

Jason nodded his shaggy blond hair. "I know," he agreed. "I've had chances, but I always felt like I should help Ally."

"I understand," Cameron said. "Of course you'd want to help her. She's been like a friend to you. But it's time for you to stand on your own two feet and build a stable life. You don't deserve to live on the edge all the time. Besides, if you got yourself into an established firm, there wouldn't be this feast-or-famine drama, wondering whether you're going to get paid or not." He paused, then softly said, "Do you understand what I mean?"

"Yes," Jason said, "and you're right. I'm tired of living on the edge. Most of my friends have bought apartments and settled down, but I'm still living like I did when I first started out."

"You're better than that," Cameron said. "You owe it to yourself to do something about it, don't you see?" Cameron knew if he played his cards right, he could turn Jason's head in the right direction. All it would take was a few whispered words, making him think Cameron was in love with him. Just a few words and some hot sex, and Cameron would bet he could convince Mr. Goody Two-shoes to steal Allegra Sheridan's designs.

Cameron got to his feet and went around to Jason's side of the table. He put his hands on Jason's broad shoulders and began massaging him. "Maybe I could help you out," he said.

Jason trembled with excitement and fear at the touch of Cameron's hands. It wasn't that he'd never had such an experience, but he was still unsure of himself and scared of his own urges.

"What would you think, Jason," Cameron said in a dreamy voice as he continued to massage the younger man's shoulders, "if you worked with me for a while at Cameron Creations? You'd have a regular salary, all the fringe benefits, and you wouldn't have to stay if you didn't like it." His hands moved beneath Jason's sweater and moved toward his nipples, kneaded his flesh gently. He bent his head down toward Jason's and whispered into his ear. "On the other hand, if you liked it, you could stay. Even get rid of that dump you live in and stay here with me for a while."

Jason could hardly control his breathing and felt the embarrassing hardening between his thighs. "I—I think . . . I'd have to think about it," he finally managed to sputter.

"What's to think about?" Cameron continued. "Huh?" He licked Jason's ear and brushed his fingers across his nipples at the same time.

Jason thought he would levitate out of the chair, and when Cameron reached down and grasped one of his hands and pushed it against his own hardness, Jason didn't protest.

"Come on," Cameron said, gently tugging on Jason's hand. "Come with me."

Jason let himself be pulled up out of his seat, and he stood facing Cameron, who placed a hand on each of his arms. "I can give you everything you need," Cameron said. "Everything." He leaned in and flicked a tongue up Jason's neck, then looked at him, a sly smile on his lips. Then he nodded toward the bedroom. "Let's go in there," he said, taking Jason's hand in his.

In the bedroom, Cameron took off his towel and threw it on a chair, then took Jason into his strong arms. "Forget Allegra Sheridan," he said. "Think about your own needs, Jason." He kissed his lips. "Think about us."

When the taxi pulled up in front of her building, Allegra paid the driver and got out. On the trip downtown, she'd decided there were really only a few things she had to do to get ready for Paris, besides pack a couple of things. First, she had to sit down and pay bills. Then there were the three people she had to talk to. One was her mother, who seldom contacted her, but who would be furious if she should call while Allegra was away and discover she'd left without letting her know. Another was Todd, to let him know she would be in Paris a couple of days. And finally, Jason. He could keep everything going at the atelier while she was gone.

Since the nature of the trip had to be kept secret, she'd decided to tell them a lie. She didn't have any choice.

When she got to the door, she was surprised to find it locked. She wondered if Jason decided to leave early. But once she was in the atelier, it looked as if he hadn't been in at all.

She hung up her coat, flipped on the lights, and went straight to the answering machine. There were two messages. One from her dentist's office, reminding her that she had a cleaning coming up. The other was from Hooper and Strang, reminding her that they hadn't received her payment yet. A metals dealer. Thank God, she could pay them as soon as Whitehead's check cleared her account.

She picked up the receiver and speed-dialed Jason at home. When his machine clicked in, she hung up and speed-dialed his cell phone. But voice mail picked up that call, as well. She left a message, wondering what had happened to him. Jason was never late, much less absent, without letting her know. She hoped he was all right.

She took the big folder of unpaid bills from the filing cabinet next to her worktable, deciding that getting them ready to send out would divert her. Then she remembered that she had to call her mother.

Hoping to get it over with, she picked up the receiver and speed-dialed her number, waiting for Clarissa the Great to pick up.

"Hello?" The voice, a smoke- and booze-ravaged, low-register drawl, belonged to her mother.

"Hi," Allegra said. "I was hoping I would catch you in. How are you?"

"How is any woman in love, darling?" her mother responded, then laughed in her husky way. "But I forgot, you wouldn't know about that, would you?"

Allegra groaned inwardly. "Guess I wouldn't, Mom," she replied. "Some of us just aren't as lucky as you are."

"No," Clarissa said. "Very few, in fact. I'm the envy of every postmenopausal wench in Key West. Even a lot of the younger ones could learn a thing or two from me."

"No doubt," Allegra said. "Anyway, I called to let you know I'm going to be out of town for a couple of days. I'll be leaving next week."

"Oh, so where're you off to?"

"Paris," Allegra replied.

"Paris," Clarissa echoed. "How marvelous. It's a man, I hope."

"No," Allegra said. "It's business."

"Oh, how dreary," Clarissa said. "What sort of business takes you to Paris?"

"A magazine is featuring my jewelry, so they've offered to fly me over," Allegra said. "They'll do the photo shoot there."

"Well, maybe you'll meet a nice young man," Clarissa said. "Or a nice old one, for that matter. You're not getting any younger, you know." She laughed.

Allegra would have liked to slam the receiver down in her mother's ear, but she restrained herself. She knew that if she did hang up on her, Clarissa would dog her on the telephone until she'd extracted an apology.

"You're so right, Mom," Allegra said, "but some of us just aren't as lucky as you are." Then to get her own dig in, she added, "Over and over again."

"Well," Clarissa said, bristling, "my choices in men may not have always been ideal, your late father being a prime example, but at least I've had my pick of what's available. I'm not growing old alone, like so many women do."

"That's so wonderful for you, Mom," Allegra said. "How is . . ." She actually had to think for a moment to come up with her latest stepfather's name. ". . . Ben? Is he well?"

"He's divine," Clarissa said in an enthralled voice. "Absolutely divine. So . . . attentive to all of my needs. So charming. And such a . . . *man.*" She cackled her smoky laugh.

Allegra wanted to gag. Her mother was a sixty-five-year-old teenager. Bleached blond hair. Always darkly tanned. Face lifted, breasts lifted, and liposuctioned, she chain-smoked, drank like a fish, and lived for Men, with a capital M. She'd never really been there for her daughter, but Allegra tried to keep up some semblance of a relationship. Clarissa, after all, was the only family she'd ever known.

"Well," she said, "I'd better run, Mom. I have a lot to do before I leave. I just wanted to let you know I'll be gone in case something comes up. Jason will be here if there's an emergency or something."

"Jason!" her mother cried. "I don't know why you don't hire a straight one, if you've got to have a man working for you. But no, my brilliant daughter has to go out and find some New York fairy to work for her. It's no wonder you're not married."

"Sorry, Mom," Allegra said, barely able to restrain her anger, "but I have to run. I'll let you know when I get back."

"You do that," Clarissa said. "And don't get into any trouble in Paris." She laughed again. "Like you would."

" 'Bye, Mom," Allegra said sweetly.

"Yeah, till later," Clarissa said.

Allegra hung up the telephone, put her head in her hands, and sighed. She wondered why she even tried.

She looked over at the pile of bills and decided that writing checks, which she was loath to do, would be a relief after talking to Clarissa. She retrieved her company checkbook from the cabinet and placed it on the worktable. She began riffling through bills for the rent to pay first.

She'd just picked up the pen when the telephone rang.

"Atelier Sheridan," she said.

"Ally, it's me, Jason."

"Where are you?" she asked. "I've been worried about you. Are you okay?"

"Yes," he replied. "I—I have to talk to you about something."

"I'm all ears," she said.

"No," Jason replied. "I mean in person."

"What is it, Jason?" she asked. "Are you sure you're okay?"

"I'm okay, Ally," he assured her. "It's . . . just . . . that it's . . . personal."

Alarm bells went off in Allegra's head. "Do you want to come to the atelier?"

"I—I . . . yes," he finally said. "I'll come right now. Is that okay?"

"Of course, Jason," she replied. "I'll be here."

"See you in a few."

Allegra replaced the receiver, more mystified than ever.

She poured herself a glass of water and began writing checks, stamping the bills PAID, and filing them away. After thirty minutes or so, she heard the door to the atelier open, and hurriedly finished the check she was writing. "Just a second, Jason," she said, not turning around to greet him.

There was no response, and then suddenly arms came from around her back, embracing her in a powerful hug. "Hey, babe. Good news. I have a big surprise for you."

Allegra felt her tension melt away. "A surprise? What?"

"I bought a building on West Broadway," Todd said. "I bought it for us."

Allegra's mind began to spin. What the hell was he talking about?

"It was very expensive," he said, as if reading her mind, "and so I've been negotiating with them for months. I decided to keep the penthouse duplex for us and thought that together we could do a real number on it. Terrace, the works."

Allegra listened now with mounting fascination. Todd had talked about them living together before, but he'd never brought up anything like this. It represented a huge step for him—and for her. Keeping the best floors in the building for *them?* What he was proposing was actually scaring her.

"We could have a great time doing it," Todd went on, "carving it up however we want. We could even have a pool on the roof along with the terrace if you'd like."

"Are—are you sure about this?" she asked nervously. "You've—you've never brought this up before."

"I'm sure, Ally," he said. "And I want to hire a general manager to take some of the workload off me, so I can spend more time at home with . . . with you. I wouldn't be working fifteen to eighteen hours a day."

She didn't know whether to believe him or not. This was such a change in his attitude—in what she'd come to think of as his very nature—that she was flummoxed. Todd the Gypsy was ready to settle down?

"Do you think you really want to do that?" she asked.

He nodded vigorously. "It would be great, Ally," he said. "I'm making the storefront into a beautiful space. An ideal space for . . . for you, if you want it."

Her head snapped up, and she looked at him with surprise. "For me?" she said. "You mean . . . do you mean—?"

Todd smiled. "I mean that you could have your own shop there, Ally. A regular retail shop. You could showcase your work. There's even room for work space in the back."

"I don't know what to say, Todd," she said in a soft voice, trying to control the tears that came into her eyes. "I—I'm a little overwhelmed."

He went down on a knee before her and took one of her hands in his own. "I know I've given you reason to doubt me," he said. "But that part of my life is over, Ally. You must believe me. I know you're headstrong and independent. You've always wanted to do this—your jewelry—all by yourself. But don't you see how this could work out for both of us? You would have your business, and I would have mine. And we'd still be together."

She nodded and looked into his earnest, green eyes. "I'm sorry for thinking the worst," she said. "I guess I'm just not ready to accept the change in you."

The door to the atelier opened, and they both turned to look toward it. Jason ambled in, his backpack hanging off one shoulder. When he saw the tableau they presented, he stopped.

"I—I'm sorry," he said. "I didn't realize I was intruding. I'll come back later."

He turned to leave, but Ally called after him. "No, Jason," she said. "Don't leave. We need to talk." She got up and went over to him and gave him a hug. "Are you all right? I was so worried when you didn't come in or call."

"I'm okay," Jason said. "I had a doctor's appointment and completely forgot to tell you."

"Are you sure you're okay?" Todd asked, getting to his feet and putting a hand on Jason's shoulder.

"Yeah," Jason replied. "It was just a routine physical."

"Good," Allegra said. "I'm glad you came in, because I needed to talk to you."

"What is it?" Jason asked. "Are we closing up shop?"

"No, nothing like that," Allegra said. "Let's sit down."

"I can wait inside," Todd offered.

"No," Allegra said. "Because I wanted to tell you, too."

"What is it?" Todd asked, taking a chair and pulling it close.

"*Jalouse,* the French magazine, called me about doing a spread on my jewelry, and they've offered to pay my way over so they can do it there in Paris."

"That's great," Todd said.

"That's unusual, isn't it?" Jason said. "Don't the foreign magazines usually have a photographer in New York do the shoot to save money?"

Allegra nodded. "Yes, but they want to do an interview, shoot the jewelry and me, and some of my design drawings. So I told them I'd love to do it, but I'd also like to style it for the magazine. That's when they offered to fly me over. So I said yes. It'll only be for a couple of days."

"When is this?" Todd asked.

"Next week," she replied.

"So just like that"—Jason clicked two fingers together—"they offered to fly you over?" he said dubiously. "That's a new one. I've never heard of such a thing."

"That's why I wanted to talk to you," Allegra said, breezily ignoring the doubt in his voice. "Just to make sure that you could hold down the fort here while I'm gone."

"Well . . . ," Jason began. "You say it's next week?"

"Yes." Allegra nodded and gave him a puzzled look.

"Well, I guess so," he said. "How long did you say it was for?"

"Just a couple of days," Allegra said. "Why? Were you planning to take time off or something?"

"I . . . well, no," Jason said, "but I wasn't sure I even had a job anymore. I mean, with the ways things have been going."

Allegra smiled. "We've had a temporary reprieve," she said. "In fact, I just started writing checks to pay our bills."

"Did you make a big sale today?" Todd asked.

"No," Allegra said. "My mother's loaning me some cash to tide us over."

"Your mother!" Jason and Todd exclaimed in unison.

Allegra nodded. "Believe it or not."

"I can't believe that . . . that witch would give you the time of day," Todd said.

"This is incredible," Jason chimed in. "Was she drunk when she promised you the money?"

"No," Allegra said, persisting in her lie. "We had a nice long talk and—"

"Oh, come off it, Ally," Todd said. "You and Clarissa have never had a 'nice' talk. What's going on?"

"Nothing," Allegra said defensively. "She has a heart, you know."

"Yeah, like Hitler had a heart," Jason said.

"I don't want to talk about it anymore," Allegra said irritably.

Jason and Todd exchanged glances, and Todd shrugged.

"So, I can count on you, Jason?" she asked.

He nodded. "I was planning to take some time off, but I'll wait."

"Where you off to?" Todd asked.

"Uh, well, not anywhere really," Jason said. "It's just been a while since I had a little time off."

"I guess," Allegra said, although she knew that wasn't true. It had been only two months since he'd visited a friend in South Beach.

"If you don't mind, I'm going to go," he said, getting to his feet. "I've got a bunch of stuff to do."

"Sure, go ahead," Allegra said. "See you in the morning."

"Yep," Jason replied.

"See you later," Todd said as Jason headed to the door.

"Later."

After he'd gone, Allegra looked over at Todd. "Do you think he was acting a little . . . weird or something?"

"Yes," Todd said. "Maybe he just doesn't feel well. Going to the doctor and all."

"He said it was routine," Allegra said, a thoughtful expression on her face. "I just get the feeling that he's holding something back."

"Ah, forget it," Todd said. He got up and went around to the back of her chair and began massaging her shoulders. "Jason's a good guy. He's probably got things on his mind like the rest of us."

"I guess so," Allegra said.

Todd leaned over and kissed the top of her head. "Will you have champagne with me tonight?" he asked.

She leaned her head back and looked up at him. "Yes," she said. "I'd love to."

"I'll even make dinner," he said.

"Ohhh," she said. "When did you start cooking?"

"When the Chinese started delivering."

Allegra laughed. "I thought as much."

CHAPTER EIGHT

The minute Todd left the next morning, Allegra went to the telephone. She dialed Sylvie's number at work.

Sylvie picked up immediately. "Hello," she said.

"Sylvie, it's Allegra," she said.

"*Bonjour, chérie,*" Sylvie said. "I'm so glad you called. I wanted to ask you a few questions before I made your reservations. Hilton says he'll pay for your stay at the Ritz, as you know."

"Yes," Allegra said. "And?"

"Well, my friend Paul owns this building and has an apartment that friends of his use. He says you can stay there. It's in the Marais. Nothing fancy, but very nice. And"—she took a dramatic pause—"I can give you another couple of thousand dollars instead of giving it to the Ritz. I know you've been a little short on money lately, so I thought I would ask."

"You're kidding," Allegra said.

"But if you want the experience of staying at the Ritz, I can certainly understand that."

Allegra laughed. "No, no," she said. "I'd be glad to take the extra cash. But does Mr., I mean, Hilton know about this?"

"*Mais oui,*" Sylvie said. "He doesn't mind at all."

"And your friend Paul. You're sure it's okay with him?"

"*Chérie,*" Sylvie said, "Paul and I do this all the time. He uses my place here sometimes, and I do the same in Paris."

"Then I'll do it," Allegra said.

"Good," Sylvie said. "It's settled. If you'll be here tomorrow around, say . . . four o'clock, I'll have your information package together. Okay?"

"Wonderful," Allegra said. "I'll be there."

"There's not a lot," Sylvie said, "but Hilton wants to tell you about procedures and such at the auction house."

"Okay," Allegra said. "The one thing that's been worrying me is security. I mean, it's a little nerve-racking to think I might be carrying around an emerald ring worth millions of dollars."

"Ah, no worry," Sylvie said. "He's already set up a bank where you can deposit it after the auction. But we'll discuss that tomorrow."

"I'll be there," Allegra said.

"See you then," Sylvie said, and hung up.

When she put down the receiver, Allegra sat there, her head spinning slightly from the prospect of the assignment she had accepted from Hilton Whitehead. Bidding on a ring of such value against some of the richest men and women in the world was daunting. Bringing the ring back to New York only added to the enormity of the task.

She quickly showered and dressed, then went into her work space. Jason hadn't arrived yet, and she took the opportunity to flip through the catalogues that had been piling up. She started with the one from Dufour, curious about Karima's jewels. She glanced through the catalogue, but decided to work on an unfinished design. Then, after ten-thirty rolled around and Jason still hadn't shown up, she couldn't concentrate and began to worry about his tardiness.

Even as she had these fretful thoughts, Jason came through the atelier door with a bright smile on his face. "I'm sorry I'm late," he said. "I had a dental appointment early this morning, and forgot to tell you about it."

What has gotten into him? she wondered. *Yesterday the doctor, today the dentist. He's never been like this.*

"I hope it went okay," she said. "Anything serious?"

"No," Jason said. "Just a cleaning." He got settled at his worktable, then looked over at her. "Do you want to show me exactly what you want me to do while you're gone?"

"Give me a few more minutes here," she said, indicating her drawing pad. "Then I will. There are just a couple of little pieces, but they have priority."

"Okay," Jason said. "Should I go ahead and start setting the rubies for the di Guaradiani brooch?"

Already absorbed in an intricate detail, Allegra nodded without looking up. "Yes," she murmured. "That's fine."

The next few days flew by in a whirlwind of activity. Meeting with Whitehead, finishing up her paperwork, handling clients, and spending time with Todd seemed to take every available minute she had.

When the day actually arrived, Todd got out of bed when her alarm went off at five thirty a.m. and made breakfast for them while she got ready to leave. A car would be there to pick her up at six for her seven o'clock departure on Hilton Whitehead's jet.

"You didn't have to do this," she said, immensely happy that he had. She knew that Todd was not an early-morning person, and had made a sacrifice to please her.

"No, I didn't have to," he said, "but I wanted to."

"I'll miss you," she said.

"I'll miss you, too," he said. "Are you all packed?"

"All ready."

"I can go to the airport with you."

"No," Allegra said. "That's silly. Riding all the way to the airport and back. You should spend the time down at your building instead." She certainly didn't want him to know that she would be leaving from Teterboro on a private jet.

"You're right," he agreed. "The contractor has a million questions."

The buzzer sounded just as she was finishing her breakfast.

Ally grabbed her shoulder bag, and Todd carried her suitcase down for her. When they reached the street, he was stunned to see a gleaming Rolls-Royce awaiting her.

"Jeez," he said. "I didn't know you'd won the lottery."

"I didn't, silly," she replied. "The magazine provided the car and driver."

"But a Rolls?" he said. "I'm in the wrong business."

The driver took her suitcase and placed it in the trunk and held the door open for her.

Todd took her into his arms and kissed her. "Call me if you get a chance," he said. "I'll miss you. And I love you, Ally."

"I love you, too," she said. She got into the car's luxurious interior, and the driver closed the door.

When the car pulled out, she blew a kiss to Todd as he waved.

After the big car was out of sight, he went back upstairs, wondering what jewelry and designs she'd taken for the shoot. He hadn't seen her pack any.

The flight to Paris wasn't too long, six hours or so, and when Allegra landed at seven p.m., Paris time, she actually felt rested after the delicious food served aboard the flight and a nap in the luxurious bedroom. At the airport a driver with a black Rolls-Royce, identical to the one that had picked her up in New York, met her to take her in quiet luxury to the studio apartment on the rue des Archives in the heart of the Marais.

She had been to Paris once before, and remembered it as the most beautiful city she'd ever visited. But she had forgotten how truly magnificent it was. Even beneath the gray wintery sky, many of the monuments and buildings she passed were lit up to dazzling effect. As the car drew near her destination in the third arrondissement, she became fascinated by what she could see of the ancient quarter. She knew that it had been a stronghold of the aristocracy before the Revolution, but its mansions had been deserted afterward. In recent years, young urban pioneers, along with the government and various institutions, began moving in, and renovating the long-abandoned buildings. The district now teemed with several museums, municipal offices, beautiful apartment buildings, and trendy and interesting shops and restaurants.

Just past a church, the driver pulled over in front of a building on the rue des Archives and brought the car to a stop.

"Here we are, Miss Sheridan," he said in English.

Allegra looked up at the building and saw that it was a lovely seventeenth-century structure much like the others that lined the street. She shouldered her pocketbook and reached for the door, but the driver had quickly rounded the car and was already opening it.

"Thank you," she said as she slid out of the car's headily perfumed leather-upholstered interior.

"Just one moment," he said, "and I'll have your luggage for you."

"Allegra," a male voice called to her.

She turned and saw a tall, thin young man with long, windblown hair coming toward her with his hand extended. He was wearing a woolen overcoat with a heavy scarf tied and tucked in as if it were an ascot.

"I'm Paul," he said. "Sylvie's friend."

"Hi, Paul," she replied. "It's so nice of you to meet me. Sylvie told me you would be here." She shook hands with him.

"No problem," he said. "I live . . . close by. Ah, here's your luggage."

The driver stood quietly with her one suitcase, a small black one on rollers with a handle. "Have a nice stay, Miss Sheridan," he said. "I'll be here to pick you up on Friday at nine."

"Thank you," Allegra said.

He tipped his hat in deference, and went back around the car and got in.

"Here," Paul said, "let me have your suitcase. I'll take it up and let you in."

"Oh, you don't have to do that," Allegra replied. "It doesn't weigh much. I didn't bring a lot, since I'm only going to be here a couple of days."

Paul smiled. "I don't mind at all," he said, "and when you see the stairs, I think you'll be glad I offered."

Allegra laughed. "That bad, huh?"

"Yes," he said. "That bad."

At a pair of black-painted double doors, he took out a key chain and held up a key. "This one is for the door if you need it," he said. "It's easier to use the keypad. The code is 2929." He pointed to the small metal keypad on the wall next to the door.

He punched in the code, opened the door, and held it aside for her, and Allegra stepped into a long dark tunnel, one wall of which was lined with mailboxes.

"This buzzer will let you out. See?" He pointed to a little round push button on the wall.

"Okay." She started down the tunnel and saw that at its end it opened onto a courtyard paved with cobblestones.

"Oh, this is so lovely," she said.

"It is nice, isn't it?" Paul replied.

Shrubbery in tubs was placed around the walls, and a leafless tree soared upward from the center. She could see one set of stairs to the left and one to the right.

"We go up these stairs," Paul said, heading right.

The stairs were made of worn limestone and oak, and the walls were dingy plaster. At the first landing, Allegra stopped and turned to Paul, who was trudging up the stairs behind her.

"On up," he said. "All the way to the top."

When they finally reached the last landing, six floors up, Allegra took several deep breaths. "I must be out of shape," she said with a laugh. "This is really a climb."

"Yes," Paul said. "See what I mean?"

"Do I ever."

He set her suitcase down and took out the key chain again. "It's this key. It's easy to remember. The one downstairs is an ordinary brass key. This one is round. It's a fancy security lock."

"I've seen one before," Allegra said. "Not exactly like that, but similar."

Paul opened the door and once again held it for her.

"Thanks, Paul," she said. She stepped into a narrow entry hall with terra-cotta sponged walls. To her left she saw a small bathroom, and straight ahead was one large room with a sofa bed, over which was draped a multicolored kilim rug; a coffee table; and a couple of chairs. Along one wall was a kitchenette, and in a corner was a television set. Large beams ran across the ceiling and down the walls. At the end of the room was one window, and Allegra went straight to it. Looking out, she could see the apartment buildings all around, with their mansard roofs and skylights.

"How do you like it?" Paul asked.

"It's so charming," Allegra replied.

"Good," Paul said. He held out a card. "Here's my telephone number if you should need anything. Feel free to call."

"I think I'll be fine," Allegra said.

"Well, don't hesitate, as I said," he replied. "I work at home, so I'm always nearby."

"I really appreciate it, Paul," she said.

"And I'll be here Friday morning," he said, "to help you down with your suitcase."

"Oh, no," Allegra protested. "You don't have to do that. I can handle it. Really I can."

"About a quarter to nine," he said, ignoring her. "I insist."

"If you say so," Allegra said. She followed him to the door to see him out.

"By the way," he said, "there's a good little bistro just downstairs on the corner. Typical fare and not too expensive."

"Thanks," she replied. "I'm sure I'll be able to find my way around."

"See you Friday, then," Paul said, and he turned and left.

After she closed the door behind him, she turned and walked back to the apartment's one big room. She shrugged out of her overcoat and draped it across a chair, then put her suitcase up on the sofa. She unzipped it and began putting away the few clothes she'd brought with her, anxious to explore a little of the neighborhood before it got much later.

Tomorrow, Wednesday, she would go to the Citibank branch with the letter of credit that Hilton Whitehead had given her. A Monsieur Lenoir was expecting her. Then she would go to the preview at Dufour to see the emerald ring and register to bid. The auction would take place Thursday at two. Friday, she was to leave on the private jet at ten thirty a.m.

Taking her toiletries kit, she went to the small bathroom, where she checked her makeup, brushed her hair, and washed her hands, before putting her coat back on and grabbing her shoulder bag and keys. Locking the door behind her, she descended the ancient staircase and went back out onto the rue des Archives.

A unique jewelry store, unlike anything she'd seen in New York or elsewhere, was practically next door. Besides selling beautiful pieces of jewelry, it sold beads and semiprecious stones and the necessary equipment for making your own necklaces, bracelets, and earrings. From there, she went on down the block, and for the next hour or more, she looked into the shop windows that lined both sides of the street. Finally, after gazing into the window of a chocolatier, whose products were both exquisite and mouthwatering, she decided to try the bistro on the corner that Paul had told her about.

Casual and boisterous, with a good-looking crowd and smiling, outrageously flirtatious waiters, the bistro was more than she'd hoped for. Prominently placed in the middle of the bar was a giant fishbowl filled to the brim with water. But instead of fish, it was filled with cell phones. To its side was a sign with a drawing of a cell phone with an X drawn through it. Another sign on the mirror behind the bar announced in French that if you left your cell phone behind in the restaurant, you would have to fish for it.

Allegra smiled and felt certain that she was going to like having her dinner here. She enjoyed a carafe of white wine, salad, roast chicken, and vegetables, with a chocolate mousse for dessert. The meal was simple but delicious, and when the waiter presented her bill, she was somewhat amazed that she had eaten so well for less than fifteen dollars. She happily used the credit card that Hilton Whitehead had provided her with, and added a very generous tip for her handsome young waiter.

Back in the apartment, she tried to call Todd, but there was no answer at his apartment or hers. She wasn't surprised. He was probably still at the renovation site. Next, she tried to get hold of Jason, but he didn't pick up at the atelier, answer his cell phone, or respond to the telephone at his apartment.

It was still early in New York City, and Allegra couldn't imagine why he would have left the atelier already. For that matter, why he wouldn't answer his cell phone. He always had it with him. Jason had not been himself lately, and now, a long way from the atelier, it bothered her more than usual. He was responsible for her livelihood while she was gone.

The telephone rang, and she started. She picked up the receiver.

"Miss me?"

"I do," she said, smiling at the sound of Todd's voice. "I feel sort of . . . lonely."

"Lonely?" he said. "You? I'd have thought you'd already have met at least a dozen hot young men who'd be more than glad to take you out and show you the town."

She laughed. "No," she replied. "I'm afraid it's not like that. I have things I have to do, and besides, I don't really know anybody here. All the Parisians I know are in New York."

"Haven't you met any of the *Jalouse* magazine people yet?" he asked.

Damn, she thought. "Not until tomorrow."

"So what did you take with you for the shoot?" he asked.

"Just a few little things," she replied. "You know, easy to travel with."

"Like what?"

"You know, my apple peel necklace, a couple of bracelets, a couple of pairs of earrings. Not much."

"I can't wait to see the results," he said. "I know they'll do a beautiful job."

"Well, you'll have to wait a while because it'll be at least three or four months before they'll publish this shoot. If they do."

"What do you mean, *if* they do?" he asked.

"You know how it is, Todd," she said. "Sometimes they decide to kill a story because something more interesting comes along. They do that all the time in the magazine and newspaper business."

"I know, but that couldn't possibly happen to my gal," he said.

"I hope not." *Oh, God, forgive me,* she thought. "How are things going with the remodeling?" she asked, changing the subject.

"Okay," Todd replied. "In fact, things are going so well, I thought I might pop over to Paris and join you. We could spend a couple of extra days together, seeing the sights."

Allegra hoped he didn't hear the quick intake of her breath. Her mind began to spin.

"Ally? Are you there?" he asked.

"Yes," she said. "Of course I'm here. I was just thinking, that's all. I've got such a heavy schedule tomorrow and the next day that I wouldn't have time to even see you. And—"

"Oh, come on," he said. "Not even at night? What're these magazine people going to do? Follow you to bed?"

"Well, I just—"

"You don't want me there, do you?" he asked, irritated.

"No, no, Todd," she said. "It's not that at all. Really. You've got to believe me."

"You don't sound very convincing," he said.

"It's just that this is business, you know? And my return ticket is for Friday."

"Couldn't you ask them just to change it?" he asked. "That way we could spend Thursday night through Sunday together, then fly back Sunday night or Monday morning."

"I don't know whether they'll be able to change my ticket or not. Plus, there's the atelier to think of. I hate to leave Jason in charge like this. I couldn't even get hold of him earlier today," Allegra said, stalling.

"Ally, you're throwing up roadblocks," he said. "Why?"

"What do you mean?" she replied, knowing exactly what he meant.

"Come on, get off it," he said. "I'm talking about the weekend. You're closed on Sundays, only open by appointment the rest of the time, and you know that Jason is perfectly fine at handling whatever comes up."

"I . . . you're right," she said apologetically.

"Look, I'll check out the flights on Thursday and let you know one way or the other," he said.

"That would be great," she said, warming to the idea. "Remember, I'll be free late Thursday afternoon, but not before then."

"Okay," Todd said.

"If you come, don't bring anything heavy," she said, after giving him the address on the rue des Archives. "It's six flights up, and there's no elevator. Plus, the stairs are lethal."

"It sounds like just the kind of old building I would love."

"You would, too," she said. "I know you would."

"We could have a blast seeing a little of Paris together," he said. Then he added, "I love you, Ally."

"I love you, too, Todd," she said.

" 'Night, babe," he said.

" 'Night."

She replaced the receiver in its cradle and took a deep breath. She felt much better now that she'd talked to Todd. Then she remembered she hadn't spoken to Jason. She dialed the atelier number. No answer. She tried his home and cell numbers. No answer at either place. She decided not to leave a message, thinking she could call him back later, but decided against that, too. She didn't want him to think she was being a hysteric about the atelier. After all, what could have happened in only a few hours?

CHAPTER NINE

A few short blocks away, Ramtane Tadjer's valet slipped the silk and cashmere robe across Ram's shoulders.

"Shall I lay out your clothes for tomorrow, sir?" Gérard asked.

"Hm . . ." Ram considered the question for a moment before answering. "Not tonight, Gérard." Tomorrow and the next day were to be very special, and he would choose his attire very carefully. For the preview and the auction, he would dress in his very best clothes. He didn't care who knew he was bidding or on what. He was willing to pay whatever it took to get Princess Karima's ring. Besides, he knew that with the stone's inclusion, some dealers and collectors would be scared away.

"Will you be having breakfast at the usual time, sir?" Gérard asked.

"Yes, the usual."

"Very good, sir," Gérard said.

Ram picked up the remote for the plasma screen television, then turned back to his valet. "Oh, one more thing, Gérard," he said. "Bring me a bottle of Armagnac."

"Very good, sir." He turned and left the bedroom, closing the door soundlessly behind him.

Ram put his arms into his robe sleeves and tied the belt loosely, then put his feet into his silk tapestry slippers. He pushed the button that activated the televison screen, and it slid soundlessly from the ceiling above the fireplace mantel, hiding a Braque painting. Positioning himself on the freshly ironed linen sheets of his Empire sleigh bed, he pushed the on button. The television was set to the news, virtually the only thing Ram ever watched.

Gérard returned with the bottle of Armagnac and a crystal snifter on a silver salver. He placed them on the bedside table, next to the carafe of water and the glass that were always at Ram's bedside and refreshed daily. Then he poured a measure of Armagnac into the snifter.

"Anything else, sir?" he asked.

Ram shook his head. "No, thank you, Gérard," he said without looking at him.

Gérard exited the room silently, closing the door behind him with only a soft click.

Ram congratulated himself on hiring the very well trained young man. Like all of Ram's household help, Gérard had once served in a very grand house, in his case that of the old Baron de Beaufre. When the baron died, Ram had pounced. Whether through death, divorce, or debts, he had secured the best help there was to be had in all of Paris. Aside from being well trained, they were hardworking, efficient, loyal, and, perhaps most important, discreet. Ram didn't have to worry about his servants gossiping, even though he gave them little fodder for spreading tales.

Gérard was the exception, since he was responsible for maintaining the apartment on the rue des Rosiers, and at times Ram relied on him for dealing with difficult mistresses or prostitutes.

He remembered the tape he had loaded earlier in the VCR, and he pushed the button to activate the machine. He picked up the snifter of Armagnac that Gérard had so thoughtfully poured and took a long swallow. Then reaching over, he twisted the dimmer on the bedside lamp until it was completely off.

Up on the big screen, Denise sprang into view, her tongue licking her sensuous red lips, her long blond hair loosened and flowing down over her pale shoulders. Her milky breasts with their large nipples were fully exposed to the camera, and when she moved slightly, her shaved mound came fully into view.

Ram immediately felt a rise in his groin. She was so beautiful. So pale and white, so blond and blue-eyed. So much the Aryan ideal. And such a slut. As he watched her, his hand slid down between his legs. It amused and aroused him to know that she had no idea her domination was being filmed.

And what I've done to her is nothing compared with what I'll do to a certain family after I have that ring in my possession. Nothing.

As the film ran, he took another long swallow of the Armagnac. His eyes glittered in the dark, aroused by lust and even more so by his power. Long before the video ended, he hit the off button, satisfied and content. He wouldn't need more of the Armagnac to sleep well tonight.

"I should be receiving a check from Dufour in about two weeks. Perhaps even less," Princess Karima said into her cell phone, her voice lowered in a breathy whisper, though she was alone in her immense bedroom. "I'll wire the money into the account in Luxembourg as soon as it's cleared my bank here. The rest is up to you."

She dragged nervously off her cigarette as she listened to her caller, her eyes bright with the excitement of conspiracy. Walking to her vanity, she crushed her cigarette in a crystal ashtray and picked up the drink she'd left there. She took a swallow, then sat down, flipping loose tendrils of hair away from her face.

"You needn't worry," she said impatiently. "I'll call you the moment I've sent the wire." She heard her bedroom door open and saw Mimi's reflection in the vanity mirror. "One moment," she said into the cell phone. She turned toward the door. "What is it, Mimi?"

"I was just going to turn down your bed, madame," her ancient maid replied.

Princess Karima waved a hand toward the old woman. "Don't bother, Mimi."

"Yes, madame." The maid executed an approximation of a curtsy on her arthritic knees and turned to leave.

"And, Mimi?"

"Yes, madame?" The old woman turned to face her employer again.

"Don't bother me again tonight," Princess Karima said. "I won't be taking any calls, no matter who they're from. Understand?"

"Of course, madame."

"Now please leave me in privacy."

Mimi turned and departed the bedroom, closing the door behind her quietly.

Returning her attention to the caller, Princess Karima apologized. "Sorry," she said. "Go on." She listened for a short time, then sighed in exasperation. "Don't be so damned paranoid. If there's any reason to worry, it's at your end, not mine."

She took another cigarette from a gold box and put it to her heavily painted lips. She lit it and took a long drag, listening to her caller while scrutinizing her exotically beautiful but mature face in the vanity mirror.

"Don't call me again," she said at last, her voice imperious. "Unless there's a dire emergency. Not until after you've taken care of business in Luxembourg. I must go now." Without another word, she depressed the END button on the cell phone and snapped it shut. After placing it on the vanity, she took another sip of the Jack Daniel's on ice and ground out her cigarette in the ashtray.

She began sliding off the four rings she wore. They were golden trinkets as far as she was concerned, not worthy of association with her exalted name and therefore not going up for auction. There was the Harry Winston diamond set in yellow gold; a plain matching band; a ruby, blue sapphire, and diamond confection; and a large peridot from Bulgari. She dropped them into a jewel-encrusted seashell. Count Fulco di Verdura had designed the seashell in the 1950s, and she had received it as a gift from Stefano several years ago. Looking down at it, she suddenly felt a sickly moment of panic, then realized it was a false alarm. The emerald wasn't there. But it wasn't supposed to be, she reminded herself.

She emitted a throaty laugh. If the men from Dufour only knew what she knew.

The world might have been informed that she was disposing of her earthly possessions, but only fools would expect a lady to give *all* of her baubles to charity.

She opened a gold compact and lightly dusted her face with powder. Flipping the compact closed, she picked up the bottle of Golconda perfume from JAR. She dabbed beneath her ears with it, trailed the stopper down her neck, then generously rubbed it between her breasts and on her thighs.

She heard the bedroom door open and looked into the mirror. She watched as the backlit figure closed the door behind him and slowly approached her at the vanity. After he crossed the room, he stood directly behind her and put his hands on her shoulders, squeezing them lightly, looking at her reflection in the mirror. Leaning down, he kissed the top of her head tenderly with his sensuous lips.

"You smell heavenly," he said softly, his voice deep, masculine, and seductive.

She turned to face him. The pearl buttons on the filmy silk chiffon gown she wore were open, exposing her ample breasts to him. Her nipples were lightly rouged. "Take your clothes off," she said, her dark eyes glinting in the soft light.

His jacket, tie, shirt, and undershirt dropped onto the floor, and he stood proudly before her, exhibiting his lean, muscular torso with its well-defined abs, his broad shoulders, and his pumped-up biceps. Naturally olive-complexioned, he was deeply tanned, and his raven black hair and dark eyes shone against his skin.

The princess feasted her eyes upon his young unblemished body, drinking in his masculine hardness, then leaned back against the vanity, her head cocked at an angle. "Light a cigarette for me," she said, indicating the gold cigarette box with a slight nod of her head.

The young man stepped forward and reached for the box, took one out, and lit it with her gold lighter. He exhaled a stream of smoke, then handed the cigarette to her. She accepted it from him, took a deep drag, smoke trailing out of her nostrils. "Now finish."

The young man slipped off his expensive loafers and socks, then loosened his belt and took off his trousers. He wore no underwear.

Princess Karima stared at his body with hauteur, but her eyes shone with hunger. She was gratified to see that he was already aroused, whether by her body or the cash he knew he would receive at the end of the evening. She didn't care which. She had no illusions about her aging body, but it wasn't her allure that was important in this transaction. It was power over him. Not to mention the physical satisfaction she would no doubt receive from his considerable endowment.

"Here," she commanded, pointing with a lacquered fingernail to her right nipple. "Kiss it."

The young man went down on his knees and leaned toward her breasts.

"Let me see your tongue," she said.

His tongue appeared, pink and wet, and she nodded her head slightly. The young man kissed her nipple lightly and began licking it, slowly and delicately at first, tracing circles around it, then more rapidly, groaning with desire as it hardened on his tongue. He began stroking himself as he licked, his breath coming in audible gasps.

"Don't touch yourself," she ordered.

The young man immediately obeyed, removing his hand from his engorged manhood, then looked up at her, awaiting a signal from her before he made another move. The whites of his eyes and his perfect white teeth stood out in contrast with his darkness, and she suddenly remembered his name. Yamal.

She spread her legs apart and boldly thrust her pelvis toward him. She enjoyed the momentary look of surprise on his face when he saw her shaved mound, then the naked lust that came into his eyes. With a finger she motioned him toward her, and when his head was nestled between her thighs, she stroked his coarse black hair as she spread her legs farther apart, giving him uninhibited access to her.

She tilted her head back as shivers of pleasure traveled up her spine and throughout her body. *The seclusion of my new spiritual path,* she thought, *is going to enhance my physical life immeasurably. Without the prying eyes of society, I'll be able to enjoy myself as never before, all the while garnering the praise of the world for my charitable acts.*

The press will compare me with Mother Teresa, she thought as she ground herself against Yamal's face, holding his curly black hair tightly.

Kitty's mouth was set in an unmistakable pout, and she barely uttered an acknowledgment of Hilton's cheerful greeting when he strode into the penthouse's master suite. Her eyes remained glued to the Italian *Vogue* she held, as if its pages provided the secret to immortality.

Hilton caught her sullen expression out of the corner of his eye as he loosened his necktie, took it off, and placed it across the back of a chair. She was pissed, he thought. He refrained from chuckling aloud, amused by her childish behavior.

He promised himself that he wouldn't tell her what he was doing. He knew it was going to be the biggest surprise of her life. But he couldn't wait to see the look on her face when he presented her with Princess Karima's thirty-something-carat emerald ring.

Staring out the floor-to-ceiling windows at the early-evening lights of Manhattan, he began undressing, whistling tunelessly. Behind him, he heard the magazine flip shut, then land on the floor with a whack.

"Do you mind?" she complained.

"What's that, beautiful?"

"The whistling," she said. "It's driving me crazy. It's not like you can carry a tune, you know."

"Why, I think you're the first woman I've ever known who complained about my whistling ability," he countered jovially.

"Then they were all deaf as doornails," she said sourly.

He gazed at her, grinning. "Thought we were going to Swifty's for dinner," he said. "Why aren't you dressed?"

She shifted on the bed and looked away from him. "I don't think I'm in the mood tonight."

"Why not?" he asked. "You were all set to go earlier today. What happened?"

"Nothing," she said in a small voice. "I . . . I just don't have anything to wear."

"What?" He laughed. "Jesus, Kitty, you've got more clothes than Bloomingdale's."

"It's not clothes," she replied.

"Then what the hell is it?" he asked, stepping out of his trousers.

"It's . . . it's my jewelry," she replied. "I . . . I don't have anything new to wear to Swifty's, and you know how those society bitches are. They'll be analyzing everything I have on—especially my jewelry—and I'll be a laughingstock if I wear the same thing twice."

"Oh, fuck," he said, laughing again. "Half of the old cows in that place can't see well enough to know whether or not you're even wearing jewelry, and the other half are wearing worn-out old pearls and mine-cut diamonds they inherited a thousand years ago. You've got more jewelry than nearly any woman in New York."

She bolted upright from the pillows against which she lay, her eyes wide with fiery anger. "That is a lie!" she cried. "I don't have anywhere near as much jewelry as most of the women in this town. Nowhere near as much."

Naked now, Hilton strode to the bed and sat down beside her. He put his hands on her shoulders and massaged her gently. "Oh, come on, Kitty," he said. "I didn't mean to upset you. I know there are women in New York with more jewelry than you've got. There's always going to be somebody with more. More money, more clothes, more jewelry, a fancier car or apartment, a bigger yacht. You name it. If you're in some kind of game where you always have to have the biggest and the best, then you've come to the wrong place. I'm not interested in playing that game."

Kitty could see that she'd gone too far, and quickly tried to mollify him. She put her hands on his cheeks and caressed them tenderly. "There is more to me than that," she said softly, an earnest expression on her face. "You know there is. It's just that . . . well, I guess I try to overcompensate sometimes because I grew up poor. And a lot of these women have had fabulous things all of their lives. I will admit that I do try to impress them, partly for me but for you, too. I want you to be proud of the woman walking beside you. I try to look my best for you all the time."

"Aw, Kitty," he said, melting at her words. "I know what you're saying. You're the most beautiful woman in New York City. I'm just afraid to see you get caught up in keeping up with the Joneses." He kissed her tenderly, inhaling her exotic scent.

Kitty returned his kiss, putting her arms around his bare shoulders. "I'm sorry for upsetting you," she whispered. "I didn't mean to. You know that."

He drew back and looked into her dark eyes. "Now, tell me," he said. "What's this all about, huh? This having-no-jewelry business."

"Well . . . ," she began, choosing her words carefully, "I . . . I admit that I do have a lot of jewelry. Not many emeralds, though."

He chuckled. "Go on," he said when she paused.

"It's just that none of it's . . . none of it's famous, Hilton. You know? It's all new. No provenance, like the auction catalogues are always talking about. And I've met women here in New York that have jewelry that belonged to Marie Antoinette, for God's sake. Or Empress Josephine."

"Somebody like Princess Karima," he said.

She nodded. "Yes, like her."

"And the auction with some of her stuff is coming up, isn't it?"

Kitty nodded again, her long black hair swinging. "This week," she said. "The viewing is at Dufour in Paris tomorrow."

"I see," he said, enjoying the harmless game he was playing with her.

She stared at him in silence, her eyes full of hope.

"Well, maybe I can see what I can do," he said. "I don't know. The estimates are sky-high, you know."

"But the provenance," Kitty said. "You can't do any better these days. This is the most important sale since the Duchess of Windsor died. Princess Karima is one of the greatest legends of our time."

"You've got a point there," he allowed. "Look," he added, pulling her to him, "I'll see what I can do, but remember: No promises."

Kitty felt something closely akin to the thrill of acquisition rush through her body.

"I understand," she said. "No promises." She brushed her lips against his. "But . . . but if it's possible, Hilton . . . I . . . I really need emeralds."

"We'll see," he said, his lips pressing against her neck.

Kitty threw her head back and thrust her chest out, offering herself to him, and he responded at once, covering her bare breasts with his lips and tongue. He soon entered her, and they made passionate, almost violent love.

When they had sated themselves, they lay entwined in one another's arms. "You're sure you want to go to Swifty's tonight?" he asked.

"Whatever you want to do," Kitty said compliantly.

He looked at her and grinned. "Well, since you don't have any new jewelry to wear, maybe we should stay in and wait till you have something to knock their eyes out. What do you think?"

Kitty almost hyperventilated with excitement. "I think you're a genius," she said, her hand sliding down to his groin. "A genius." She began stroking him, slowly, teasingly.

Hilton quickly became aroused and slid around on the bed and up onto his knees. "Here," he whispered. "Genius."

Kitty looked up and knew what he wanted at once. She opened her mouth and licked her lips lasciviously. *That emerald's mine,* she told herself as she took him into her mouth. *All mine.*

CHAPTER TEN

A llegra dressed conservatively in a simple black pantsuit with a black cashmere turtleneck sweater and high-heeled black boots, and wore no jewelry except her watch. She didn't want to draw attention to herself at the auction house preview, and even small pieces of her jewelry might catch a connoisseur's eye at such a gathering.

Anxious to get out onto the streets of Paris, she looped a thick woolly scarf around her neck, put on her heavy winter coat, took up her shoulder bag, and set off to have something to eat before visiting Monsieur Lenoir at the Citibank branch near the place Vendôme. At a small café down the rue des Archives, she took a seat at a table next to the window, where she could watch the perpetual show that paraded back and forth along the sidewalks. Ordering a croissant and a cup of caffeine-rich French coffee, she slathered the perfect, flaky croissant with butter and thick-cut orange marmalade and put two lumps of sugar, along with heavy cream, into the coffee. Surveying the crowd in the café, she noted that her fellow patrons ranged in age from about eighteen to eighty, most of them stylishly dressed, and many of them reading the daily papers.

She paid her bill and was out of the café in no time, and began the short walk to the Métro stop located at the Hôtel de Ville. It was much cleaner and seemed safer than its counterpart in New York City.

After emerging from the Métro at the Tuileries, she walked briskly in the direction of the bank. She entered the palatial building and approached a uniformed security guard. "Monsieur Lenoir?" she asked.

The guard indicated a roped-off area to her right, where several people worked behind big desks. She strode to the area, where a young woman looked up at her quizzically. "Mademoiselle?"

"Monsieur Lenoir?" Allegra repeated.

"Do you have an appointment?" the young woman asked in English.

"No," Allegra replied, wondering how the woman knew she was American. "But he is expecting me. I'm here on business for Mr. Hilton Whitehead."

"One moment," the young woman said, rising from her chair.

A tall, handsome young man with dark, slicked-back hair strode toward Allegra, his hand outstretched. He was tanned and looked more like an athlete than a banker.

"Miss Sheridan?" he asked, his eyes traveling the length of her body, appraising her in one quick moment.

Allegra shook his hand. "*Oui,*" she said.

He smiled graciously, exhibiting perfect white teeth. "We all speak English," he said. "I'm Richard Lenoir. It's a pleasure to meet you. If you'll come with me?"

She walked along beside him to a plush cherry-paneled inner office, where he closed the door and indicated a chair for her. "Please have a seat."

Allegra sat down on the comfortable leather chair at the side of his desk and removed the manila envelope in her shoulder bag.

"This will only take a moment," Monsieur Lenoir said. "I spoke to Mr. Whitehead and his assistant, Ms. Javelle, yesterday, and I just need your copy of the letter of credit, then your signature on a form."

"I have the letter of credit here," she said, handing him the envelope.

"Very good," he said, taking it from her. "Thank you."

She watched as he sat down and took out the letter of credit. He glanced at it briefly, then searched through a small pile of papers on his desk.

"Ms. Javelle faxed me a copy," he said, "but we have to have the genuine article." He chuckled, and Allegra smiled.

"Ah, here we are," he said. He held a piece of paper in his hand. "Please sign this on the line by the *X*." He handed her an expensive-looking fountain pen.

Allegra signed her name and returned the pen to him.

"Thank you," he said. "Ms. Javelle said that Mr. Whitehead would be calling me tomorrow. She said that you would be writing a very large check against this account."

"Yes," Allegra said. "And I'm sure she told you that it has to be honored immediately."

He nodded. "That's not a problem for Mr. Whitehead," he said. "He's a valued customer of ours, and we've performed this service for him a number of times. We've also arranged for a safe-deposit box in case you should need it."

"Good," she said. "I'll probably be paying a bill for him tomorrow, then bringing something by here to keep until Friday. I'm scheduled to leave that morning."

"Oh, so soon?"

"Afraid so," she said.

"You'll hardly get to enjoy Paris at all," he said. "In any case, don't worry—you won't have any problem from this end, I can assure you. Oh, and here's your safe-deposit box key."

"Thanks," Allegra said, taking the proffered key and putting it in her handbag.

"That's it, then," he said, rising to his feet from behind the desk. "It was a pleasure to meet you, and if I can be of any further assistance to you while you're in Paris, I'll only be too happy to oblige."

He smiled again, and Allegra had the distinct feeling that his offer was more than professional. "I think I have everything I need," she replied, "and I'd better get going now."

"It was a pleasure to meet you," he said, leading her toward the office door. "Maybe I'll see you again."

"Maybe," Allegra said, noticing the glint in his eyes.

As she left, she couldn't help but smile. Some women might be offended by a come-on as obvious as the handsome Monsieur Lenoir's, but she felt complimented by it.

She spied a taxi cruising by and hailed it. After she was seated in the rear, she gave the driver the address for Dufour, nearby on the rue de Richelieu in the area known as les Grands Boulevards. It was time for viewing the auction items, and suddenly she felt excited by the prospect.

The taxi soon pulled over in front of the Hôtel des Ventes Dufour. It was a venerable, gray stone neoclassical building that gave the impression of solidity and quiet old-world wealth. Inside its twenty hallowed auction rooms, however, she knew that the atmosphere could become noisy, raucous even, when the bidding escalated into a frenzy for the treasures that were put on the auction block every day at two p.m. promptly.

She paid the taxi fare and entered the building's grand façade, her heart beating quicker than usual in anticipation. She stopped at the information desk, where an attractive young blond woman wearing an Hermès scarf knotted just so around her neck looked up at her from behind tortoiseshell-rimmed glasses.

"*Vente des bijoux?*" Allegra asked in French.

"The top floor," the young woman responded in perfect English. "The elevators are just ahead."

"*Merci,*" Allegra responded. Why had she always heard Americans complain that the French insisted upon using their own language? Perhaps, she thought, when they heard her efforts, they immediately used English so as not to have to hear her butcher French. She knew her command of the spoken language was at best crude, but she was determined to use it as much as possible.

When she stepped out of the elevator a few moments later, she found herself in a hallway with several doors leading into a very large exhibition/auction room. Walking through the nearest one, she was confronted by a crowd of well-dressed, immaculately groomed men, primarily of middle age and older, and their counterparts, perfectly coiffed and designer-dressed women, primarily of a comparable age, although there were a few younger beauties.

Conversation was whispered throughout the room, and all eyes were glued to the various displays of jewelry in glass cabinets. The most important pieces were exhibited singly in glass or Lucite boxes on pedestals. Allegra knew that the ring she was looking for would be in one of these single display cases, but rather than focusing on it at once, she made a perambulation of the room, studying the displays in the less important cabinets first.

As she so often felt at auctions in New York, she was stunned by the staggering amount of the world's beautiful and costly objects that were available at any given time for those who could afford such luxuries. After a half hour or so of scrutinizing the assembled jewelry, her eyes had already taken in almost as much as she could absorb. Dazzled by the king's ransom on display, Allegra decided it was time that she had a look at the ring she would be bidding for, then register to bid.

She went to a display case where she saw an auction catalogue, and flipped through it until she saw the ring. It was lot number twenty-four. She put down the catalogue and looked around the large room. She casually moved from the display cases that contained the less expensive lots, and meandered around the room, focusing on the single displays.

Arriving at lot number twenty-four, she stopped behind a man and a woman who were looking into the case. Princess Karima's thirty-four-and-a-half-carat emerald shimmered against the black velvet on which it was set. Clearly, the princess's ring was not just any emerald. Its dark green color, clarity, and cut were the very best. Allegra thought it was probably from Colombia, though that wasn't necessarily the case. Emeralds came from mines in several countries, including India, Brazil, and Egypt. On the surface, it appeared to be perfect, but that was seldom ever true with emeralds. Flawless ones were extremely rare, and oil was commonly used in the business to fill cracks, enhance color, and hide other flaws.

Anxious to see the stone up close, she looked about for a guard with a key. Spotting one nearby, she approached him. "Monsieur," she said, pointing toward the display case. *"L'émeraude, s'il vous plaît?"*

The guard looked at her, then removed the key chain on his belt and went to the case. Allegra opened her shoulder bag and took out the suede case that held her loupe. Fortunately, the couple who had spent a long time looking at the ring had moved on, so she would be able to examine it without interference from anyone else.

The guard opened the case, took out the ring, and handed it to Allegra. She positioned the loupe in her right eye, and brought the ring toward the loupe slowly. She studied it intently for several moments, turning it this way and that with her fingers, before exhaling a deep breath. She hadn't realized that she'd been holding it until now. Removing the loupe, she continued to examine the ring as it shimmered magnificently in her hand.

She was puzzled by it, and a little uneasy for some reason, though she wasn't certain why. Something about this stone rang a little bell somewhere in the back of her brain.

One thing was certain. The emerald was not flawless. Its color and cut were perfect, but the stone itself had a flaw that no one had tried to conceal, which she thought odd. The vast majority of dealers the world over would have used oil to fill the flaw.

She replaced the loupe in her eye once more, and brought up the emerald. Focusing on the flaw, she felt a chill run up her spine, and the hairs on the back of her neck stand up. She'd never seen anything like it in her life.

She took one more look, then handed the ring back to the guard. *"Merci, monsieur,"* she said.

"You're welcome," he responded in English.

Allegra went back to the catalogue on the display case. She found the page with the emerald and looked at the picture. Then she looked at the copy, which mentioned the flaw. She saw that no provenance beyond that of Princess Karima was provided. Absolutely nothing.

It was as if the stone didn't exist until Princess Karima bought it. But that wasn't so odd. After all, catalogue copy often read like that, ignoring any previous owners who weren't famous, or rich, or both.

Before registering to bid at the auction, Allegra was tempted to ask to speak to one of Dufour's jewelry experts for more information about the ring's provenance. Surely they knew more than they'd published in the catalogue. But after considering such a move, she decided against it. Her mission was to bid on the emerald. That was all. And she didn't want to draw undue attention to herself by asking about the ring, either.

She could imagine the news spreading like wildfire throughout the auction house. *A young woman is asking about Princess Karima's emerald. Watch out for her.* One expert would tell another, word would inevitably spread to potential buyers, and all eyes would be upon her tomorrow.

She went to one of the ladies behind a display case. Another blonde. Another Hermès scarf perfectly knotted about a neck. But a scowl on her face.

"S'il vous plaît," Allegra began.

"I speak English," the woman said, interrupting her.

"Where do I register to bid?" Allegra asked.

"On the ground floor," the woman said. "You will see it near the information desk."

"Merci," Allegra said cheerfully, despite the woman's disagreeableness, and turned and walked to the elevators. On the ground floor, she looked around and spotted the registration desk. She went to it, got the appropriate forms, and filled them out. The perfectly groomed blonde behind this desk took them, filled in some blanks, then told her, *"Vingt-neuf."*

"Excusez-moi?" Allegra said.

"You will have paddle number twenty-nine," the young lady said irritably.

"*Merci,*" Allegra said, ignoring her tone. She turned and left the auction house.

She stood outside on the rue de Richelieu, breathing in the fresh air. Something still niggled at the back of her mind. Something about the flaw in the emerald. But she could not for the life of her put her finger on what it was.

She began walking down the rue de Richelieu with no destination in mind. Despite the gray skies and the brisk, chill wind, she enjoyed the splendor that was Paris. Before long, she found herself passing the Bibliothèque nationale and approaching the Palais Royal. Allegra idly wandered through arches into the garden that lay hidden within the confines of the former palace's walls. It was now bereft of green but nevertheless beautiful due to its formal structure. She decided to stroll all the way around the colonnade that lined the four sides of the garden, and was happy to discover that interesting shops lined the stone walk.

She passed a number of elegant-looking dress shops and found herself entranced by the finery exhibited in their windows. A store that sold both antique and contemporary men's vests exhibited fabrics that nearly made her swoon. Coin shops and dealers specializing in military decorations abounded, along with a few dealers in modern art. She idled in front of Le Prince Jardinier, where beautiful and expensive gardening tools and clothing were sold; ogled the exquisite restaurant Le Grand Vefour, one of the most expensive in Paris; and then stopped and stared into the showcase at Jules Levant Joaillier.

She had heard of the legendary Levant, of course, and had seen pieces of jewelry that he'd designed in years gone by up for auction at Sotheby's and Christie's. Lingering in front of the windows, she was stunned by the quality and lavishness of the jewelry. This was not a shop where one could purchase a relatively inexpensive trinket—a fountain pen or cigarette lighter, for instance—and then boast that it had come from Jules Levant. It sold nothing inexpensive and had never created an affordable line for those who weren't rich, like Tiffany, Bulgari, and even Harry Winston, of late. No, Jules Levant Joaillier obviously operated in the belief that there were always enough rich people to keep its doors open, without its having to stoop to serving the hoi polloi.

Allegra decided to treat herself to something more than a peek in the shop's windows, even though she knew she couldn't afford the least expensive bauble in the place. She buzzed the highly polished brass bell set in the doorframe and waited to be given entry. When she heard the door buzzer, she pushed on the door and stepped into one of the most exclusive realms in the world of jewelry.

A shop of moderate size, it was decorated in a pinkish beige that Allegra knew served as a good background for the jewelry. The air was delicately scented with a provocative aroma that conjured up the Orient. On a magnificent ormolu-embellished *bureau plat,* she saw an enormous vase that contained dozens of pale pink roses and white French lilacs that beckoned to her. A huge crystal chandelier hung from the center of the ornately plastered ceiling, dripping hundreds of reflective prisms. The walls were lined with cabinets and on the plush carpeting sat showcases, all filled with treasures.

As she stood there deciding where she should begin her tour of the cases, she was unaware of two men and a woman observing her on a video monitor in an office behind the salesroom.

"A window-shopper," sniffed the woman, Madeleine de Chantérac. "One wishes they would waste someone else's time."

"I'll let her waste mine," Ali Noureddin said, starting for the door.

"No," said Ram, staring at the monitor. "You keep busy here, Ali. I'll see to the young woman."

He opened the office door and called out to the showroom. "One moment, mademoiselle."

Allegra searched for the owner of the cultured voice, but saw no one. Removing her black calfskin gloves, she walked toward a showcase and began inspecting the jewelry within it. Necklaces, bracelets, and earrings with enormous stones, beautifully set, greeted her eyes. Allegra could see why Jules Levant was legendary. The jewelry was magnificent down to the smallest piece. She knew that the shop had altered its designs very little over the years, and she could see why. The designs were classic, and the settings were of secondary importance. They were mere containers for the stunning stones they held.

"Mademoiselle?"

Startled, she looked up. On the opposite side of the display case stood one of the most handsome men she'd ever seen. His hair was the darkest black, slightly graying at the temples, his skin was like honey, and his dark eyes could be described only as liquid, bedroom eyes. His sensuous lips held a smile that made her want to smile back. *And probably happily married to one of the chic, thin women that crowded Parisian sidewalks,* she thought.

"Hello," she finally said in English, forgetting to try her French.

"Ah," the man said, smiling. "You are American."

"Yes," Allegra replied. "I'm—I'm just looking around if you don't mind. Your store is so . . . so magnificent."

The man nodded slightly. "Thank you," he said. "Look around all you like. What brings you to Paris?"

"Oh, I'm just doing a little sightseeing, you know," Allegra said.

"Ah, I see," he said. "No doubt you will do some shopping."

"Maybe," she said. "Nothing major, though."

"Well, if there's something here you would like to try on, don't hesitate to let me know."

Allegra laughed. "I don't think so," she said. "I'm just a poor working girl."

"All the more reason to try a few things on," the man replied. "Every woman should experience wearing the world's most expensive jewels, don't you think?"

His charm disarmed her completely. "I agree with you wholeheartedly," she said, "but I don't want to waste your time."

"You never know. Perhaps someday a husband or a lover will bring you back to Jules Levant and buy something for you."

Todd's face flashed in Allegra's mind, but she couldn't imagine him bringing her into this shop and purchasing something for her.

"I doubt it," she said in a good-natured voice, "but it's fun to look anyway."

"I see you were looking at the ruby ring," the man said, reaching down into the showcase from behind. "This one surrounded with diamonds." He held the ring up for her inspection. "The ruby is 25.70 carats."

"It's really beautiful," she said. "Is that a Burmese ruby? I should say, is it from Myanmar?" She reached into her shoulder bag, her fingers searching for her loupe.

"We all still think of it as Burma, don't we?" he said, looking at her quizzically. "But how did you know? Women who wear the finest jewelry often know very little about it."

"It's fairly obvious, isn't it?" Allegra replied. "Most of the best rubies come from Myanmar. Plus, the color of this one is exquisite. It's not too bright, like the stones from Vietnam, Afghanistan, or Pakistan, and it's not too brown like Thai stones. It's a perfect red. At least, I think it's a perfect red." She looked up at him and smiled. "Plus, I've studied gemology."

He laughed. "What a rare creature you are."

"Why's that?" she asked.

"It's very unusual for such a beautiful woman to take up such a study, don't you think?"

Allegra felt herself blush. "I . . . well, thank you, but surely there're lots of good-looking women who study gemology."

"I can assure you that you are wrong," he said, smiling. "There are a soupçon of attractive women in the business, but most of them are, shall we say, flinty-eyed?"

Allegra laughed again. "That's probably true," she allowed. "Do you mind if I look at it with my loupe?"

"Not at all," he said, handing the ring to her, "but I can assure you before you look that the stone has not been heat-treated for inclusions. It is perfect."

"Oh, I believe you," she replied, bringing the stone toward the loupe in her eye. She stared into the stone, turning it in different directions, then took her loupe out and put the ring on the counter. "This is one fantastic stone," she said, "and so are the diamonds that surround it."

"Try it on," he said.

"Oh, no," Allegra said. "I shouldn't. . . ."

"I insist," Ram said gently. He picked up the ring. "Let me have your hand."

Allegra let him take her hand in his and immediately felt embarrassed. This simple action seemed intimate somehow.

"There," he said. "It's a perfect fit, and I think it looks spectacular on you. You make the ring even more beautiful than it is."

Allegra felt herself blush again. "You're . . . you're awfully nice to say so," she said. "Do you mind my asking how much this ring sells for?"

"Around a million euros," he replied. "Give or take a few."

"My God," Allegra said. "I don't think I've ever worn anything that valuable before. Oh, well, it's a little out of my price range this week." She laughed. "Besides, I've always been partial to emeralds. I think they look better with my coloring."

"You're probably right about that," he agreed, "and I have an emerald I would like to see on you."

He let go of her hand and moved down to another showcase.

"No, really," Allegra protested. "I know you must be busy, and I've really got to get on my way."

"First you must try on this ring," he said. "For me." He looked at her. "I must see it on your finger."

"Well . . . okay," Allegra said, shrugging. "If you say so." She had to admit that this was fun. Even being in the jewelry business, she didn't often get to try on pieces that sold for this much money. What was more, the man's charm and looks were magnetic, and she didn't feel a rush to leave the shop.

"Here," he said. He held the ring in the palm of his hand with his fingers closed around it so that she couldn't see what it looked like.

When he opened his hand, Allegra gasped. "Oh, my God," she exclaimed. "This is amazing. I think it's the biggest, most beautiful emerald I've ever seen."

He looked very pleased with himself. "Try it on," he said. He held the ring between his thumb and a finger, ready to put it on her finger.

Allegra let him slide it on. The fit was slightly large, but no matter. Simply wearing this magnificent stone was mind-boggling. She stared down at it in quiet reflection, wondering what it would be like to be able to own something of such grandeur. To be loved by the kind of man who could afford such a gift and be thoughtful enough to buy it.

"What do you think," the man asked, smiling patiently.

"I think it's overwhelming," she said, looking up at him. "The woman who will someday wear this will be a very lucky woman, I think."

"It's a very special emerald," he said, "for a very special lady, and I think it's *you*."

"I would like to think so, but I can't picture myself as quite this grand," Allegra replied. She thought about the emerald she would be bidding on tomorrow, and she wished that she could share that information with him. Wouldn't he be excited to learn that she was almost certainly going to be the high bidder on Princess Karima's emerald? However, her lips remained sealed.

"I have an idea," the man said.

"What's that?" she asked, only half paying attention as she continued to study the sight of the emerald on her finger.

"I will take you to lunch," he said, "and you will wear the ring there."

"Oh, no. I couldn't," Allegra protested.

"Oh, but you could," he replied. "We will simply walk a few steps around the arcade, right here in the Palais Royal, and have lunch together at Le Grand Vefour."

Allegra remembered her recent view through the restaurant's windows and the resplendent room with its glorious murals. She knew that it was one of the most expensive restaurants in Paris, if not the world, and his invitation was tempting.

"Come," he said, "you must say yes."

"I—I can't," she said. "I really appreciate your offer, but it's impossible. I—I have engagements I have to keep today."

"I thought you were simply sightseeing," he persisted.

"Yes, but . . . but I have to make some telephone calls," she said, hearing the lame excuse for what it was. "And I have to see a couple of friends before they leave town," she added.

"That's too bad," he said. "Perhaps another time, then."

"That would be wonderful," she replied. "I'd really better get going now."

"So soon?"

"Yes," she said, pointedly looking at her watch. "I'm going to be late as it is."

The man extended his hand across the showcase. "I am Ramtane Tadjer," he said, "and it is a pleasure to have met you."

"I'm Allegra Sheridan." She laughed and shook his hand. "It was wonderful to meet you and have the opportunity to try on some of your beautiful creations."

He shrugged his shoulders. "It was nothing," he said. "All my pleasure, I assure you. Getting to see my jewels on such a beautiful young lady who is worthy of their perfection was a treat for me. I usually see them on the arthritic, age-spotted fingers of the very old ladies who can more often afford my merchandise."

"Well, thank you very much," Allegra said.

"Please take my card," the man said, slipping a gold card case from the inside breast pocket of his suit. He flipped it open and took out a heavy cream-colored vellum card with his name, address, and telephone number engraved—not cheaply embossed—on it. "This is my personal card," he added, "and you must feel free to use it at any time."

Allegra took the card from him as she searched through her shoulder bag for her own case. When her fingers finally touched upon it, she pulled it out, opened it, and handed him one of her cards. "This is my business card," she said. "I'm afraid that's the only one I have."

He took it and looked down at it. "Atelier Sheridan." He recited the address and telephone number. "You may be surprised to hear from me one day."

"It would be a pleasure," she said. "I could show you around town if you're in New York."

"I'm in New York often," he said, "so I may take you up on the offer. In the meantime, if you have a free moment in Paris, don't hesitate to phone me. We could have dinner, perhaps. Or just a drink."

"Thank you, Mr. Tadjer," Allegra said.

"Ram, please," he replied. "My friends call me Ram."

"Oh, that's a wonderful name," she said. "My friends call me Ally."

He nodded. "Ally," he said, trying the name on his tongue. "I think I will call you Allegra, if you don't mind. I think it befits you more."

Allegra smiled. That was the first time she'd ever heard that. "Whatever you prefer," she said. "Now I really must get going." She turned toward the door.

"Don't hesitate to call," he said.

"I won't," she said.

He came from behind the counter and walked toward the door with her, opened it, and bowed slightly as she stepped out onto the walk. "Ciao, Allegra," he said.

"Ciao, Ram." She sketched a wave in the air, then walked purposefully toward the nearest exit from the Palais Royal's arcade.

Her bootheels beat a loud staccato on the stone walk, resonated about the plaster and brick walls, ceilings, and arches. When she had gone through a passage and back out onto the street, she stopped and leaned back against the building for a moment.

Oh, my God, she thought, breathing deeply, as if she had been deprived of oxygen. *He's so charming and handsome. But I've pledged myself to Todd. The former philandering Todd. Or so he says.*

Allegra straightened up and started walking down the street, not knowing where she was going, but determined to quit thinking about the very sexy Ramtane Tadjer and the man she was fairly certain she was in love with, Todd Hall.

Wandering aimlessly, she finally decided that she would return to the apartment to change clothes, have something to eat, and try to get hold of Jason and Todd.

Allegra slammed down the telephone in a mixture of anger, curiosity, and worry. Jason had answered at none of his numbers, and he should have been in the atelier by this time. In any case, he was once again incommunicado, wherever he happened to be, and Allegra was disturbed by this new behavior of his.

Pacing the small studio, she fretted, but came to the conclusion that it was a waste of her time. She decided to try to get hold of Sylvie.

She picked up the telephone and dialed the New York number.

"Hilton Whitehead's residence," Sylvie said.

"Sylvie, it's Allegra."

"Ah! I'm so glad you called," Sylvie exclaimed, her accent more pronounced than usual.

"What—?"

"It's Todd," Sylvie growled. "When I came in this morning, he had left a message on the answering machine. Which I ignored, of course. But he's already called again."

"Todd! But how—?"

"You tell me," Sylvie said. "How *did* he get this telephone number? Surely, Allegra, you did not give it to him."

"No, of course not," Allegra replied defensively. She was seeing a side of Sylvie that she'd never seen before. "How could you even think such a thing? I haven't told—"

"Never mind," Sylvie said. "However he got it, he did, and he's going to drive me crazy."

"What the hell is going on?" Allegra asked.

"Dear Todd is worried about you," Sylvie responded. "He doesn't seem to believe your story about going to Paris for a photo shoot, and he thinks I know something."

"You didn't tell him anything, did you?" Allegra said.

"Of course not," Sylvie said. "I played completely dumb. Anyway, he is very persistent, and I finally told him not to ever call me here again."

"Good," Allegra said. "I can't imagine why he called there. He's bugging me about changing my ticket, so that he and I can spend the weekend in Paris together, then fly back together Monday."

"*Mon Dieu,*" Sylvie swore. "What did you tell him?"

"I told him I would see about it," Allegra said, "but that I didn't think it was possible."

"Do you want to do that?" Sylvie asked.

"No," Allegra quickly replied. "Well . . . I mean, it would be nice to spend the weekend in Paris with him, but if I have the ring . . ."

Sylvie paused a moment, thinking the situation over. "The ring will be in the bank?"

"Yes, but—"

"But nothing," Sylvie said. "I can talk to Hilton and unless he has plans for the weekend, I'm sure he won't mind your staying until Monday. I'll just have to alert the pilot. You and Todd can have a fun weekend together."

"Are you sure about this?"

"I'll talk to Hilton right now," Sylvie said.

"Oh, God," Allegra said.

"What?"

"Then I'll have to explain to Todd why we can't fly back together," she said. "If he wants to try to get tickets on the same flight. I mean, I can't tell him I'm flying on a private jet."

"Before you worry about that," Sylvie said, "let me talk to Hilton. I'll call you back in a few minutes."

"Sylvie, you're so great," Allegra said.

"Just doing my job, *chérie,*" she said. "Besides, Todd sounds very much like a young man who's madly in love. How can I resist trying to help?"

Allegra replaced the receiver in its cradle and stared into space, a puzzled expression on her face. Sylvie seemed to have accepted the delay awfully quick. Allegra wondered what Hilton Whitehead would have to say. The ring was certainly a major purchase after all, and one he would probably want brought back to New York immediately. She would have to wait to see. In the meantime, it occurred to her that she would be responsible for the ring all weekend if Whitehead agreed to a change in plans.

Oh, well, she told herself, *it's going to be in the safe-deposit box. What could possibly go wrong with it in the bank?*

Her reverie was interrupted by the telephone's shrill ring, and she picked up the receiver. "Hello."

"It's Sylvie, *chérie.*"

"Already?" Allegra replied, surprised.

"Yes, and I've got good news for you," Sylvie said. "I just hung up from talking to Hilton, and he says that it's fine to return next week. He'll send the plane on a little errand, so you and Todd can have a romantic weekend."

"Oh, thank you so much, Sylvie," Allegra said. "That's wonderful.

Now I have to figure out how to explain us not being able to fly back together."

"One step at a time, *chérie,*" Sylvie replied. "I must run. The two of you have fun."

"Thanks," Allegra said. "I'm sure we will."

She disconnected with Sylvie, then dialed Todd's cell phone number. He picked up on the first ring. "It's me," she said.

She heard the unmistakable sound of him kissing into the receiver. "Hello, you," he finally said.

Allegra laughed. "You're silly."

"I'm in love," he replied.

"Are you packed?"

"Are you serious?"

"Yes."

"I'm nearly there with bells on my—"

"Forget about the bells," she said. "Just come."

"I'll do that, too," he said. "I'm so excited, Ally."

"I am, too," she said, "and I'll see you soon. I'd better go now."

"I love you."

"And I love you." She hung up the receiver and hugged her arms against her chest. *I do love him,* she thought, *and it feels so . . . good and so . . . right.*

CHAPTER ELEVEN

W hat . . . ? Where . . . ? Abruptly Allegra sat up in bed, momentarily disoriented by where she was. A frisson of fear, brief as a flash of light, ran up her spine. As she fully awoke, she smiled at the reassuring sunshine pouring through the window shutters.

Drawn by the sun's first appearance since she'd been in Paris, she relinquished the comfort of the bed and went to the window. She pulled the shutters apart and looked over the nearby rooftops, observing that almost all of them were a uniform gray metal in the mansard style. Directly opposite her, beyond the small ironwork balcony and the French doors that led to it, she could see a woman running a vacuum cleaner in a large apartment with avant-garde furniture and large abstract canvases on the walls. Below, the sidewalks were crowded with pedestrians, and the street was a steady stream of motorbikes, scooters, and cars.

She wondered about the time, suddenly aware that the sun was high in the sky and the street life was too hectic for the early morning. She turned and glanced at the alarm clock on the little African stool at the bedside. The clock read ten-thirty, and Allegra wondered how she could have slept for so long.

Worried about time, she dashed into the bathroom, put on her face, and fixed her hair with record speed, then quickly dressed. Hurrying down to the street, she went straight to the café where she'd breakfasted the day before. As she waited for her food, she glanced through a copy of *Le Monde* that lay on an empty chair next to hers.

On the front page, prominently positioned, was a photograph of Princess Karima on the arm of Stefano Donati, her former lover. The picture was a few years old, Allegra guessed, and the woman was stunningly beautiful. Donati, while not handsome in a traditional sense, exuded breeding, money, power, and polish even in this newsprint photograph. The couple was dressed in formal attire as if going to or leaving a ball. Allegra could see that the princess was wearing a necklace of many large stones, a bracelet to match, and several rings, the emerald the most easily identifiable among them.

The article reported the upcoming auction, of course, but its thrust was the new spiritual path that the princess had taken. She was moving to a small millhouse in the countryside outside Paris, it said, and selling all of her other properties.

Sipping her coffee as she read, Allegra was impressed by the article, but was curious as to what could have led such a worldly woman to make such an about-face in the way she chose to live her life. Fear? Allegra wondered. Fear, as a believer, that she wouldn't receive a reward in the afterlife unless she changed her ways? Or was it something as simple as boredom? The woman had seen and done nearly everything humanly possible in her lifetime. Perhaps this path would provide a diversion for a jaded woman.

It was after noontime when Allegra left the café and hailed a cab. She told the driver to drop her off at the Madeleine, realizing that she would have time to slow down and walk to Dufour from there, sightseeing along the way. After she had paid the fare and walked for several blocks, she felt calm and relaxed, distracted by the sunlit boulevards. However, when she reached the intimidating gray stone facade of the auction house, she felt her pulse begin to race.

What have I gotten myself into? she asked herself. *What is a simple jewelry designer with hardly a dime to her name—let alone the pedigrees of the bidders that will be in the auction room today—doing here? How could I have had the audacity to tell Hilton Whitehead that I could do this?*

She walked up the limestone steps to the grand entrance, and strode into the building. She ignored the guards and the well-dressed people standing in small gaggles, chatting in soft voices, as if in a church. She went to the registration desk, where she picked up her paddle for bidding. Even the young lady behind the desk spoke in hushed tones. *Vingt-neuf.*

Twenty-nine. The sibilant sounds of whispers followed her as she went to the elevator. Well, this was sort of a church, Allegra reminded herself, as she ascended to the auction room. A temple, if not to God, then to mammon. And this temple offered the closest thing to heaven that could be found on earth as far as its customers were concerned.

When she reached the auction room, she went straight in and walked down to the second row of folding seats that had been set up. She took a seat on the aisle. She was not going to allow the auctioneer to ignore her bids. She would be front and center, where she and her paddle couldn't be missed. There would be no excuse for overlooking her. Certainly not in front of a room full of curious people. And there would be a lot of curiosity. About everybody that bid today, of that she was certain. She shrugged out of her overcoat, leaving it on her shoulders, then loosened her scarf and removed her gloves. Glancing at her watch, she saw that the auction would begin in about five minutes.

God help me, she silently prayed. *I've got to be successful. For Hilton Whitehead. For my business. And for myself.*

Allegra's head was swimming, and her heart was beating rapidly. She felt her body stiffen with anxiety and made an effort to relax, but it was all she could do to maintain the carefully composed picture of cool reserve that she had adopted for the auction. Appearing to be a nonthreatening observer as opposed to a serious bidder was more difficult than she'd imagined. The auction audience, buyers and onlookers alike, was in an extremely excited state, loudly oohing, aahing, and gasping as prices climbed, and clapping enthusiastically when individual lots of the princess's jewelry were sold.

And sell they did. Lot after lot was auctioned off at a rapid-fire pace, usually taking no more than a minute to achieve an astronomical price and bring the suave auctioneer's hammer swinging down for a dramatic pound on the lectern. Not a single lot had gone unsold thus far, an auction world rarity, and Allegra was stunned by the prices that people were paying for jewels that were not necessarily very valuable.

Lot number sixteen, for example, was approximately fifteen tiny unset diamonds, worth no more than fifty dollars each, Allegra surmised, for a total value of approximately seven hundred fifty dollars. Dufour, clever salespeople that they were, had arranged the tiny stones on a piece of black velvet in the shape of a *K,* obviously for *Princess Karima,* and Allegra had watched in amazement as the bidding for them reached seventeen thousand dollars before the auctioneer swung his hammer high in the air and brought it down.

As lot number twenty-four, the emerald ring, approached, Allegra looked down at her watch. Not twenty minutes had yet passed, and she wished now that the ring had been later in the auction. *Oh, well,* she thought, *it's better to get the suspense over with.* She was practically sitting on the edge of her seat when the auctioneer announced lot twenty-four.

In French, he quickly informed the audience that the thirty-four-and-a-half-carat emerald had been a gift to the princess from her companion of many years, Stefano Donati. It was therefore, he summarized, one of the most important pieces of jewelry in the princess's collection. The bidding started at one million euros and, before Allegra knew what was happening in the lightninglike pace of bidding, had reached twenty million.

Suddenly she felt a cold sweat break out on her face and neck, and she realized that she'd better get in the game before it was over. She raised her black paddle with its white number twenty-nine high in the air and left it there unwavering. The auctioneer's eyes briefly made contact with hers before surveying the rest of the room in one swift appraisal. Allegra didn't follow his gaze, but kept her eyes glued to him, her paddle still unmoving. She couldn't see who else was bidding, or whether there were several bidders or a handful, but over the beating of her heart and the adrenaline that shot through every vein, she heard the auctioneer say, *"Trente.* Do I have *trente-cinq? Trente-cinq. Quarante. Quarante."*

For an instant his gaze caught hers, and he nodded almost imperceptibly. *"Quarante-cinq. Quarante-cinq."*

His eyes swept the room, and she saw him nod toward the tables of young ladies and gentlemen who were manning the telephones set up for call-in bidders. Gasps filled the room. Obviously someone had phoned in a bid of forty-five million euros.

Allegra nervously clenched her jaw and held her paddle with knuckles white and tight. *It's got to end,* she thought. *It's got to. I can't stand the tension. Oh, God, help me.*

The bidding abruptly slowed, and the auctioneer began to cajole the audience, using his considerable charm, accusing them of being too poor or too cheap to bid any higher. There was laughter around the room.

Then she heard, *"Quarante-six."* Soon followed by *"Quarante-sept."*

*   *   *

In a small room next to the auction gallery, Princess Karima watched the activity from behind a large window that appeared to be a mirror in the auction room. Her heavily made-up eyes gleamed darkly as they focused first on Ramtane Tadjer, who was seated in the rear of the auction room, and then the young woman with the strawberry blond hair, seated near the front. She flicked the ash off her cigarette into the porcelain ashtray at her side, then took a long draw of it, before exhaling a plume of smoke through her nostrils.

Who is she? she wondered, although she was certain she knew the answer to her question. She was obviously American, and she was no doubt bidding for a rich American. But who could that American be?

A long, lacquered nail tucked a stray hair into the cream cashmere turban that was wrapped around her head, completely concealing all but an inch or so of black hair at her forehead. She wore it with a deceptively simple but elegant cream cashmere suit from Valentino Couture. Small pearl studs adorned her ears, and a simple gold watch was at her wrist. Otherwise, the princess wore no jewelry. In her lap were black calfskin gloves and a black alligator pocketbook, both from Hermès, and her feet were shod in medium-heeled black alligator pumps. From one hand dangled a pair of large, dark sunglasses in black frames, and in the other was her cigarette.

On one side of her sat Prince Albert de Guermantes, a jewelry specialist with Dufour, who remained quiet but attentive during the auction, his focus on the princess rather than the auction itself. The prince, who despised cigarette smoke, sniffed and shifted in his seat, but endured the princess's noxious fumes. He was there as a representative of the house should the princess have any questions or any special needs. Should she want a drink, for example, the prince would scramble to accommodate her.

On the other side of her sat the Honorable Marcus Setville-Penhurst, a handsome, darkly tanned, and much sought-after bachelor in his forties. Scion of a venerable British family that had managed to hang on to a grand country house, a town house in London, and a fortune in art and antiques—despite the burdens of death duties and taxes—he was one of Princess Karima's most frequent companions, although it was well known among their set that he preferred the company of men after dinner parties had ended and the long dark hours of the night began. He was watching the proceedings without much real interest, thankful that he'd swallowed a two-milligram Xanax before escorting the princess through one of Du-four's rear entrances.

Princess Karima slipped a cell phone out of her alligator bag and flipped it open.

"Who the devil are you calling?" Marcus asked, looking at her.

"Mimi," she replied without returning his glance. "I forgot to give her some instructions." She dialed her housekeeper's number.

"But *now*?" Marcus said incredulously.

She waved him to silence with a hand. "Mimi," she said into the cell phone, "we'll be going to the country this afternoon. Get everything ready." She listened a moment, then said, "No, it won't be long. That jeweler from Jules Levant—you know the one—and a young American woman are bidding against one another. I don't know her. She's attractive, thirtyish, all in black with strawberry blond hair. But I must go. See you soon." She flipped the phone closed and replaced it in her handbag.

"What the hell does that old hag care about all this?" Marcus asked, staring at her with curiosity.

"Shhhh, *chéri*," Princess Karima chided, putting a finger to his lips. "We must see who gets my emerald ring, mustn't we?"

Allegra desperately wanted to see who was bidding against her but didn't dare take her eyes off the auctioneer. Was it just one person? Two or three? She had no idea, but she kept her paddle high.

"*Quarante-huit.*"

She held her breath.

"*Quarante-neuf.*"

The room fell totally silent.

"*Cinquante.*" The auctioneer surveyed the room over the rims of his half-moon glasses, a serious expression on his face now. Finally his gaze fell on Allegra and rested there.

"*Cinquante et un.*"

There was a collective gasp; then Allegra heard the hammer fall with an explosive bang on the lectern.

"*Vendu!*" exclaimed the auctioneer. "To the young lady in the second row."

Allegra realized that he was smiling at her from behind the podium. *Oh, my God,* she thought. *I got it. I got it. I got it!* She heard the wild applause from the audience and, looking around, saw that all eyes were upon her.

Lowering her paddle, she picked up her shoulder bag, shrugged into her coat, stood up, and, putting a smile on her face, quickly walked up the aisle toward the back of the room, aware of the sea of eyes that still stared at her with curiosity and of the many whispered comments traded behind hands held at mouths. She failed to notice the only person in the room whom she had previously met, and didn't see him leave his seat as she hurried out of the room into the hallway. She had to pick up the ring and get it to the bank right away. In the hallway she pressed the elevator button. Yesterday, she had neglected to ask where the cashier and pickup areas were, but she assumed they were downstairs.

On the ground floor, she went to the information desk. The young blonde, Hermès scarf tied around her neck, looked up at her. "Mademoiselle?"

"*Le caissier?*" Allegra asked.

Pointing a finger down a hallway, the young lady replied, "Down the hallway to the end, then to the left. You can't miss it."

"*Merci,*" Allegra replied.

She turned and followed the young lady's directions, aware of the guards and staff staring at her and whispering as the crowd had upstairs. Then she saw the video monitors that were mounted on the walls, televising the auction upstairs.

Aha! So they know I'm the woman who just dropped about sixty-five million bucks on an emerald ring, she thought with amusement.

Turning left where the young lady had indicated, she saw the long mahogany cashier's counter straight ahead. An elderly woman, heavily made-up and with hair dyed a pitch black and pulled back into a bun, looked at her through the thick lenses of her glasses. Her eyes were magnified into huge, almost frightening black saucers. "Mademoiselle?" she said in acknowledgment, her garish red lipstick clownish in the way it attempted to create lips where there was nothing more than a thin line.

"*Lot vingt-quatre,*" Allegra said, smiling and trying not to stare.

"*Oui, mademoiselle,*" the woman said with a nod. "You wish to pay for it?"

"*Oui,*" Allegra replied, placing her shoulder bag on the counter. She reached inside it and withdrew the envelope with the check she was to use.

"*Un moment.*" The woman turned and went to a long counter with an array of computer equipment behind her. Underneath the counter was a lengthy row of filing cabinets. The woman began pushing computer keys, slowly, looking from the keyboard to the monitor with every tap of a key.

Allegra riffled through her shoulder bag for a pen and didn't see the man who had followed her from the auction room. He stood just around the corner of the hallway, his eyes riveted to her back. Her fingers found a pen, and she pulled it out of the bag, then stood patiently waiting while the elderly woman did the necessary paperwork. She didn't know what the total charge would be after the tax and buyer's commission were added.

After what seemed an interminable wait, the old woman turned from the counter with a sheaf of papers and stapled them together in front of Allegra with a heavy pound of her fist. She laid the papers down so that they were facing Allegra. Then with a long, red-lacquered fingernail she tapped at the total amount due at the bottom of the top page.

The amount was so unreal to Allegra that she almost laughed. Instead, she wrote out the check, and handed it to the woman. The woman gave it the briefest of glances, as if she saw checks for such astronomical amounts every day, then looked over at Allegra, her purple-shadowed eyes steely.

"I must call your bank, Mademoiselle Sheridan," she said, "to make certain that the funds are available."

"Of course," Allegra said agreeably. "If you ask for Monsieur Lenoir, he can take care of it immediately."

"I'll only be a moment." She turned and went down to the end of the counter and through a doorway, closing the door behind her.

Allegra heaved a sigh. She turned and looked around, propping her elbows on the counter behind her. She was glad to see that the pickup area was a short distance down the hallway. Hopefully, she would be finished with her business at Dufour in a few minutes and would be on her way back to the bank.

"Mademoiselle?"

Allegra turned and faced the elderly lady, who held the paperwork and check in liver-spotted hands. "Yes?" she said.

"Everything is settled," the woman said. She tore off a copy of the invoice and handed it to Allegra.

Allegra took the invoice from her. "*Merci,*" she said, noticing for the first time that the woman wore a ring on nearly every finger, each one of the rings enormous and several of them loose on the woman's aging fingers.

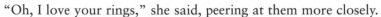

"Oh, I love your rings," she said, peering at them more closely.

"*Merci,*" the old woman replied, spreading her hands. "There were all gifts, *chérie*. From lovers." She winked at Allegra conspiratorially, her eyelashes so heavy with mascara as to appear spidery.

Allegra laughed. "You must've had quite a few."

"One can never have enough," the old woman said.

Allegra smiled. "I guess not," she said, humoring the woman.

"I know it to be true," the woman said. She leaned on the counter. "Now, then," she said, "I know you must be in a rush to show off your new bibelot. Pickup is just down that hallway."

"*Merci,*" Allegra said.

The old woman nodded. "Enjoy it, *chérie*. Life is short."

Allegra turned and went down the hallway to the pickup counter. There was one man behind the counter, and two or three others in the room behind him, putting together boxes and filling them with various kinds of padding.

The counterman looked at her appraisingly. "May I help you?" he asked in English.

"*Lot vingt-quatre,*" she replied, handing the man her invoice.

He looked at it, then looked at her. "It will only take a moment," he said. He walked over to a small safe, unlocked it, and searched inside, then withdrew a small box.

Allegra recognized the box immediately. It was the same pinkish beige that Jules Levant Joaillier still used.

The man brought it to the counter and opened it. "Is this the lot you placed the successful bid on, mademoiselle?"

Allegra glanced down at the ring. The same simple but elegant yellow gold setting, and the same beautiful dark green stone. She took her loupe out of her shoulder bag, then picked up the ring. With her loupe in her eye, she brought the emerald toward it. Expecting nothing out of the ordinary, she was stunned when she saw that the emerald was virtually flawless.

What the hell? she wondered. She looked at it again, closely scrutinizing the stone from various angles. She could only come to one conclusion, and a ripple of fear ran up her spine. *This is definitely not the same emerald I was shown at the exhibition. What's going on here?* If anything, this stone probably had more intrinsic value than the emerald in Princess Karima's ring. Only its value was a fraction of what Princess Karima's ring was worth because it had not belonged to her.

I can't believe this, she thought.

There was only one thing she could do, and that was protest. "Monsieur," she said, taking the loupe from her eye and setting the ring on the counter. "There has been a mistake."

"A mistake?" the man said. "What do you mean, mademoiselle?"

"What I mean," Allegra said, "is that this is not the same ring that I saw in the auction preview. This is not Princess Karima's ring. It is not the ring I was bidding on."

"But that is impossible," the man replied.

"I want to see an official of Dufour immediately," Allegra said in a no-nonsense voice. "Preferably a jewelry expert."

"Certainly, mademoiselle," the man said.

"At once," Allegra emphasized, her brain swirling with questions.

The man picked up a telephone at one end of the counter and dialed a number. "Monsieur Lorrain," he said, "this is René in pickup. We have a problem that requires your immediate attention." He listened for a moment, then replaced the receiver in its cradle. "Monsieur Lorrain, one of our jewelry specialists, will be down momentarily," he said.

"Good," Allegra said. *Jesus,* she thought. *Why did I ever agree to such a harebrained scheme as this? And what in the hell will I tell Hilton Whitehead?* Her mind was still swirling with a multitude of questions, and there had better be some answers forthcoming.

"Mademoiselle Sheridan?" A distinguished man of sixty in a handsome chalk-striped suit and gray tie approached her. He extended a hand. "I am Edmond Lorrain. I understand there's a problem?"

Allegra shook his hand. "Yes," she said. "There has been a mistake. This is not the same emerald that I saw in the preview."

Monsieur Lorrain shook his head. "Oh, but you are mistaken, mademoiselle. I don't see how that is possible." His reply was cool in the extreme.

"I don't know how it is, either, Monsieur Lorrain," she said, "but it is true. This is definitely not the same emerald. The setting is identical as far as I can tell, but this is not the same stone."

"Mademoiselle Sheridan," he said with the patience of a parent dealing with a recalcitrant child, "what you are saying makes no sense. Now, why don't you—?"

"It certainly doesn't make any sense," she said angrily, "but I am a gemologist, Monsieur Lorrain. With a great deal of experience, I might add, and I won't have my knowledge insulted by you or anyone else when it comes to gemstones." She pointed at the offending box that held the ring. "I'm telling you that this is *not* the same emerald. I will swear in a court of law that it's not. The inclusion that defined Princess Karima's stone is not there." She looked at him with fiery eyes. *Does this pompous ass think I'm an idiot?*

"Oh, so you're a gemologist," he said. "I see." He looked at her with interest. "And you were bidding for yourself, mademoiselle?"

"That's none of your business, Monsieur Lorrain."

The man swallowed and his face reddened.

"Excuse me," a man's voice interjected. "Perhaps I can help?"

They both turned toward the dark, handsome man standing behind them, a smile on his sensuous lips. "Ah, Mademoiselle Sheridan," the man said. "I thought I recognized you."

Allegra was so surprised to see the handsome jeweler that she stammered, "Oh, uh, well, it's nice to see you again, too."

"Monsieur Tadjer," Lorrain said, offering his hand. "You know this young lady, I take it?"

"Indeed, I've met the very beautiful and charming Mademoiselle Sheridan," Ram replied. He turned his attention to Allegra. "Are you having some sort of difficulty, mademoiselle?"

"I'm here to pick up lot twenty-four," Allegra replied, relieved by his sudden appearance, "and the stone in the ring is not the same stone that I saw in the auction preview."

"I saw the ring at the preview as well," Ram said. "What if I take a look? You don't mind, Monsieur Lorrain, do you?"

"Certainly not," Monsieur Lorrain replied stiffly, "but I can assure you that Mademoiselle Sheridan must be mistaken. We've never had such a problem here at Dufour."

Ram removed a loupe from the breast pocket of his suit and picked up the ring. After positioning the loupe in his eye, he brought the emerald up to it, in exactly the same manner Allegra had. After a moment his mild expression became puzzled, and then an angry scowl contorted his features. He removed the loupe. "This is definitely not the same emerald," he said, looking at Monsieur Lorrain, his dark eyes flashing. "It is certainly not Princess Karima's emerald. There is no question about it."

Monsieur Lorrain looked crestfallen. Under no circumstances could the opinion of Ramtane Tadjer of Jules Levant Joaillier be dismissed.

"I—I can't imagine what has happened," he said. "This . . . this . . . I—I . . . if you'll give me just a moment, allow me to call upstairs to the department."

"Of course," Ram said.

Lorrain turned and went through a doorway in the pickup area, closing it behind him.

Ram turned his attention to Allegra. "It's so lovely to see you again," he said.

"I'm certainly glad to see you," she replied. She meant what she said and realized that it wasn't only because of the ring. "I don't know what's going on here, but this Mr. Lorrain sure isn't in any hurry to admit that Dufour has made a mistake."

"It is very curious," Ram replied, delighted with her distress since he could take a part in her rescue. "But whatever the mistake is, I'm sure that Dufour will rectify it. They have a reputation to protect, after all."

"What could have happened?" she asked, looking at him quizzically. "It's . . . it's crazy. The stone is so easily identifiable with its inclusion. This makes no sense. Anybody who knows anything about gemstones would be able to tell the difference right away with one glance through a loupe."

Ram shook his head thoughtfully. "No, it doesn't make any sense, I agree. It'll be interesting to see what Lorrain has to say."

"I can't imagine," Allegra said, still anxious and cross with Monsieur Lorrain's condescending manner.

Ram smiled and took one of her hands in both of his. "Don't worry," he said. "They'll straighten this out. I'm certain of it."

Allegra was surprised by his familiar gesture, but a frisson of excitement surged through her at the feel of his warm hands on hers. She had to admit that she liked the feeling. It was reassuring and protective, and she could use a little protection right now. She made no move to disengage her hand from his. "Thanks for your support."

He gently squeezed her hand, then released it. "It's nothing. But what a surprise to see you here," he said. "And bidding on Princess Karima's most famous ring. You are a very surprising and, I think, clever young woman." He smiled again. "You were trying on jewelry in my shop yesterday and didn't even mention that you were here for this auction."

Allegra was temporarily speechless. "I . . . I didn't deliberately mislead you," she finally said. She wanted to change the subject because she didn't want to explain why she was here or whom she was bidding for. She knew that there was going to be a lot of speculation in the Parisian press concerning the mystery woman who had successfully bid on Princess Karima's ring and whether the ring was for herself or someone else. She wasn't about to explain the circumstances to this man or anyone else. That was up to Hilton Whitehead to do after delivery.

"No," he agreed, "you didn't mislead me, although you *did* seem to delight in trying on jewels that were relatively inexpensive—even cheap—compared with what you've just bought for yourself today."

Allegra smiled. She wasn't about to fall into his trap and give away any information. "I was delighted," she said, "and it was awfully nice of you to let me try on some of your wonderful pieces."

"I enjoyed seeing the jewels on someone so beautiful," he replied. He eyed her thoughtfully. She was indeed a clever woman, he reflected. He would have to work very hard to discover whom she made the purchase for, but he didn't really care. What was of vital importance was to part Allegra Sheridan from the emerald before it ever left her hands and reached its new owner.

Monsieur Lorrain came through the doorway and approached them with a neutral expression, giving away nothing of what he felt. When he reached them, he bent forward and sotto voce said, "I'm terribly sorry, Mademoiselle Sheridan. You are right, of course. I have the ring here." He took a box from the pocket of his suit jacket.

"What on earth happened?" she asked him.

Lorrain explained. "Because the emerald is worth so much, the insurance company wanted an astronomical amount of money to insure it while it was in our hands."

"Yes," Ram said. "I can well imagine that the insurance costs for this exhibition were huge."

Lorrain nodded. "So we came up with the idea of creating a duplicate of the ring to save money. The insurance company was satisfied, and our costs were considerably lowered." He paused and looked at Allegra. "Well, it was *nearly* a duplicate, obviously. You very smartly and correctly knew it wasn't Princess Karima's ring." He handed Allegra the pinkish beige box from Jules Levant, and she held it in her hand.

"Surely anybody else who'd placed the successful bid for the ring would've known," Allegra said.

"Perhaps," Lorrain said, "but you'd be surprised how many clients don't really know much about stones. I'm certainly glad that it was you because you've prevented Dufour from committing a grievous error."

"It would've been a great injustice to an unaware buyer," Ram said. "The buyer would've ended up with a ring with no provenance whatsoever instead of having Princess Karima's, with all of its sentimental value."

Lorrain nodded. "I'm afraid so. In any case, it was difficult to keep the ring under constant supervision, as you can imagine," he said. "More than any other single piece of jewelry, it was being photographed by many different photographers for magazines and papers and our own catalogue. It even went on a small tour with some of her other jewels to help drum up interest, you know. So we created this one to take its place. We saved a fortune on the insurance, and no one was the wiser."

"I see," Allegra said.

"The guards upstairs made the mistake of sending the wrong ring down to the vault for you to pick up." He shrugged expansively. "So you see? It was a simple mistake by one of the guards. I'm awfully sorry, mademoiselle."

Allegra didn't know what to think of his explanation. She hadn't had time to think it through, but something about it didn't sit well with her. His story made sense, but something told her that she would have questions for him later on.

"It's straightened out now," she said, "so we might as well forget about it." She smiled. "But I do want to look at this one, if you'll pardon me a minute."

Lorrain looked surprised, then slightly miffed. "Of course," he said.

Allegra opened the box, took out the ring, then put the loupe to her eye. She brought the emerald up to the loupe and knew immediately that she held Princess Karima's ring in her hand. The inclusion was unmistakable. Removing the loupe, she slipped it into its suede sheath and placed it back in her shoulder bag, then tucked the ring into the slot in its box. She put the box in her shoulder bag as well. "Thank you, Monsieur Lorrain," she said. "I'm satisfied now."

"Once again, mademoiselle, I'm awfully sorry for our mistake," he said, "and would love to see you return to our auction house. I hope you'll not hold it against us here at Dufour."

"Oh, no," she said, "of course not." *Wait till I tell Hilton Whitehead about this,* she thought. *He's going to have everything he's ever bought here reevaluated.*

Lorrain had gathered up her paperwork from the pickup counter, put it in an envelope, and handed it to her. He pocketed the duplicate emerald ring; then he offered his hand, and Allegra took it. "It's been a pleasure," he said, "and I repeat, I hope we see you again."

"Good-bye, monsieur," Allegra said, smiling widely.

Lorrain nodded, turned, and went back through the doorway into pickup again.

Allegra turned to Ram. "And thank you very much for your help," she said. "I don't know what I would've done without it, and hope that some-day I can repay you."

"You can repay me right now," Ram said.

"Gladly," Allegra said, "but how?"

He looked at her, his most disarming smile in place. "By letting me take you to tea. It is close to teatime."

"Oh, but . . . ," Allegra began.

"I won't take no for an answer," Ram said. "Not under any circumstances."

"But I really am in a hurry," she protested, starting to walk down the hallway. "I have to get to the bank."

"Ah," Ram said, nodding. "To keep the emerald safe." He glanced at his watch and noted that the banks wouldn't be open much longer.

"Yes," Allegra said worriedly.

Ram stopped her with a hand on her arm. He looked at her with what was clearly a feigned expression of disappointment. "But you wanted to repay me," he said.

Under other circumstances his expression would have been comical, but Allegra was too anxious to laugh. "I'm sorry, but I really must get to the bank," she reiterated as she started toward the door again.

"Then allow me to take you to the bank myself," Ram persisted. "I have a car waiting outside and can get you there very quickly."

"Well . . . I—I don't know—" Allegra began.

They reached the door to the street, and Ram held it wide for her. They descended the steps to the street together. The moment they reached the sidewalk, a midnight blue Bentley pulled over to the curb. A chauffeur in livery got out and hurried around the big car to open the rear door.

Allegra looked up at Ram. "You're certain it would be no trouble?"

"No trouble at all," he said, "and you wouldn't have to worry about the ring's safety."

Allegra couldn't get the ring to the bank fast enough. "Okay," she said. "If you're sure."

Ram smiled and indicated the car's open door.

Allegra got in and, despite her anxiety, noted its warmth and comfort. The Connolly leathers on the seats were in the same dark blue as the car's exterior lacquer, and their scent was like an expensive perfume.

"Which bank is it?" Ram asked, leaning into the car.

"It's Citibank," she replied. "I've got the address here." She began rummaging in her handbag.

"Don't bother," Ram said. "I know where it is." Allegra heard him issuing orders to the chauffeur sotto voce in rapid-fire French, but she understood nothing other than the word *Citibank*.

Ram slid onto the backseat next to her, and the chauffeur closed the door, then returned to the driver's seat. The big car began moving down the street.

"It will only take a few minutes," Ram said in a reassuring voice.

"This is awfully nice of you," Allegra said.

"It's my pleasure," he said. "Perhaps afterward you will join me for a drink. What do you say?"

"I have a friend coming in this evening," Allegra replied. "Otherwise I would love to. We're supposed to go out to dinner and—"

"I see. The cards are stacked against me," he said in an amused voice. "A young man, no doubt?"

Allegra smiled and nodded. "Yes."

"Coming in from New York?"

Allegra nodded and smiled again. "Yes."

The car came to a stop, and she looked forward through the windshield worriedly. A red light. Looking down at her watch, she realized that the bank would soon be closing.

Ram patted her arm. "We'll get there in time," he said. The car began moving again. "See? On our way already. It's very close, so you needn't worry."

Allegra appreciated his efforts to reassure her, but she couldn't help but fret. *A sixty-five-million-dollar ring is in my shoulder bag, and I'm not supposed to worry? Sure.*

The car suddenly picked up speed and began weaving in and out of traffic as it entered one of the Grands Boulevards. Allegra clenched her hands together, twisting them nervously, but almost as quickly as the chauffeur had accelerated, he slowed down and pulled the car over to the curb. Before she knew what was happening, he had opened the door, and Ram had gotten out.

"Here we are," he said, leaning in toward her.

"I'm coming," she replied, scooting across the seat. Allegra got out of the car and looked around. "But—" she almost wailed.

"What is it?" Ram asked with concern. "What's wrong?"

"This isn't the right bank," Allegra groaned incredulously.

"But this is Citibank," Ram said smoothly.

"Yes, but this isn't *the* Citibank," she retorted. "Not the one where I've made arrangements. The one near the Madeleine." She looked at her wristwatch. "Oh, my God. What am I going to do?"

"Quick," Ram said. "Get back in. We'll get you there."

Allegra did as she was told. Ram slid in beside her, giving the chauffeur orders at the same time. After making an illegal U-turn, he sped down the boulevard in the opposite direction. Allegra wrung her hands anxiously and repeatedly looked down at her wristwatch as if doing so would make time stand still.

"I'm terribly sorry," Ram said, "but it's only a short drive from here. Gérard will try to get you there on time. I should've let you give me the address after all."

Allegra nodded but didn't reply. *What if we don't make it?* she wondered, clutching her shoulder bag tightly. *What am I going to do then?* She felt her body stiffen every time the car slowed down, and at red lights she had to control the impulse to jump out and run, even though she didn't know the way to the bank and knew that she couldn't beat the car there.

"I feel so awful about this," Ram said. "It's such a ridiculous mistake."

"It's not your fault," Allegra said, attempting a smile. "You've done nothing but try to help me."

"I've only done what any decent person would do," Ram replied.

Gérard suddenly swerved toward the curb and braked, throwing them both forward. Ram grabbed her arm. "Are you okay?" he asked.

"I'm fine," she said.

"Citibank," Gérard said, before getting out of the car to open their door.

"Oh, my God," Allegra exclaimed. "I didn't realize—"

"Just in time, I think," Ram said.

Allegra didn't hear him. Ignoring the traffic, she opened the door on her side of the car and was out and on her feet, running toward the bank. When she got to the door, she shoved against it, but the heavy glass door wouldn't budge. The bank was already closed.

"Oh, no," she groaned, slumping against the door. "Oh, my God. What am I going to do?"

She sensed Ram behind her, then felt him take her by the arm. "Come with me, Allegra," he said. "It will be okay."

CHAPTER TWELVE

In the backseat of the car, Allegra sat stunned with fear. Clutching at her shoulder bag, she felt her pulse race and a sickening knot in her stomach. She was at a loss as to what her next move should be. She knew that she had to protect the ring, but she didn't have any idea of how she was going to do that. When Ram spoke, she almost jumped, so wrapped up in her thoughts was she.

"Wh-what?" she said.

He twisted on the seat to face her. "You don't have to be afraid, Allegra," he said. "I can keep you safe."

She looked at him and swallowed. She didn't know what to believe or what to say.

"Gérard is not only my chauffeur but my bodyguard. He's very well trained, too. Don't forget, I'm a jeweler, and as you know I handle a lot of expensive merchandise, so I have to have a bodyguard."

"I understand," she replied.

"So as difficult as it is, try to put yourself at ease," he went on. "You are safe with me."

"Thank you," she said. She took a deep breath and exhaled. "I—I don't know what to do now," she confessed.

"Listen," Ram said. "I'm a member of a club in the Marais. It is one of the safest places in Paris."

"A club?" she said.

"Only the most privileged are allowed in this club," Ram continued. "We could go there. You would be safe, and we could decide what to do."

Allegra wanted to believe him, but she didn't know whether she could trust him or not. Yet, she thought, he'd done nothing but help her.

"I—I don't know," she finally said. "Are you sure the ring will be safe there?"

Ram nodded. "It's as safe as any bank, believe me. It's a quiet, elegant club for people who belong to the Musée de la Chasse et de la Nature."

"It's like a hunt club?" she asked.

"Yes," Ram replied.

"It doesn't sound like the safest place to me," Allegra replied doubtfully, clutching the box with the ring in her hand.

"It is," Ram insisted. "It's for people like me who ride. Actually, I don't get to participate in many of the hunts. I'm too busy with my work. But I can assure you it's one of the most private and safest places in Paris."

Allegra couldn't think of what else to do. "I—I guess we could go there," she said.

Ram told Gérard what to do, and he pulled away from the curb and began driving through the streets of Paris at a reasonable speed. At an intersection, Ram grabbed her arm to hold her as Gérard was forced to slam on the brakes. "Sorry," the driver said from the front seat. "Someone pulled out in front of me."

"You're okay?" Ram asked Allegra.

"Yes," she said softly. Despite her fear for the safety of the emerald, she once again felt that frisson of excitement when he placed his hand on her, and she also felt protected, as if no harm could come to her while she was with him.

"Look," he said, pointing out the window past her. "Here we are."

Allegra turned her gaze to the window and looked out. A grand mansion with enormous gates leading into its cobbled courtyard greeted her eyes. "Oh, it's magnificent," she said.

"It's the Hôtel de Guénégaud," he said. "Built by Mansart in 1654 for one of the king's counselors."

The chauffeur drew up to the gates, and an attendant looked out from the gatehouse. When he saw the car, he came out and opened one of the giant gates to allow them to pull into the courtyard. They were surrounded on three sides by the limestone mansion with its elegant floor-to-ceiling windows after the driver stopped the car.

"See how safe it is?" Ram said.

Allegra nodded. "It certainly looks that way."

They got out of the car and stood together in the courtyard for a moment, looking around them at the magnificent house. "It's the only house left in Paris by Mansart," Ram said. "I should say the only one left in its entirety. So much was destroyed after the Revolution."

"It's gorgeous," Allegra said.

"Come, let's go in," he said. "We can have a drink and if you like, I can show you around the museum. I think you'll find it interesting."

He turned and nodded to Gérard, then led her through a door to the right of the courtyard and into a large sitting room with many multipaned windows looking out onto the courtyard. No more than ten or twelve people, all expensively but conservatively dressed and well groomed, sat about the room in twos or threes. The walls were paneled with intricately carved boiserie, a grand Savonnerie rug was placed on the *parquet de Versailles* floors, and antique chairs, tables, and chests representing different periods furnished the room in luxury. Paintings, primarily of animals, hung on the walls.

"This is so beautiful," Allegra said, momentarily distracted from her worry.

"It is well done, isn't it?" Ram replied. "Let's have a seat and order, shall we?" He indicated a Louis XIII chair with needlepoint flame stitch upholstery.

"Thank you," Allegra said as she sat down. She felt like a queen taking a seat on her throne in this palatial atmosphere.

Ram had no sooner sat down opposite her than a waiter arrived. "Monsieur Tadjer," he said. "Lovely to see you."

"Hello, Maurice," Ram replied. He looked at Allegra. "What would you like? Tea or something a littler stronger perhaps?"

When she didn't reply at once, Ram touched her arm. "I'm sorry. I was . . . I was in another world," she said. The ring still preyed on her mind, despite the elegant surroundings.

"Tea or something stronger?" Ram repeated indulgently.

"Oh, I think . . . something a little stronger sounds very good," Allegra said.

Ram smiled. "My thoughts exactly," he said.

"A vodka martini," Allegra said. "With a twist."

"And I'll have a Scotch neat," Ram said.

The waiter nodded. "*Merci,*" he said.

"I have to make a quick telephone call," Ram said. "Do you mind?"

"Of course not," Allegra said.

He got to his feet. "I'll only be a moment," he said.

Allegra watched as he walked to one end of the long room and went through a door. *What a wonderfully generous man he has been,* she thought. *So handsome, so suave, so sexy, and yet he seems so gentle and kind.* She was certain that had he not come to her aid, she would still be at Dufour, battling it out with their experts and making emergency telephone calls to Hilton Whitehead in New York.

That was when it suddenly occurred to her that she hadn't yet called him to let him know that she had placed the winning bid on the ring. She would also have to tell him that she hadn't been able to put it in the bank vault. Allegra dreaded to think of what his response would be to that piece of news, but he would surely come up with some solution to the problem.

The waiter arrived with the drinks on a silver tray. He placed Allegra's martini in front of her on the small marquetry table that sat between her chair and Ram's, then placed Ram's Scotch across the table from hers.

"*Merci, monsieur,*" Allegra said.

"You're welcome," the waiter replied with a smile. He disappeared on silent feet.

Ram came through the door at the end of the room and strode quickly toward her. She noticed that he was tucking a cell phone into the inside breast pocket of his suit jacket.

"Sorry," he said, quickly taking his seat opposite her. "I don't like business interfering with pleasure, but sometimes it's a necessity."

"That's all right," Allegra said. "If you'll excuse me a minute, I have to use the powder room. Which way is it?"

"See the door at the end of room?" He indicated the door he had just come through.

"Yes," she said.

"Go through that door, and just to your left is a powder room."

"Thanks," Allegra said. She quickly rose to her feet. "I'll be right back."

He nodded. He watched her walk the length of the room and admired her beautiful, long legs. The way she walked had just the hint of a swing in her hips. So sexy. So confident. Such a pity she had the ring. Such a waste. Too bad he couldn't have a little fun before it was all over.

He took a sip of his Scotch and felt it burn a fiery path down his throat and into his stomach. He glanced at his watch and sighed impatiently. *I wish she'd hurry up*, he thought. *I want to get this over with.*

Allegra took the cell phone out of her shoulder bag and dialed the number for Hilton Whitehead in New York. Sylvie picked up on the second ring.

"Hilton Whitehead's," she said with her slight accent.

"Sylvie, it's Allegra."

"Ahhh!" Sylvie exclaimed. "Tell me the good news."

"I've got it," Allegra said.

"*Magnifique!*" Sylvie said. "I'll let Mr. Whitehead know right away."

"But there's a hitch," Allegra said, getting to the point.

"What is that?" Sylvie asked.

"I didn't get to the bank in time to put the ring in the safety-deposit box."

"You what!" Sylvie exclaimed.

"You heard me," Allegra said. "The bank was closed by the time I got there. Please tell Hilton what's happened and ask him what he thinks I should do. It's very . . . frightening to be carrying around a sixty-five-million-dollar ring."

"Of course," Sylvie replied. "He's not here now, but as soon as he comes in I'll tell him." There was silence for a moment, then, "So you have the ring with you?"

"Yes," Allegra said. "In my shoulder bag. And I don't know what to do with it."

Sylvie could hardly believe her ears—or the golden opportunity that had just been dropped in her lap.

"Are you at the apartment?" she asked.

"No," Allegra replied, "but I'm on my way there." She didn't think it was necessary to tell Sylvie about the mix-up at the auction house and Ramtane Tadjer's help. At least not yet.

"Good," Sylvie said. "If I were you, I'd go tuck the ring away in the apartment right now. After all, who would think to look there?"

"Anybody who knows that I'm there and that I have the ring," Allegra said.

"Which is no one but me," Sylvie said. "So there's no problem."

Allegra knew this wasn't true but agreed. "Yes," she said. "I guess it's the best thing to do now."

"In the meantime, I'll try to locate Hilton and give him the news."

"Okay. I'll call you when I get back to the apartment. I'd better go."

"An excellent idea," Sylvie said. "Hide it in the apartment right away, and I won't have to worry about it."

"I'm worried, too," Allegra said. "I hope you can get hold of him soon."

"I'll start trying him the instant we hang up," Sylvie said, only her plans didn't include Hilton. Sylvie needed to get hold of Paul to tell him about the great opportunity that had come up.

"Good," Allegra said. "Till later, then."

"Ciao."

Allegra pressed the END button, shut off the power, then flipped the tiny cell phone closed and put it back in her shoulder bag. She'd thought that talking to Sylvie would help allay her fears, but suddenly she felt more worried than ever. Hilton Whitehead wasn't in, and it might be a while before she heard from him. She took a deep breath and pulled the powder room door open, heading back to the lounge.

As she approached the lounge, she saw Ram in the distance. *He brought me here, but is it really safe? And is he really harmless?* She realized that she knew almost nothing about him, a very frightening prospect. Nevertheless, she forced a smile to her lips. "Hi," she said, rejoining Ram. "Sorry to be so long."

"That's quite all right," he said. He lifted his Scotch in a toast, and Allegra followed suit, picking up her martini and raising it into the air.

"To your success at the auction today," he said.

"Thank you," she said. She didn't want to say anything else, as she didn't want to encourage discussion about the auction. She took a sip of her martini and set it down. "So this magnificent house is devoted to the hunt? It is a fascinating building," she said in an attempt to change the course of the conversation.

"I'll show you the rest," he said. "Why don't we go now? We can come back to our drinks. How's that?"

Allegra took another sip of her martini, stalling for time. The club was immense, and there was almost no one about. She wondered if she was just being paranoid because of the ring and reminded herself that he had behaved like a perfect gentleman since the moment she met him.

"Okay," she finally said, taking another quick sip and setting the glass back down.

They got to their feet. "We have to go around this way," Ram said, taking her arm and leading her down the room toward the midsection of the building. "We'll begin at the beginning," he said.

They eventually arrived at a small stairwell, and he stopped. "Just beyond here you can see the little entry room and bookshop," he said.

Allegra followed his gaze and was surprised to see that it was so small with just a cashier reading quietly. "They don't sell souvenirs, do they?" she said. "Like in so many American museums."

"Only the books," he said. "Now we go upstairs."

Looking up, Allegra saw that no one was in the ancient stairwell. This place was so quiet and empty. She felt a shiver go down her spine, but Ram immediately distracted her by pointing out the stairwell's decoration.

"See the beautifully painted tiles?" he said.

Allegra nodded and hesitantly began up the stairs with him. "There are so many," she said, "and the paintings are wonderful. I love the dogs."

"They were nearly all painted by Desportes or Oudry," he said. "Two of the greatest animal painters."

At the top of the stairs, he led her into a room full of antique weapons and their accessories. Rifles, crossbows, arrows, pistols, muskets, powder horns, the majority of them made from highly polished wood or steel and elaborately decorated with silver, gold, and bronze, filled glass cases and lined the walls. Allegra couldn't help wondering if should she be getting a message. But her fears were soon diminished by the artistry employed by the weaponry makers.

The decorations on many of these instruments of death had been done by master craftsmen. They were both frightening and beautiful, she thought, and despite their artistry, they still made her feel uneasy. "Some of these are like pieces of fine jewelry," she told Ram. "In fact, there are very few jewelers today who can do this kind of elaborate metalwork."

"I thought you would enjoy them," he said.

In a hallway, she stopped to look at a pair of paintings. "They're by Rubens and Brueghel," she said with surprise. "Working together."

"Yes," he said. "Have you noticed anything . . . funny about them?"

Allegra turned back to them, then smiled. "Oh, I see," she said. "There's a dog in each one licking its privates."

Ram smiled. "Exactly," he said. "Most visitors never see them, and I think it's a pity."

She had to admit they were amusing but wondered why he felt com-

pelled to point this feature out. Had it to do with a naughty sexual sub-
text?

Before she could give this any thought, he led her on to the next rooms.
"Oh, my God," Allegra exclaimed, coming to a standstill. "This is almost
too much." She shifted her gaze from the room to Ram before she looked
ahead once again.

Confronting her was an enormous white bear, poised for eternity on its
hind legs, a ferocious expression on its face. It merely served as an intro-
duction to the contents of the room. Taxidermic animals of all kinds were
grouped about the room in various configurations. Wild boars, leopards,
cheetahs, lions, tigers, deer, foxes, creatures she'd never even heard of. Allegra felt another chill run down her spine. She began to worry anew for
her safety and that of the ring.

She finally turned to Ram. "They're beautiful," she said, "but this almost makes me sick. To think that these were all living creatures that've
been shot just to satisfy some man's ego. Just for a kick."

"I know what you mean," Ram said, "but many of these animals were
killed before the animal rights activists we have today began raising people's consciousness about needlessly slaughtering animals." He paused
thoughtfully, then added, "And before we became aware of disappearing
species."

She noticed a plaque that thanked an Arab prince for his many contri-
butions to the collection. "I . . . suppose it's a good thing that the museum
exists," she said, "so that there's a public place where people can see what
they probably never would otherwise."

"You look a little pale," Ram said, taking her arm. His face was etched
with worry. "Why don't you stand at one of the windows and take a little fresh air? There's one over there that's open a crack." He gestured
toward it with a hand.

Allegra shook her head. "No, really," she said. "I'm fine."

Ram tugged gently on her arm nonetheless, drawing her toward the
window. "Maybe you should get some air anyway," he said, cajoling her.

Allegra hesitantly let him lead her to the window and took a deep
breath of air, closing her eyes as she did so. Suddenly she heard the crash
of broken glass, followed by a dull thud. Her eyes jerked open instantly.
Pieces of shattered glass hit her right shoulder, and she let out a cry. "What
the—?"

She was immediately distracted by a woman's distant scream, which sounded as if it came from somewhere in the museum. She caught a glimpse of a uniformed guard dashing down a stairwell from another room.

"Down!" Ram shouted, pulling her toward him, where he was crouched against the wall. *That fucking Ali,* he thought. *I should never have relied on him to do something as simple as this.*

Allegra clutched her purse tightly as she almost fell on top of him, but caught herself against his shoulder, then crouched beside him. The unmistakable sound of running feet pounding the cobbles of the courtyard below and the urgent shouts were amplified by the enclosure created by the walls and gates and carried up to the room.

"What—what's happening?" she asked Ram, looking at him in near panic.

"I don't know," he said, a worried expression on his face. "Some lunatic on the loose, I guess."

"But—but the . . . glass . . . what—?"

"I don't know," Ram insisted. "My guess is somebody took a shot at something or somebody, and it hit the window."

From the courtyard below, there were more shouts. Allegra wanted to crawl to the window and see if she could see anything, but common sense told her that would be a very silly thing to do under the circumstances. The windows were floor-to-ceiling, and she would make an easy target for a lunatic. Craning her neck, she could see where the windowpane had been broken, and she followed the natural trajectory of the bullet.

The guard who had been on duty returned, hurrying down the hallway toward them. "Monsieur Tadjer," he said as he approached. "Are you okay?"

"I think so," Ram replied. "Allegra? Any damage?"

She shook her head. "No, nothing," she replied, looking down at her shoulder where the glass had hit her. There was no blood, not even a tear in her sweater.

"Very good," the guard said. "The coast is clear now. You are free to leave."

Ram helped Allegra to her feet. "What the hell is going on?" he asked the guard.

The guard shrugged. "We have no idea, monsieur," he said. "A man came into the courtyard and fired a shot then ran back out again. That is all we know. The police are chasing after him now, but I doubt they will find him. He got a good head start before they were alerted."

"Did anybody see it?" Allegra asked.

"I don't know if anybody actually saw him fire a shot," the guard replied.

"He shot into this room," Allegra said.

"You are certain about that, mademoiselle?"

"Absolutely," Allegra responded. "Look." She showed him where the shot had come through the window.

"*Mon Dieu,*" the guard swore. "You could have been injured."

"I was standing in the window when it happened," she said.

"That was probably coincidental," Ram interjected. "It was probably one of those animal rights terrorists, just shooting randomly inside the courtyard to scare people."

Allegra looked at him quizzically. "Do you really think so?" she asked.

"It wouldn't be the first time these weirdos have tried to scare people away from the museum."

The guard nodded vigorously. "They are an unsavory element, and I wouldn't put anything past them."

Allegra looked at the broken window again, then scanned the room once more. Then she saw it. Almost directly behind where she'd been standing, on a level with her chest, a magnificent antelope was posed in a leap. The beautiful khaki-colored hide on its side clearly had a hole in it. She walked over to the antelope for a closer inspection of the hole, then walked around the animal. On the opposite side was a much larger hole, this one surrounded by shredded hide. She suddenly felt a shiver of fear run through her body and thought she would be sick.

"What is it?" Ram asked, looking over at her.

"It's . . . it's . . . come look at this," she said. She looked at the wall behind the antelope and saw another hole in the plasterwork there, cracks spread out around it in a spiderweb pattern.

Ram and the guard joined her, and she pointed out what must have been the bullet's entry, exit, and eventual landing site.

"I'll have to call downstairs to my superior immediately," the guard said. "Excuse me." He turned and left the room and went out into the hallway, where he picked up a telephone on the wall.

"I think we should be going," Ram said. "I need a drink or something to calm down."

"But what about the police?" she asked. "Don't you think we should talk to them and tell them what we know?"

He shook his head. "The guard here can show them everything. Besides, you are a visitor in our country, and you don't want to get mixed up in a police affair. What if they want to detain you for questioning?"

Allegra hadn't thought of that and knew that there was truth in what he said. Nevertheless, she felt that leaving the scene before telling the police everything she knew would be an irresponsible act.

"Don't worry about it," Ram said. "We were simply in this room when it happened. We certainly don't want them to think either of us was a target, do we?"

The thought hadn't occurred to Allegra until this moment, and as remote as it seemed, it wasn't altogether impossible, was it? She was carrying around an emerald worth sixty-five million dollars. An emerald that she'd casually tossed into her shoulder bag as if it had been a tube of lipstick. She felt a knot of fear twist her stomach.

"Okay," she said. "Let's vamoose. And in double time, too."

Ram took her arm and led her out into the hallway past the guard. He was still speaking on the telephone, but motioned toward them with his free arm to come back. Ignoring him, they calmly descended the nearest staircase to the ground floor. Straight ahead was the small museum entrance and bookshop. The elderly woman whom they'd seen manning the cash register earlier was not in evidence. She'd probably taken refuge in the staff's lounge or in one of the museum's offices. They walked out into the tiny vestibule that led directly to the entrance gates.

Beyond the gates, the big Bentley sat at the curbside, softly purring like a big cat, as exotic and rare as some of the beasts in the museum. With a hand in the small of her back, Ram propelled her toward the car quickly, and not waiting for the chauffeur, who was getting out to open the door for them, he pulled it open and practically shoved her into the car. Allegra was nonplussed by his sudden aggressiveness, even though she had every reason to hurry out of the museum if she was unwilling to be detained by the police.

"Gérard," Ram said, "get moving. And fast." He turned to Allegra as the driver gave the car gas and sped off down the rue des Archives. "I don't mean to alarm you, but the quicker we're away from here, the better. If the police want to question you, they'll be searching this area very soon."

Allegra nodded, but knew if the police wanted to question her, all they had to do was get in touch with Ramtane Tadjer. Everyone at the museum saw them together, and he was a member of the club. She knew one thing for certain: if she wanted to avoid the police, she would have to extricate herself from the charming company of Ram and get back to the apartment.

"I understand," she said to Ram. "I think it would be best if you dropped me off a couple of blocks from here. I have to get back. My friend will be coming in soon."

Ram slid an arm across the leather seat just above her shoulders. "Why not stop by my place for a quick drink first?"

Allegra shook her head. "No," she said. "Really. My friend is expecting me, and I have to get back."

"Where is it you are staying exactly?" he asked.

Allegra almost blurted out the address, which was only a few short blocks in the opposite direction on the rue des Archives, but something— some self-protective instinct told her to hold back. "I—I . . ."

The blast of police sirens suddenly seemed to surround them, and Allegra saw that two policemen on motorcycles had pulled up even with the Bentley. When she turned to look, she saw that there was a police car behind them.

"*Merde!*" Ram swore, slamming a fist against the seat. "The police. It'll be hours before we get away from them."

The look of fury on his handsome face was almost scary, but Allegra tried to remain calm. "Oh, well," she sighed. "I guess I'll have to call my friend and have him wait on me."

"Don't breathe a word about the auction or the emerald," Ram said hurriedly.

"Don't worry," she said. "I won't." She slid a hand inside her shoulder bag and gripped the ring tightly. Perhaps it was a coincidence that someone fired a shot into the club while she was there. Standing at the window, no less. But Allegra didn't think so, and with that realization, she felt her stomach twist into a sickening knot again. *Somebody may have tried to kill me to get the ring,* she thought. *Not only that, but Ram took me to the club where the shot was fired. He might have set it up. Would he have done such a thing?* she wondered. She didn't know, but she certainly didn't feel safe with him any longer.

CHAPTER THIRTEEN

onneur, one of the two policemen who had been questioning her in the club's lounge, flipped a notepad shut and smiled at Allegra. "You have my card in case you think of anything else, Miss Sheridan. I'm sorry we've had to detain you," he added in slightly accented English, "but that should wrap it up. You've been very helpful, and we appreciate it very much."

"You're welcome," Allegra replied. "If I'd thought I could tell you anything useful, I would never have left the museum, Monsieur Bonneur." She knew that wasn't quite true, but she wanted to get out of there as quickly as possible. They had only asked her a few questions, and for that Allegra was grateful. She could see Ram looking toward her from the far end of the lounge, where another pair of policemen were questioning him. He smiled, but she thought that he looked anxious and impatient.

"Could you thank Mr. Tadjer for showing me the museum?" she said to Bonneur. "I would myself, but I really have to run." *I've got to get back to the apartment and hide the ring,* she thought, *and I've got to find out what Hilton Whitehead wants me to do with it.*

"Of course, Miss Sheridan," Bonneur replied. He looked at her with a curious expression. "But I'm sure he'll be ready to leave in a few minutes if you want to tell him yourself."

"I really have to run," Allegra said, giving him her best smile.

"Would you like for a policeman to escort you back to where you're staying?" he asked.

"No, but thanks," Allegra said. She waved toward Ram and saw him stand up abruptly and pull out his cell phone. Pointing to her wristwatch, she waved again and fled out the door to the courtyard.

Once outside, she walked briskly toward the gate, training her eyes straight ahead, determined to give the very handsome Ramtane Tadjer the dodge. As she sailed out the gates, she saw the Bentley parked at the curb-side again, its engine running and Gérard, the driver, standing beside it.

At that instant, he turned around, and his eyes widened in recognition. Without a moment's hesitation, he rushed around the big car toward her, and Allegra, ignoring him, began to run down the rue des Archives. Gérard reached out with one muscular arm and grabbed her arm with his hand.

"Mr. Tadjer wants you to wait for him here," Gérard said, a smile on his lips.

"I'm sorry," Allegra said, "but I've got an appointment." She tried to jerk her arm free, but his grip on her was so tight she could hardly move. She could feel the ring box squeezed against her, and began to panic. He pulled her toward the car, and she stumbled in her high-heeled boots. "Let me go!" she cried, struggling against him.

Suddenly Gérard's grip loosened on her arm, and she watched in horror as he slumped to the sidewalk. Then she saw blood spreading across the breast of his uniform jacket. Allegra stifled a scream and began to run down the street as fast as her feet would carry her, her eyes focused straight ahead of her and her hand clasped around the ring box buried in her purse. She was aware of passersby staring after her, but she didn't care. The apartment was only two blocks away.

She didn't stop to catch her breath until she had reached the big black doors on the street. Gasping for air, she reached out and punched the security code on the little steel buttons, then shoved on the door. It didn't budge.

She took a deep breath, then tapped in the numbers once again, more carefully this time. The door gave when she pushed on it, and she slipped inside the passageway and slammed the door closed behind her. She rushed through the dark tunnel and hurried up the stairs to the apartment after she reached the inner courtyard. Fumbling in her shoulder bag for the key, she nearly jumped out of her skin when the door across the little hallway opened.

A young woman smiled. "Hello."

"H-hi," Allegra stammered breathlessly. She attempted a smile. Her fingers felt the key, and she withdrew it from her shoulder bag. In a moment of panic, she searched further until she found the suede box. As she unlocked the door, the young woman began descending the stairs, turning once to stare at Allegra with curiosity. *She probably thinks I'm crazy,* Allegra thought.

The door swung open, and she stepped into the apartment, locking the door behind her. Slumping against it, she realized that her heart was pounding and she was covered with sweat and shaking. As she caught her breath, her eyes darted about the little studio wildly. *Nothing out of the ordinary here,* she thought. *Thank God.*

When the nervous shaking had all but ceased, she went into the living room, dropped her shoulder bag on the sofa, and took off her coat and scarf, draping them over the back of a chair. She glanced at her watch. She still had an hour or more before Todd was due to arrive, plenty of time to shower and change, but that was out of the question right now.

She knew she should call Sylvie again and tell her that someone might be trying to kill her to get the ring, although she wasn't absolutely certain about that. Should she call the police about Ram's driver being murdered right before her eyes? But when she considered the almost certain possibility of being detained by the police in a foreign country in a homicide investigation, she decided that calling them would be a last resort.

Trying to clear her mind of all the conflicting thoughts and emotions that offered no immediate course of action, she decided that first things first: where to hide the emerald?

She sat down on the sofa and riffled through her shoulder bag until she found the small pinkish beige box. Opening it, she stared down at the huge gem, which returned her gaze with a mute and magnificent sparkle. *Why are you so special?* she asked it. *Why would someone try to kill for you? Why you with your imperfection?*

With a heavy sigh she shut the box, hiding the emerald from view.

Now, where do I hide it? she asked herself anew.

The oft chosen plan of hiding within plain view would definitely not work in this case, she decided. Clever as it might seem in movies or mystery novels, the ring was too big, too extraordinary, and attracted far too much light to be effectively hidden within view. Scanning the studio's single large room, she could immediately see that it offered very little in the way of a hidey-hole. Even the kitchen area, positioned as it was against one wall, didn't offer more than a single drawer, which was filled with silverware and other kitchen implements. There were no cabinets, only simple open shelves upon which basic provisions and dishware and the like had been artfully arranged.

She got up and walked into the hallway. The one closet there was small, with a single shelf above a rod for hanging clothes. It could be thoroughly searched in a minute. She walked on into the bathroom. She'd put her bag containing all of her bath and cosmetic essentials on the vanity and had chosen towels from a large wicker basket on the floor by the shower.

Running her gaze over the bathroom walls, she could instantly see that the room offered a multitude of possibilities. The ancient walls and pipes had been concealed behind built-in cabinets of various heights and widths with doors featuring intricate cutouts in a Moorish pattern.

She began opening all of the doors and inspecting the contents. Most of the cabinets, she discovered, were filled with a plethora of shampoos, conditioners, scented bath oils and powders, and other grooming essentials. Near the floor, they were stuffed with cleaning materials. One turned out to be a laundry hamper, in which she saw piled T-shirts and underwear, all male. *Paul's?* she wondered. He'd said he lived nearby, but why would his underwear be here? Maybe he used the apartment occasionally, she decided, dismissing the thought.

She returned her attention to the cabinets. *Any one of these shelves would do,* she thought. They were all stuffed with so many bottles and tins and boxes that it would take forever to do a thorough search for the ring, should anybody undertake one. She'd left the laundry hamper open and started to close it when it occurred to her that it offered a good temporary hiding place, as well. Rummaging through someone else's soiled underwear would not be an appealing task to most people. Reaching down into the hamper, she pulled out one load of the dirty laundry and placed it on the floor, then reached in to pull out the rest. Her hand struck against something hard, and she pulled out the rest of the laundry slowly, looking down into the deep hamper with curiosity.

Gasping aloud, she let the laundry slip out of her hands and fall to the floor. Lying in the bottom, dully gleaming in the bathroom's soft light, was a gun. *"Jesus!"* she exclaimed. "What the hell is sweet little Paul doing with a gun?" After staring at it a moment, she reached in and picked it up.

It was small but heavy in her hand. She turned it over and over, looking at it closely. She had no idea what kind of gun it was or precisely how to use it, but she suddenly realized that it might be useful.

What the hell am I going to do with a gun? she asked herself.

Almost as if it were a snake, she gingerly held the gun between two fingers and gently replaced it in the bottom of the laundry bin. She picked up the dirty laundry and tossed it back in the bin atop the gun, then shoved the bin closed. *Scratch that idea,* she thought.

Eyeing the open cabinets again, she saw a roll of bandage tape, and she knew what she would do. Taking the tape out, she quickly taped the box with the emerald firmly closed, wrapping the tape around it three or four times to make certain it wouldn't come open. Then looking into the open cabinets again, she decided to tape the box to the backside of one of the many pipes running up and down the ancient walls, where it would be concealed by the contents of the cabinets. Getting down on her knees, she chose the one that was the most difficult to see and get to.

She ran three strips of tape across one side of the box, leaving the ends of the tape sticking out, then carefully positioned the box on the back of a large pipe. Holding the box in position with one hand, she secured the tape to the pipe with the other, making certain that it was tight against the pipe. Sitting back on her haunches, she studied her handiwork. Only the most discerning eye would see the pieces of tape reaching around from the back side of the pipe. After she repositioned the multitude of bottles, tubes, and boxes on the shelf, she couldn't see even the pipe, much less the ends of the tape sticking to it.

She stood up and closed all of the cabinet doors, then washed her hands in the sink, satisfied with the hiding place. She glanced at her wristwatch again. *Oh, my God. I'd better hop in the shower if I'm going to be ready by the time he gets here.*

She quickly shed her clothes, showered, and dried her hair. She applied a bit of eyeliner, mascara, shadow, and blusher, and before leaving the bathroom, she liberally daubed perfume at her ears, the cleavage between her breasts, and her wrists.

After wrapping a towel around herself and looking at her reflection in the mirror again, she decided that she looked and felt refreshed, as if nothing out of the ordinary had occurred today.

Princess Karima's dark eyes were ablaze with fury, and there was a tremor in the hand that held the cell phone against her ear. It clicked irritatingly against her pearl earring, which only increased her anger.

"What do you mean?" she asked in a quiet but threatening voice. She took a deep breath, trying to control the rage she felt, fearful that Marcus would overhear her. Although he was mixing drinks in the distant salon, she knew that he loved nothing more than spreading vicious gossip. Despite their friendship, he would gleefully get word out among their set that he had heard Karima have a tantrum after the auction, thus feeding speculation concerning her real feelings about selling her possessions.

When she had listened to the fateful words once again, she abruptly felt something snap in her mind, and forgetting Marcus for the moment, she shouted into the receiver. "You idiot. You filthy little *shit*! You're incapable of doing anything right. I don't want to hear of you or see you ever again!"

She snapped the cell phone shut and flung it toward the desk, where it clattered against a vase of flowers before landing against a basket piled high with the day's mail. She tore off the turban that still encased her lush black hair and threw it to the floor, giving it a swift kick with her shoe. She lit a cigarette with shaking hands. Exhaling a stream of smoke toward the bedroom ceiling, she felt tears in her eyes. Not one to cry, Princess Karima was startled by this emotional reaction to the awful news.

She looked about the magnificent bedroom where she and Stefano had plotted the extraordinary course of their lives together. He had been the great love of her life, and the emerald ring—more than any of the many other priceless gifts he had showered upon her—had represented that bond between them as had nothing else.

Taking another long drag off her cigarette, she glanced at the clock on her desk. She had to get ready to leave for the millhouse in the country immediately, she realized. Marcus was waiting for her, and she must, to all appearances at least, carry out her plan as she had announced it. Marcus was no small part of it. She knew that he would report on her activities after the auction.

As she slowly undressed and then put on the simple black cashmere sweater and slacks that Mimi had laid out for her, she began to feel better. Perhaps the ring was not lost to her after all. She could manage to get it back from the odious American lady. The failure this afternoon certainly didn't mean that future efforts would not succeed. She would simply have to put someone more adept in charge of retrieving the ring.

She stubbed out her cigarette in an ashtray, then slipped into flat, supple leather driving shoes. Marcus would be driving, but these were more comfortable after wearing heels most of the day. After refreshing her makeup at the vanity, she picked up the large silk Hermès scarf Mimi had selected—she would wear it for the drive with large dark glasses, a dramatic look for any paparazzi lurking about—then tossed her cigarettes in a carryall and picked up her quilted black Barbour jacket.

At the door to the bedroom, she took one final glance around. She might never see this magnificent room again, but she felt little regret. The plan for the next stage of her life was a brilliant one, and this house would play no part in it. Closing the door, she walked to the salon, where she would have a quick drink with Marcus before leaving what had once been an extraordinary love nest for the chaste simplicity of her millhouse. There, she would formulate a plan for securing the emerald. Of one thing she was certain: she would go to her grave with it on her finger.

Allegra hadn't heard the apartment's telephone the two different times it rang while she was in the thunderous shower. She had been enjoying the powerful jets of water from the enormous saucerlike chrome showerhead as they pummeled her body, massaging the day's kinks and worries away. When the loud knock came at the door, however, she had finished showering but hadn't had time to dress yet. She rushed toward it with a towel tied around her torso, released the locks, and swung it wide, prepared for Todd's smiling face and strong arms.

"Ahh, Allegra," Paul said nervously, trying to avoid looking at her towel-draped body.

She held the towel tightly against her breasts. "Oh, Paul," she said. "So sorry. I wasn't expecting you. I—"

"I'm terribly sorry," he said, remaining in the doorway. "I tried to phone, but no one answered so I thought you must be out."

"Come in," Allegra said, gesturing expansively with a hand.

"I'll only be a moment," Paul said. "I realized that I forgot . . . I forgot to show you how to operate the coffeemaker." He coughed a laugh. "And it's a little complicated for Americans who've never used one like it. Sylvie called and said you'd be staying over the weekend."

"Yes, but coffee's not a problem," Allegra said. "Uh, let me throw on something quickly."

"Sure." Paul turned and walked down the hallway toward the apartment's single room, leaving the door ajar behind him.

Allegra ducked into the bathroom. "I've been going out for breakfast

and don't drink much coffee anyway. You don't have to worry about it."
She took the towel off and, neglecting a bra, slipped into the low-cut
black ruffled Yves Saint Laurent blouse that she knew Todd would find
alluring.

"I'll just be another minute," she called to Paul.

"That's okay," he replied. "Take your time."

She unrolled the black leather miniskirt that she'd packed in tissue
paper, and put it on, pleased to see in the mirror that it had survived her
small carry-on with hardly a wrinkle.

She padded out of the bathroom toward the living room. Paul stood in
the middle of the room with a lost expression on his face. *What's with
him?* she wondered. *He's really an odd character.*

"About the coffeemaker—" Paul began.

"Oh, Paul, really," Allegra said, sitting down to put on her very high
black Christian Louboutin heels. "I'll not use it at all."

There was a knock at the still open door, and Allegra and Paul looked
down the hallway in unison.

Allegra jumped up. "Todd." She rushed down the narrow hall. His
arms encircled her, and they kissed. Allegra loved his familiar warmth, his
masculine scent, and the protective feeling of his arms. He jerked abruptly,
and looking up, she saw his eyes focus across her shoulder on Paul, who
remained standing in the room.

"Oh, Todd. I'm sorry," she apologized. "This is Paul. Paul is Sylvie's
friend who owns the apartment."

Todd took her hand in his and walked to Paul. "Hi," he said, extending his free hand with a smile. "It's nice to meet you, Paul."

With a slight nod of his head, Paul took his hand but held it lightly
rather than shook. "I hope you have a pleasant stay in Paris," he said.

"I'm sure we will," Todd said, his eyes turning to Allegra. He squeezed
her hand affectionately.

"Well, I won't keep you," Paul said. "I know you must have a lot to . . .
see and do. I came by to show Allegra how to use the coffeemaker, but she
doesn't seem interested in using it. I'll be on my way."

He started toward the hallway, but turned and looked at Allegra. "You
don't mind if I use the loo, do you?"

"Of course not," Allegra said. "It is your apartment, after all." She
laughed.

Todd's gaze swept the small apartment.

"I'll just be a second," Paul said, going into the bathroom.

Allegra looked up at Todd and saw the intent look in his eyes as he continued to survey the room. "What?" she asked. "Why so serious?"

Todd ignored her momentarily, then whispered, "Where did you hide the loot?"

Allegra yanked her hand out of his and stiffened. "Wh-what are you talking about?" she said in a low hiss.

"Don't play games with me." His voice was still a whisper. "I know you're here to buy something for Hilton Whitehead."

Allegra remained silent, her eyes ablaze with fury.

"Tell me," Todd growled quietly, "and I mean now."

She looked away from him and didn't respond.

Todd placed his hands firmly on her shoulders and leaned in close, his mouth at her ear. "There are minicams in this place. Somebody's been spying on you." He nodded toward the hall. "Probably that little creep that's in the head."

"But—but . . . are you sure?" Allegra sputtered.

He nodded, looking into her eyes. "Now tell me where the hell you hid the loot."

Allegra returned his gaze. "In—in the . . . bathroom," she finally said.

Todd's lips formed a momentary smile. Then he let her go. "Sit down and stay in here."

"But what—?"

"Allegra, please just do as I say for once."

She saw the serious set of his face and sat down on the couch.

Todd went down the hallway and locked the apartment's door, then stood blocking the exit, arms folded across his chest. Soon the bathroom door opened, and Paul stepped out. Even from the sitting room, Allegra could see the look of surprise on his face.

"I'll be going now," the young man said, trying to maneuver around Todd.

"I don't think so," Todd said.

"Why? What—what's going on?" Paul asked, looking at Todd, then down the hallway to Allegra.

With one beefy hand, Todd grabbed him by the neck and practically lifted him off the ground as he walked Paul into the sitting room. Paul clawed wildly at Todd's hand, but to no avail. Thin and weak, he was no opponent against Todd's strong, worked-out body.

Allegra watched with widened eyes and started to get to her feet. "Todd, what the hell—?"

He motioned to her with the flat of one hand. She sat back down with a frown on her face.

He loosened his grip on Paul's neck, but didn't release him. "Before you go," he said, "I want what you took out of the bathroom."

Paul's hooded eyes were barely open, and he was limp in Todd's hold. He licked his lips, and said, "I . . . I don't have anything from the bathroom."

Allegra could see beads of sweat on his face and the almost spastic tremor that took hold of his body.

"Don't play games with me," Todd said.

"I—I don't have anything," Paul mewled pathetically. Sweat was now rolling down his face, and his eyes were wide with fear.

Todd gave his neck one good hard squeeze, and Paul yelped. With his free hand, Todd yanked Paul's jacket off his shoulders and threw it to the floor. "Search his pockets, Ally," he ordered. "And pat down the lining good."

Allegra sat still, but only for a moment, hating being part of this violent scenario. It wasn't so much the authority in Todd's voice that got her moving but the thought that he knew what he was talking about. She scooped up Paul's jacket from the floor, quickly searched the pockets, then laid it down flat on the couch and began patting it down.

With his free hand, Todd was patting down Paul's upper body. Arms, chest, back, stomach.

Allegra looked up at Todd. "There's nothing," she said.

"You're sure?" he asked.

She nodded. "Absolutely."

Todd clawed at Paul's belt, undoing it with alacrity, then yanked down the zipper at his fly and tore open his pants, sending the button rolling across the floor.

Paul began to squirm in his grip. "Please," he whimpered. "Please. Don't do this. Please." His eyes beseeched Allegra, but she turned away, unable to bear the pathetic look on his face.

"Aha," Todd said calmly. "What have we here, Paul?" From Paul's Jockey shorts, his pulled the small box labeled JULES LEVANT JOAILLIER and held it up toward Allegra.

She gasped, and Paul's body slumped in Todd's powerful grip. Tears were running down his wan cheeks.

Allegra took the box from Todd's hand, and he released Paul, who almost stumbled to the floor.

Allegra opened the box to make certain that the ring was still inside. Nestled within the pinkish beige suede, its dark green shimmered up at her—almost with an impish wink—and she felt her body go limp with relief.

"It's here," she said to Todd.

He nodded, watching Paul reach over and take his jacket from the couch. When he'd put it on, he wiped the sweat and tears from his face with a sweep of both hands and stood stiffly.

"You did this for Sylvie," Todd said, stating a fact rather than asking a question.

Paul's eyes briefly lit on Todd's. Then he studied the floor as he redid his zipper and belt.

Todd took a step toward him, and Paul flinched. "I repeat. You did this for Sylvie, didn't you?"

Paul's mouth opened and closed, but nothing came out.

"You had a minicam in here and one in the bathroom, watching to see if Ally hid the ring here, didn't you? You have a place with monitors, upstairs or downstairs. Don't you?"

Todd took another step toward him, ramming the fist of one hand into the palm of the other. Paul looked up at him, flinched again, and then took a step backward.

"You were watching her. Invading her privacy. Like some filthy pervert. Only you couldn't see her while she was in the shower because that's a blind spot on your monitors, and you thought she'd gone out."

His eyes fell to the floor, and Paul remained silent.

Todd drew back his arm and balled his hand into a fist again. "You make me sick," he spat. "I'd like to tear you to pieces."

"No," Allegra cried. "Todd, don't. We've got the ring. Just let him go. Please."

"Tell me, Paul," he said. "Tell me now, or I'll break your fucking nose. You did this for Sylvie, didn't you?" He moved closer to him, using his body to intimidate him.

Paul nodded slightly.

"Say it," Todd growled.

Paul nodded with more vigor. "Yes," he finally muttered. "For Sylvie."

Todd relaxed his fist and crossed his arms over his chest. "I'm going to rip the fucking minicams out, and I want you out. I don't want to see your face again."

When Paul didn't move at first, Todd shoved him with a hand. "Get the fuck out!" he yelled.

Paul scurried down the hall to the door. His hands fumbled at the locks as he tried to open the door. Todd was close on his heels.

Paul was over the threshold in one awkward step and didn't pause in the hallway outside before starting down the steep, curving steps.

"We'll be out of here tonight," Todd shouted at his back, a finger pointed at him. "Your keys'll be in the kitchen sink." He slammed the door, locked it, and turned back to face Allegra, who stood watching from the sitting room. Her face was drawn and white.

CHAPTER FOURTEEN

He walked slowly toward her, then took her into his arms. "Oh, Jesus, I'm so glad to see you," he said, hugging her tightly.

Allegra's tense body shook slightly and tears came into her eyes, but she fought them back as he stroked her shoulders.

"It's going to be okay, Ally," he said tenderly. "I'm here for you."

She slowly relaxed into his warm embrace. "I—I'm glad to see you, too," she said, "but I'm having trouble believing what just happened." She drew back and looked up into his eyes. "I'm having trouble believing everything that's happened in the last few hours for that matter." She squeezed his shoulders with her hands. "Including how you found out so much."

"I think we'd better sit down and have a little talk, Ally. I want you to tell me everything. You've obviously put yourself in some danger here, and I want to know exactly what's going on," he replied.

Releasing her, Todd moved a chair over against the far wall, stood up on it, and yanked the minicam off the wall near the ceiling. Plaster chips rained down on the floor, and the tiny camera hung loose on a wire. He jerked again, tearing the camera off the wire.

"There," he said. "That little shit can't watch us now. If he's got the balls." He got down off the chair and tossed the camera on the floor. "Be right back. I'm going to get the one in the bathroom, too."

Allegra heard plaster falling in the bathroom and felt a chill run up her spine when Todd returned with the minicam dangling from a length of wire in his hand. "It was like I thought," he said. "The camera was aimed so it could see nearly everything in the bathroom but the shower." He threw the camera toward the corner where the other one had landed.

He joined her on the sofa, where she had taken a seat. "Now," he said, "everything. From the beginning. Leaving nothing out. Okay?"

She nodded. "Yes."

"Good," Todd said. "First, get comfortable, and I'll pour us a little champagne. How's that?"

"Champagne?" she said. "Where did you get that?

"Had the driver stop on my way in from the airport and got us a nice, chilled bottle." He pulled it out of his black carry-on bag. "Something to keep that tongue of yours well lubed, loose, and . . . true."

"I'll tell you the truth, Todd," she promised. "Why confide in you if I'm going to lie?"

"That includes no sins of omission," he said. "I know you well enough to know that you might leave a few important details out." He winked at her playfully, then turned and went to the kitchen counter. He set the bottle down, took two wineglasses from the shelf, then ripped off the foil and took off the wire covering the cork. The cork suddenly flew off and popped against the ceiling before landing on the floor.

"Whoa!" Todd exclaimed, quickly grabbing a glass for the champagne bubbling out of the bottle. He filled both glasses and took one to Allegra.

"Mademoiselle," he intoned formally.

"Thank you, monsieur," she replied.

He sat down next to her and clinked his glass against hers. "To us," he said, looking into her eyes.

"To us," she echoed.

They both took sips of the champagne. "This is delicious," Allegra said.

"It is, isn't it?" he agreed. He set his glass down on the little table and clapped his hands together. "Now," he said, turning and looking at her, "why don't you start at the beginning."

Allegra didn't like what she was about to do because she felt that she was betraying a trust. She had promised Hilton Whitehead not to tell anyone what she was doing. But, she reasoned, circumstances had changed considerably since she'd made that promise in his New York penthouse. She had performed her duty to him in Paris, and since then had been a witness to two shootings, both of which might have been attempts on her life. Now, to top it off, Sylvie and Paul were apparently in cahoots to steal the ring.

She began to tell Todd everything. Sylvie approaching her for White-head. Coming to Paris to bid on Princess Karima's ring. Staying at Paul's apartment at the instigation of Sylvie. Meeting Ramtane Tadjer at Jules Levant Joaillier, then seeing him at the auction, where he verified her assertion that Dufour was attempting to give her the wrong ring. Going to the museum with him, where a shot was fired through a window in the room where they were standing. Rushing from the museum only to see Ram's chauffeur shot on the street in front of her. Running back to the apartment and hiding the ring, only to discover Sylvie and Paul's plot to steal it.

When she was finished, Todd, who had listened to her story without interrupting, stared at her blankly. She could tell that his mind was working overtime, however, and she knew that he was going to have questions. But first, she wanted the answer to a couple.

"How did you figure out what I was doing?" she asked.

Todd shrugged. "It was simple," he said. "You left the Dufour auction catalogue on your bedside table for one thing. I saw you and Sylvie having a tête-à-tête at the club that night we went dancing. Then you've had all these conversations with her in the last couple of weeks. I know you're acquainted, but not that close. I also know she works for Hilton White-head, the only person I can think of who could afford to buy anything in that catalogue. Then, you were picked up in a Rolls-Royce to go to the airport. Plus, *Jalouse* magazine did not have a photo shoot scheduled with you." He took her hand in his. "I feel bad about calling them to check up on you, but I was getting really concerned."

Allegra wanted to be angry with him, but it was hard to work up any real anger toward someone who had been looking out for her welfare.

"I guess I would never make a very good spy," she said.

"I wouldn't suggest that you go into that line of business," he replied, his hand massaging her back. "But I think there are a couple of things we ought to do right away."

"What?" she asked, turning to him.

"Get out of here and check into a hotel, for one," he said. "And the other is to call Hilton Whitehead and tell him exactly what's happened. He ought to know, Ally. I think you may be risking your life for him, and he should know about it. And he's got to know about Sylvie right away."

Allegra nodded. "Oh, God," she said. "I hate doing this to her—"

"To her!" he exclaimed. "Think about what she was trying to do to you."

"I know," she said, although the full impact of Sylvie's betrayal hadn't yet registered in her mind.

"I wonder . . . ," Todd began, his eyes focused on some distant, indefinable point.

"What?" she asked.

"This guy Tadjer sounds very suspicious to me. You say the ring originally came from the shop he owns. He was at the auction. He came to your rescue at the auction house. He took you to the bank, but too late. Then he takes you out for a drink and you nearly get killed."

"It doesn't look very good, does it?" she replied. "But, on the other hand, everything he did might have been perfectly innocent." She sighed and said in an exasperated voice, "I just don't know what to think."

Todd took her hand in his. "Nothing right now," he said. "Let's get your stuff together and get out of here. We'll find a hotel. Then we'll call Whitehead from there."

"Okay," Allegra said. "First, let me run to the loo." She got to her feet. "I'll be right back, and it'll only take me a minute to get packed."

She went down the hall to the bathroom, closed the door behind her, and took the lid off the big wicker hamper. Then, pulling the dirty linens out, she tossed them on the tile floor until she saw the gleam of metal at the bottom of the hamper. She lifted the small snub-nosed pistol out and looked at it, thinking it might come in handy.

Hardly believing what she was doing, she slipped it into the toiletries bag still perched at the edge of the bathroom sink where she'd left it, then quickly gathered up her various articles and cosmetics, and stuffed them into the bag. She zipped it closed, then replaced the dirty linens in the wicker hamper. Finally, hoping to fool Todd, she pulled the chain that dangled from the old-fashioned toilet tank mounted on the wall near the ceiling.

She took her toiletries bag, opened the bathroom door, and went back out to join him. He was already on his feet, his overnight bag in hand.

"I'll just be a couple more minutes," she said, stopping at the closet.

Sylvie slowly replaced the receiver in its cradle and began tapping her carefully manicured fingernails on the desktop. She felt as if all the nerves in her body were stretched as taut as piano wires.

Jerking open a desk drawer, she rummaged out a pack of unfiltered Camels. Her hand shook as she lit one with the gold-plated Cartier lighter that Paul had given her for Christmas. Taking a long drag, she blew out a stream of smoke and watched it poison the pristine air in the brightly lit office. Hilton would have a fit, but Sylvie knew her run with him was over.

Racking her brain to come up with a solution to her dilemma, she couldn't think of a satisfactory explanation to give Hilton Whitehead. She could play the innocent girlfriend who had told the sweet, harmless boyfriend she'd left in Paris about the auction setup and place the blame on Paul, professing to be guilty only of giving away a secret she shouldn't have. But if Hilton Whitehead decided to investigate, she knew that Paul wouldn't take a fall for her. *No*, she thought, *the little shit would start screeching like a spoiled schoolgirl that I planned the whole thing.*

With a final tap of her nails, she quickly got busy. Pulling open a desk drawer, she took out a small metal box and opened it with the key that had lain in the drawer next to it. There was always at least five thousand in petty cash that she used for tipping building employees, catching cabs, and sundry duties. Not much, she thought, but it was a start. She took the cash out and stuffed it in an envelope, then shoved the envelope in her handbag.

From another desk drawer, she took out two checkbooks, one small—a personal account of Whitehead's—and a large one for one of his business accounts. Flipping to the back of the small one, she carefully tore out ten checks. Any more than that and it might appear obvious that checks were missing. She opened the hard-covered business checkbook and flipped to the back of it. After opening the metal ring binder, she took out five pages of checks, fifteen in all. She folded these along the perforations, then stuffed them along with the personal checks in another envelope. Between the two accounts, she estimated that she ought to be able to garner another few thousand this afternoon if she worked quickly, going to different bank branches to cash them. His signature was no problem. She'd signed it countless times.

She replaced the checkbooks in their drawer and went to the small hidden closet in the paneling. She retrieved her coat and put it on. Before she left, she sat down in her chair and unzipped an inside pocket in her handbag, extracting an Altoids tin from it. She opened it very carefully and looked hungrily at the white powder inside. With a fingernail, she scooped up a portion of the powder, then lifted it to her nose. She snorted the powder up one nostril, then licked at her fingernail, making certain that she'd left none of the precious powder there. Using the Hermès scarf in her coat pocket, she wiped at her nose. No telltale traces of powder would be seen by anyone.

She replaced the tin in its pocket and zipped it shut, then closed her handbag. She could already feel the crystal meth beginning to work its magic in her system, could feel her spirits lift, could feel a pleasant urgency about completing her tasks. Knowing that she would succeed.

She left the office quietly, went to the elevator, and pushed the button. A night flight to Paris, she thought dreamily. Then she and Paul could drive to their beautiful little hideaway in Provence. The idea of holing up in Saint Rémy appealed mightily after the hectic pace and vulgarity of New York. Just the two of them for a few days to decide what they would do and where they would go from there.

The elevator arrived and she stepped in, her eyes glittering with the possibilities that lay ahead. Allegra had done her a favor. It was time for Sylvie to escape the country she thought uncouth, primitive. It was time for her to get back to a civilized place where people knew how to live.

CHAPTER FIFTEEN

The little cell phone on the bedside table rang and rang, but Hilton shut his ears to its relentless chirping. Kitty, her silky black hair splayed out across his hips, was slowly working her knowledgeable tongue around his engorged shaft, and he was completely absorbed in her every sensuous flick and lick. He thought that he would explode at any minute, but he was trying with all of his might to hold off because he wanted to mount her at the last moment and release himself inside her. He knew that she would love that, and he wanted to give her as much pleasure as she gave him.

When he felt the tip of her tongue delve into the tip of his cock, he knew that it was now or never. He put his hands under her arms and drew her face up to his, then began kissing her passionately as he rolled her over onto her back and mounted her. Her large breasts pressed against his chest as he entered her, and Kitty moaned as his hands caressed her hard nipples and his shaft filled her. Her body immediately responded, moving urgently against him, engulfing him in the sweet nectar that anxiously awaited him between her honey-colored thighs.

Hilton groaned with desire, his whole being focused on the ecstasy of the moment, and he began moving rhythmically against her, quickening his pace, unable to control the passion that held him in thrall. When Kitty cried out and began to tremble beneath him as waves of orgasm overcame her, he exploded in a final plunge.

He held her tightly, completely enraptured by this woman who gave him such sensuous pleasure, and lay catching his breath as she gasped beneath him. When at last they had both recovered, he eased off her, but kept his arms around her shoulders, kissing her tenderly, his lips brushing her eyes, her ears, her nose, her cheeks, her neck, her lips.

"I think you're possibly the best thing that ever happened to me," he said with a smile.

"I *know* that you're the best thing that ever happened to me," Kitty said softly.

The cell phone began its relentless chirping again. "Damn," Hilton swore.

"That's your private number," Kitty said. "Hadn't you better get it?"

Hilton glanced over at the offending instrument. "Yeah," he said, "but it's probably nothing. There are only ten or twelve people with that number."

"It might be important," Kitty said.

"Might be," he agreed, "but not more important than this."

Kitty laughed. "No, not more important than this."

The phone continued to ring. "But somebody is certainly persistent," she said.

"Aw, shit." Hilton reached over for the phone and depressed the TALK button. "Hilton Whitehead," he said.

"Mr. Whitehead," the voice said. "It's Allegra Sheridan."

He immediately sat up in bed. "Hey," he replied. "What's going on? Everything okay?"

"Yes. No. I mean, something's happened that you should know about right away. In fact, a lot has happened that you should know about."

"What is it, Allegra?" he asked, as Kitty stroked his back. He gently brushed her hand away and got out of bed, blowing her a kiss on the way to the bathroom. He didn't want her to overhear this conversation.

Allegra told him about Sylvie and Paul and then, at Todd's urging, about meeting Ramtane Tadjer and the subsequent shootings. "And you and your boyfriend are okay, Allegra?" he asked worriedly when she had finished.

"Yes," she said. "We're fine. I'm just glad that Todd flew in. If he hadn't, Paul would be gone with the emerald."

"Jesus!" Hilton expelled a breath of air that was almost a whistle. "I don't believe this. Sylvie, of all people."

"I'm really sorry to have to tell you," Allegra said. "I can hardly believe it, either. We've known each other for quite a while, and I thought we were friends."

"Well, I'm sorry you've been put through all this," he said. "This Tadjer. You say he owns Jules Levant?"

"Yes," she replied.

"He worries me a hell of a lot more than Sylvie and Paul," Whitehead said. "I can take care of her from this end. She may still be downstairs in the office in fact, but I don't like the idea of you seeing any more of Tadjer. Do you think he has any idea where you are?"

"No," Allegra said. "Not unless he's got some spies watching me. We got a taxi outside the building, then drove all over Paris while Todd used the cell phone to find a hotel room."

"Where are you?"

"Practically around the corner from where we started out," she said, blurting a short laugh. "At the Hôtel de la Bretonnerie."

"And you're pretty certain nobody knows where you are?"

"Absolutely," she said.

"When we hang up, I'm going to get on the phone," he said. "If we have to, we'll get the Sûreté, Interpol, whoever we have to involved in this."

"I wish you wouldn't do that," Allegra said. "If you do, then I'm going to end up being stuck here for days. With the emerald. And, like you said, you can take care of Sylvie from your end. If the police get involved here, then they're going to be talking to Dufour, Tadjer, the museum staff, me, and God only knows who else. I really could be kept here for days until they decide to let me leave. Todd, too, since he's involved now."

"I see what you mean," he said. He didn't like the idea of not following through with an investigation into the purported mix-up at Dufour, Tadjer's involvement, and the rest of it. There was one consideration, however, that was paramount in his mind: the emerald.

"Listen, Allegra," he finally said. "The only important thing right now is to get the ring to New York safely. We'll try to find out what we can about Tadjer and the shootings, but we'll wait until you and the ring are back here. Okay?"

"That's fine," Allegra said with relief. "I wish I could follow through here and find out what's caused so much interest in this emerald."

"Forget about it," Whitehead advised. "Your job was to buy the ring and get it back. That's all. So get it to the bank the first thing in the morning. Monday, after the driver picks you up, get it out of the bank on your way to the plane. You understand?"

"Yes," she replied. "Understood. It's just the rest of the night that worries me."

"Listen to me," he said.

Allegra heard him out before finally hanging up the telephone.

"Feel better now?" Todd asked.

"Not really," she said. She told him about her conversation with Hilton Whitehead. "I don't think I'll feel better till the ring is in New York."

"In the meantime," Todd said, "why don't we get something to eat?"

"That's a great idea," she replied, wishing that she really felt that way.

When they stepped outside the Hôtel de la Bretonnerie, Allegra stood on the narrow sidewalk, nervously looking both ways, deciding in which direction to walk. Even with Todd at her side, she felt vulnerable, especially outdoors.

"Does it feel uncomfortable?" she asked him.

"No," he said, smiling, "but if I do a sort of a duck walk, you'll know why." He put a big arm around her shoulder and gave her a pat with his hand. "What say we go . . . that way?" He pointed with a finger.

"Sure, why not," Allegra said, and they began strolling down the street, Allegra looking to see if she could detect a noticeable difference in Todd's walk.

"I don't think your average Joe—or your average thief—is going to look for an emerald ring where I've got it tucked away."

As they walked arm in arm down the rue Sainte-Croix de la Bretonnerie, neither of them was aware of the dark eyes monitoring their every movement from the direction of the rue Vieille du Temple. The sidewalks were crowded with window-shoppers and restaurant and bar patrons coming and going from the multitude of trendy establishments that lined the block. As Allegra and Todd fell into the leisurely pace of the pedestrians surrounding them, yet another pair of eyes were observing them from the direction of the rue des Archives.

"Look," Todd said. "What do you think about this place, huh? Looks like it might be really good."

"I love it. It's so tiny and quaint," Allegra said. "Let's look at the menu and see what they've got."

They stood in the window, looking at the menu posted there, oblivious to the attention focused on them from just down the block.

"Looks like pretty basic French fare to me," Todd said.

"And reasonably priced, too," Allegra said. "Plus this place is practically next door to the hotel. Just think. We can eat and then go collapse."

Todd kissed her cheek. "I don't know if we'll collapse when we get back to the room. What do you think?"

She looked at him. "No," she said, "I didn't mean literally. What I meant was that the bed's a stone's throw away."

He kissed her again. "You're definitely my kind of woman."

He opened the door, and they stepped inside the small restaurant. The room was noisy with the lively conversations of twenty or more diners, and the smells emanating from the food were like perfume. The maître d' approached them immediately.

"Two for dinner?" he asked, looking from Allegra to Todd.

Todd nodded. "If you have a table, we'd love it."

"Follow me," the maître d' said, turning and expertly skirting his way through the small maze of tables toward a back corner. When he reached the tiny table, he turned to them. "Will this suffice?" he asked.

"It's perfect," Allegra said, noticing the romantic candlelight and the little vase of fresh flowers on the table.

After they were seated and had ordered a carafe of the house white wine, they studied the menu. "I think I'll have a salad and the duck with seasonal fruit," Allegra said.

"Same here," Todd said. "Then the chocolate soufflé for dessert."

"Me, too," she said.

Todd reached across the tiny table and took her hand in his. "I can't tell you how happy it makes me to be here with you."

Allegra smiled. "I'm thrilled that you're here, too," she said. "And you saved my neck today."

"That was nothing," he said. "Even if Paul had gotten away with the emerald, you'd have put two and two together in no time, and Whitehead would've had him tracked down some way."

"Maybe," she said, "but you never know. Anyway, tonight you're my hero."

He gently squeezed her hand. "You're always my heroine."

They ate and drank with relish, enjoying the basic but delicious French cuisine, and when they were back out in the cool air of the rue Sainte-Croix de la Bretonnerie, they walked arm in arm.

They reached the hotel and went into the little lobby with its ancient beams and antique furnishings. They had failed to notice the men across the street, one directly across from the hotel, speaking into a cellie, the other down the block, speed-dialing a number on his cell phone.

Mimi, a Provençal-patterned scarf knotted around her gray hair and a heavy apron covering her from ample bosom to arthritic knees, shuffled into the old mill's beamed salon. In her thick, gnarled hands was a heavy silver tray laden with smoked-salmon sandwiches made with trimmed toast, lots of capers, thinly sliced onion, freshly squeezed lemon juice, and a mere hint of Neufchâtel cheese, just the way the princess liked them. She'd heard laughter on her way in from the kitchen, and it warmed her heart. There had been little reason for joy in her mistress's life of late, and she was glad that Marcus Setville-Penhurst—useless *perverti* she considered him to be—could bring tears of laughter to the princess's eyes.

She set the tray down on the massive oak coffee table, then straightened her back and cleared her throat.

"What is it, Mimi?" Princess Karima asked. Clad in a white silk caftan trimmed with gold braid, she lay sprawled on one of the tapestry-upholstered sofas, her black hair loose and flowing below her shoulders. She held a crystal old-fashioned glass of Jack Daniel's in one hand and a cigarette in the other. Kitty-corner to her, Marcus lay on a matching sofa, holding a glass of Scotch on his stomach.

"The man called from Paris," Mimi said. "He found the lighter you lost."

Princess Karima bolted upright. "Wonderful," she exclaimed. "And?"

"He said not to worry. He will take care of it for you."

"Did he say when?"

Mimi shook her head. "No, madame, but he assured me it was not a problem."

"Thank you, Mimi," Princess Karima said. "If he should call back, I want to speak with him."

"Yes, madame," Mimi said. "Will there be anything else?" She looked from the princess to Marcus, who lay staring at her with a blank expression.

"No, not tonight, Mimi," the princess said.

The old woman turned and shuffled back out of the room.

"What was that all about?" Marcus asked when Mimi had disappeared into the kitchen.

"I left a gold lighter in a restaurant the other day," Princess Karima told him airily. "That must have been the maître d'. They'll send it to me here."

"Remarkable," Marcus replied. "I should have thought it would've been pawned the minute you were out the restaurant door."

"There are a few decent people left in this world," the princess said, swirling her drink around in its glass.

Marcus laughed. "Introduce me," he said. "I've yet to meet them."

"I can't share everything with you, Marcus, darling," she replied. "A woman must have her secrets if she doesn't want to appear to be common."

"How right you are," Marcus said. "Though I do wish you would share the telephone number of that young man you've told me about."

Princess Karima threw her head back and laughed. "Never!" she said through her laughter. "I would never see either of you again." She took a sip of her drink, then set the glass down on the coffee table, her body tingling with excitement.

How odd that Marcus should mention him now, she thought. *Just when I've had a call from him. He's proving to be such a useful young man. In more ways than one. He has found the young American woman, and if anybody on the planet can get the emerald out of her, he can.* She lay back against the soft cushions and took a long drag off her cigarette, looking thoughtfully at the fire that burned on the ancient stone hearth.

It had been very clever of her to hire the young man for the job, she decided. He was handsome, charming, smart, and very sexy, and he was also a heartless, merciless hustler. Yes, he was perfect for the work, even if unproved outside the bedroom. She could hardly wait for the morning, for he would surely make his move tonight.

Ram flipped his tiny cell phone shut and placed it on the table next to the sofa bed in the little apartment on the rue des Rosiers. His lips smiled as he looked at the ceiling thinking about Allegra Sheridan. What a stupid girl. She might be beautiful in that American way, but she was also very careless. And the man Ram assumed was her boyfriend must be a typical Neanderthal American male. Probably clean-cut and good-looking, but thickheaded and uncivilized, without a bone of sophistication in his body. They were right in the neighborhood, only a few blocks away, when they could have been out of the country. Gone. And the emerald gone with them.

He reached for the pack of cigarettes on the table and lit one, blowing a plume of smoke toward the ceiling after inhaling deeply. He would have the emerald after all, he thought. Plus, he could hardly wait to get his hands on the girl. She had caused him no end of problems. He'd wasted the entire evening with the police after Gérard had been killed, and he had no more idea than they about who was responsible. The one thing he was certain of was that it had to do with the emerald.

He wondered who else could be after it, though it really didn't matter. What was important was that he would have it soon. Kadar would see to that. He'd been on her trail ever since she and the boyfriend had left the apartment on the rue des Archives, and Kadar would figure out a way to get to them in their little love nest at the hotel tonight. Otherwise, he would be there to greet them when they left it in the morning. Like Ram, Kadar had grown up in les Bosquets, the bleak projects that were the perfect breeding ground for ruthless killers. Kadar would get the job done.

He heard the toilet flush and looked toward the bathroom. The girl opened the door and, when she saw him staring at her, smiled tentatively before walking toward him, her pert young breasts bouncing slightly against her skinny rib cage. Under the sheer black thong that was the only thing she wore, he could see that she was completely shaved, and he felt a powerful stirring in his groin.

Hmmmm, the perfect antidote to all my problems, he thought, relishing her pale skin and nubile young body, her long blond hair and hungry, painted mouth. She was pathetic, really. Nothing more than a cheap, strung-out street urchin. And he would make her beg for whatever he chose to give her. She deserved it.

Yes, she is the perfect antidote. The perfect receptacle for all of my frustrations, and nobody will miss her after I'm finished. He pulled the sheet off his muscular body and pointed with an index finger to the weapon aroused between his thighs. The girl's eyes suddenly widened in surprise, then he saw her pause as a ripple of fear ran up her spine, but she continued toward him, as he knew she would. The thought brought a smile to his lips. Women. They were all alike. All of them had a price, and this one was a bargain.

CHAPTER SIXTEEN

In the small lobby of the Hôtel de la Bretonnerie, the clerk behind the desk looked up at the young man who approached from the door to the street. *"Oui, monsieur?"* he said, taking in the young man's extraordinarily handsome features and his expensive clothing.

"What room is Mademoiselle Sheridan in?" he asked. "I'm an old friend, and I would like to surprise her."

The middle-aged clerk shook his head and fussed with a lily in the elaborate flower arrangement that decorated the desk. "I'm sorry, monsieur," he said. "We have no Mademoiselle Sheridan registered here."

"Surely there's some mistake," the young man said, smiling, exposing his perfect white teeth. "She told me that she and her boyfriend would be here tonight and that I should meet them here after dinner."

The clerk shook his head again, and he smiled indulgently. "You said you wanted to surprise her, monsieur, eh?"

"Well, not really. It's just that I'm a little early, you see," the young man lied glibly.

"Your friend must have meant another hotel," the clerk said. His hand fingered the fresh hundred-euro note that Todd had slipped into his trouser pocket only a short time ago.

"She didn't mean another hotel," the young man persisted. "I saw her here."

The clerk's eyes became steely. For the first time, he became aware of the hard glint in the young man's eyes and the muscular body that his clothes could hardly contain, and he regretted that he was manning the desk by himself tonight. There was no one else around with the exception of Mustapha, the bellman, who was probably down in his basement room smoking.

"If you'll excuse me," he said to the young man, "I have work to do, and I think you'd better leave now. Your lady friend is not here."

He turned his back to the young man and slipped a message into one of the pigeonholes mounted on the wall. Suddenly he felt his collar grabbed from behind, and he almost lost his footing as he was jerked backward, as if he were a marionette. He tried to shout for help, but he was choked by his own tie and collar. As he drew his hands up to his neck, he felt only an instant of excruciating pain. It shot through his entire skull as if it had been crushed by an enormous rock. Then he slumped unconscious to the floor.

Yamal put the pistol back in its shoulder holster and went around the counter to look for the registration book. Shoving the clerk out of the way with one foot, he found the book in plain view on a shelf just below the countertop. Picking it up, he looked at the day's entries. There weren't many, since it was not the tourist season, and this was a tiny out-of-the-way hotel.

His dark, glittering eyes were rewarded almost immediately, for there it was: *Sheridan/Hall, room 103*. He looked in the pigeonholes on the wall and saw the key was in their box. He pocketed it. Then before he started up the steps, he went to the glass door that gave onto the street. He flipped the brass lock on it, shutting out any possible arrivals. Going up the staircase a step at a time, he removed his pistol from its holster once again and stopped briefly to make certain that the small silencer was fitted on it properly.

At the top of the stairs, he saw a sign indicating that room 103 was to the left. On silent feet he crept down the carpeted hallway until he arrived at the door. He tried the handle. Locked. Taking the key out of his trouser pocket, he put it in the lock and turned it quickly and silently.

The door gave, and he pushed it open, stepping into the darkened room and shoving the door shut behind him at the same time. Holding the pistol in front of him with his right hand, he reached with his left and felt on the wall for a light switch. At first he felt nothing; then his hand brushed across it. He pushed it with a finger, but nothing happened. The room remained in darkness, except for the faint light coming in from a

THE PARISIAN AFFAIR ❧ 181

window across the room. He advanced toward the foot of the bed, his pistol still out in front of him.

His eyes had adjusted somewhat to the darkness, and he could make out the shape of two distinct lumps in the bed. He aimed the pistol toward the one on the left and fired twice, then switched to the right, and fired two more times. The pop-pops made by the pistol wouldn't draw any attention. They could've been champagne corks to anyone who might have heard them.

Going to the left, he found the cord on the bedside lamp, and felt down it until his fingers brushed the switch. He flipped it, and the lamp immediately lit up. Yamal looked at the bed to make certain they were both dead, before setting about to find the emerald.

He snapped the cover back with a flick of his wrist, and his eyes widened in surprise and disgust.

"Fuck!" he spat in disbelief.

The bed was empty, with the exception of the extra pillows and blankets that had been arranged to make it appear as if a couple were sleeping there.

Yamal looked about the room, almost as if he were expecting someone to be standing in a corner snickering at his failed attempt, but the room was deserted.

Giving the bedside table a furious kick that knocked the lamp off and broke its bulb, he put his pistol back in its holster and quietly went back to the door. Opening it, he looked both up and down the hallway and, seeing no one, stepped out and locked the door behind him. At the top of the stairway, he paused and listened. Not a sound came from the lobby on the ground floor below.

He'd only been a couple of minutes, and knew that the old man could still be out. He considered searching the hotel for Allegra and Todd, but realized that they never intended to stay there. They were obviously in cahoots with the clerk who had taken their key and let them out the back door after they made the bed look like they were in it.

Convinced that a further search would be a waste of time, Yamal went down the curving stairs. Nothing had changed in the lobby. A glance behind the counter satisfied his curiosity about the desk clerk. He still lay in a silent clump as if he were a pile of dirty laundry the maid had dropped and left. Yamal walked around the counter and replaced the key for room 103 in its box, then retraced his steps. He started for the glass door that led to the street when he saw a man try to open it, then shake it by the handle when it wouldn't open.

Yamal sauntered to the door as if he owned the hotel, switched the lock, and opened it.

The man outside stepped back and turned his face away as if he'd changed his mind about entering the lobby, but Yamal paid no heed. He put his hands in his pockets and began whistling as he sauntered off, merging into the still busy sidewalks along the rue Sainte-Croix de la Bretonnerie.

Kadar patted down the sides of his hair, then entered the small lobby and looked about but saw no one. He didn't find it strange that the lobby door was locked, only that no one came to lock up again. He went to the desk and rang the bell, but no one appeared. He waited a minute and rang it again. Still no one.

He looked around the small lobby again, then stretched to his tiptoes to look over the counter to see if he could locate the hotel's registration book.

He was shocked to find the clerk. Looking over his back once again, he could see that no one was about. He darted around the counter and checked the clerk. Out cold. He caught sight of the registration book, lying open on a shelf beneath the countertop, and picked it up, his eyes quickly scanning down the page of the most recent entries. They stopped when they hit *Sheridan/Hall.* He looked up at the wall of pigeonholes and saw the key for room 103 there and took it out.

Kadar hurried around the reception desk and up the flight of stairs to the *premier étage,* his sneakered feet silent on the carpeting.

She felt him explode inside her, and Allegra arched against him with all of her might as wave after wave of contractions overcame her. *Oh, my God,* she thought ecstatically. It was as if the world had shifted somehow, had changed in some fundamental way, and she was at its epicenter, surrounded by a cocoon of warmth and love such as she had never known.

Todd wrapped her in his strong arms and peppered her face and neck with kisses. "Oh, Ally," he whispered, "I love you."

"I love you, too," she breathed, returning his hugs and kisses. "I . . . can't believe this."

"What?" he asked softly, his lips settling at her ear, where his tongue traced little circles. "What can't you believe?"

"This . . . you . . . us," she said in a breathy voice. "It's so . . . wonderful, so perfect."

He hugged her to him more tightly. "You're so wonderful, so perfect," he said. "I feel as if we've reached some new . . . I don't know. Some new level. A new plane. We're closer now than we ever were." He kissed her lips tenderly, then drew back slightly, his eyes reaching into hers. "I've never been so happy."

"You really mean that, don't you?" she said, looking at him in wonderment.

He nodded, his black hair falling over his eyes. "I've never meant anything more strongly. I've never felt anything this powerful in my life."

She kissed his lips then and hugged him passionately. "I feel the same way," she said. "I feel like . . . like we were meant to be somehow."

"Yes," he said. "We were meant to be together. Always and forever."

They kissed again. Then he drew back and looked into her eyes with a smile of such happiness that it almost brought tears to Allegra's eyes. To inspire such love and to feel such love for another human being must be the greatest of all gifts imaginable. It brought such joy to her heart that she couldn't begin to describe it. She thought that she had felt it before with Todd, but not like this. Not this powerfully.

"What are you thinking?" he asked.

"Oh . . . just . . . just how in love I am."

He laughed.

"What are you laughing at?" she asked, punching him playfully on the arm.

"Nothing. I'm just so happy."

She smiled. "Maybe it's just getting to sleep in this magnificent suite."

"Aren't you glad we followed Whitehead's plan and sneaked out of the last hotel?"

"Yes, especially after seeing that suspicious-looking character talking on a cell phone across from the hotel. I know we did the right thing."

"The right thing would have been for me to kill the bastard," Todd growled.

"Well," she said, smiling, "I'm safe now, aren't I? You're here with me, and the emerald is safely stowed away in our room safe."

"Yeah," he said with a grin. "I kind of miss it in my shorts. The man with the sixty-five-million-dollar crotch."

Allegra laughed. "I think it's better off in our safe here at the Ritz, don't you?"

"Yes," he agreed, "and that's where it should stay until we leave."

She looked around at the grandeur of the suite. "I feel like a real princess in a palace. I've always heard about the Ritz, but I never dreamed it was quite *this* palatial."

The bed was a magnificent canopied affair, draped in silk, and the walls were boiserie, the carved wood highlighted in gilt. On the *parquet de Versailles* floor were Aubusson carpets, and the furnishings were all antique, very fine French pieces upholstered in silks and satins. Huge bouquets of fresh flowers were on consoles and tables, and at the bedside was an opened bottle of Louis Roederer Cristal champagne with two Baccarat crystal flutes, now half empty.

"Well, I'm sure it's not all like this," Todd said. "I think this is the most expensive suite in the place. The bellman told me it was the Duke and Duchess of Windsor Suite. They stayed here before they moved to Paris permanently."

"Well, no wonder I feel right at home," Allegra said in jest.

"Yes," Todd said. "Only you're much more beautiful that the Duchess of Windsor ever was."

"And you're a lot better looking than the duke was," she countered with a yawn.

Todd brushed her lips with a kiss. "I think it's time to hit the hay. I can tell you're worn out, and I'm a little jet-lagged myself."

She nodded, her eyes beginning to droop. "I'll just brush my teeth and wash my face," she said. "Then I'll be ready to call it a night."

"Me, too," he said.

They got out of bed, and rather than use the separate bathrooms provided by the suite, they went hand in hand to the same one. When they finished in the opulent bathroom, they padded back to the grand bed, switched out the lights, and slipped under the covers, their naked bodies cuddled together. It was only moments before they were both sound asleep and the worries of the day were at bay.

It wasn't a sound or a movement that woke her from a deep sleep. It wasn't anything external, in fact. It was something Todd had said earlier in the evening that rang an alarm bell in her dormant brain and in one swift instant roused her to complete wakefulness. For several moments she lay still, not daring to move, listening to Todd's rhythmic breathing. His arms were no longer around her, and he'd rolled onto his other side.

She knew why Princess Karima's emerald was so important. Beyond its value as a gemstone and its enhanced worth for having belonged to the princess, the stone must be one of the most historically important gems in the world.

I know what I must do, Allegra thought. *I'm going to try to prove it. No matter what it takes, I'm going to get to the bottom of this. It may not make any difference to Hilton Whitehead or anyone else, but it does to me.*

Besides, if she told him what she knew, he would put professionals on the case, and she'd be left out in the cold. And he'd said it himself: her job was to buy the ring, then get it to New York. No more. Allegra knew she had to go it alone on this. With Todd's help, she would try to prove the ring's origins, and perhaps one day it could be returned to its rightful owner.

With that comforting thought, Allegra turned on her side and closed her eyes. Although she was still excited by what she knew, she fell into a deep sleep again, certain that she'd come to the right decision and preparing herself to take on the challenge.

CHAPTER SEVENTEEN

Breakfast in bed was unlike anything Allegra had ever experienced. When she woke up, Todd had already showered and shaved, and was clad in one of the hotel's complimentary bathrobes. He had also ordered breakfast for them, and his timing was psychic. Allegra had hardly run a brush through her hair and donned a matching robe before there was a knock on the suite's door.

"Who on earth?" she asked, appearing at the bathroom door as he went to answer the knock.

"We'll see," Todd replied.

When the waiters arrived, laden with silver trays, Allegra looked over at Todd and smiled. "I should've guessed," she said.

He returned her smile. "Why not?" he asked.

"Why not, indeed," she said, knotting the robe about her waist.

He took her hand. "Let's eat in bed," he said. "Unless you'd rather that they set the table."

"I think the bed is an excellent suggestion."

"We'll have breakfast in bed," he said to the waiters.

"*Oui, monsieur,*" one of the waiters replied.

After they were settled on the grand silk-swathed bed, the waiters, acting in unison, placed trays on fold-down legs before them. Coffee was poured, croissants and various rolls were put on the trays, with accompanying condiments, and the waiters left after asking if they needed anything else.

"This is heavenly," Allegra declared after taking a bite out of a buttered croissant. "I think it must be the best croissant I've ever eaten."

"Thought you might enjoy it," Todd said, sipping his coffee. He set his cup down and looked over at her. "So what do you want to do today?" he asked. "Have you decided?"

Allegra had known he was going to ask this question, and she had given her answer considerable thought. "I was thinking that maybe I might do some shopping," she said.

"Shopping?" he exclaimed, looking at her as if she'd lost her mind. "For what?"

"Clothes, the odd accessory. You know, girlie things." She took another bite out of a croissant, waiting for his response.

"Allegra," he said. "We're in Paris, for God's sake. Why on earth do you want to go shopping? I mean, there's the Louvre, the Picasso, the Pompidou, and a million other museums. There's . . . there's a million things you've never seen before, you've never done before, and you want to go *shopping*? In *Paris*?" He looked at her with an incredulous expression.

She looked at him, feigning surprise. "But don't you see? That's the point. Being in Paris, I mean. I can get things here I can't get anywhere else in the world."

"Like what?" he asked, mystified. "They've got all the same stores in New York. Gucci, Prada, Yves Saint Laurent."

"Of course they do, silly," she said. "But I don't mean places like that. I'm talking about little boutiques that New York doesn't have. Places that will have all sorts of things I could never find anywhere else."

"I don't believe this," he said. "You could see some of the greatest art in the world, and you're talking about looking for clothes."

He was reacting exactly as she'd hoped he would. Now if only the rest of her plan would work out as well. "Todd, sweetie," she said, turning to him, "how often will I have somebody else's American Express card to use in Paris?"

"Jesus," he said. "You know there's no way you're going to get me to go shopping with you."

"Oh, Todd," she said. "Don't be upset with me. You can do something you'd like to do while I'm busy. I won't be all day, you know."

He gently brushed a finger down the side of her face as if to placate her. "I'm not upset. We can go our separate ways, then meet somewhere for lunch or whatever."

"That's a fabulous idea," she said. "What do you think you'll do?"

"Oh, I don't know. Maybe just do a lot of walking. Looking at buildings and stuff. You know how I love architecture, and there's so much to see here."

"That sounds fun," she replied.

"What about lunch?" he asked. "Do you have a place in mind?"

She shook her head. "No, not really. You?"

"I was thinking about Le Grand Vefour," he said. "It's supposed to be one of the best restaurants in Paris, and I'd like to see what it looks like inside. I've seen pictures, but I've never seen the real thing."

"Sounds wonderful," Allegra said, wondering if he knew that the restaurant was in the Palais Royal, where Jules Levant Joaillier was located.

"What time?" he asked after taking another sip of coffee.

"Oh . . . let's give ourselves plenty of time this morning," she said. "Around one thirty?"

"Okay. I'll see if I can get reservations."

She leaned over and gave him a kiss. "You're a prince," she said, "and I love you."

"Is that because I'm an accommodating prince?"

"That, too."

They finished breakfasting, then began dressing for the day. Todd called Le Grand Vefour and secured reservations. Allegra hadn't paid any attention to him while he was getting ready, and when he appeared in the bedroom wearing a suit and tie, she was dumbfounded.

"My God," she said. "Look at you. You're dressing up like that to go for a walk?"

"Well, we are going to Le Grand Vefour for lunch," he said, "and it's a dressy place, from what I hear."

"Oh, you're right," she said. "I didn't think about that."

"I might as well dress now instead of coming back here and changing," he said.

"You look so handsome," she said, giving him a kiss.

"And you look beautiful," he replied.

"You really think so?" She looked down at her simple black cashmere sweater with matching cashmere slacks. Around her waist was a black alligator belt with a closure in the shape of a frog. It was made of brushed gold, with peridot eyes, and it was an attention grabber against the black.

"Are you fishing for compliments?"

She nodded. "A lady can't get enough," she replied, twirling once in her high, black heels.

"Well, you are one beautiful lady, and you look especially beautiful today."

"Thank you," Allegra replied. "Are you ready?"

"Ready."

They donned their coats and left the suite together, then descended to the small but regal lobby. They were about to step out onto the place Vendôme when Allegra abruptly stopped.

"What is it?" Todd asked.

"I don't believe it," she said. "I have to go to the bathroom. You go ahead."

"I'll wait," he said.

"That's ridiculous," she protested. "Start your walk, and I'll take care of my business."

"If you say so," Todd said with a shrug. He gave her a kiss. "I'll see you at one thirty at Le Grand Vefour."

"I'll be there," she replied.

Todd went through the doors and out onto the place Vendôme, and Allegra went straight back upstairs to their suite. In a matter of minutes she had the ring out of the room safe and in her shoulder bag. Her first order of business, she'd decided, was to get the ring to safety once and for all. Allegra went back down to the lobby. The doorman hailed a cab for her on the place Vendôme, and she was off to her first stop. Taking the cell phone out of her shoulder bag, she dialed the number for stop number two.

Todd glanced into the shop's windows before going inside and was glad that he had dressed up. He probably wouldn't be given the time of day if he had come in dressed in ordinary street clothes. *It's like Van Cleef & Arpels,* he thought. *A lot of expensive merchandise and a lot of attitude. They check you out before they let you in.* He looked at his reflection in the glass and adjusted his tie slightly, then strode to the door confidently. When he saw a buzzer for entry, he pressed the button and waited. The buzzer sounded and he pushed the door open.

He felt as if he were in a pinkish beige cocoon of extraordinary luxury. A huge, sparkling crystal chandelier was suspended from the center of the ceiling, and the jewelry was displayed on the walls and, directly in front of them, in cabinets that formed a semicircle around the room. Two enormous flower arrangements in crystal vases sat at opposite ends of the counter. Behind it, directly ahead of him, stood a woman somewhere over the age of sixty, he estimated, although it was difficult to determine due to her auburn-dyed, perfectly coiffed hair, liberal use of makeup, and smooth, wrinkle-free skin. She had once been a beauty, he thought. She wore a beige Chanel suit with heavy braid trim on the jacket. Beneath it was a simple silk blouse down which several strands of pearls cascaded. A Maltese cross of various colored enamels with a large ruby center was pinned to her jacket. Todd immediately sensed that beneath her surface polish and hauteur was a woman who was lonely, unhappy with her station in life, and possibly in need of a friend. She was a woman who would welcome his attention.

He approached her, and her lips spread in a close approximation of a smile. *"Bonjour, madame,"* he said.

She nodded slightly. *"Bonjour, monsieur.* May I assist you?"

Todd wondered if he looked American, although he was grateful that she spoke English. *"Oui, madame,"* he replied. "At least I hope so."

"Yes?" She looked at him questioningly, her thinly penciled brows arching.

"I came to Paris for the auction at Dufour yesterday," Todd said. "I was interested in Princess Karima's emerald ring, you see."

The woman's eyes lit up, and he could see that they were blue and still held the capacity for liveliness, perhaps even mischief. "So were many others," she said, smiling now. "It is a very beautiful ring. It came from this shop, you know."

"Yes, I did know," Todd said. "That's why I came here. I was not the high bidder."

"How unfortunate for you," she said, "but there were many bidders, monsieur, were there not? Princess Karima's property is highly prized."

"Yes, indeed," Todd said. "I had no idea. Anyway, I'm getting engaged and my fiancée has a passion for emeralds."

"Don't we all?" the lady said with a hint of laughter in her voice.

"Yes, well . . . ," Todd said, looking at her and smiling charmingly, "I'm hoping to be able to find an emerald ring like the one at the auction for her, and I thought that since the ring had come from Jules Levant, perhaps you could help me. I know I can't get a replica, but maybe something about the same size and color."

The lady's eyes suddenly took on an intensity he had not seen in them before. She was taking him seriously now, probably calculating her commission.

"Your pearls and cross are very beautiful, by the way," Todd said to her.

One of the woman's hands went to her chest, and she fingered the pearls with perfectly manicured nails that were painted a lustrous beige. *"Merci, monsieur,"* she said, looking up from the pearls and over at him. "These, and my Maltese cross, were a gift from my late husband."

"He had exquisite taste."

She looked back down at the pearls. "Yes . . . yes . . . he was known for his taste," she said in a faraway voice. She emitted an almost soundless sigh, but Todd heard it. Was it wistful? Or had he had taste and lacked something more . . . substantial? Perhaps something to fall back on so that she wouldn't have to work in this shop?

"I hope I can find something as beautiful for my fiancée," he said. "I wanted the emerald for her so much."

The woman returned her full attention to him. "You must be very much in love, monsieur."

Todd assumed a sheepish expression. "I . . . I really am," he said.

The lady smiled. "She's a very lucky young lady, and I'm certain that we can find something for her," she said. "We have many beautiful things, including emeralds, in the shop."

"As I said, I would be particularly interested in an emerald about the same size and color of Princess Karima's."

"Yes . . ." The lady looked off into the distance as if lost in thought. "We've had several over the years," she finally went on. "I'm trying to think what we've got in stock presently." Her eyes wandered into the distance again, then returned to him. "I know," she said. "Before I start bringing out everything in the shop, I'll show you our book."

"Your book?"

"Oh, yes," she replied. "We have a book that pictures all of our stock. The stock that we have currently. Even the jewels we've sold in the past. Everything at Jules Levant is documented, Monsieur . . . ?"

"Oh, I'm terribly sorry," Todd said. "I'm Todd Hall. It's nice to meet you." He put his hand over the counter, and she shook it with surprising strength.

"Monsieur Hall," she said. "I'm Madame de la Montarron. Jacqueline. It's a pleasure to meet you, also."

Her hand, he noted, was birdlike in its skinniness, age-spotted, wrinkled, and knotted at the joints. Her face must have been lifted several times, for it was sixty while her hands were at least seventy.

"Documented?" he said.

"Yes, of course," she said. "All truly great jewelers document their stock. Their stones and jewelry. Here at Jules Levant Joaillier, we've documented every single item we've bought and sold for . . . well, as long as I can remember . . . even before I was here."

"You've been here a long time?" he asked.

She nodded. "Yes. Since before Monsieur Levant died. After his wife died, I came in to help out off and on, then when Monsieur Tadjer took over, he asked me to stay on full-time. I know so many of the clients, you see."

"Of course," Todd said. "You must be indispensable."

She laughed. "I'm afraid no one is indispensable, but I have been here a long time. Well, wait here a moment, and I'll get our book. If you like, have a seat at the table over there." She nodded toward an ornate *bureau plat* that sat in a small area behind the semicircular display cabinet.

She turned and went through a jib door hidden in the paneling, and Todd, trying to hide his excitement, began to peruse the contents of the cabinets. After a few minutes, he could see that the shop was truly world-class and sold only the best and most expensive merchandise. Going to the *bureau plat*, he sat down in a suede-upholstered, gilt-wood bergère and gazed about the shop. He could see at least three video cameras, and he was sure that there were more. They were motion sensitive, silently following any activity from their mounts up near the ceiling. He had been on camera ever since walking in the door.

Madame de la Montarron appeared from behind the jib door, carrying two large books bound in leather the same pinkish beige that was everywhere. She set them down on a counter, closed the jib door, then picked them up again and walked to the *bureau plat*. She placed the books on it, then sat in a chair opposite Todd.

"Now, Monsieur Hall," she said with a secretive smile, "I'm going to show you things few customers of Jules Levant Joaillier ever get to see. We'll start with the emeralds, shall we?"

Todd nodded. "Madame de la Montarron, I would be honored."

If I hadn't worn slacks, she thought, *this is when I'd show him a little thigh. As a reward.* Instead, Allegra heard herself cooing to the handsome banker, "I appreciate your help so much, Monsieur Lenoir. I don't know what I would've done without you." Then, as a reminder of exactly whom he was ultimately dealing with, she added, "Neither will Hilton—Mr. Whitehead—when I tell him about it."

Lenoir smiled disarmingly. "It was nothing," he said, his gaze traveling up her crossed legs to her breasts, where his eyes lingered before finally looking into hers. "And I told you I would be glad to be of service. Are you absolutely certain there's nothing else I can do for you? I would be glad to show you a bit of Paris. Or perhaps take you for a drive? I could show you some of our more . . . rural delights."

His eyes swept up and down her body again, and Allegra felt as if he'd undressed her and had a long, lascivious look at every inch of her bare flesh. She could imagine him drooling in anticipation of enjoying the pleasures that she had to offer. *Well, I asked for it,* she thought. *I've practically thrown myself all over him to get him to do what I asked.* But it was a pity, she reflected, that a man as handsome as he was and as charming as he could be was also as obviously hungry for sex. There was something repellent about his paying so much attention to her.

"I wish I could," she said, "and it's awfully nice of you to offer. But I have a full schedule, I'm afraid." She looked pointedly at her wristwatch. "In fact, I'd better get going or I'm going to be late." She rose to her feet.

Allegra held out her hand, and Monsieur Lenoir took it in both of his and caressed it. Allegra quickly withdrew it and picked up her shoulder bag and coat. "I really must hurry," she said, turning toward the door.

"Let me help you into your coat," he said, following close on her heels.

"Thanks, but I have to fly," she said, putting it on as she rushed out. "Mr. Whitehead's going to be calling me," she said, turning to him, "so it's essential that I get back to the hotel in time. You know how it is with these billionaires."

"I see," Monsieur Lenoir said, disappointed. Then his face suddenly brightened. "Please give him my best regards, and tell him that we're only too happy to have been of service."

Allegra smiled. "Thank you again, Monsieur Lenoir, and I'll be sure to tell Hilton what a help you've been."

He nodded. "Good-bye, and have a good stay in Paris."

Allegra swept out onto the sidewalk and began walking with a quick stride, taking deep breaths of air. *God! I'm so glad to be out of that place and away from that appalling man,* she thought. *How could somebody so good-looking and so well-placed be so creepy?*

She started looking for a taxi and, when she saw one, raised her hand high into the air. *Now if only my next appointment works out as well,* she thought hopefully.

Todd had spent over an hour sitting at the ornate *bureau plat* with Madame de la Montarron, and it was all he could do to control his growing excitement. He hadn't known that Jules Levant would have document books, nor would he have imagined that he would actually get to look at them—and have a running commentary from a woman who had personally handled or sold many of the jewels. Madame de la Montarron had excused herself for a moment to help a promising-looking middle-aged woman who'd come into the shop, the only customer who'd appeared in the time he'd been here, with the exception of a couple who'd indicated that they were merely browsing.

He rubbed at his eyes with his fingers, feeling practically blinded by the countless photographs he'd seen and the staggering quality, size, and colors of the jewels involved. He'd known that Jules Levant was one of the world's premier jewelers, but he hadn't been prepared for how magnificent and, in many cases, important their jewels were. Their clientele had always been the richest people in the world, the crème de la crème of international society.

Madame de la Montarron had happily pointed out jewels that she'd sold to celebrities, royalty, and the merely rich, often telling him anecdotes about the people involved, or sharing patrons' peccadilloes or eccentricities she'd discovered during the process of selling jewelry. All of that had been very interesting, even fascinating in some cases, but it was something else entirely that had at first merely piqued his interest and then begun to excite him to a near fever pitch.

He couldn't wait to see Allegra, to tell her what he had found out. She wasn't going to believe it. She would probably be angry with him because he'd gone behind her back to do his own investigation. But he felt he had no choice. He certainly didn't think it would be wise to put her in the proximity of Tadjer, a vital consideration, and who else was there to do the work he'd done? Besides, he thought with a smile, who else could've gotten the cement-haired Jacqueline de la Montarron to open up Jules Levant's document books and her life as a saleslady there?

One thing he was sure of: when Allegra heard his news, she would forgive him anything.

Allegra exited the taxi on the winding cobbled lane and looked up at the ancient building where he lived. It resembled a tenement in New York City, and the neighborhood, or this small area of it, was reminiscent of certain blocks on the Lower East Side. Across the lane was a shop that sold Hebrew literature, yarmulkes, menorahs, and other material of Jewish interest. There was a kosher delicatessen on the corner, and street vendors sold falafel and all sorts of food from blazing braziers. This was a Marais she hadn't seen before.

She turned her attention back to the building and saw that the buzzers for individual tenants were mounted next to the door. Names were scribbled on little pieces of paper in tarnished brass slots beneath each buzzer. She found the one for Solomon Weiss, number seven, and pressed it. She waited for the door to buzz, her hand at the ready to open it, but there was no response. She pressed the buzzer again, holding it down longer this time, but there was still no response. *What the devil?* she wondered. *I hope nothing's happened between the time I called and now.* The thought made her stomach turn.

She knew the man must be at least eighty-something years old, and she knew that he wasn't in good health. He had told her so only a short while ago when she'd called him from the taxi. His voice had been so weak it seemed he was exerting a great effort to merely speak with her.

The buzzer suddenly sounded, and she quickly turned the handle and pushed on the door. It was very heavy and scrapped against the stone floor as she pushed it open. Once inside, she faced a long, dark tunnel at the end of which she could see a garden.

Aha, she thought. *It's like the situation at Paul's apartment.* She went through the tunnel and out into the garden. There were several small trees and a number of potted plants struggling toward the gray light of Paris above. Old bicycles were chained here and there, and through the opaque glass set in what appeared to have once been a greenhouse, she could discern the figure of a woman setting a table. Through an opening on her right, she saw the staircase the elderly man had told her to take. She climbed the decrepit curving stairs, noting that they were made of stone and oak as those in Paul's building were. The walls were peeling plaster, and old electric lines ran across them like drapery swags.

When she reached the fifth floor, she stopped on the small landing and caught her breath. Her feet had begun to ache in the four-inch heels she'd worn. *How on earth does the old man ever get up and down these steps?* she asked herself. On the landing she noticed a water spigot that emptied into an dented, tarnished copper basin mounted on the wall. It was probably the only source of water when the building went up, she thought.

When she reached the sixth-floor landing, the door to apartment number seven stood ajar, and just inside it, she saw an ancient bent man who'd once been tall. Wisps of snow-white hair stood out straight all over his head, giving him the appearance of a man who'd stuck his finger in an electric socket. His brushy white eyebrows weren't concealed by the thick glasses on his large nose, and his mustache was slightly yellowed around his lips. He was wearing a shirt and tie, both a little rumpled, over which was a gray cardigan sweater. A paperback book poked up out of one of its pockets. In his hand was a wooden cane with a silver handle. He stared at her with rheumy eyes surrounded by a mass of wrinkles.

"Mr. Weiss?" Allegra asked.

He nodded. *"Oui, mademoiselle,"* he replied. "Please come in." He opened the door wider and stepped to the side.

Allegra stepped into the apartment and put her hand out. "I'm so glad to meet you, Mr. Weiss," she said.

He took her hand and moved his up and down a fraction of an inch, then let it go. "I'm always glad to make the acquaintance of a beautiful young woman," he replied.

Allegra saw the smile on his lips and the twinkle in his eyes. "Thank you," she said. "I'm so grateful that you'd let me visit with you."

"Come this way," he said, slowly going down a narrow hallway, his cane thumping against the bare wood floor.

She followed him into a large, stuffy, overfurnished room whose walls were covered with drawings and paintings. The four windows were all shuttered, permitting little light into the room. She saw that books were everywhere: on shelves, on tables, chairs, and couches, and in high piles on the floor.

"Please, Mademoiselle Sheridan," he said, "make yourself comfortable." He indicated a tufted, leather-covered chair, its upholstery torn and its springs coming loose.

Allegra sat down gingerly on the chair and looked around the room. *It looks English,* she thought. *Edwardian.* There wasn't a single piece of furniture that appeared to be French. "This is a fascinating apartment," she said. "You must love to read."

"Yes," he replied. "Always have. My late wife and I, both of us incurable readers." He had seated himself in a chair similar to hers and looked over at her with a steady gaze. "But I don't assume you came to listen to me ramble on about my personal life. It's my career at Jules Levant you want to know about, isn't it?"

Allegra nodded. "Yes, Mr. Weiss," she said. "I did some reading on the Internet this morning and discovered that you worked for Jules Levant for many years."

"Yes," he said in a wistful voice, his gaze directed at some distant point. "I was there practically from the beginning. We were very close, Hannah, Jules, Elisse—my late wife—and myself. After Hannah and then Jules died, Ramtane inherited the business, and I worked for him for some years until I decided it was time for me to retire." He drew in his gaze and looked at her. "But you don't want to listen to me reminisce. You want some sort of very specific information is my guess. Am I right?"

Allegra nodded. "Well, yes," she replied, a little startled by his directness. "I . . . I came to Paris to bid on a ring that Jules Levant sold several years ago."

"Ahhh," he said knowingly. "Princess Karima's."

"Yes," Allegra said.

"So you're the beautiful and mysterious young American woman who placed the successful bid?"

Allegra felt herself blush. "Well," she replied, "I did place the successful bid."

He chuckled. "Your modesty is refreshing, Mademoiselle Sheridan," he said. "But do go on. Tell me what it is you want to know."

Allegra told him everything that had happened up to this point in Paris.

Monsieur Weiss shook his head and muttered under his breath as she told her tale, but didn't interrupt her. When she was finished, he pushed himself to his feet and shuffled over to a tray of bottles, carafes, and glasses that sat on a bookshelf. He turned to her and asked, "A glass of wine, mademoiselle? Regrettably, it's a *vin ordinaire,* but not a bad Bordeaux."

"Yes," she said, "that would be lovely."

He poured two glasses of wine from a carafe, and Allegra noticed that his hands shook slightly. She got up and crossed to him, and he held a glass up for her. "Thank you," she said.

"You'd better taste it first," he replied with a chuckle.

They returned to their chairs and sipped the wine. "It's quite good," Allegra said.

"Palatable," he said. Then he looked at her with a serious expression. "I have several immediate thoughts about what you've told me. Allow me to express them. Then you may ask me whatever it is you think I might be able to help you with. First, the business at Dufour is absolutely execrable. Someone in the auction house was involved, of course, but the more important question is, who was this person working for? Princess Karima? Ram Tadjer? Some other interested party? Naturally, I don't know the answer, but my guess would be that the princess or Ram was trying to pass off a copy of the ring to you."

"Why one of them?" she asked. She took a sip of the wine.

"Princess Karima because she didn't want to let go of the ring," he replied, looking at her through his thick lenses. "She's rich beyond belief and will never want for money, but that ring held a very special place in whatever heart she's got. Donati, the Italian, was more than a great love affair to her. He gave her entrée—legitimacy, you might say—to international society."

"It sounds to me like she does have a very big heart," Allegra said. "Getting rid of all of her possessions and setting up this charitable foundation."

"Ha!" the old man exclaimed. "Nothing but public relations. I don't know what it is, but the princess has something up her sleeve. For one thing, she's only divesting herself of her Paris holdings. I know that amounts to many millions of dollars, but she's got plenty besides. Her millhouse they keep referring to in the press is a multimillion-dollar pile in the forest of Fontainebleau."

"So you really believe that she might be responsible for Dufour trying to pass off a copy of the ring to me?" The thought hadn't even occurred to Allegra, and she was genuinely surprised with this information.

He nodded. "Absolutely."

"And Ram . . . Ramtane Tadjer?" she said.

"He went there expecting to get the ring," Weiss said, "but he was overlooked for you."

"What do you mean, 'overlooked'?" she asked.

"I'm certain he would have outbid you, but at the last minute the auctioneer simply failed to recognize him and let you win the ring."

"Are you serious?" she asked, appalled that such a thing could take place.

He nodded. "Happens all the time," he said with confidence. "The auctioneer didn't want Ram to have the ring even if it meant letting you have it for a million or few less."

Allegra was silent for a moment, digesting this tidbit. She didn't know whether to believe the old man or not, but this was yet another angle she hadn't considered.

"But there's something more important," Weiss said.

Allegra looked over at him. "What's that, Monsieur Weiss?"

"Something that I think you may know a bit about, since you are a jewelry designer." He paused and took a sip of his wine. "Ram has been buying back certain jewels that were sold over a period of years by Jules Levant Joaillier," he went on, "and Princess Karima's ring was yet another of these purchases."

Allegra felt gooseflesh run up her arms. Monsieur Weiss had just fit in a missing piece of this puzzle for her. "And do you know what those pieces of jewelry are?"

He set his wineglass down and looked into her eyes. "Mademoiselle," he said, "all of the jewels he bought back were emeralds. All the same size."

"Do you have any idea as to why he might have bought them back?" she asked.

"Not the faintest. None. You may know more about that than I do. I was simply a cutter—one of the best, if I say so—and a polisher and setter. I know stones, but I'm not a designer nor am I a historian or even a salesman. I've never worked in the front of the store. Hardly ever set foot there, in fact."

Allegra looked puzzled and then, thinking aloud, said, "He sold all of these emeralds, but then set about buying them back. They're all the same size, so they almost definitely belonged together at one time. Belonged to the same person."

Monsieur Weiss nodded. "Yes," he said, "but who that person was? I don't know. And why he wants them back? I don't know that, either."

"Do you know who he sold them to initially?" she asked.

He shook his head. "No," he said. "I never paid much attention to that sort of thing. I loved the stones. Cutting them, polishing them, setting them to perfection. The rest I left to the others."

Allegra took a sip of her wine, then set the glass down. "I wonder if there's a way to find out," she said.

"Ramtane Tadjer knows," Weiss said, "but I would advise you to stay well away from him. Especially considering what you've already told me. One thing I'm sure of, Mademoiselle Sheridan." He pointed a finger at her. "He'll stop at nothing to get that emerald. Nothing."

Allegra felt a sense of dread. "But then there's the princess, too," she said.

He nodded. "Both of them are lethal."

"You're really serious about that?"

"Absolutely." He nodded emphatically. "You can tell yourself—and I can't blame you for doing so—that I'm just a crazy old Jew. That Ram and the princess are of Arab descent, and that I have it in for them. But you'd be wrong, mademoiselle."

"I don't think that would've even occurred to me, Monsieur Weiss," she said honestly.

"Well, it would to a lot of people," he replied. "But I have my reasons for mistrusting them. Especially Ram. I was there when the Levants took him in. I saw his rise within the company, and I might add that he deserved it. He was a relentless worker and brilliant young man. But I was also there when Jules died and left everything to Ram, and I think there was some . . . I think there were extenuating circumstances."

"What do you mean?" Allegra asked. "Are you implying that—?"

"Think what you will," Weiss said. "But in my opinion, Ram might have helped poor Jules along."

Allegra almost stared openmouthed. *Surely not,* she thought. *If he had been taken in by them, adopted for all practical purposes, what would he have to gain by hurrying Jules Levant to his death?* It didn't fit with the Ramtane Tadjer she'd met. He seemed far too intelligent and patient a man to risk losing everything—when he knew he was going to get it anyway—by trying to speed up the process.

"And the princess?" she said. "Why would you mistrust her?"

"I can't really give you any tangible evidence of her . . . shall we call it lack of character, for want of a better phrase? No. She has done nothing reprehensible that I can name. Not yet, in any case."

"Then why do you mistrust her? Why do you question her motives concerning her charitable foundation?"

He shrugged. "Call it instinct, mademoiselle," he said. "An unsatisfactory answer, I know. But this I do know: the princess is a woman rife with resentments. She is a woman who has suffered grave emotional damage in the past. And I think she's the last person on earth to follow some spiritual course. No. I think she's much more likely to be planning some sort of revenge on those who've wronged her."

Allegra didn't know what to believe. Were Monsieur Weiss's thoughts merely the ramblings of an ancient, resentful man? But, she asked herself, what did he have to gain by sharing these thoughts with her? He certainly seemed to have his wits about him, and he didn't seem to have any particular ax to grind.

"Are you in contact with Monsieur Tadjer any longer?" she asked.

He shook his head. "No," he replied. "Ram has no use for an old man like me." Then he smiled and a sly look came into his eyes. "But I have seen him from time to time over the years, though he doesn't know it."

Allegra looked at him with curiosity. "What do you mean?" she asked.

"Ram still has the little apartment in this building that Jules and Hannah gave him all those years ago."

Allegra's eyes widened in surprise. "An apartment here? In this building?"

The old man nodded. "Yes," he said. "They did the same for him that they did for Elisse and me. After they took him in, they gave him an apartment here, and even though he lives like a pasha in his great mansion a few blocks away, he's kept his little place here."

"That's incredible," Allegra said.

"Not really," he replied. "You see, he brings women here. Women that he'd prefer not to take to his home, I assume."

Allegra swallowed and sat silently, digesting this news in silence. Finally, she said, "It sounds a bit . . . unsavory."

Monsieur Weiss laughed softly. "The least of his less appetizing characteristics, I should think. Many men here keep mistresses or girlfriends, as I'm sure they do in America, but I don't think that's precisely the case with Ram. It's been many women over the years, so I'm told and so I've observed. But that's neither here nor there, is it?" He sipped the last of his wine and set the glass down. "I hope I've been of some help to you, mademoiselle."

Allegra was glad for the opportunity to excuse herself. "I'm sure you have," she said, "and I can't thank you enough for your seeing me today. It was very kind and generous of you to share your time with me, and I've enjoyed meeting you very much."

"It was a pleasure to meet you, too, Mademoiselle Sheridan," he replied. "I hope you find what you're looking for."

"I think I will," she said, "and partly because of you." She rose to her feet. "Please don't get up. I can let myself out."

"No, no," he replied, pushing himself up out of his chair. "I may be old, but not so infirm as to have to be uncivilized."

Allegra followed him down the hall and waited for him to open the door for her, then smiled and gave him her hand to shake. He took it in his and merely held it for a moment. "You're a lovely young woman," he said. "Come again if you want. It would be a pleasure to receive you."

"Thank you, Monsieur Weiss," Allegra said. "It would be a pleasure to talk with you again." Her reply was heartfelt, and even though she was in a rush to meet Todd, she was reluctant to leave him.

When she finally reached the street, she felt a powerful sadness sweep over her. *He's so old and alone,* she thought, *yet so interesting and lively.* She doubted that she would ever see him again. Looking about for a taxi, she saw that there was none about and started walking, hoping she was aiming in the direction of a major thoroughfare. She wondered whether she should tell Todd about what she discovered today, and couldn't make up her mind. One thing for certain was that she was more obsessed than ever with the emeralds and more determined to find out what was going on.

CHAPTER EIGHTEEN

Allegra trotted along the arcade at the Palais Royal toward Le Grand Vefour. When she reached the restaurant, she rushed inside and saw Todd already seated at a table for two in the grand dining room. He saw her and immediately got to his feet. The maître d' didn't fail to notice.

"Mademoiselle Sheridan?" he said.

Allegra nodded. "Yes," she said. "I see my party back there."

"Would mademoiselle like to hang up her coat?"

"No," she replied. "I think I'll keep it on." It had been breezy and gray outside, and she hadn't quite recovered from the chill.

"As you wish," he said. "Please follow me."

At the table, he pulled her chair out, and Allegra seated herself. The maître d' handed her a menu, and she thanked him. He poured her a glass of champagne from a bottle that rested in an ice bucket on a stand next to the table. "Ah," she said, "elixir of the gods. Thank you, monsieur."

The waiter nodded, then left the table.

Todd sat back down and beamed across the table at her.

"You look happy about something," she said, smiling.

He reached across the table and took her hand. "I'm just so happy to see you."

"Well, I'm glad to see you, too," she replied.

"But I had no idea this place was practically next door to Jules Levant Joaillier when I made the reservation."

"Do you think we ought to leave?" she asked, looking around her, tak-

ing in the grand restaurant's elegant designs painted on the glass and mirrored ceiling.

"I don't think we have to take a drastic measure like that," Todd said.
"In fact, I happen to know that Ramtane Tadjer is not in the shop today,
so I don't think we run the risk of seeing him."

Allegra lifted her eyebrows in surprise. "And how do you know that?"
she asked, shrugging out of her coat and putting it around her shoulders.

"Just wait till I tell you what happened," he said in a soft but gleeful
voice. He took a sip of his champagne. "I had a run of good luck while
you were out shopping." His expression abruptly changed. "Where are
your shopping bags?"

"I couldn't find anything I wanted," Allegra lied glibly.

He stared at her for a long moment. "Allegra," he said, "do I look like
I was born yesterday? You're in Paris, and you couldn't find anything you
wanted?" He set his champagne glass down. "Now try telling me the
truth."

"First, you have to tell me your news," she countered. "You're being
very mysterious, and I gather you were up to a lot more than a walk
around the streets of Paris. How do you know that Ramtane Tadjer is not
going to be in the shop today, for example?"

"I thought I'd try to help you find out more about the emeralds," he
said slowly and cautiously.

Allegra's eyes burned into his.

"I figured that Tadjer knows what you look like, but nobody at Jules
Levant has ever seen me before," he said quickly.

Though Allegra was peeved, her ears perked up. "Go on."

"So I went there and acted as if I were a customer looking for an emerald ring," Todd said. "In fact, I told the saleslady that I'd come to Paris to
bid on Princess Karima's ring."

Allegra almost sputtered champagne. "You *did*?"

Todd nodded. "She bought my story hook, line, and sinker, but what's
more important is that she took a shine to me." He paused and smiled
with self-satisfaction.

"I see," Allegra said. "All the ladies do, don't they?"

"A lot of them do," he said teasingly, "but it wasn't what you're thinking. This woman must be seventy, at least. Anyway, she offered to show
me their document books."

Allegra almost levitated out of her chair. "Their document books?" she exclaimed. When she realized that she'd used a raised voice, she immediately lowered it and looked about. "I can't believe this."

The waiter appeared. "Are you ready to order?"

"We'll be a few more minutes," Todd replied.

When the waiter disappeared, Allegra said, "You've got to tell me. What did you find out?"

"A lot," he said. "Over the years, Jules Levant has handled several emeralds of the exact same size and color as Princess Karima's. I made a list of who they were sold to."

"Oh, Todd! Oh, you're unbelievable." She leaned across the table and planted a kiss on his lips.

He beamed once again. "The saleslady wasn't even aware that I made the list," he said. "She was so busy telling me anecdotes about the people who bought them."

"Who?" Allegra asked. "Who did buy them? And how many people were involved?"

"I'd have to look at my list," Todd said, "but I remember that there were a brooch and a bracelet. Then a necklace. Earrings. And the ring that was Princess Karima's. And all of the pieces were bought by different customers."

Allegra's mind was spinning. The emeralds had to be part of a matched set. All the same weight and color. Very rare. Especially for emeralds. And Jules Levant—or Ramtane Tadjer—deliberately broke them up, even though they would've been more valuable if they'd been sold all together.

"So," he asked, looking at her with obvious pride, "how'd I do, huh?"

"You did brilliantly," she said. "Absolutely brilliantly." She took a sip of her champagne, then set the glass down. "I can't wait to have a look at that list."

Todd fished a piece of paper out of the inside breast pocket of his suit jacket. "Have a look."

Allegra practically tore it out of his hands.

The brooch. Costas Stephanides, she read. She knew who the rich Greek was, of course. No doubt, he'd bought the brooch for his mistress, that Greek actress, what's her name. Marina Koutsoukou.

The bracelet. A General Ramondo González-Viega. Allegra didn't know who he was, but she knew she could find out without much trouble.

The necklace. A Parisian, Vicomte de Rabe, had bought it for his *vi-*

comtesse. Allegra knew her name from the society and fashion press. She was one of those rich, thin social butterflies whose every movement was recorded, whose taste in clothes and decoration were emulated by women everywhere.

The earrings. William Cosgrove Hutchison. A New Yorker. Allegra searched her mind. She knew that she'd heard the name, but she couldn't quite place it. Probably one of those quiet, old-money New Yorkers who neither wanted nor got much publicity.

The list accounted for a hell of a lot of thirty-four-and-a-half-carat emeralds. Especially of the same color. She couldn't begin to calculate what they would be worth if they were reunited and sold as a set. Princess Karima's ring was the only anomaly. It was the same size and color, but it had its unique inclusion.

She looked over at Todd. "This is fabulous," she said. "I still can't believe you did it." She formed a kiss and blew it across the table.

The waiter approached again. "Do you need more time?" He poured more champagne for them both.

"I think we're ready," Todd said. "What if I order for us both?"

"Perfect," Allegra said.

"We'll both have the lamb," he said. "Rare."

"No appetizers, monsieur?"

"No, thanks," Todd said. He looked over at Allegra for confirmation, and she nodded.

"Very well," the waiter said, and he disappeared.

"Now," Todd said, "you've got to tell me what you've been up to, all right?"

"Well . . . I did a little research on the Internet," she said, deciding not to tell him about her visit to the bank and using Monsieur Lenoir's computer while there.

"Uh-huh," he said. "What kind of research?" he asked.

"Looking at stuff about Jules Levant Joaillier," she replied.

"And?"

"And I found out that a man named Solomon Weiss used to work there," she replied. "He was a cutter, polisher, and setter. I also found out that he was still alive and living here in Paris."

Todd looked excited. "And you went to see him? What did you find out?"

"He's a widower, well into his eighties, and lives on the rue des Rosiers. It's a little Jewish neighborhood in the Marais."

"Odd, isn't it?" Todd said. "You were staying in the Marais in Paul's apartment. You went to a museum in the Marais where you were shot at twice. We checked into a hotel in the Marais, then checked out. Now this Weiss character turns up in the Marais. The neighborhood keeps popping up."

"Yes," Allegra said, "and get this. Ramtane Tadjer has an apartment in the Marais. In the same building that Monsieur Weiss lives in. The Levants gave it to him when they took him in years ago, and he's kept it."

"Jesus," Todd exclaimed. "Him again. There you were in the same building where he lives."

"No, no," Allegra said. "He doesn't live there. He has a mansion a few blocks away, Weiss said, but he keeps the apartment for assignations."

"Oho," Todd said, smirking. "So our Mr. Tadjer is either married or he won't do the dirty at home."

"I guess," she replied neutrally, although for some reason the thought of the handsome, charming jeweler involved in clandestine, sordid-sounding escapades didn't sit well with her.

Their food was served, and as they ate the delicious lamb and vegetables with gusto, Allegra told him about her visit with Solomon Weiss. When she had finished her tale, Todd sat thoughtfully eating the last of his meal before responding. He finally said, "You know, it's as if you found one giant piece of a puzzle, and I found the other. We know to whom these emeralds have been sold and that Tadjer has been buying them back over the years. Though Madame de la Montarron didn't mention anything about him buying back any of the jewels she showed me."

"She may not even know," Allegra offered.

"True," he responded. "She probably doesn't. She would've mentioned it. I mean, once she got started talking it was like floodgates had opened, and she wouldn't stop."

"But it's odd that Solomon Weiss knew," Allegra said. She shrugged. "It's probably not even important, but I'm curious."

"Well, madame certainly knew that Tadjer was bidding on Princess Karima's ring," Todd said.

"Everybody in Paris knows that," Allegra said. "But it was a very special case, being the princess's and all."

"Now what do we do with what we've got?" Todd mused aloud.

"Good question," Allegra said. "And where did the emeralds come from? And why does Ramtane Tadjer want them back?"

Todd looked at her with thoughtful eyes. "How do we find out?"

"I'm not sure," she said, "but my enquiring mind wants to know." She put her knife and fork down. "That was wonderful. Do you want dessert?"

"I'll have something if you do," he said.

"I think I'd rather get out of here, fabulous as it is, and go back to the hotel. Brainstorm a little bit."

They left the restaurant, walking hand in hand in the arcade of the Palais Royal, avoiding the section where Jules Levant was located.

"How did you extricate yourself from the saleslady?" Allegra asked.

"I told her I was having lunch with my fiancée," Todd said. "She appreciated the idea of two young lovebirds meeting for lunch at Le Grand Vefour."

Allegra laughed. "I guess that's a very French reaction."

"I guess so," he agreed, "but she does expect me to return to the shop later today or Monday."

"She's going to be disappointed. She won't get to see you again."

Todd squeezed her hand affectionately. "Maybe," he said. "Then again, maybe not. They do have some really nice jewelry."

"Oh, don't even tease about that," Allegra said. "It is all magnificent, but it's priced accordingly."

"Can your feet handle the walk back to the hotel in those heels?" Todd asked, looking down at her stilettos.

"Sure," Allegra said. "They've had a good rest, and it's not that far."

He brushed her cheek with a kiss. "It's so wonderful to be here in this beautiful city with you," he said.

"Even if it's gray and chilly?"

"Who cares about the weather?" he said, kissing her cheek again.

"Not me," she said, stopping and kissing him on the lips.

With their eyes only for each other, they failed to see that they were being watched, and when their walk finally took them back to the place Vendôme and the Ritz, they didn't realize that they'd been followed.

Sylvie paced in Paul's ground-floor apartment, her heels click-clacking a loud tattoo on the cold limestone floor, plumes of blue gray smoke encircling her in a fog before lifting to the ceiling.

Paul sat on the sofa watching her, his body hypertense. Sylvie had both fascinated and scared him, and today, her histrionics were almost proving too much for his already frazzled nerves. The generous snorts of crystal meth she'd offered him had increased his body's state of alertness but simultaneously made him feel as if his concerns weren't important anymore, even though intellectually he knew that wasn't true.

Clack! She had made another turn in her to-and-fro path, and his body jerked involuntarily. He watched her take a long drag on the unfiltered Gauloises she was smoking and send another noxious plume of smoke into the room.

He'd been in love with her for years, and had always wondered what appeal she'd found in him. She could have anyone. And though Sylvie wasn't exclusive to him, he was grateful for whatever time she deigned to give him.

They had met at le Rosey, the exclusive boarding school, and as unlikely as their friendship might seem to outsiders—he, a reticent, unattractive nerd; she, a stylish, bubbling social butterfly—they had found a common ground at once. They both felt like misfits at the expensive school, and together they sought escape in recreational drugs. Not that they were exceptions among the student body, but they developed an intimate relationship that lasted for years, even if it was almost entirely dependent on Sylvie seeking him out, rather than the opposite. She had, and still did, come to him after debauched evenings with boyfriends and pull him into bed and make passionate, if drugged, love, telling him how superior he was to the rich but thuggish boys who had gotten their rocks off then fled the scene.

"You're like me, Paul," she would say. "Sensitive and caring. Creative. Artistic. Not like those animals." All this while they fucked again and again, sometimes for hours on end, until their bodies could no longer perform, and they collapsed into long, drugged sleep.

Their time together had of necessity been lessened by her work in New York, but she often visited Paris, and Paul often make the trek to New York to see her. He would do anything for her, and while he knew that the reverse was not true, it didn't matter to him.

"Do you have any vodka?"

At first her question didn't register, although he saw her stop and whirl around and look at him. He saw her beautiful painted lips move and the inquisitive look on her elegant face. He was so distracted by the powerful drug that he simply looked up at her with a blank expression.

"Do you have any vodka?" she repeated in a louder voice.

"Oh, yes, of course," he replied, jumping off the sofa and going to the refrigerator. He opened it and took a bottle of Stolichnaya out of the freezer, then poured two glasses nearly to the brim. He handed her one and smiled. "Here."

Sylvie took it and raised it to her lips immediately, taking a long sip, then shuddering slightly. *"Magnifique,"* she said, returning his smile.

Paul took a swallow of the vodka and enjoyed the burning sensation as it traveled down his throat to his stomach. "Why don't we sit down," he said, "and relax a bit."

Sylvie kicked off her heels and sat down on the couch, pulling her feet up under her. She patted the space next to her. "Here, darling Paul. Sit here. We must talk."

He sat down next to her, waiting for what would come next. He never knew. Sylvie was unpredictable, to say the least.

She reached over and stroked his face with her fingers, her nails scraping along his cheek lightly. "I want you to help me," she said.

He looked at her. "Help you do what?" he asked.

Her eyes narrowed. "I want to get back at Allegra," she said. "I want to pay her back for ruining my life in New York."

"I think we'd be wise to leave well enough alone, don't you?"

She didn't respond but took a sip of the vodka.

"I mean, look at it this way, Sylvie," he said. "You're lucky you got out of New York without Whitehead stopping you. We're both lucky to be sitting in this apartment instead of some fucking police station today. He might decide to pursue you. Us. Have you thought about that?"

Sylvie shrugged. "He won't," she said. "I'm sure of it. He doesn't really care about a few thousand dollars, only that fucking emerald for Kitty. Besides, he liked me. He liked me a lot."

"You didn't . . ."

"Don't be a fool," she said. "Of course not. He isn't my type, and it might've ruined a good working relationship. He paid me an enormous salary, and I did a great job. That was all there was to it."

She put a hand on his thigh and rubbed it gently. "Let's forget about him," she said. "He doesn't matter. That bitch Allegra does. She and her boyfriend. They ruined my life, and what's worse, they humiliated you. For that I will never forgive them."

"But . . . but it's pointless," he said. "Besides, what can we do? They'll be going back to New York on Monday, and we don't even know where they are."

Sylvie smiled mischievously. "Oh, I bet I do."

Paul looked at her. "So where are they?"

"At the Ritz, of course," she replied. "That's where she was supposed to stay to begin with, and I'm sure that after talking to Hilton, that's where they went."

"Well, then we might as well forget it," he said. "The Ritz is like a bunker. We'd never be able to get at them. What could we do anyway?"

"Something . . . ," she said slowly, "something to make her life miserable."

"But what?" he asked.

"Something simple . . . like . . . like throwing acid in her face," Sylvie said.

Paul froze. "I—I think you're going too far," he said. "Sylvie, we could really get in trouble. I don't like this."

She put her glass down and put her hands on his shoulders. Looking into his eyes, she said, "Trust me, Paul, darling." She kissed his lips. "Nothing will happen to us." Kiss. "Nothing." Kiss. "We'll be off in Provence tomorrow or the next day without a care in the world."

He started to pull away, but she held him with her hands. "No, Sylvie," he said. "I really don't like this. I—I think it's the drug talking."

She laughed. "That's ridiculous," she said. "But so what if it is? I want to do it. And we can do it. It's very simple. I have it all worked out." She took her hands off his shoulders and placed them on his thighs, where she began massaging him slowly and gently. "Just this one little last thing before we head down to Saint Rémy," she said, "and start a new life . . . together."

He looked into her eyes. "Together? You mean—?"

"I meant what I said, Paul," she replied. "Yes. The two of us. Together in Saint Rémy. We'll start a new life there. Away from the rat races of New York and Paris. We can garden and decorate the house and live healthy lives."

Paul looked into her eyes and saw the dreamy expression they held. He didn't know whether to believe what she said or not, but he wanted to. He wanted to with all his heart.

"Whatever it takes," he said, "we'll do it. Together."

Cameron had already been to the gym and showered, and now as he changed clothes, Jason watched, enraptured by the sleek, buff body with its hardened, defined musculature.

Cameron turned and flashed a smile, his perfect white teeth exposed. "What are you thinking about?"

"Oh, nothing," Jason replied sheepishly.

"Don't lie to me, boy toy," Cameron said, ruffling his hair affectionately. "I can always tell, you know."

"Well . . . I . . . I was just thinking about how lucky I am," Jason admitted.

"And why's that?" Cameron asked, although he knew the answer to his question.

"Because you . . . you . . . love me," Jason said, looking up into his eyes.

Cameron, his legs spread wide in front of the chair where Jason sat, leaned over and placed his hands on his shoulders, then lowered his lips to Jason's and kissed him. It was a long, tender kiss, and Jason felt himself falling under the spell that Cameron had cast over him.

Cameron stroked his face with one long finger, then drew back. "You're going over to the atelier this morning, aren't you," he said. It wasn't a question but a command.

Jason nodded. "I'm ready to leave."

"Then you'll come straight back here?"

"Yes," Jason said, "but it'll take me a while. At least a couple of hours. Maybe more. There're tons of designs."

"Just make sure you photocopy everything," Cameron said. "And I do mean everything. Whether it's in a bound drawing book, a notepad . . . in the safe, on the wall. I don't care. Just photocopy them all."

"Don't worry," Jason replied. "I will."

"And while you're at it," Cameron added, "why not take a few loose stones?"

Jason suddenly went pale and felt his stomach knot. "Cameron, wait a minute," he said nervously. "That wasn't part of the deal. You didn't say anything about taking any stones."

Cameron ruffled Jason's hair again. "Aw, come on," he said teasingly. "She's not going to miss a few stones. A little diamond here, a little ruby there." He made little picking motions with his hands.

"She might," Jason said.

"Don't give me that," Cameron said. "Not even Allegra Sheridan has a count of every single stone she's got in stock." He stroked Jason under the chin. "I've been there with you, baby," he said. "I know what the place is like. And believe me, she isn't going to miss a few carats of this and that. So just slip a few in your pocket." He leaned down and kissed his lips again. "For me, baby," he said, looking into his eyes. "For me."

Jason was both repulsed by and inescapably drawn to Cameron, his monumental ambitions, his rapacious desires, his insatiable body, and he knew that he would do whatever Cameron asked of him, even if it meant alienating the best friend he'd ever had. He knew Allegra would never forgive him once she found out that he copied her designs.

"I'd better get going," he said, getting to his feet.

"Good boy," Cameron said, playfully patting his ass. "I'll be here when you get back, and we'll have a little celebration. So put a smile on your face."

"Okay."

Thirty minutes later, he was in the atelier, rapidly stuffing drawing pads and notebooks into his backpack and a large duffel bag he'd brought with him for the purpose. He'd taken several drawings out of their frames and would have to replace them after he'd finished. This was going to take longer than he'd thought.

It seemed Allegra saved every design she ever came up with. Many of them he recognized, of course, but he was surprised to discover that there were dozens and dozens she'd never shown him.

Jason quickly filled the backpack and then stuffed the duffel bag as fast as possible. He was going to Brooklyn to photocopy everything. He didn't want to risk the possibility that any of the places in the neighborhood would know that he was copying Allegra's work.

When he was finished, he went to the safe and opened it. From various pouches, he took a small handful of precious and semiprecious stones. Only three or four from each suede pouch. He knew that the only way she could substantiate the theft would be to go through all of her invoices, then count stones, subtracting those that had been used in pieces they'd created since the purchases had been made. It would be an arduous task, enormously time-consuming and tedious.

His cell phone rang, and he quickly grabbed it from its holder on his belt. But as he always did nowadays, he checked caller ID before answering. Jason felt a sudden prickle of heat about his neck and face when he saw the number. It was the same overseas one that he'd seen displayed innumerable times in the last two or three days. *Allegra*. He stared down at the number for a moment, then slipped the cell phone back in its holder.

He began to work faster, shoving the stones in the left-hand pocket of his Levi's. It had been empty, and the stones wouldn't get mixed up with the cash in his right-hand pocket. He closed and locked the safe, then shouldered his backpack and picked up the duffel bag.

Thank God Cameron had given him the cash to take a taxi to the wilds of Brooklyn. Now if he'd just get lucky catching one back without having to wait forever. Oh, well, he thought, Cameron had taken care of that, too. If taxis were scarce, all he had to do was call a limo service and give them Cameron's account number, and he'd be picked up and delivered back to Manhattan in a matter of minutes.

Jason considered himself one lucky guy as he let himself out of the loft. He hurried, anxious to get to Brooklyn and back. Back to the lover who was beyond his wildest dreams.

"Excuse me, Marcus," Princess Karima said, "but I must take this call."

Marcus nodded, but he didn't fail to notice the gravity in Karima's voice as she got up from the table and left the dining room. Like everyone who knew her, he was fascinated by the press releases concerning her selling off assets and the new spiritual path she claimed to be following, and like those who knew her best, he hadn't believed a word of them. Gossip had been rife, of course, and speculation among the international set had reached epidemic proportions.

When she'd asked him to accompany her to the auction and to the country afterward, he'd been thrilled. Anybody who was anybody would be asking him out. The invitations would pour in because, of course, everyone would want to pump him for information. *If Princess Margaret were still alive,* he thought, *she'd already have been burning up my phone line.*

But as he lit a cigarette and took a sip of the extremely fine wine they were having with lunch, he was more puzzled than ever over the whole affair. Karima, who had always seemed easy to read as far as he was concerned, had suddenly become something of an enigma. She was more high strung than usual, and a bit less forthcoming. When he'd broached the subject of her charitable foundation last evening, she'd given him the brush-off. Merely told him that her "men in Geneva" were taking care of everything. Then when he'd asked about this new spiritual path, she'd replied in a most mysterious fashion. "I've reached an age," she'd said, "at which inner peace is important to me, Marcus, darling, and I'm consulting various advisers, testing the waters, seeing what's best for me."

Had she not stared directly into his eyes with such fiery intensity, he would've laughed aloud. But he hadn't dared. Karima had seemed deadly serious, and the last thing he wanted to do was incur her wrath, for her tantrums were legendary.

He got to his feet and wandered into the salon, cigarette and wineglass in hand. And all these phone calls that she had to take in private, he thought, taking a drag off his cigarette. She'd never been like this before.

He took the last sip of wine in his glass, put his cigarette out in an ashtray, then went back to the dining table to pour another splash into his glass. The crystal carafe was empty. He pushed past the swinging doors that led into the butler's pantry and looked on the shelves and in the cabinets there. Nothing. He shoved on the door that led into the kitchen to look for Mimi, but she was nowhere about.

Then he heard Karima's voice, raised in anger, and saw that the door leading out to a porch was ajar. He stood still and listened, wondering what she was upset about. After a moment, he could hardly believe his ears. Princess Karima was speaking Arabic! He knew for certain because he'd known princes from various Arab states while he was a student at Eton and then at Oxford. But he had never in the thirty-odd years he'd known Karima ever heard her speak in her native tongue.

He continued to listen, not understanding what she was saying, but hearing her repeat "Yamal" any number of times. Marcus abruptly felt very uncomfortable, and he turned and went back through the door as quietly as possible. Eavesdropping was one thing, but this was another, he decided. Something very odd indeed was going on, and he didn't want to be caught overhearing whatever it was.

In the dining room he set his wineglass on the table, then went out into the entrance foyer and took his quilted Barbour jacket off its hook. He put it on and slipped quietly out the front door. He strode across the stone terrace, down the steps, and out onto the pea gravel drive, then headed around the right-hand side of the house toward the service entrance. The gardens in the rear of the estate were a closer walk that way, and although it was too early for much activity in the way of blooms, he could admire their beautiful layout, the statuary and pool, and the well-kept forests that surrounded them.

He stopped to light a cigarette, then followed the drive, gazing at the magnificent conifers that lined it. Rounding the end of the house, he thought he heard voices, and saw the tail end of an unfamiliar car parked at the end of the drive. As he got closer, he saw that the car was a Ferrari. On he walked, smoking, enjoying the cool outdoor air despite the overcast skies.

As he approached the car, he heard the voices again, and he saw a tall, muscular young man with pitch-black hair and a dark complexion. Marcus stopped in his tracks. As the young man spoke, he turned and drew on a cigarette, so that Marcus could see his profile, his high, prominent cheekbones and aquiline nose, his square jaw and sensuous lips. Marcus marveled over the best-looking man he'd ever seen. Then it dawned on him that he must be the young man Karima had told him about. The extraordinarily expensive hustler. Who was obviously doing well for himself considering he was driving a Ferrari.

He and Princess Karima were engrossed in conversation, but Marcus couldn't hear what they were saying. She stood at the door to the enclosed porch as the young man stood in front of the car. Realizing that once again he was intruding upon the princess's privacy, Marcus slowly backed up, willing the gravel not to crunch beneath his shoes—an impossibility, of course. However, they were so preoccupied that they didn't hear him, and as luck would have it, neither of them had seen him. When he was safely out of earshot and sight, he sped up his pace and returned to the terrace at the front entry.

Christ! he thought for the hundredth time. *What is she up to? She wasn't on the telephone at all, but talking to this staggeringly handsome young man.*

He let himself into the foyer, took his jacket off and put it on its peg, then went back to the dining room and sat down. He almost jumped when Mimi came into the room.

She stared at him with her wrinkled up little eyes, then said, "You have been out, monsieur?"

"Out?" Marcus echoed. Then he forced a laugh. "Oh, just smoking a cigarette on the terrace."

"Do you need anything, monsieur?" she asked, her eyes still trained on him harshly.

"I would like some more of that divine wine we were having with luncheon," Marcus said.

"Very well," Mimi said, coming to the table and picking up the carafe.

"Will Princess Karima be returning to table?" he asked. "I hope nothing is . . . amiss?"

"My mistress will be back shortly," the old woman said. "I will bring your wine."

"*Merci,* Mimi."

Marcus wished he felt at liberty to ask Karima what was going on. But that was out of the question. He would have to discover an answer to this mystery another way. Of one thing he was certain. The young man he saw talking to her was anything but a spiritual adviser, although he had to admit that he would gladly worship what he'd seen of him.

He mustn't let on that he had seen or heard anything. The better to hear and see more. And he hoped that Mimi hadn't seen him out near the service entrance.

What a coup it would be to be able to go back to Paris, then on to London and New York, with his tales of the latest in the princess's life. The world was dying to know—the world that *counted,* at any rate—and if he played his cards right, he'd be able to dine out on this weekend with the princess for years to come.

"What was his name, Jacqueline?" Ram demanded.

The older woman's forehead, though practically incapable of wrinkling from the Botox injections, did so now. "I've told you," she replied in exasperation. "I do not know." She wondered how many times he was going to ask her and of what possible importance it could be. The stranger was a very handsome young man in love, looking for an emerald ring. Harmless, very polite, too—a rarity for an American.

"Tell me everything again," Ram said, pointing a finger at her. He was in a furious state, like nothing Madame de la Montarron had ever seen before.

She slowly repeated everything, and when she was finished, she could swear that she saw smoke pouring out of Ramtane Tadjer's nostrils. He had been in a rage ever since he'd come into the shop. He'd made several cell phone calls in his office, then come charging after her as if she were some sort of common thief.

"You will never, ever again show anyone the document books without my explicit permission," he shouted at her. "Never! Do you understand that?"

"What am I to do when our prize customers ask to see them?" she asked, regaining a bit of her composure. "One of the Saudi or Kuwaiti princes, a Niarchos or Goulandris? One of the royals? Tell me that, please."

"In cases such as that," he replied in a calmer voice, "you will do as you have always done, Jacqueline." His voice began to rise, and his face began reddening again. "But with a stupid young American nobody like the one today, you will not give him the time of day." He slammed a hand down on the *bureau plat*.

The roses in the heavy crystal vase on the corner of the desk quivered, but Jacqueline de la Montarron merely glanced up at him with an imperturbable expression. *What an uncivilized heathen,* she thought. *Showing his true stripes.*

"I should think," she said at last, "that if a young man came in and told you he had been bidding for Princess Karima's emerald at Dufour you would pay more than a little attention to him. Would you not?"

He glared at her. He wanted nothing more than to slap her patrician face. But he wouldn't allow his emotions to rule the day. He needed Jacqueline de la Montarron, almost as much as she needed him. Women like her weren't necessarily rare, but she had made herself indispensable over the years at Jules Levant. Some of the most valued customers would deal with no one but her. She came from their world, after all. She not only knew many of them, knew their likes and dislikes, their families, and their idiosyncrasies, but she knew a great deal about jewelry, too. She was one of *them,* he reminded himself, except that she had been left penniless by her philandering husband.

He took a few deep breaths to calm himself and sat down at the *bureau plat* across from her. "You say he was staying at the Ritz?"

"Yes," she said with a nod.

"And he was definitely the young man you pointed out to me? The one leaving Le Grand Vefour with the young lady?"

She nodded again. "I expected him to bring the young lady into the shop after lunch," she said, "but perhaps they had other plans." She smiled, imagining what those plans might have been, hoping that the young lady was worthy of such an attractive, attentive, and altogether charming young man.

"I am going to leave now," Ram said. "I have a great deal of business to take care of. I trust you will do as I've said. If the young man returns— or the young lady—you will call me immediately."

"Of course," she replied.

"And you will keep the document books here in this office unless a customer known to us comes in and wants to see them?"

"Yes," she said, patting the side of her cement hairdo.

"Good. See to it that you do." He turned and left the office and went down the hallway to the front of the shop. Jacqueline de la Montarron rose to her feet, as regal as a swan, and followed along behind him at her customary pace, mentally calling him a slew of filthy epithets a lady of her position would never say aloud.

Kitty stood at the closet in nothing but a short silk kimono, riffling through the clothes neatly hanging inside. Her movements were quick and angry, and she didn't try to go quietly about her search for something to wear, even though Hilton still slept in the big bed. Wooden hangers clacked against one another, and plastic rippled and swished loudly, and his continued snoozing only fed her fury all the more.

There was nothing in the goddamned closet for her to wear. Anything she would want to put on was at her apartment. She was sick and tired of running back and forth between her place and Hilton's. The waiting game was beginning to wear thin. Waiting for him to ask her to move in.

She continued angrily slamming one hanger against the next as her eyes quickly scanned one garment after another. She was sick and tired of her wardrobe, too. Today, she planned on doing something about that. In a major way. She would start at Dior, picking up every John Galliano creation she could get into. From there she would probably go to Roberto Cavalli, and if there was anything in the store that she didn't own, she would buy it. Versace, ditto. Then go downtown to Alexander McQueen's place in the meatpacking district and make a raid on his stock.

She would steer clear of the jewelers. That was a man's territory as far as she was concerned, and the principal reason for her anger this morning. She had called Dufour in Paris yesterday and discovered that Princess Karima's ring had been purchased by a young woman the auction house refused to identify. The mere thought that another woman was in possession of the ring was like an insidious disease in her mind. It would suddenly creep up on her, this horrible thought, and make rational thinking or behavior utterly impossible. She had never wanted anything so much in all her life, and now someone else owned it. Another woman.

Bang! Clack! She slammed the hangers with increasing speed, so intent upon her search for the outfit that would suit her mood today that she didn't notice Hilton had sat up on his elbows and was staring at her with a frown.

"What the hell are you doing?" he finally asked.

She didn't respond to him, but kept rummaging through the clothes as if she hadn't heard him.

Hilton watched her for a moment, annoyed by her childish fit of pique, then threw off the bedcovers and got to his feet. He padded across the room to her, put his arms around her waist, and nuzzled her neck with his chin before kissing it.

"Don't!" she exclaimed, stiffening. "Just . . . just leave me alone!"

He continued lavishing kisses upon her neck, disregarding her outburst.

Kitty gave up looking through her clothes and stood still and mute, trying to calm herself. She didn't want to upset Hilton, not at this stage of the game, and he wouldn't appreciate her anger the first thing in the morning. Finally, she turned in his arms and faced him.

"Good morning," he said with a smile.

"I . . . good morning," she replied.

"What's got your goat the first thing this morning?" he asked, looking into her eyes.

Kitty looked away, carrying on a debate about what to say. Perhaps she should level with him. It was a unique tactic, but Hilton would appreciate her honesty. He was old-fashioned that way.

Kitty looked up into his eyes and put on her best lost-little-girl look. "I—I'm sorry, Hilton," she said. "I'm acting like a spoiled brat."

You always do, he thought. "Tell me what it is," he said, kissing her lips.

"I—I . . . oh, it's . . . silly and useless and not important," she said, her voice quavering.

"Come on," he cajoled, kissing her again. "Tell me what it is. Anything that upsets you is important to me, Kitty. You should know that."

"I . . . oh, I just can't get Princess Karima's ring out of my mind," she replied. She felt his arms loosen about her and saw the look of—what? disappointment?—that came into his face. "I know it sounds ridiculous," she quickly went on, "but you know how she was always my idol."

"I know," he replied, trying not to sound irritated. Hilton was getting tired of listening to her. She just wouldn't let up. But he was still determined to save his surprise. He wanted to give the ring to her next week and propose at the same time. If he told her about it now, all of his plans would be spoiled.

"Dufour wouldn't tell me who got the ring," Kitty said, "but I know that *you* could find out."

"Why would they tell me?" he replied in a nonchalant voice.

"You know very well, Hilton," she said. "They'd tell you anything you want to know, with your money and power."

What she said was accurate, of course, but he had to use a delaying tactic. Even though he was quickly growing weary of this game—and her obsession with the ring—he needed something to distract her. "Maybe I'll give them a call," he said. "I can't call until Monday, but I'll see what I can do."

"Would you really?" she asked enthusiastically, her hips pressing against him.

"For you," he said, "you bet I will." He kissed her again and slid his hands inside the kimono.

"Oh, Hilton," Kitty said in a breathy voice, "you're so good to me."

He knew what she said was true, but he was beginning to wonder if she deserved it. His hands stroked her breasts tenderly, then his fingers thrummed her nipples until they were hard. "Hmmm," he said, kissing her in earnest now, "why don't we get back in the sack, Kitty. You don't have anything you have to do this morning, do you?"

She shook her head, her hands stroking his rounded buttocks in circles. "No, Hilton," she whispered. "Nothing. Nothing at all."

He drew her toward the bed. Even though he was becoming bored with her childish antics, he still enjoyed her beautiful, voluptuous body. But he was beginning to ask himself if the physical pleasure she gave him was worth all the expense and irritation. Nobody had ever satisfied him physically as Kitty did, but he was starting to realize that he wanted more. And Kitty was incapable of giving more.

He heard the buzzer and slowly pushed himself out of his chair and went to the button on the wall panel near the front door. *It's Maurice,* he thought. *He's brought me something for my dinner. A little early today, but who can complain?* The people at the delicatessen across the street had been wonderful to him since Elisse's death, bringing him food, helping him up and down the stairs when he had to go out—a venture seldom risked of late—picking up and doing his laundry. It was nothing short of a miracle these days, he thought. This sort of kindness and generosity. It restored his faith in humankind.

He unlocked the door to his apartment and heard the sound of footsteps on the steep stairs. Leaving the door ajar, he slowly shuffled down the hallway and returned to his chair. He turned the radio's volume down a notch. Fauré's *Requiem*, such a sublime piece of music.

He heard the screech of his door opening all the way, then heard it close. He called to the young man, "I'm in the salon, Maurice. You're early today."

He sensed rather than heard movement at the doorway leading into the salon and turned his head in that direction. Behind the thick lenses of his glasses, his eyes narrowed. "You!" he exclaimed, his voice barely above a whisper. "What are you doing here? What do you want?"

The man stepped into the room and stood over Monsieur Weiss with a smile on his lips. "How are you, Solomon?" he asked.

"As if you cared," the old man replied.

"You've got that right," the man replied. His gaze swept around the room before he crossed to the old tapestry-covered sofa and picked up a throw pillow, then retraced his steps to Monsieur Weiss. He stood with his legs spread wide, and looked down at the old man sitting in his leather-upholstered chair. The visitor's face was blank, devoid of emotion.

Solomon Weiss looked up at him, then allowed his eyes to rest on the pillow. "So this is what it's come to, is it?"

The man did not reply. He took the glasses off Solomon Weiss's nose and put them on top of the radio. Then he brought the pillow up with both his hands, and brought it down hard on Weiss's head, pushing him against the chair's back. Weiss emitted a whimper that was quickly muffled, and began to struggle against the pillow. But it was useless. The younger man held it against his face with such force that Weiss could hardly fight against it. His arms and legs flailed pitifully at the air for a few moments, then went limp. A few moments later, his body slumped in the chair.

The younger man removed the pillow from his face and returned it to the sofa where he'd found it, fluffing it up a bit. Then he picked up the old man's glasses from the top of the radio and put them back on him. He felt for a pulse, but there wasn't any. He turned the radio up slightly and removed his latex gloves, shoving them in the pocket of his jacket.

He turned and left the room, walked down the hallway, opened the door, and let himself out, then closed the door behind him.

CHAPTER NINETEEN

"The first thing we have to do," Allegra said, pacing the Savonnerie rug of the bedroom in their Ritz suite, "is to try to talk to everyone on the list you made. All of these people who've bought those emeralds from Jules Levant over the years." She took a sip of the champagne that had been awaiting them, courtesy of the management, when they returned to the suite.

"Why?" Todd asked from his perch on the silk-draped bed. He'd taken off his suit and was spread out in his Jockey shorts. "What difference does it make?"

"I want to know if they still have them," Allegra said. She was wearing one of the hotel's robes, and she adjusted the tie.

"But why?" Todd persisted. He sipped his champagne and set the glass down.

"Ramtane Tadjer is trying to get them all back," she said. "I don't know why, except for the obvious worth they'd have if they were reunited, but—"

"Wait. Hold up a minute," Todd said. "You say 'reunited.' You can't be sure they were ever part of a set, Ally."

"You're right," she said, "but because of their distinctive similarities, my professional opinion is that they were together at one time. Then they were split up for whatever reason, and sold separately over the years." She didn't want to tell him yet that she had a very good hunch about why. Todd might decide that they should stay out of the whole affair.

"And now this Tadjer character is trying to get them all back," Todd stated.

"Exactly," Allegra said.

"Why?" Todd asked.

"They'll be much more valuable that way. A huge matched number of emeralds. And they may have an extremely important provenance."

"So that would make them even more valuable," Todd said.

Allegra nodded. "Yes. They could've belonged to Marie Antoinette or somebody as famous. You can imagine what that would do to their value. You saw what people were willing to pay for Princess Karima's ring alone."

"But I wonder why Tadjer sold them off in the first place if that's the case," he said, his practical mind at work.

"He wasn't in control then. Jules Levant was."

"A small detail that I forgot," Todd admitted.

"But the number one reason that they were sold separately was that Jules Levant got them by some irregular means."

"Stolen?"

"Maybe. Or whoever was selling them didn't want anyone to know," Allegra said. "Anyway, I'm going to get started on the telephone. Using the hotel switchboard will be easier, if more expensive. But since we're not footing the bill, why not? The Vicomte de Rabe is right here in Paris. I'll see what I can find out there."

She picked up the receiver at the bedside and dialed the switchboard. "This is Mademoiselle Sheridan," she said. "I would like to be connected with the Vicomte Philippe de Rabe's residence, please."

"One moment, mademoiselle," the operator said, without missing a beat.

Allegra put her hand over the receiver. "They're so used to important names at the Ritz, the operator didn't give it a second thought."

Todd grinned.

The number began ringing, and Allegra removed her hand from the receiver. The phone was picked up on the second ring. *"Bonjour,"* a female voice said.

"Bonjour," Allegra replied. "Le Vicomte de Rabe, *s'il vous plaît.*"

There was a momentary silence, then, *"Le vicomte* is deceased," the voice said.

"Oh, my, I'm terribly sorry," Allegra said. "Is it possible to speak to the *vicomtesse?*"

"Who should I say is calling?"

"My name is Allegra Sheridan," she replied. "I'm doing an article and research on jewelry, and one of the pieces that I'm writing about belongs to the *vicomtesse*."

"One moment," the woman replied.

Allegra crossed her fingers and held them in the air for Todd to see. Todd responded by crossing two toes and holding them up for her to see. She almost laughed aloud.

"Madame Sheridan?" The voice bespoke cultivation, sophistication, and glamour all in those two words.

Allegra wouldn't correct her for saying *madame*. "*Oui*," she said.

"I can speak English," the *vicomtesse* said. "What is it that you want to know, madame?"

"I'm doing some research for a magazine on emeralds," Allegra replied, "and I saw the magnificent emerald necklace that the *vicomte* purchased several years ago from Jules Levant," she said.

"Yes?" the *vicomtesse* replied.

She's not going to make this easy, Allegra thought. "I hope I don't appear to be nosy," she said, "but I wondered if the necklace is still in your possession. You see, I'm tracing the provenances of several very important emerald jewels as part of the article. If you don't want your name mentioned, then I'll certainly honor your request."

"I see," the *vicomtesse* replied. She cleared her throat before continuing. "I'm afraid, madame, that you've called the wrong party."

"Excuse me?" she responded.

"My late husband did not buy the emerald necklace for me, madame," the *vicomtesse* said. "He bought it for his mistress."

Oh, my God, Allegra thought with horror. *What have I done?* "I—I'm sorry," she said. "I had no idea."

"Of course not," the *vicomtesse* said. "Why would you? Should you want to pursue this further, I suggest you call Danielle Dandois. If you'll wait a moment, I'll give you the number."

"Thank you," Allegra said.

There was silence for a few moments; then the *vicomtesse* came back on the line. "Have you a pen and paper?"

"Yes," Allegra replied, quickly taking the pad and pen from the bedside table.

The *vicomtesse* gave her the telephone number. "I wish you luck," she said afterward. "I'm afraid Danielle is . . . shall we say she is not always terribly responsible about things."

"I can't thank you enough," Allegra said.

"Think nothing of it," the *vicomtesse* replied, then hung up the receiver.

Allegra turned and looked at Todd.

"What?" he asked.

"I'm mortified," she said, and told him what had transpired.

Todd couldn't help his laughter. "Jesus, this is really opening a can of worms, isn't it?"

Allegra nodded. "I suppose so. No, I know so. Well, on to the next call."

"How about a kiss first?" Todd said. He didn't know whether it was the champagne or simply Allegra's allure or his own body's greedy lust, but he felt incredibly horny.

"How about it?" she replied.

He took her into his arms and kissed her passionately. When he drew back, she sighed. "Ah, such a temptation. But first things first. Let me make this call."

He slipped an arm around her waist again. "Okay," he said, "but try to hurry, huh?" He kissed the back of her neck. "I've got a monster in my pants."

Allegra laughed and slapped his arm playfully, then dialed the number the *vicomtesse* had given her.

The telephone rang four times before it was picked up. "Danielle Dandois Antiquaire," a male voice answered.

Allegra was momentarily flummoxed. She hadn't realized she was going to reach a business. "Madame Dandois, *s'il vous plaît*," she said.

"Who is calling, please?" the man asked.

"My name is Allegra Sheridan. I'm afraid that Madame Dandois doesn't know me. The Vicomtesse de Rabe gave me her number." Allegra was certain that the *vicomtesse*'s name would get her through to Madame Dandois.

"In regard to?" the man asked with a nasty tone.

"It is a personal matter, monsieur."

"Hold, please."

After a moment a woman's voice came on the line. "Yes, this is Danielle Dandois. How may I help you?"

Allegra gave her the same pitch she'd given the *vicomtesse*. When she was finished, Danielle Dandois burst into gales of laughter. "Sorry,

Madame Sheridan," she said. "I can't help it. The *vicomtesse* will be stewing about this for weeks to come." She laughed helplessly again. "But I'm afraid I can't help you," she finally said.

"Oh?" Allegra said, her heart sinking.

"No, madame," the woman replied. "You'll have to call that bastard Ramtane Tadjer. He owns Jules Levant Joaillier. He bought the necklace from me when Philippe died. I got a good price from him, too, even though the bargaining went on for weeks."

"I see," Allegra said. "So he has the necklace."

"As far as I know," the woman replied. "I never cared for it, really. Not to my taste. I only wore it for Philippe. So Ram, the awful bastard, actually did me a favor taking it off my hands." She laughed again.

"Thank you very much for your help, madame," Allegra said.

Allegra replaced the receiver in its cradle. She turned to Todd, who looked at her quizzically. "Ramtane Tadjer bought the necklace from her," she said.

"That's great," he said.

He hugged her, then kissed her lips. "Why don't you take a break and I'll make the next telephone call?"

"You don't have to do that," Allegra said. "I started this and—"

"I'm here to help you," Todd said. "Remember? Here, give me the list, and I'll try to get one of them."

Allegra handed it to him, and Todd looked it over. "What if I try the Greek. Costas Stephanides. I always loved that actress he shacked up with. What's her name?"

"Marina Koutsoukou," Allegra replied. "But you're not going to be able to get hold of Stephanides, because he died several years ago."

"You're positive about that?"

Allegra nodded. "Yes, so we have to try to get hold of Marina Koutsoukou somehow or other."

"Were they ever married?" Todd asked.

"I don't think so," Allegra said. "I know he had this huge place on Mykonos, the Greek island. It used to be in all the magazines."

"I guess I could start by seeing if I can get a number for a Stephanides on Mykonos," Todd said. "Here. Why don't we change places. You spread out while I make this call."

"You're a sweetheart," Allegra said, giving him a kiss. She climbed onto the bed from the edge and propped herself against the pillows.

Todd scooted over to sit on the side of the bed, then picked up the telephone receiver and dialed the switchboard. "I want to place a call to the residence of Costas Stephanides in Mykonos, Greece," he told the operator. "I don't have the number."

He turned and winked at Allegra.

The operator came back on the line. "The number is ringing, monsieur," she said.

"*Merci,*" Todd replied, then turned to Allegra. "It's ringing," he said with surprise.

The phone rang and rang and just when Todd had about given up, a woman picked up. "*Kalimera,*" she said.

"*Kalimera,*" Todd replied, using one of the five Greek words he knew. "Do you speak English?"

"Of course," came the reply in what was almost a snarl.

"Hi. My name is Todd Hall, and I'm writing an article on important emeralds," he said. He was glad he'd had the champagne. It made lying so much easier.

"So?" came the impatient reply.

"I was trying to get in touch with someone in Mr. Costas Stephanides's family, because—" he began.

"I am Arianna Stephanides," the woman said. "His daughter."

"Wonderful," Todd said enthusiastically. "Perhaps you can help me. Your father bought a very important emerald brooch from Jules Levant Joaillier several years ago, and—"

"Get to the point," the woman said in a rude voice.

"Sorry," Todd said apologetically. "The brooch is to be featured in my article along with other emeralds, and I wondered if you still have it."

"Why would I tell you?" the woman snapped. "You could be a thief for all I know."

Todd, fearing she would slam the telephone down, quickly spat out a rush of words. "I'm only a writer. A simple *student,* really. I'm calling from New York City. I couldn't steal it if I wanted to. I'm just doing an article on emeralds. And this brooch is—"

"I don't have the emerald," the woman said in her harshest voice yet. "My father's whore has it. Call the bitch."

She slammed down the receiver with a bang that reverberated in Todd's ear. He turned to Allegra. "Je-sus, I'm great with the ladies," he said.

"What happened?" Allegra asked.

He told her.

"Then we have to try to locate Marina Koutsoukou another way," Allegra said. "I wonder if she still lives in Mykonos?"

"One way to find out," Todd replied, and he dialed the switchboard again. He gave the operator the instructions.

The phone was picked up after the second ring. *"Kalimera."* It was a man's voice.

"Kalimera," Todd said. "Do you speak English?"

"Of course." The reply was almost a snort of derision this time.

"I'm trying to locate Marina Koutsoukou," Todd said. "I'm writing an article on important emeralds, and one of them is a brooch that Costas Stephanides gave her. I won—"

"Madame Koutsoukou is not here," came the snapped interruption.

"Do you know where I could locate her?" Todd asked politely. "This article is—"

"Madame is in London."

Todd took a deep breath, wondering how he got involved in this. But any misgivings he had were swept away when Allegra ran a hand down his back and tickled his butt.

"Is it possible to get her number there?" Todd asked. "This is very important."

"Madame's number is not given out to total strangers," the man said with satisfaction.

"But Costas Stephanides's daughter gave me this number," Todd said. "She realized how important this is, and—"

"Arianna Stephanides gave you this number?" the man asked incredulously.

"Yes," Todd said.

"Well, perhaps, I could give madame your number," the man said, "and she could call you if she wants to."

"That would be wonderful," Todd said. "I'd appreciate it. I'm at the Ritz hotel in Paris," he said, and he gave the man the number.

"Very well," the man said. "I'll call madame. She will call you if she sees fit to do so."

"Thank you so much," Todd said.

"You're welcome, sir," the man said.

Todd hung up and turned to Allegra. "Well, if you haven't already gathered what that was about, keep your fingers crossed. 'Madame'—as her manservant, or whatever he is, calls her—may be phoning us from London."

"That's fabulous," Allegra said, throwing her arms around him. "For that, you deserve a kiss."

"At least," Todd said, turning and taking her into his arms. They kissed playfully at first and then, becoming quickly aroused, Todd slipped his hands inside her robe and began stroking her bare flesh, drawing her closer to him.

Letting the business at hand slip away, Allegra allowed herself to enjoy Todd's gentle caresses, his passionate kisses, and her body's response. She slid her hands up and down his hard, muscled back, and up into his raven black hair as his lips moved from hers down to her neck. His tongue licked a path down to her breasts.

"Hmmm," she breathed, letting Todd pull her robe off her shoulders. She helped by unknotting the belt about her waist, exposing her nakedness to him.

Todd sat up on the bed and quickly pulled down his shorts, then took them off. He was already fully aroused and fell upon her immediately, his hands everywhere at once. Allegra hummed with delight. She hadn't realized that her own carnal desires had been so urgent, but now she gave herself up to the moment entirely. As his tongue laved her nipples, they hardened instantly, and she reached down, taking his swollen cock in her hand, stroking it gently, savoring its throbbing power.

Todd groaned at her touch before sitting up on his knees. With his hands on her breasts, he slid down, his tongue moving down her torso slowly, slowly, to her thighs, where he licked and kissed her with abandon. Allegra arched up to meet him, and almost cried out when his tongue found her golden mound. He teased her mercilessly until he finally entered her, licking and kissing her, making her writhe in ecstasy.

"Ah . . . ah . . . Todd," she moaned with pleasure. "Ahhh . . ."

He could wait no longer to mount her. He reared up, then lowered himself atop her, entering her slowly, his mouth on her lips, kissing her deeply, with an all-consuming passion. Allegra spread her legs wide as his manhood filled her. Then she drew them back together again, relishing the feel of him inside her.

They began moving together, slowly at first, in a controlled rhythm, trying to draw out the sensual pleasure, but as desire overcame them, they began moving with lusty abandon until Allegra felt the contractions of orgasm begin.

"Ahhhh . . . Todd," she cried out. "Ohhhh . . . I'm . . . I'm . . ."

Her orgasm propelled Todd to his own, and in a final thrust, he moaned his pleasure as his seed burst forth. His body momentarily stiffened, and then, as if all his tensions were diffused, every muscle in his powerful body relaxed, seemed to melt into her, and he began gasping for breath even as he peppered her face with kisses.

"I . . . love . . . you, Ally," he rasped. "Oh . . . God . . . how I love you."

She hugged him to her tightly, her hands on his back. "I . . . love you . . . too . . . Todd," she said in a breathy voice.

He rolled to his side, taking her with him, still inside her and reluctant to withdraw. Looking into her eyes, he swept her hair back, away from her face, and kissed her lips tenderly.

The telephone rang, and they both tensed. Then Todd laughed, and Allegra smiled. "I'd better get that," he said.

She nodded.

"It had better be Marina Koutsoukou," he said. "To take me away from you."

Paul rummaged in the laundry hamper but didn't feel the familiar cold metal of the gun. Alarmed, he picked up the hamper and dumped its contents onto the tile bathroom floor.

"*Merde!*" he swore. He kicked at the heap of dirty laundry with his shoe. "That bitch! She's stolen my pistol."

Sylvie rushed down the hallway from the living room and looked into the bathroom. "What the hell?"

"I had a pistol hidden in here," Paul said, his face stricken.

"What?" Sylvie exclaimed. "It's not there?"

Paul shook his head. "I can't believe this."

Sylvie stepped into the bathroom and put a hand on his shoulder. "Calm down," she said. "We don't have to have it."

Paul looked as if he was going to cry. "Do you know how hard it was to get hold of that?" he said. "I had to steal it from my grandfather. He— he . . . if he knew . . ."

Sylvie patted his hair with a hand. "Don't worry, Paul. Your grandfather will never know. He's practically senile."

"I have to be so careful," Paul said, whining. "He gave me this building. What if he changes his mind? What if he decides to take it away again?"

"That's not going to happen," Sylvie replied. "Come on. Come back to the living room with me." She took his hand and tugged at it. Paul left the bathroom reluctantly, as if remaining there would somehow make the pistol reappear.

When they were seated on the sofa, Sylvie fished around in her shoulder bag for the little Altoids tin and extracted it with a benevolent smile. She opened it and used a fingernail to scoop up a tiny amount. "Here," she said. "Have another little snort, Paul."

He shook his head. "I don't know. . . ." He was still high from earlier and angry that he'd been unable to make love to Sylvie. The drug had made an erection impossible. And now, the loss of the pistol.

"Come on," she cajoled. "What's the harm? There's plenty more in your apartment downstairs. I'm going to have some. You have to keep up with me, don't you?"

Paul looked at her, and Sylvie smiled. "Okay," he said. He took her hand and carefully lowered a nostril to her fingernail, snorting all of the powder. "Hmmm," he said, leaning back against the sofa.

Sylvie scooped up some more in her fingernail and quickly snorted it, then replaced the Altoids tin in her bag, this time putting it in the little zippered compartment. When she was done, she reached over and gave Paul a kiss on his cheek. "Cheer up," she said. "It's not the end of the world. We don't want the gun anyway. We don't want to get into that kind of trouble."

"God, no!" Paul exclaimed. "I had no intention of using it, Sylvie. It's just that . . . well, I had it in case, you know."

"In case of what?" she asked.

"You know. If some dealer got out of hand or . . . who knows?"

"Oh, don't be paranoid," she said. "Nothing's going to happen to you or me." She lit a cigarette from the pack on the coffee table. "I think we should go get your car and take a ride over to the Ritz."

"Fine," he said, "but what are we going to do there?"

"Wait for Allegra and her stupid boyfriend to come out," Sylvie said, blowing smoke through her nostrils.

"I guess so," Paul said. "But what're we going to do if we do see them?"

"I have an idea," Sylvie replied, "that will get the ring into our hands."

When Todd picked up the telephone, he wasn't prepared for the reality of Marina Koutsoukou's deep and throaty voice. The gravelly rumble was tempered by years of liquor and cigarettes, and one of her most valuable assets.

"Meester Hall," she said.

"Yes," he replied. "Thank you very much for getting back to me, Ms. Koutsoukou."

"My houseman, Dimitri, said that you'd spoken to Arianna Stephanides," she said.

"Yes," he replied. "I'm doing an article on important jewels, emeralds specifically, and I've been trying to track down the emerald brooch that her father gave you. I'm following several pieces of jewelry. Where they came from and where they are now."

He heard a deep and heavy sigh, as if her entire body's strength had been summoned up to heave its world-weary and sad sound. "I don't have the brooch, Meester Hall."

"Oh, I see," Todd said. "Do you mind my asking what's happened to it?"

"I sold it," she said. "After Costas died, I needed some cash to tide me over until I could get work. He helped me spend the money I'd made from films, then left me with nothing."

"How awful," Todd said.

"It wasn't awful at all," she replied dramatically. "I expected exactly what I got. *Nothing*. We had a marvelous time together while he was alive, and that's what counted, Meester Hall. Who cares about emeralds? It is the heart that matters. But that is not why you asked me to call, is it?"

"Well, no," he said truthfully. "I'm trying to trace the emerald, as I told you."

"Christie's," she said. "It was auctioned off at Christie's. In Geneva." She burst into laughter. "As 'property of a lady.' Is that not ridiculous?"

"Was that for anonymity?" he asked.

"Of course," she said. "I couldn't let the studios know I needed money, or they would've tried to take advantage of me."

She paused, and Todd heard her take a long draw on a cigarette. "That sexy young Arab bought it," she went on, her voice suddenly full of innuendo. "The one Costas bought it from. I don't remember his name. He came from that famous jewelry store in Paris. He came down to Mykonos. To the house in Aghios Stephanos. If I hadn't been so happy with Costas, I would've seduced him then and there." She erupted into deep, throaty laughter, then coughed. "Anyway, he bought it back. What he's done with it, I don't know."

"I really appreciate your getting back to me," Todd said. "You've been very helpful."

"I don't know how I've been helpful," she replied, "but you're welcome, Meester Hall."

She hung up.

"Tell me what she said," Allegra asked anxiously, although she was certain she already knew pretty much what Marina Koutsoukou had said.

Todd smiled. "Exactly what we expected. She sold the brooch at Christie's in Geneva, and 'that sexy Arab' bought it."

"She said that?"

Todd nodded and told her about the conversation.

"I bet we're going to hear the same story from the general and the guy in New York," Allegra said.

"Probably," Todd agreed. "If they've been forced to sell."

"Through death or divorce or . . . whatever," Allegra added. She looked at him thoughtfully. "I hope we can get hold of the general. He might be difficult, living in exile in Miami. There might be old enemies after him. The man in New York. What's his name?"

Todd looked down at the list. "Hutchison. William Cosgrove Hutchison."

"He shouldn't be too much of a problem," Allegra said. "At least I don't think so."

"Want me to try him?" Todd asked.

"I'll do it," she said. "We can take turns. How's that?"

"Fine," he said. "As long as we get some dinner in a while. Are you getting hungry?"

"Yes. I think sex makes me hungry."

"We don't want you getting too fat," he joked, "so maybe we better cut it out. What do you think?"

"I think I would be a very happy fat woman," she said.

Todd leaned over and kissed her.

"Wait," she said, drawing away and laughing. "Let me try Hutchison in New York. Okay?"

"Sure," Todd said amiably. "I think I'll jump in the shower."

"Maybe I'll join you," she said, "if this doesn't take too long."

"This might be a very long shower."

"Go," she said, laughing.

He kissed her cheek and hopped off the bed. Allegra picked up the list. She dialed the switchboard and gave the operator the instructions.

After a while, the operator came back on. "I have three W. C. or William C. Hutchisons," she said in barely accented English. "Do you know the address?"

"No," Allegra replied. "Can you tell me what addresses you have?"

"One on West Ninety-fifth Street," she replied. "One on Moore Street, and one on Park Avenue."

"Let's try the Park Avenue number," Allegra said, considering it the most likely bet.

Moments later, the telephone was picked up. "Hello," a man said. His voice was that of an elderly man, and a cranky-sounding one at that.

"Mr. Hutchison?" she asked.

"Who's asking?" he replied unpleasantly.

"My name is Allegra Sheridan, and I'm doing an article on important emeralds. Tracing their history, that sort of thing, and I wondered if you're the same William C. Hutchison who bought a pair of emerald earrings at Jules Levant in Paris several years ago."

"Damn right I did," he said with a chuckle, "and it was one of the worst mistakes I ever made."

"Oh?" Allegra replied. He sounded as if he'd had a few drinks. She didn't know whether that boded ill, but she ventured on. "May I ask why?"

"She was the sweetest little thing you ever met," he said, "until I put a cap on her spending. She turned into a virago. Never saw anything like it. Those earrings were a wedding present, and when we got divorced they went with her. No prenup. Stupidest thing I ever did."

"How awful," Allegra sympathized. "Do you know if she still has them?"

He chuckled again. "I know that she most certainly does not. She may've taken me for a ride, but she didn't take me to the cleaners. Sold the damn things because she needed money. Which gives me no end of pleasure to contemplate. Sotheby's in Monte Carlo. 'Property of a lady.' Should've said 'property of a tramp,' if you ask me."

"I see," Allegra said. "You don't happen to know who bought them, do you?"

"I most certainly do," he replied. "The same slick operator who sold me the damn things. Owns a jewelry store in Paris. You know the one . . . ?"

"Jules Levant?"

"That's it," he said. "Convinced Lily they were extremely important, matched the way they were, and talked about how they were probably from Cleopatra's mines in Egypt."

"That's fascinating," she said.

"Umpteen thousands of dollars fascinating," he replied. "So, you're doing an article?" he asked, almost as if it were an afterthought. "What's this for?"

"I'm a student," Allegra replied. "It's a school paper."

"Well, young lady, I'd appreciate it if you refrained from using my name," he said.

"Yes, sir," she replied. "I promise I won't do that. Thank you very much, Mr. Hutchison. It's been a pleasure to talk to you."

"Good-bye," he said.

The phone went dead in her ear, and Allegra hung up. "Three down and one to go," she said aloud. From the open bathroom door, she could hear the roar of the shower, and she thought about Todd and the soothing hot water sluicing down his naked body.

She got to her feet and padded to the bathroom on bare feet. Slipping out of the bathrobe, she suddenly felt a slick, wet hand reach out and grasp the back of her neck.

"You—you prick!" she exclaimed, before bursting into laughter. "You scared me half to death."

Todd, his soaked hair plastered to his forehead, grinned. "Come on in, little girl," he said, pulling her toward him. "The big bad wolf has something just for you."

"I can't imagine what that might be."

Soon his arms were wrapped around her, and the water was streaming down them both, its roar not quite covering up the gasps of delight and moans of ecstasy that escaped their lips.

"Give me the keys," Sylvie demanded. "I'm going to drive."

"I don't think that's a good idea," Paul retorted. "It's an antique and worth a lot of money." He glanced at the 1953 Mercedes-Benz 300 S roadster with a measure of pride. Its dark green paint—so dark it was almost black—gleamed, despite being slightly dusty, and its natural-canvas convertible top was virtually pristine. All of its chrome retained its high luster, even the wheel rims, which shone against the big whitewall tires.

Fortunately, it had seldom been driven outside the environs of his grandfather's château and those of his neighbors in the Loire Valley.

"Oh, get off it," Sylvie said. "I can drive as well as you can. Probably better." She held out her hand. "Give."

"I really don't like the idea," Paul said. "My grandfather would have a fit if he knew I'd let anyone else drive it."

"Face it, Paul," Sylvie snapped. "Your dear old grandpapa probably wouldn't even know *you* if you drove out to see him in it. He's moldering away in that leaky old château. Boozed up all the time."

"Sylvie," Paul protested, "you're stoned on crystal meth, and this car—"

"You are, too," she snapped back, "and probably a lot more stoned than I am. I've never had an accident, and I'm not going to have one now." She grabbed his hand, trying to snatch the keys from him.

Paul finally relented with a massive sigh. He loathed these scenes with Sylvie and would concede to practically anything to avoid them. "If anything happens—"

"Nothing's going to happen," she replied. She gave him the benefit of a huge smile. "I know exactly what I'm doing. Now, get in. Let's go."

Paul opened the door for her, and she slid onto the natural-colored leather of the car's seat. He went around and got in on the passenger side. "It's not an automatic," he warned.

"Tell me something I don't know." Sylvie started the engine and put the big car into reverse. "Wouldn't it be fun to put the top down?" she said, backing out of the parking space.

"It's too cold for that," Paul said, stating the obvious. He idly brushed dust off the dashboard's beautiful wood trim. He must remember to get a cover for the car. Even though it was garaged at enormous expense, the city's air crept in and coated it with grime.

Sylvie pulled out onto the street and made a right, and eventually turned onto the the rue Vieille du Temple, heading toward the rue de Rivoli, on which she went westward. He noted gratefully that she drove with confidence, handling the big, heavy car as if she'd driven it many times before.

"Where are we going?" he asked.

"I told you before," she said. "Place Vendôme. The Ritz."

"Sylvie," he said mildly, "the Ritz is like a fortress, and they'll never let us in."

Sylvie laughed and slapped the steering wheel with a hand. "We're not going inside," she said, glancing at him out of the corner of her eye.

"Then what are we going to do?"

"Wait," she said. "They'll be coming out for dinner in a little while."

"We could be there for hours," he replied in a whine.

"No, Paul," she said patiently. "Mark my word. They'll be going out to dinner soon. They're Americans."

The traffic wasn't too heavy, and they reached the rue de Castiglione quickly. Sylvie turned right and headed straight for the place Vendôme, which was a short distance north.

"We won't be able to park," Paul said.

"You'd be surprised," Sylvie said. "With this car and my flirting with a gendarme? We could probably idle near the Ritz for a long time."

"I don't think so," Paul replied.

Sylvie drove into the immense place Vendôme and around the huge bronze-wrapped column, commemorating the Battle of Austerlitz, at its center. Napoléon's statue, so often removed and replaced, looked down from its top as she slowly pulled down the block from number fifteen, the elegant entrance to the Ritz hotel. Pulling over, she shifted into neutral but didn't turn off the engine.

"Now we watch," she said to Paul, "and if you see them first, let me know."

"What I see," Paul said, "is a gendarme already coming this way."

"Not bad looking, either," Sylvie said, unbuttoning her blouse down toward the waist. She wasn't wearing a bra, and when she pulled her blouse apart, little was left to the imagination regarding her breasts. "Just keep your mouth shut."

She lit a cigarette and rolled the window down, waiting for him. "Hello," she said with a big smile as he approached. He was frowning until he glimpsed her almost completely exposed bosom.

"Mademoiselle," he said, leaning in close to her, "you are not permitted to park here."

"We're waiting for my poor grandpapa," she replied, "and we'll only be here a couple of minutes, I promise. He's up from the country and staying at the Ritz. He can't walk more than a few feet, so I'm trying to stay out of the way until my *maman* brings him down to the car."

"Just a couple of minutes, you say?" the gendarme replied, his eyes reluctant to stray from her breasts.

Sylvie nodded. "I promise," she cooed. "Then we'll be out of the way."

"Make sure you are," the gendarme said. He tapped the car with a gloved hand, then went on down the block.

"You're shameless," Paul said, trying to suppress a laugh.

"Don't take your eyes off the hotel entrance," Sylvie said, opening her shoulder bag. "I'm going to give us a quick little snort."

"But the gen—!" Paul began.

"Ha," she said, unzipping the compartment in her bag where she kept the tiny Altoids tin. "He'd probably take some if I offered it to him. That and a few minutes in the backseat."

"You're crazy," Paul said.

"No," she retorted, "I'm practical."

"Are you ready?" Todd called to her in the bathroom.

"One second," Allegra answered. She checked her makeup in the mirror one last time, then dabbed perfume behind her ears, letting her finger trail down to the neckline of the simple black sweater she'd put on. That and her miniskirt would have to do again tonight. She had packed for only a couple of days, but she was pleased that the few things she had brought were elegant, appropriate, and even sexy. She flipped off the light and left the bathroom, returning to the bedroom, where Todd waited.

"I'm glad we decided to go casual tonight," Todd said. "I really didn't want to put that suit back on."

"Well, you look great," she said, kissing his cheek, "and I think casual is all I could handle."

"Do you want to try the general one more time before we leave?" he asked.

They'd tried his number in Miami several times after showering, but so far there had been no answer. Surprisingly, there hadn't been an answering machine, either.

"I left word with the operator to stop trying him until we get back to the hotel," she said. "The concierge will let her know when we're back. Besides, I'm fairly certain that we're going to hear the same thing from him that we've heard from the others. Let's go find a place to eat. I'm starving."

They left the suite and took the elevator to the ground floor, then walked out onto the place Vendôme. There were almost no pedestrians about and very little traffic. The evening was chilly, and there was a brisk breeze.

"This neighborhood is so . . . ritzy," Allegra said with a laugh. "And a tad cold, if you know what I mean. I hope we can find something that's not quite so fancy close by."

"I'm sure we will," Todd said. "Why don't we walk until we see something that looks good?"

Todd took her hand in his, and they started walking in a northerly direction. Dusk had already descended, but the huge square was well lit.

"Wait," Allegra said, noticing the statue of Napoléon. "Let's go over to the column. I want to see it up close."

"Fine," Todd said.

They changed direction and started walking east, to the enormous column. Just before they reached it, Allegra heard the roar of a motor and turned to look in its direction.

"What the hell?" she asked, stopping, squinting against the glaring lights.

Todd turned to look, but like Allegra he could see nothing but blinding headlights aimed directly at them. "Ally!" he yelled. "Ally, get out of the way!"

Allegra heard him, but she was frozen to the spot. The car was almost upon them, and the area surrounding the column was directly in front of them. Todd jerked her hand in his, causing her to lose her balance.

She felt her high heels slide, then her feet slip out from under her. She could see the grillwork of the roaring car and could swear that she felt the heat of its engine.

But it was the pain in her legs that made her cry out. "No!" she yelled as her legs scraped against the rough stone.

Suddenly she was lifted into the air, and before she knew what was happening, she felt the breath being knocked out of her as she landed with a thud against stone.

"Fuck!" she heard Todd groan. She didn't move for a moment, trying to get her bearings. When she did, she realized that she was on top of him and that they were inside the fence that surrounded the column.

"Are you okay?" he asked, trying to sit up.

"I—I think so," she said, scooting off of him. "Are you?"

"Yes," he said. "Shit. We're both going to be sore tomorrow." He was sitting up now, and Allegra was sitting next to him.

"What the hell was *that* all about?" she asked, looking at him.

"I'll give you one guess," he said, shaking his head as if to clear it of cobwebs.

"I think you saved my life," Allegra said.

He carefully got to his feet, then reached a hand down to her. "Or you saved mine," he said. "You saw the damn thing coming at us first."

Allegra took his hand and gingerly rose to her feet. "Oh, God," she said. "We really could've been killed, Todd, and it's all my fault for getting us involved in this."

He hugged her to him. "I didn't have to get involved in this," he said. He looked down at her. "Are you sure you're okay? Your legs?"

Allegra peered down. "Torn panty hose," she said. "Maybe some scrapes. It's nothing." She looked back up at him. "Are you okay? You took the brunt of the fall with me on top of you."

He shrugged. "I'm all right," he said. "Did you get a look at the car?"

"I could hardly see a thing," she said. "You?"

He shook his head. "No. Just the lights."

"I saw the grille," Allegra said, "and it looked . . . well, it looked old-fashioned. But I don't know what it was."

Todd looked around them, his gaze sweeping the grand square. Nobody had stopped to stare at them as he would have expected. "I wonder if anybody saw what happened."

"Who knows?" Allegra said. "Besides, I don't think we want to involve the police."

"You're sure about that?" he asked. "Somebody just tried to run us down."

"I know, but please, let's just go and eat," she said.

He hugged her again. "Do you want to go back to the hotel and order room service instead?"

"Maybe that's a good idea," she said, nodding.

Todd helped her over the fence, and they started to walk back across the square to the hotel. In the near distance, they heard the familiar roar of a car again.

"I don't fucking believe this!" Todd said, as Allegra scrambled back over the fence toward the safety of the column.

"Look!" she cried. "That's it! The car."

The car barreled toward them, but swerved at the last second, the driver obviously thinking twice before crashing into the bronze-sheathed column. "They're nuts!" Todd exclaimed. "Fucking nuts."

The car roared on toward the rue de la Paix. As they watched, it seemed to suddenly stop. Then they heard a huge explosion. Metal and glass were propelled skyward, and another explosion followed the first. A fireball rent the evening darkness, and their faces were lit up by it. Suddenly the square came to life. People started running toward the scene of the accident from every direction. They heard screams and shouts, and in a few moments the unmistakable sound of emergency vehicles, the police and ambulances both.

Allegra squeezed Todd's hand, and he put an arm around her, hugging her to him. "I don't want to do this," he said, "but I think I ought to go take a look. Why don't you wait here a minute."

"No!" Allegra exclaimed. "I'm going with you. I'm not staying here."

Once again he helped her over the fence, and they hurried north toward the rue de la Paix. As they neared the scene of the accident, they could see that it wasn't the car that had tried to run them down that had caught fire, but the car that it had broadsided. The police had started to direct traffic away from the area and shouted at pedestrians to stay back. The scene was still chaotic, however, and they got close enough to brave the intense heat and smoke thrown off by the fire.

The Mercedes-Benz's convertible top reared up into the air almost perpendicular to the car, and the driver was clearly visible in the hellish light cast by the fire. Allegra gasped, and threw her hand to her mouth. "Oh, God, help us," she whispered. She turned her head and buried it in Todd's shoulder.

"Sylvie," Todd said simply.

Reflected in the fire's orange light and the whirling red and blue of the police cars, fire trucks, and ambulances, which were already arriving, her face was unmistakable. The driver's-side door was thrown wide open, and her left arm dangled out of the car. The steering column had been driven up into her chest, pinning her back against the seat, and her head was thrown back at an odd angle, her bloody neck and breasts partially exposed. There was no sign of life, and Todd had no doubts that she was dead. Her chest had been crushed and her neck most likely broken.

Todd, an arm still around Allegra, guided her toward the other side of the car to get a better view of the passenger. Even with the car's top thrown open, it was difficult to see from this angle, though it was apparent that the passenger had gone through the windshield.

"Oh, Jesus," he exclaimed when they had rounded the rear of the car and walked toward the front. He immediately turned around, propelling Allegra along with him, hoping that she hadn't seen what he had. The upper half of Paul's body was splayed across the car's once magnificent hood, and his head was almost entirely severed from his torso. Fiery light reflected off his open eyes.

Allegra was silent, but her body began to involuntarily shake. Her stomach lurched, and for a minute she thought she was going to throw up. But she fought it down and clung to Todd. He quickly walked her away from the scene, an arm protectively around her shoulders.

CHAPTER TWENTY

They went straight up to the suite, through the sitting room, and into the bedroom. Todd guided her to the bed, where he sat her down.

"I'm just going to get us a drink," he said.

Allegra nodded and tried to smile up at him.

He went to the minibar, where he got two bottles of Scotch and ice cubes, then retrieved glasses and poured them both drinks. He handed her one, and Allegra gladly took it.

"Thanks," she said.

He sat down next to her and put an arm around her shoulder again. "You going to be okay?" he asked. "I could always get the hotel doctor to give you something."

Allegra shook her head. "No, I'll be fine," she said. She took a sip of the drink and felt its fiery trajectory down her throat and into her stomach. "I think this will do the trick."

Todd sipped his drink and stroked her back with his hand. They talked about the awful accident for a while, wondering how Sylvie could end up with a creep like Paul.

Finally, Todd said, "You know you aren't responsible in any way for this."

"I know—" she began, but the telephone rang.

"I bet that's the call you had in to the general," Todd said. "You want me to take it?"

"No," she said. "I'll do it." She picked up the receiver. "Hello?"

"Mademoiselle Sheridan," the operator said, "I have your party on the line."

"Thank you," Allegra replied. She heard a click. "Hello," she said again.

"Yes?" The voice was a woman's with a pronounced Spanish accent.

"I'd like to speak to Ramondo González-Viega," Allegra said.

"Who is this?"

"My name is Allegra Sheridan," she said, then repeated the same story she and Todd had told the others.

"I am Dorisita Luisa González-Viega," the woman said in a pompous voice. "The general, I am his wife. He is in the hospital."

"Oh, I'm so sorry," Allegra said, surprised to hear that a woman who was once in such a high position in her former country spoke broken English. She'd met so many South Americans in New York who were fluent in English. "I'm calling at a bad time. I hoped that the general could help me."

"The general, he is dying," the woman said. "The cancer, you know."

"That's horrible," Allegra replied. "I'm so sorry," she repeated.

Suddenly, the woman began weeping, then progressed to sobbing. Allegra continued to hold the receiver to her ear, wondering what she should say. Finally, she ventured, "Senora González-Viega, I wish there was something I could say to help you."

"Ahí, no," the woman managed through her sobs, "there is nothing nobody can do. Momento."

Allegra heard her move the telephone, then blow her nose away from it.

"Senora Sheridan," she said after she'd finished, "I can probably tell you what it is you want to know."

"I don't want to bother you," Allegra said, and she meant it. If this poor woman couldn't deal with her questions now, she would call another time or forget it altogether. She was fairly certain that Ramtane Tadjer had the emeralds anyway.

"No bother," Senora González-Viega said. "If my husband was here, it would be a bother. He don't like to be reminded of the emerald bracelet. He's a man, you know? So proud. And he love to see me wear the bracelet. In front of his friends. He always point it out."

"I can understand that," Allegra said. "It's a magnificent bracelet."

"Sí, sí, sí," Senora González-Viega replied. "Big, big emeralds. You never saw so big emeralds, senora." Her voice was full of pride and enthusiasm, as Allegra was sure her husband's would have been.

"Yes," Allegra said. "Huge emeralds. And matched."

"*Sí,*" Senora González-Viega replied. "Important, this matching, they say. My husband get the bracelet in Paris. At Jules Levant, the fancy jeweler, you know? I wear night and day. Then the revolution, it come. We come to Miami to our condo here on Brickell Avenue."

"You were very lucky to escape," Allegra said, feeling like a hypocrite. She remembered that General González-Viega had been one of those responsible for the "disappearings"—the rounding up, killing, and burying of protesters in unmarked graves—in his native country.

"*Sí,*" Senora González-Viega replied. "Very lucky. They kill many peoples, but we get to Miami. The general, he put money in bank here. The Espiritos Santos Bank, you know? On Brickell Avenue. Very safe. But not enough. We think we go back soon. That my husband, he will be savior of country. But that doesn't happen. So here we are in condo and the money, it's running out."

"I am sorry for you," Allegra repeated, knowing there was nothing else she could say under the circumstances if she wanted to find out what happened to the emeralds.

"*Sí,* is terrible life now," the senora said. "So, we sell the bracelet at Sotheby's. My husband, he say the jeweler in Paris bought it."

"At least you had something to sell," Allegra said, thinking that her words of comfort sounded awfully lame to her own ears.

"I survive a lot of things," the woman said, "and I survive this, too."

"I'm sure you will," Allegra said, hoping to draw the conversation to a close. "And I'm so grateful to you for taking the time to talk to me."

"*De nada,*" she replied. "I wish you good luck, senora. Better luck than I have."

"*Gracias,*" Allegra replied.

The woman hung up the telephone, and Allegra heaved a sigh of relief, then turned to Todd.

"So now we've established that Ramtane Tadjer has all of the emeralds except the one in the safe here," Todd said.

Allegra didn't say anything, just sat in thoughtful silence for a while.

"There's something we've neglected," she said finally.

"What's that?"

"Dufour giving me the wrong emerald," Allegra said. "Princess Karima had the last one, and something tells me that the 'mix-up,' as it was called, wasn't a mix-up at all. Someone was in cahoots with the princess. I would love to see her reaction when I tell her that Dufour tried to give me the wrong ring."

"How the hell are you going to do that?" Todd asked.

"Pay an unannounced visit," Allegra said.

"We'd never get in to see her."

"I bet I would if I showed up on her doorstep and told her I was the woman who bought the ring." She turned to Todd and smiled. She decided it wouldn't be smart to tell him that Solomon Weiss had said the princess was lethal.

"You are one clever lady," he said, returning her smile. "I think you're right." He paused in thought. "But do you know where she is?"

"The newspapers said that she was leaving Paris after the auction for her old millhouse in the country. The forest of Fontainebleau. Said she would be living there full-time after selling her mansion."

"Do you know where that is?" he asked.

Allegra shook her head. "No, but we'll find it."

"How?"

"Rent a car first thing in the morning and head to the forest of Fontainebleau. Drive around till we find it. You know, stop and ask. Say we're lost. Tell people we're invited there for lunch or something and lost our direction."

"You really think that'll work?"

"Sure," she said. "People in that neck of the woods will know exactly where the princess's place is."

"Maybe. Maybe not," he answered.

"You game?" she asked.

He winked. "I'm in."

Ram took a puff of one of the Cuban cigars he occasionally allowed himself, held the smoke briefly, then blew it out in a long blue gray streamer into the dimly lit magnificence of his library. The *hôtel particulier* on the rue Elzevir was quiet tonight, the servants either out or retired to their private quarters, and after the exertions of the previous night with the young street hooker and his activities earlier in the day on the rue des Rosiers, he felt both exhausted and paradoxically energized. His dream was coming closer to a reality, and that thought alone was enough to create a tension in his loins that must be released.

He fleetingly thought to call one of his girls and pay another visit to the rue des Rosiers. But no sooner had the thought come to mind than he nixed it. He didn't want to be in the vicinity when Solomon Weiss's body was discovered, if it hadn't already been. He knew that neighbors regularly looked in on the old man and that the delicatessen across the street provided him with meals. He didn't think anyone would suspect foul play, but he didn't want to make himself available for the idle questions of a nosy neighbor.

Then again, tonight would be a good time to visit the apartment again. Not only for another night of satisfying his erotic desires but to retrieve the emeralds, settings, and photographs that had been stored for so many years in the little safe hidden away in the apartment.

Over the years, he'd considered removing them to the jewelry store, but had always decided against it. The store was sometimes a beehive of activity and offered too many opportunities for a slipup. What if he neglected to put his keys away and inadvertently gave one of his employees the opportunity to see what his private safe contained? For the same reason he'd never brought the cache to rue Elzevir.

Now, however, with his scheme coming so close to its inevitable end, it was time. Time to bring the emeralds, settings, and photographs here to rue Elzevir. He could take one of the girls there, then dismiss her and bring back the treasures to the *hôtel particulier,* where eventually—perhaps in the next few days—he would himself reset the stones in their original settings.

He took another puff on the cigar, relishing its rich flavor. Yes. He could have Kadar check out the situation on the rue des Rosiers when he had finished his shift at the hotel. Most likely, the body had been discovered and carted away, and everything in the old building had returned to normal. Besides, he needed to talk to Kadar to get an update on the Sheridan woman and her boyfriend.

He picked up his cell phone and pressed in the number.

Kadar picked up on the second ring. "Hello."

"Can you talk now?" Ram asked him.

"Just a moment," came the reply. Then, "Let me call you back in a minute."

"Hurry," Ram said.

"Don't worry," Kadar said.

Ram pressed the END button and sat waiting. In anticipation of the upcoming night, he flipped through the Hermès address book on his desk.

Who will it be tonight? he asked himself. *Which one of the beauties will have the privilege of my company?* Then he saw the name: Josette Clement. *Perfect,* he thought. She was pale, strawberry blond, tall, and slender. *She's much like the American, Allegra Sheridan.*

His cell phone rang, and he picked it up. "They keep you busy there, I see," Ram said.

"Yes," Kadar replied. "They work us like dogs in this palace."

Ram chose to disregard the negativity of his reply. He had gotten him the job there, and although he understood Kadar's plight, he would prefer to hear his gratitude rather than his gripes. "Are the Sheridan woman and her boyfriend in their suite or have they gone out?" he asked.

"They went out a little while ago," Kadar said. "But I told you that tonight it will be impossible for me to get into their suite," he added impatiently. "It will have to be tomorrow. This manager—"

"I haven't forgotten," Ram interrupted. "Tomorrow night is fine. In the meantime, I have a little errand for you to run tonight when you get off work."

"What?" Kadar asked.

"Take a run down to rue des Rosiers," he said. "Then call me and let me know if there are any police around or any activity in the building. Anything out of the ordinary."

"I'll go straight from here," Kadar said.

"Good," Ram replied. "Then tomorrow morning before you go on duty, I want you to come by here and pick up something for the Sheridan woman and her boyfriend."

"What time?" he asked.

"Oh, say about eleven. How's that?"

"Fine," Kadar said. "I'll be there."

"See you in the morning," Ram said. He pushed the END button on his cell phone. Then from a drawer in the desk at which he sat, he took a single piece of very heavy ecru vellum writing paper and an envelope. He had one bit of business to take care of before he called Josette Clement.

Picking up his gold Jules Levant fountain pen, a gift for special customers, he began writing. *This will do it,* he thought with satisfaction. *Kill two birds with one stone.*

Cameron flipped through the drawings slowly, examining each one, his eyes bright with intensity. Jason anxiously sat next to him on the couch, only glancing at them when Cameron remarked on something in particular, but kept his eyes averted for the most part.

He had been greeted as a returning hero when he got back from Brooklyn with the drawings and the precious stones he'd taken, though Cameron's face had fallen when he realized that Jason had not helped himself more generously to Allegra's store. Cameron, however, had recovered quickly and reiterated his praise of Jason's accomplishments. Then he'd drawn him into the bedroom, where he had slowly taken off Jason's clothes, removing them almost as if they were engaged in a sacred ritual, before he slipped out of his own.

"Look at this," Cameron said enthusiastically, pointing to a drawing of a cockerel. "Why didn't I think of that? It's so simple but so brilliant. Everybody has done them, but not like this. Of course, to mass-produce it, we'll have to change the specs. All the precious stones become fakes or semiprecious. The eighteen-carat gold has to go. Ten carats at best. More likely, gold tone."

Jason looked down at the drawing and could remember the first time he'd seen it. He and Allegra had been working alone in the atelier, and when she'd finished it, she'd asked him what he thought. "I love it," he'd said. "It's so . . . you. Lighthearted and fun, but elegant." Allegra had been thrilled with his response and had kissed his cheek.

"What's with you?" Cameron asked. "You're so quiet."

Jason shrugged. "Nothing," he said, looking at his lover. "I'm fine."

"I don't think so," Cameron said. "I think you're having second thoughts. Are you feeling guilty?"

Jason shrugged again. "No, not really," he lied.

"Well, don't," Cameron said, pointing a finger at him. "It's not permitted." He laughed, and Jason attempted a smile. "What you did is admirable," Cameron went on. "She's been ripping you off for years, paying you peanuts for all your hard work, and this is the least you deserve."

He paused, seeing how Jason was reacting. "Besides, she probably won't even recognize her own work once it's mass-produced." He laughed again, but stopped when he saw that Jason was not really amused.

Sliding an arm around his shoulders, Cameron pulled him toward him. "Listen to me," he said. "You're with me now, you hear? We're a team. We'll set the world on fire together. Just the two of us." He kissed his forehead.

Jason felt himself falling under his lover's spell again, as surely as if

Cameron had given him some kind of magic potion that made him irresistible. "Do you really mean that?"

"You have to ask?" Cameron said. He shook him. "Don't be insulting. This is me you're talking to." He pointed a finger at his own chest. "And I don't lie. I don't cheat. Not on my man." He smiled. "And that's you." He pointed his finger at Jason, then kissed him again.

"Now, what do you say we go out tonight?" he said. "I want to show you off. Show everybody what I've got. What we've got together."

Despite the guilt eating away at him over betraying Allegra, a new sense of pride surged through Jason. "Go where?"

"Out to dinner," Cameron said, "then out to a couple of bars, maybe a couple of clubs."

The thought of being seen out as a couple would have thrilled Jason under different circumstances. He'd envied other couples for so long. Now he would be seen out with a star hunk. Handsome, built, and brilliantly intelligent. And he knew everybody who was anybody. But Jason didn't know if it was possible for him to enjoy being out with Cameron now.

"I . . . I think I'd like that," he finally said hesitantly, compounding his guilt by lying.

"You've got it," Cameron said, ruffling his hair. "It'll be like shouting it from the rooftops." He leaned over and kissed Jason again.

Jason returned the kiss because he felt it was obligatory, but without enthusiasm.

"Hmmm," Cameron murmured, drawing him closer and running his hand down Jason's torso to his thighs. "We've got plenty of time, hours even, before we have to get ready. Let's make the best of it."

CHAPTER TWENTY-ONE

The car they leased was a tiny dark blue Renault. Allegra had the map the rental office had provided spread out on her knees, while Todd was tucked in behind the steering wheel, his long legs surprisingly accommodated by the car. Their route looked simple enough. From the Porte d'Italie, they took the A6 to the N7, which would take them to Fontainebleau, about an hour's drive from Paris, they were told.

"All you know is that her place is somewhere near Fontainebleau," Todd said as they whizzed down the highway through the Île-de-France.

Allegra nodded. "I saw it in a magazine once, and it was mentioned in the auction catalogue," she said.

"From the looks of the map, that covers a huge territory. I don't know if we have any kind of chance of actually finding it," Todd said skeptically.

"We'll find it," Allegra responded with confidence. She glanced at him and smiled. "I bet all we have to do is have a glass of wine in Fontainebleau or one of the nearby towns and ask around."

"It may take quite a few glasses of wine, huh?" Todd joked.

"And lunch and stopping for gas and who knows what else?"

"The lunch part sounds good to me," he said. "My stomach's already growling."

"Mine, too," Allegra confessed. After getting up late, they'd had a quick breakfast of buttered croissants and coffee, so they could get on their way.

When they arrived in Fontainebleau, they discovered that restaurants and cafés abounded, lining the main street and the side lanes.

"What if we park and look around," Allegra said.

"Fine with me," Todd replied. Since it wasn't the tourist season, the streets were practically empty and parking was easy. They got out of the car and strolled down the rue de France hand in hand, stopping to look at menus posted in windows and on chalkboards out of doors. Finally, they decided on Croquembouche, a moderately priced and attractive restaurant.

"There are quite a few people," Allegra said, "and lots of waiters and waitresses."

"Which means we'll have a lot of people to ask?" Todd said.

"Exactly," she replied.

Their waitress, a hip-looking young woman with wildly dyed hair, took their wine orders, and before she left them to look over the menu, Allegra stopped her. "I saw that Princess Karima has a place near here," she said.

The young lady looked at her with lifted brows that were plucked into narrow lines. "Yes?"

"I thought you might know where," Allegra tried.

"*Non,*" she replied, shaking her head slowly. "This Princess Karima, she is famous?"

"*Oui,*" Allegra said. "Very rich and famous."

The waitress shook her head again, a grave expression on her face. Then suddenly her eyes lit up. "Ah," she said, "Guy will know. He knows everything. Especially if it's anything to do with rich people or famous people. I will send him to you."

Before she returned with their wine, one of the waiters sidled up to their table. He was about eighteen, Allegra thought, with hair that was gelled up into little blond-tipped spikes. "Fleur says you want to know about Princess Karima," he said in heavily accented English.

"Yes," Allegra said. "I heard that she has a house near here."

"Yes," he said. "She has even been here to eat. She is so beautiful," he went on, "but you can tell she has had the cosmetic surgery."

"So she must live close by?"

"It's not far," he said. "An old mill converted into a house. It's magnificent. In the forest with lots of gardens."

"Do you know how to get there?" Todd asked.

"Of course," he said, sounding offended. "You have to go to Melun, then from there toward Meaux." He looked at them and sighed. "But you are American. You don't know the area. I will draw a map and bring it to you."

"That would be wonderful," Allegra said.

"I'll be back soon. We're busy, so I have to go." He hurried off.

"He's starstruck," Todd said.

"And we're in luck," Allegra replied.

They were nearly finished eating before the waiter returned. "Here," he said, handing Allegra a slip of paper. "This is it." He pointed down to a star he'd drawn on a penciled map. "You can't miss it."

"Thank you so much," Allegra said.

Todd had already taken a ten-euro note out of his pocket and discretely palmed it into the young man's hand.

"Thank you, monsieur," he said, and he hurried off again.

They finished eating and paid the tab, anxious to get on their way. In less than half an hour they'd reached Melun and turned onto the N36, headed northeast toward Meaux.

"I hope she'll let us in," Todd said.

"She'll let us in," Allegra said. "Once she finds out who I am."

Princess Karima's cell phone rang, and she picked it up. "Hello?"

Marcus noted the quick change in her demeanor, from smiles and laughter and a languid pose on the silk-velvet-upholstered chaise to the wrinkled forehead of a frown and stiffness as she suddenly sat up. Rapidly slipping her feet into the tapestry mules on the floor at the side of the chaise, she got up and, ignoring Marcus, swept out of the conservatory, the caftan she wore fluttering behind her. In her wake, Marcus detected the scent of the Golconda perfume she perpetually wore.

The mysterious telephone calls didn't seem to stop, and if there was one thing Marcus hated, it was a mystery. He rose to his feet and approached the French doors that led out to the garden. He thought he might have a walk about the elegant parterres, but even as he put his hand on the door handle, Princess Karima glided back into the conservatory.

"So sorry, darling," she said, all breathless cheer. "I had to take a call from one of my dreary accountants. You know how they are."

"I do indeed," he said, turning to her. "Dull and unimaginative. Always want to spoil the party."

Karima laughed. "Exactly."

From behind them, they heard Mimi's heavy tread. "Madame?" she said.

"Yes, Mimi," Karima asked. "What is it?"

"There is a call from the gate," she said in a grumpy voice, as if the call had disturbed her. "A woman wants to see you."

Karima looked at her in surprise. "What? Here? Who is it?"

"She says her name is Allegra Sheridan," Mimi replied.

"I know no such person," Karima said huffily. "Send her away."

"She said she bought your emerald ring at Dufour," Mimi replied, "and that she needs to speak to you about it."

"What?" Princess Karima and Marcus exclaimed in unison. They exchanged glances. "What on earth is she doing here?" Karima wondered aloud.

Marcus shrugged. "Who knows? Maybe she simply wants to meet you and is using the ring as an excuse."

Princess Karima lit a cigarette and paced the limestone floor thoughtfully before turning back to Mimi. "Tell her I can see her briefly."

"She has her fiancé with her," Mimi said.

"Wouldn't she just?" Karima replied. "Show them both in."

Mimi turned and left, and Karima looked at Marcus with a puzzled expression. "How on earth do you think this American woman found me?"

"I've no idea," Marcus responded, "but it's certainly no secret that you have a place here. I warned you about allowing magazines to publish pictures."

"But who would ever expect something like this? The audacity to simply arrive on my doorstep."

"She's American," Marcus said. "You know how they are. So aggressive. So uncivilized."

"That's one of the things I like about them, actually," Princess Karima replied. "They're not weighed down with all that European snobbery and obsession with ancient bloodlines. Some of them have been very nice to me over the years."

"You're right, of course," Marcus said. "I was speaking in a general sense. I can think of several delightful Americans we know. Very rich ones, naturally."

Karima laughed. "Well, in any case, I'm glad you're here with me to face this . . . this creature who got the ring."

Mimi shuffled back into the conservatory with Allegra and Todd following behind her. "Mademoiselle Sheridan," Mimi said, "and Monsieur Hall."

Princess Karima and Marcus looked them up and down, and Allegra felt as if she'd been appraised by a couple of shrewd horse buyers, examining her for potential track or breeding abilities.

"I apologize for being so rude," Allegra said, "barging in like this, but I was dying to meet you and your number wasn't listed." She had decided to play the starstruck fan, one of the devotees of Princess Karima's beauty, wealth, and style. She put out a hand to shake. "I'm Allegra Sheridan, a jewelry designer from New York City, and this is my fiancé, Todd Hall."

Princess Karima offered her hand and let Allegra hold it for a moment, then repeated the gesture with Todd.

"This is my friend, the Honorable Marcus Setville-Penhurst," Princess Karima said, indicating him with a wave.

"So pleased to meet you," Marcus boomed in his plummiest old Etonian voice, shaking both of their hands vigorously.

Princess Karima noticed that Allegra wasn't wearing the ring, but wasn't surprised. She assumed she would have put it in her room safe in the Duke and Duchess of Windsor Suite at the Ritz.

"Please," she said, "now that you're here, won't you have a seat?" She indicated chairs grouped near the chaises she and Marcus had occupied. Then she turned to Mimi. "Mimi, please bring a bottle of the Louis Roederer Cristal."

"*Oui, madame,*" Mimi said, then turned and left.

"Oh, you mustn't go to any trouble," Allegra said. "We'll only be a minute. Really."

"It's the least I can do," Princess Karima said graciously, seating herself on the chaise longue again. "You paid a great deal of money to get to wear my ring, and by doing so you've made an enormous contribution to my charitable foundation. Your money will help so many of the less fortunate."

Allegra and Todd had taken chairs facing the chaises, and Marcus, fascinated with Karima's show of hospitality, spread out on his chaise longue again.

"I have to confess that I didn't buy the ring for myself," Allegra said.

"Oh?" Princess Karima said. "Who did you buy it for?"

"I'm sorry, but I'm not permitted to say," Allegra replied.

Princess Karima looked thoughtful for a moment, then said, "It's a pity

I won't get to know who it is who's helping my foundation, Ms. Sheridan. Nor will I know who the woman is who will wear the ring."

"I don't think it will remain a mystery for long," Todd said. "We belive the owner is waiting until he gives it to his companion."

"Ah, so he's saving it for a surprise," Marcus said amiably.

"I think so," Todd said.

"American, I suppose," Marcus said.

"He is, yes," Allegra said.

Mimi shuffled into the conservatory with a silver tray laden with tulip-shaped glasses and a bottle of chilled champagne. She set it down on a table and began pouring the wine. When she finished, she handed one glass to Allegra, then to each of the others, before turning and leaving the room.

"A toast," Marcus said, raising his glass. "To Ms. Sheridan for placing the successful bid at Dufour."

"Yes," Princess Karima chimed in. "To your success," she said, lifting her glass.

They all sipped the champagne.

"It's too bad the ring is not for you, Ms. Sheridan," Princess Karima said. "You are a very beautiful young woman, and it would look perfect with your coloring."

"Thank you," Allegra said. "I've always thought that you are one of the world's most beautiful and stylish women."

Karima laughed. "You're very kind," she said, "but you're speaking of a woman who no longer exists. That Princess Karima is now considerably older and hopefully wiser." She shifted her gaze to Todd. "It's a pity, Mr. Hall, that you didn't buy the ring for your fiancée." Her eyes were full of mischief.

"It was a little beyond my budget," Todd said with a laugh.

"I daresay it was beyond most everyone's budget," Marcus allowed.

"But if I'd had the money, I certainly wouldn't have hesitated to get it for Ally," Todd said. He reached over and took her hand in his, smiling.

"How lucky you are, Ms. Sheridan," Princess Karima said. "To have such a handsome young man in love with you."

"I—I, yes," Allegra said. She'd never been one of those girls who'd followed Princess Karima's life in the society press, but she had to admit the woman was not only stylish and a great beauty but also formidable. The thought of taking her on as an opponent was frightening.

"Do you work in America?" Marcus asked.

Allegra nodded. "I'm a jewelry designer," she replied.

"How interesting," Princess Karima said. "Do you work on your own?"

"Yes," Allegra said. "So far at least."

Princess Karima shifted her gaze to Todd. "And you, Mr. Hall. Do you have some sort of occupation?"

"I'm a landscape designer," Todd lied. "And I have to tell you that I'm stunned by what I can see of your gardens."

"Oh, it's far too early to see them at their best," Princess Karima said. "They will be lovely in late spring and early summer."

"But the bones are fantastic," Todd said enthusiastically. "The layout is exquisite."

"Yes," Marcus said. "I've always thought the same thing. They're so perfectly laid out that they're beautiful even in the midst of winter. Karima is responsible for that."

"You mean that you designed them yourself?" Todd asked.

Princess Karima nodded. "Yes, with a little help."

"Unbelievable," Todd said. "They look as if a world-class landscape designer had done them."

"You flatter me, Mr. Hall," she said. Then after a pause, she asked, "Would you like to see them?" Her dark eyes questioned him.

"I would love to," he said, "if it's not too much trouble."

"Come along everyone," Karima said, rising to her feet. "Let me get a coat, and we'll all take a stroll so you can see more."

She swept out of the room, and Allegra, Todd, and Marcus got up.

"Karima takes her gardens very seriously," Marcus said. "They give her great enjoyment."

"And peace," she said, reentering the conservatory in a dramatic floor-length sable coat with a hood. "They are a wonderful place to sit and contemplate life."

She smiled and went to one of the French doors, which Marcus opened. Princess Karima went out onto the terrace, followed by Allegra, Todd, and finally Marcus.

"Let's go around and start in the knot garden, shall we?" the princess said, leading the way.

They had walked for several minutes, when Allegra abruptly stopped. "I'm sorry," she began. "Is it all right if I run back to the bathroom, then catch up with you? I'm afraid I can't wait."

The others stopped and looked at her. "Of course," the princess said after a beat. "Go through the conservatory and the dining room. You'll reach a hallway. Turn to your right and go down the hall. You'll see one on your left."

"Thank you," Allegra said. She turned and rushed back along the well-tended gravel path toward the terrace. When she reached the conservatory doors, she looked back. They were around the corner of the huge house, out of sight.

She hurried through the conservatory and dining room, then down the hallway. The expensive scent the princess wore lingered in the air and unnerved Allegra slightly. It was almost as if she were present, watching Allegra's every step. On her right, the first door she came to was ajar. Looking in, she saw that it was a moderately sized room and obviously used as an office. A large desk was positioned in front of a window. Behind it was a chair that faced the doorway.

Allegra looked up and down the hallway, then went into the room and walked around the desk. She peered down at the neat stacks aligned on its gleaming surface. Among them were piles of expensively engraved invitations, magazines, catalogues, bills, personal correspondence, and—

What's this? she wondered.

Leaning down for a closer look at a letter-size stack, she saw that at the top of it was a copy of a wire transfer from a Paris bank to a bank in Geneva. For several million euros. *Must be her foundation,* she thought. Quickly thumbing through part of the small stack, she saw that there were innumerable like transfers, all of them for millions of euros and all from Paris to Geneva.

My God, she thought, realizing that the breathtaking amounts added up to over a hundred million euros, *she's really serious about this charitable foundation. Whatever it is.*

She thumbed through several more of the wire transfers, but suddenly stopped. She felt a chill run up her spine, and the hairs on her arms stood up. Why she had such a reaction, Allegra couldn't really say, but what she saw presented a conundrum. The lower half of the stack was made up of similar wire transfers, but they were all from the bank in Geneva to a bank in an Arab state. It seemed extremely odd to Allegra that these huge sums of money were being transferred first to Switzerland, then to an Arab country.

Why not send the money directly to the second bank? she wondered.

Why go through Switzerland? A quick second look showed her that the amounts were identical in every case. Fifteen million, for example, would be sent to Switzerland, then fifteen million wired to the Arab bank.

Allegra looked over at the open doorway, then back down at the desk. A black alligator address book beckoned to her. She opened it and flipped through, but nothing leaped off the pages at her. It was like anyone's address book, complete with scratched-out addresses and telephone numbers and new ones written in their place. Then just as she was about to replace it, a piece of notepaper fell out. On it were three names: Ali, Hassan, and Nessim. Each was followed by a telephone number. She took a pencil from a silver holder and jotted down the bank account numbers of the Swiss and Arab banks first, then the three names with their corresponding phone numbers. That done, she folded the piece of paper and put it in her pocket. Giving the desk one final sweeping glance, she didn't see anything else that appeared to be of interest.

She went back to the doorway, peeked out, and looked both ways. No one. Out into the hallway she went, then realized that she actually needed to go to the bathroom. *Maybe it's my nerves,* she thought. She found it where Princess Karima told her it would be, quickly made use of it, then hurried back out to the conservatory.

She was startled by the elderly maid, who was emptying ashtrays into a silver silent butler. The old woman looked up at her with suspicious, narrowed eyes. "Mademoiselle?" she asked.

"I was just using the loo," Allegra said with a smile.

The old woman continued to stare at her but didn't say anything, and Allegra rushed on outside with the irrational feeling that the maid knew she had been snooping. *She gives me the creeps,* she thought, anxious to be with Todd again. When she caught up with Todd and the others, they were walking through a formal parterre. Its walks were pea gravel, and the beds, all lined with small formally clipped boxwood, were planted with hundreds of rosebushes.

"There you are," Marcus said cheerfully.

"Are you okay?" Todd asked. "We were beginning to worry about you."

"I'm fine," Allegra said with a smile. "Now at any rate."

"You found everything you need?" the princess asked.

"Yes, thank you," Allegra said.

They walked on, the princess telling Todd about the various roses that would eventually be blooming, and he in turn asking her questions about them. After strolls through several garden "rooms," the greenhouses, and a small portion of the park, they returned to the conservatory, where Marcus refilled their champagne glasses.

"You've been awfully generous with your time," Todd told the princess, "and it's been a wonderful experience for me."

"I'm glad you've enjoyed it," she replied graciously, lighting a cigarette.

"I wondered if you would mind clearing up something for me?" Allegra asked.

"What's that?" Princess Karima asked, blowing a stream of smoke into the light-filled room.

"After I placed the successful bid on your ring at Dufour, I went to pick it up, and they gave me a ring that wasn't yours."

"What?" Princess Karima exclaimed, sitting up in her chaise longue.

"Yes," Allegra said with a nod. "They told me that they had made duplicates for photographic purposes and to save on insurance costs and so on. Your pieces were so valuable they didn't want to let them out of the auction house. They didn't want to take any chances."

"Oh, I see," Princess Karima said.

"I think it's awfully odd that they gave me the duplicate, don't you?" Allegra said.

"It's preposterous," Marcus burst in. "Absolutely outrageous."

"It was merely a mistake," Princess Karima said with a shrug. "They are so busy, you know. Mistakes are made."

"But a mistake like this?" Allegra said. "If I weren't a gem expert and hadn't examined your ring prior to the auction, I could have easily left there with the wrong ring."

"I have no idea what could have happened, Ms. Sheridan," Princess Karima said. "If you have questions, ask the people at Dufour, not me."

"Oh, I'm sorry," Allegra said. "I didn't mean to imply that you had anything to do with their deception or—"

"Deception!" the princess exclaimed. "That's hardly likely, Ms. Sheridan."

"Oh, I think it is," Allegra said. "I think they were deliberately trying to pawn off a ring on me that wasn't the one I'd bid on. I'm wondering why they would try to keep yours."

"This is nonsense," the princess said as if she had a bad taste in her mouth. "Absolute nonsense. You don't know what you're talking about." She smashed her cigarette out in an ashtray. "It was merely a mistake." Then she added in an emphatic voice, "Which they corrected."

"Only after I confronted them about it," Allegra persisted, "and Monsieur Ramtane Tadjer from Jules Levant came to my rescue."

"Ramtane. . . ," the princess began, her voice drifting off. Then, "He knew about this?"

Allegra nodded. "He saw what was happening, and he looked at the ring with his loupe, too. He knew at once that I'd been given the wrong one."

"He's the owner of Jules Levant," the princess said to Marcus.

"Oh, I know who he is, darling," Marcus said.

"Well, Ms. Sheridan," the princess said, "I wish I could answer your question, but I think it was merely a mistake. Nothing more or less." She rose to her feet. "Now, if you don't mind, I have a busy evening ahead of me." She looked from Allegra to Todd.

They quickly put their champagne flutes down and got up, knowing the dismissal for what it was. Nothing more would be learned from Princess Karima.

"Thank you so much," Todd said. "I really appreciate your hospitality after our barging in like this."

The princess merely shrugged.

"It was so wonderful to meet you," Allegra added. "You're such a generous person."

Princess Karima looked at her as if she didn't know whether she was being sarcastic.

"I wish you both luck," the princess said. "It will be interesting to find out whom you've bought my ring for. I hope the woman who wears it will be worthy of it."

"I'm certain she will be," Allegra said. "And thanks again."

Mimi appeared as if she'd been summoned out of thin air. She indicated the doorway into the dining room with a hand.

"Good-bye," Todd said.

"Good-bye," Princess Karima and Marcus said in unison.

Allegra and Todd followed Mimi to the front door, then made a beeline for the little car, where they buckled up before Todd drove them down the gravel lane to the ornate iron gates. The gates opened as they approached, and he sped past them and out onto the highway.

"Jesus!" Allegra exclaimed. "Am I glad that's over."

"How'd you do in the house?" Todd asked.

"I'm not sure," she said, then told him what she'd come across on the desk.

"It could be nothing," Todd said, "but on the other hand it could be a huge story."

"I know," she said. Then, taking the slip of paper out of her coat pocket, she read the names off to him.

"Same case," Todd said. "Could be nothing, but might be something really big."

"I'm not sure what to do with any of this information." She took a deep breath and let it out. "I'm just glad to be out of there."

"You did wonderfully," Todd said, placing a hand on her knee and squeezing it. "I loved you playing an adoring fan of hers, then getting a little tough about the problem at Dufour."

"And you were great as a landscape designer," she said. "I was about to believe you myself."

Todd laughed.

They drove on toward Paris, discussing the information they had, wondering what to do with it. "Not even Hilton Whitehead is going to be of much use when it comes to Swiss bank account numbers," Todd said, "or those in the Arab bank."

"No," Allegra agreed. "Getting information out of them would be next to impossible, even for a government, much less an individual. I just think that it's really odd that she transfers first to Switzerland, then to the Arab bank. It makes no sense to me. Unless, of course, she wants the money immediately available for distribution in Arab countries." She looked over at Todd. "Do you get the impression from what you know of her that she would be doing charity work in the Middle East?"

Todd shook his head. "The opposite from what I've read. She's tried to erase her connection to the Middle East since she was young, making herself as European or international as possible."

"Maybe she's had a change of heart," Allegra said. "Maybe she's going back to her roots."

"Maybe," Todd said, "but you'd never know it from the way she lives. I mean, look at what the newspapers and publicity releases call the millhouse. It's really a huge estate worth millions of dollars, and it must cost a fortune to maintain. It's not like she's taken a vow of poverty or anything."

"No, but as luxuriously as she lives," Allegra said, "she really has cut back." She paused thoughtfully. "I'm more confused than ever, but one thing I'm fairly certain of: she knew about the ring switch at Dufour. She defended them just a little bit too much as far as I'm concerned."

"I'm not sure," Todd said. "She seemed surprised about it to me."

"No, I don't think she was surprised for one single minute. I think she knew about it."

"Maybe you're right," Todd said. "Female intuition and all that, but she would've fooled me."

"It's going to be interesting to call these telephone numbers and see what happens," Allegra said, looking at the slip of paper.

"That's something Hilton Whitehead may be able to help us with," Todd said. "Tracing the numbers."

"Do you really think so?"

"Maybe," Todd replied. "He's got connections all over the world in the communications industry."

"Then we should give him a call," Allegra said.

She rummaged through her shoulder bag until she had her cell phone in hand. "Besides, I want to tell him about Sylvie and Paul."

"If he doesn't already know," Todd said.

The yacht was a floating palace, but unlike so many of the newly built temples to luxury that plied the warmer waters of the planet, it still had the air about it of being a ship. There was little plastic or fiberglass to be seen, nor were there waterfall chandeliers or fountains, tons of marble, or glitzy fabrics and furnishings. In their place were lots of teak and mahogany, high-maintenance brass and nickel, and natural fabrics on the furnishings. If the choice of materials used in its construction and decoration were old-fashioned, it still had every technological wonder available, including a Global Positioning System; two-way satellite communication; a digital navigation system with tracking software and 3-D charts; sonar; radar; and high-speed Internet connectivity capable of downloading large files, streaming video, and voice and video teleconferencing. Aside from the numerous large-screen plasma TVs and CD players and an onboard library for entertaining oneself, the vessel was equipped with a helicopter, speedboats, Jet Skis and Seascooters, and Windsurfers.

It was not yet enjoyable yachting weather in the northeast, and normally the pleasure palace would have been in the Caribbean until summer. Hilton Whitehead had decided, however, that the occasion merited bringing the yacht from Saint Bart's to New York for a party cruise around Manhattan. He had quickly had the invitations hand delivered to titans of industry and society all over the world for the party, and he looked forward to using the occasion to announce his engagement to Kitty. At the same time, he would surprise her with the emerald ring that had belonged to Princess Karima.

The yacht had arrived yesterday, docking in New Jersey because there wasn't a slip in Manhattan that would accommodate its vast length. Today, while the crew and caterers were busy preparing the huge vessel for the party the day after tomorrow at twilight, he had brought Kitty to New Jersey while he oversaw the details of the party.

"You astound me sometimes, Hilton," Kitty said, looking at him over the top of the latest issue of Italian *Vogue,* which she was devouring as if it were the Bible.

He looked down at her, spread out on a blue-and-white-striped couch in the main salon. "Why's that?" he said, smiling.

"You have all these experts working for you, but you have to come out here to make certain they do everything right," she said. "I don't get it. What are you paying them for?"

He pointed a finger at her. "God is in the details, Kitty, and don't forget it," he said amiably. "I want this party to be perfect, and the only way to do that is be here and make sure nothing's overlooked."

She sighed with exasperation. "I don't see what's so special about this party," she replied. "Just a bunch of businesspeople and a few high-society snobs. Why are you trying to impress them? You're more important than any of them."

"Well," he said, "it's sort of a special party."

She licked a finger and flipped another page of the magazine. "I don't see anything special about it," she said, looking down at the page, studying it with concentration.

"You will," he said. "You will."

"Oh, really, Hilton," she replied. "You make it sound so mysterious. What are you going to do? Announce a new acquisition? A new merger?"

"Maybe," he said.

"Personally," she said, "I think the best parties are those people have for no reason. Just to have a good time. So many of your parties are like boring business meetings for the men to have pissing contests and the women to make ridiculous small talk. A few of them try to outdress each other, but most of them look like cleaning women in borrowed clothes. Really, they're the most boring people on earth."

Hilton felt his jaw clench. Kitty was being a pain in the ass. If she only knew that all of this fuss was on her account, she might feel different, but he wasn't even certain about that. He knew that she couldn't stand most of his business associates or their wives, couldn't even abide most of the high-society folks he was friendly with. Kitty was more drawn to dissipated, self-indulgent hedonists who lived for parties and little else.

"Look," he said patiently, "this party is important, and I hope you'll enjoy it. I know some of the people aren't very colorful, but most of them have really done something with their lives."

"Ha!" she said. "Make money. That's all most of them have ever done, and they don't even know how to spend it."

"Kitty, that's ridiculous," he said angrily. "They just don't spend it the way *you* would. They give away millions of their money every year to very good causes. Some of them have started foundations for charity, built hospitals, orphanages, schools, museums—all kinds of things that may not be particularly sexy but make this world a better place."

Kitty knew that she'd gone too far again, and decided she'd better backtrack quickly. "I didn't mean to upset you," she said. "I'm very sorry, Hilton." She sat up on the couch and then rose to her feet and padded over to him. "Please forgive me." She kissed him. "I just get a little bored with some of these people, you know. I know they're very nice and do good things. I didn't mean to put them down."

Hilton looked down into her eyes. No one had ever satisfied him sexually as Kitty did, but he'd come to decide lately that she was a con artist. He was beginning to ask himself if he could live with that. But now, seeing the plea written on her exquisitely exotic face and feeling her magnificent body next to his, he found it difficult not to tolerate her episodes of selfishness and vanity.

She pressed her breasts against him and put her arms around him, stroking his long back and ass. "Please," she purred, looking up into his eyes. "Hilton, I know I'm a naughty girl, but I'll try to be better for you. I promise." She kissed him again and held him tightly.

He felt the chemical attraction that he had no way of controlling. He returned her kiss, and his body immediately responded to her seductive power. Kitty moaned as his tongue sought out hers, and let one of her hands trail around to his thighs.

Hilton's cell phone rang, and they both jerked slightly. "Damn," he said, drawing back from her. "I have to get this."

"Not now," she pleaded. "Do you?"

"Have to." He released her and took the cell phone off its belt clip. "Hilton Whitehead," he said as Kitty retreated to the couch and spread out in a come-hither pose.

"Hey," he said, suddenly smiling. "Give me just a second. I want to talk to you, but I've got to go to my stateroom. This place is a madhouse."

"You're on a boat?" Allegra asked.

"Yeah," he said. "Docked in Jersey. I'm getting ready to throw a bash the day after tomorrow and was hoping you and Todd could get here in time for it."

"That sounds like fun," Allegra said. "Is this the—?"

"It is," Whitehead said. "Just a second." He had reached his stateroom and went in and locked the door behind him. "Now," he said, "we can talk in privacy. Tell me what's going on."

"Well, there have been some little developments," Allegra said. "First, I wanted to tell you about last night. I'm sorry to say that Sylvie was killed in a car accident."

"Killed?" he gasped.

"Yes," Allegra said, "and her friend Paul, too." She told him the entire story. How Sylvie was trying to run down her and Todd, and the fiery conclusion to her efforts.

When she finished, Hilton Whitehead exhaled a heavy sigh. "It was so pointless," he finally said. "She was a good kid, deep down inside, I think. She was a great employee, and I'm really mystified by this."

"I feel the same way," Allegra said.

"I'm glad you let me know," Whitehead said. "I've been more or less out of touch getting ready for this party."

"There's something else," Allegra said.

"What's that?"

"Today, Todd and I paid a call on Princess Karima."

"You *what*? I don't believe it."

"Yes. I wanted to see her response to the supposed mix-up at Dufour," Allegra said. She gave him the details of their adventure.

"You two are something else," he said with a chuckle. "I ought to hire you to work for me."

Allegra laughed. "I don't think we could take much more of this."

"I probably won't be able to get hold of anybody at Dufour today," Whitehead said, "but Monday I'll start calling in some favors. I know a couple of people on their board, and we might be able to get to the bottom of this."

"There's one more thing I thought you might be able to help us with."

She told him about the wire transfers and the telephone numbers. "When I looked at the wire transfers," Allegra said, "I also saw her address book. These names and numbers fell out of it."

"Hang on a second," he said. "Let me get a pen and paper."

Allegra waited silently, noting that they were already nearing the Porte d'Italie and would be back at the hotel in a short time.

Whitehead came back on the line and she gave him the names and their corresponding numbers. "I don't know if finding out who these people are will get us anywhere or not," she said. "They could be gardeners, but something tells me they aren't.

"You know, this Princess Karima is beginning to smell like a rat. She's obviously funneling money into an Arab bank and wants it kept quiet," Whitehead said. "Listen, I'll get on this right away, then give you a call. It'll take at least an hour or two, but I'll get back to you."

"Thanks a lot, Hilton," Allegra said.

He hung up, and Allegra pushed the END button, flipped the cell phone shut, and looked over at Todd. "He's going to get to work on those telephone numbers right away," she said.

"I hope he can find something out," Todd said. "If nothing else, it would be nice to know what's going on with the princess."

Allegra could see the twin towers of Notre-Dame in the distance. "It'll be nice to be back at the Ritz," she said. "I want to take a shower and have a nap. How about you?"

He glanced at her and smiled. "I like the idea," he said. "I like it a lot. We can save water and shower together."

Allegra laughed. "Ah, ever the conservationist."

"Oh, yes," he agreed. "It's the only way to go."

CHAPTER TWENTY-TWO

Jason awoke with a pounding headache and a cotton mouth. His body felt leaden, and he wanted nothing more than to go back to sleep. It was the awful dehydration that finally forced him out of bed and into the kitchen, where he chugalugged three glasses of water, one after the other. He went into the bathroom then and looked at himself in the mirror. His hair was a rat's nest, his skin blotchy, and there were telltale circles under his bloodshot eyes. The groan that escaped his lips was almost a squeak. His throat was still parched.

Retracing his steps to the kitchen, he poured a glass of orange juice and drank it down in one swallow, then wiped his mouth on the back of his hand. He had never had a hangover like this before in his life. But then, he reminded himself, he'd never had so much to drink, mixed with all those drugs. He slumped into a chair at the small kitchen table, his throbbing head in his hands.

The evening had begun with Cameron taking him to three very popular bars, all of them packed with hot guys. He'd bought him drink after drink—Scotch and water—and enthusiastically introduced him to some of the most eligible men in New York. Cameron had shepherded him through the maze of glitzy, expensive gathering places like a prize bull, and when they finally left for the restaurant, Jason had never shaken so many hands or been kissed by so many handsome men.

At the restaurant, they had joined three couples, a famous fashion designer and his partner, a well-known interior decorator and his friend, and a enormously rich Wall Street investment adviser and his boy toy. There had been more cocktails, followed by exorbitantly expensive wine with dinner, topped off by after-dinner drinks.

As midnight approached, Jason began to flag and was ready to go back to the apartment and hit the sack. "We've only begun," Cameron told him. "The night's young." That was when he herded Jason into a bathroom stall at the restaurant and took a small tin of cocaine out of his jacket pocket. He handed Jason a straw. "Take a good healthy snort up each nostril, baby," he said.

Jason had second thoughts. He'd smoked marijuana a few times years ago, but otherwise he'd never experimented with drugs. Cameron persisted, however, and Jason finally did as he was told. He felt the cocaine almost immediately. It was as if it exploded in his brain. Suddenly he no longer felt tired. His body, in fact, seemed to vibrate with energy, and he couldn't wipe away the smile that had come to his lips.

"We're off to the clubs now," Cameron said. Thus began an odyssey through Manhattan's hippest dance clubs that lasted till the early hours of the next morning. Hours of dancing and necking with wild abandon. Hours of drinking one drink after another. Hours of snorting cocaine. Hours of downing ecstasy. Hours of sniffing amyl nitrite.

Jason poured another glass of orange juice and sipped it this time. The water and juice combined were beginning to quench his thirst. Now if he could get rid of the excruciating throb in his head, he would feel a little more human. He got up from the table and quietly went back into the bedroom, then tiptoed into the bathroom. In the medicine cabinet he found a bottle of aspirin. He took three 375-milligram tablets, swallowing them down with a small glass of water. Tiptoeing back through the bedroom, he glanced at the bed and stopped in his tracks.

Cameron and another man, whose name he couldn't remember—Gary? Greg? Gray?—were curled up together, Cameron's arms thrown across the young man's shoulders. They both slept soundly, the picture of satiated bliss, undisturbed by Jason's presence.

Jason thought he was going to be sick. He remembered Cameron's luring the young man back home with them. The way his eyes and hands had been all over the stranger's body. His constant reassurances to Jason that it meant nothing. "Everybody does it, right?" he'd said. "It's nothing, baby. He'll just make our own sex even better."

Jason quickly left the bedroom and returned to the kitchen, where he sat back down at the table. He put his head in his hands and felt the sweat beading on his forehead and a discomforting feeling in the pit of his stomach. Grabbing a tea towel, he wiped his face, then sat staring into space.

Tears suddenly sprang into his eyes, and trying to control the impulse to cry, he brushed at them with his fingers. He realized now that Cameron, while he might genuinely find him attractive, had simply used him as a way to gratify his own ravenous sexual desires. His protestations of love had meant nothing.

Tears began to run down Jason's face, and sobs began to shake his body. He put his hands over his mouth to try to keep from making any noise. *I was such a fool,* he thought. *Such a blind idiot. He's been using me for sex like some kind of toy and, much more important, to get hold of Allegra's designs.*

Because, truth be told, Jason finally had to admit that Cameron had run out of ideas. That, or he was simply too lazy to come up with them and then follow through with their execution. He was looking for a shortcut, the easy way out, and he'd found it when he met Jason. He'd lured Jason with sex and vows of undying love, and Jason had fallen for it hook, line, and sinker, becoming his willing accomplice in the theft of Allegra's work.

How could I have been so stupid? he wondered. *How could I have gotten mixed up with someone so unscrupulous? How could I have failed to see that he's nothing but a fraud?*

Jason felt as if he needed to take a long, hot shower, to wash away the memory of the man. He got up and pulled a length of paper towel from its holder and blew his nose, then leaned back against the granite kitchen counter, listless and miserable. He had never felt as lonely in his life as he did at this moment, he realized. What he would give to have a friend to talk to. But there was no one. Allegra had always been that person, and now he'd betrayed her trust.

As the throbbing in his temples gradually dissipated and he became more clearheaded, he realized what he had to do. And nobody would stop him. He'd seen the error of his ways, and he was going to try his best to correct the mistakes he'd made.

He went into Cameron's study, where they'd stacked the Xeroxes of Allegra's designs, and began putting them in his backpack and the duffel bag, which were still on Cameron's desk. When he finished that, he opened the desk drawer into which he'd seen Cameron drop the bags of precious and semiprecious stones. He recalled how Cameron had done it with a carefree flourish of his hand, as if the stones were worthless garbage. Jason took the little bags of stones out and put them in the backpack.

He left the study and placed the backpack and the duffel bag near the front door, then tiptoed back through the bedroom to the bathroom. There, he retrieved his shaving gear, toothbrush, and sundry items, shoving them all into his leather travel kit. He crept into the bedroom then and quietly gathered the clothes he'd worn the night before, not forgetting his shoes and socks.

He dressed in the kitchen, then got his coat out of the closet in the entrance hall. Starting for the door, he changed his mind and went back to the kitchen. On a notepad used for grocery lists, he penciled a note to Cameron:

> Cameron,
> I'm leaving and taking the Xeroxes and stones
> with me. I've left some clothes. You can keep
> them, although I hardly think they're your style,
> but I'd appreciate it if you had them sent to my
> apartment. I don't want to discuss this with you
> or see you again. Please don't try to contact me.
> Jason

*   *   *

Ram stepped into his library on rue Elzevir and crossed to the gilt console that served as a drinks table. Pouring two fingers of Armagnac into a cut-crystal old-fashioned glass, he downed it in a single swallow. He didn't want to drink too much, though. He wanted to be in top form for the upcoming evening. He was excited and energized by the mere thought of what lay ahead.

He crossed the rug to his large Napoleonic desk and sat down behind it. Last night had been a successful evening, he thought as he lit a cigar. Josette had provided temporary satisfaction, but it had been nothing more than an amusing diversion. He was glad he'd called and brought her here, not something he usually did. She was elegant and sophisticated and always had the latest gossip, as she had connections in the highest levels of government, industry, business, and society. She had assuaged his sexual appetite in a ladylike fashion, as she was paid a small fortune to do, and now she would delight her powerful and wealthy clients with tales of Ram's prowess, his opulent home and exquisite tastes, and his generosity. Josette, however, had served only to whet his voracious appetite. It was tonight that would bring him the kind of satisfaction that people seldom achieved. He was certain of that.

Opening a drawer in the desk, he took out the small plastic bag that was tucked beneath a small pile of old invitations. Ram held the bag up and examined it in the light of the gilt bronze *bouillotte* lamp on his desk. Inside were gel capsules, each containing a finely ground powder commonly known as the date rape drug. There was enough in each capsule to knock out the average individual for several hours. Kadar was an invaluable resource for such substances.

He slipped the plastic bag into the pocket of his suit jacket, then patted the pocket affectionately. It wouldn't be long, he thought, until he heard from Allegra Sheridan and her boyfriend. Then the fun would begin. And the final stage of his plan would be set in motion.

He got up from his chair and walked to one of the French doors that overlooked rue Elzevir. Last evening he'd decided against bringing the emeralds, their original settings, and the photographs here. He'd left them in the safe at the apartment on rue des Rosiers. He was glad now. Pushing aside the drapery, he gazed out over the street beyond the *hôtel particulier* opposite. *I'll take them to rue des Rosiers after we've dined here,* he thought. *The curious couple can see why the emerald is so important. It will be their last treat before they disappear from the face of the earth.*

Todd pushed the hotel room door open and let Allegra walk in first. When her heel caught on something, she looked down and saw a large ivory vellum envelope. Bending over, she picked it up.

"What's this?" she said, wondering aloud.

Todd, close on her heels, looked at it. "I don't know, but it has your name on it."

Allegra tore the envelope open and pulled out the sheet of heavy writing paper, eyeing it suspiciously. She turned to Todd. "I don't believe it," she said. "Listen to this. *Dear Ms. Sheridan, I would be honored if you and your friend would dine with me this evening at my home. It was a pleasure meeting you, and I thought we might get together to discuss your design career. Jules Levant is always looking for young, innovative designers, and perhaps we could talk about possibilities before you return to New York. I will send my car for you and your friend at seven thirty. If you can't make it, please phone me at the number below to let me know. Paris, by the way, is a small town, and I was delighted when I heard you were staying at the Ritz! I hope I'm not intruding on you in any way and hope you and your friend can come. Best regards, Ramtane Tadjer."*

She looked at Todd with amazement after she'd finished reading the note. "I don't believe this."

"How the hell does he know where we are?" Todd said.

"Paris is a small town," Allegra said sarcastically.

Todd sat down and took off his shoes. "Either we've been followed or he has spies all over the place."

"I guess it should give me the creeps," she said, "but I wonder. . . ." She looked off thoughtfully as she slipped off her heels.

"What?" Todd asked, looking up at her.

"I'm just curious about this business of 'possibilities,' " she said.

"Do you think he's actually serious?"

Allegra shrugged.

Todd studied her face, then smiled indulgently. "Allegra," he said, "listen to me for a minute. Think about the conclusions we've both come to about this guy. He's been buying back all these emeralds, and he tried to buy back the one you've got. Right?"

She nodded.

"And somebody tried to take a shot at you at that museum. Right?"

She nodded again. "Probably," she allowed.

"There's no 'probably' about it," Todd said, disgust creeping into his voice. "This guy's dangerous, and we both know it."

"But he's asked us both for dinner," she said.

He stared at her. "You just want to see if you can find out something, don't you?"

"Well . . . I am curious," she said. "Aren't you?"

Todd looked down at the floor, then back up at her. "Yes and no," he finally said. "I don't want to put you in any danger."

"Oh, come on, Todd," she said. "I'm a big girl. Besides, didn't we just come from a little trip to the country to see Princess Karima, who's definitely mixed up in this emerald chase? Agreed?"

He nodded. "But this guy. I don't know. . . ."

"Look," Allegra said, trying to reason with him, "whatever else you can say about him, I don't think he's completely crazy. He's a major jeweler. Well-known and highly respected. He'd never try anything in his own house. Plus, we're not going to have the ring with us. It's safe. So what've we got to worry about?"

"I think we've got a lot to worry about," Todd said, "but since you're determined to try to get to the bottom of this business, I think we're going to dinner at"—he took the invitation from Allegra—"Mr. Ramtane Tadjer's." He smiled at her.

Allegra returned his smile. "We've got time to shower and change," she said, looking at her wristwatch, "and maybe have a drink before his driver picks us up."

"Why don't we have a drink first," Todd said, "then shower and dress? What do you think, huh?"

"I think you have some hanky-panky in mind," Allegra said.

Todd got up and walked around to the back of her chair and put his hands on her shoulders. He began gently massaging them. "What gave you an idea like that?"

Hilton Whitehead hung up the telephone and stood staring into space. He was worried for Allegra Sheridan and Todd Hall, and knew he had to reach them immediately. He'd known they might be playing with fire, but he'd never suspected anything like this.

As he picked up the telephone in his stateroom to call them, there was a knock at the door. "Later," he called out. "I'm busy now."

"Hilton," came Kitty's voice through the door, "it's me. Let me in." After a moment, she added, "What are you doing in there?"

He walked to the door and opened it. "Listen," he said, "I've got to make an important telephone call. I'll be out in a minute."

Kitty frowned. "Why can't I sit in here with you while you make it?" she asked. "It's crazy out there"—she pointed to the hallway—"with those caterers and decorators and all. I'm just in the way."

"Okay," he said, "but please sit quietly and don't disturb me. This may be a matter of life and death."

Kitty's eyebrows arched. "Life and death?" she repeated. "What in the world are you mixed up in?"

"Nothing," he said. "Now just sit. Please. And keep quiet."

Kitty sashayed over to the couch and sat down. Reaching for a magazine on the coffee table, she stared up at him as he placed the telephone call. He was pacing the carpeted floor of the owner's suite like a caged animal.

"Allegra," she heard him say. "Todd. Call me the instant you get this message. I want you two on the plane pronto, and I mean that. These names and telephone numbers you gave me? All three of these guys are mixed up in terrorist organizations. A couple of them with links to al-Qaeda. I want you—"

Hilton looked at the telephone in his hand as if it were a snake. "Goddamn it!" he exclaimed. He started to throw the phone down, then thought better of it.

Kitty jumped to her feet. "What is it, Hilton?" she demanded. "What's going on?"

"No more message space," he said.

"That's not what I mean, and you know it," she said.

He turned away from her and sat on the edge of the bed. "I've got a couple of people running an errand for me, and they may be getting in over their heads."

"What's this about terrorist organizations?" she asked. "And al-Qaeda? Huh?" When he didn't respond, Kitty stamped her foot. "Tell me, Hilton. This sounds extremely dangerous to me. What the hell is going on?"

"Don't worry about it," he said glumly. "This isn't dangerous for you or me. It's these two working in Europe I'm worried about."

"You're sure?" she said.

He nodded. "One hundred percent."

Kitty heaved a sigh of relief. "I thought maybe you were some kind of target," she said. "Those people are crazy, you know? Just because you're an American and rich, I thought maybe somebody might be after you."

"Oh, for God's sake, Kitty," he said impatiently. "That's crazy. I'm not a target. This has nothing to do with me."

Kitty sat down on the bed next to him. "Thank God," she said, her fingertips brushing his chin. "I wouldn't want anything to happen to you. To us."

He turned and looked at her. "Yeah, well, what about this couple? They could be in a lot of trouble."

"As long as we're safe," Kitty said.

"You really don't care about these people, do you?" he said.

Kitty brushed his lips with a kiss. "Of course I do," she said. "If they're important to you, then they're important to me."

Hilton Whitehead once again found himself wondering if what Kitty said had an ounce of truth in it. He wondered if she really cared about anyone other than herself.

"Look," he said, taking her hand and gently squeezing it. "I've got to make some more telephone calls. Business calls. I won't be too long. Why don't you take a swim in the pool or something?"

Kitty knew she'd better leave him alone now. "Okay," she said brightly. "I just thought you might want some company. Maybe I'll . . . I'll go watch a movie or something."

"That's a good idea," he said. "There're a bunch of new DVDs. I won't be too long."

She got up and went to the door, then turned and blew him a kiss. "I'll see you in a bit," she purred.

He nodded. When she was gone, he locked the door again. He had to make sure that the plane was in France and ready to go. He also needed to call the Ritz and leave a message at the desk just in case Allegra neglected to check for messages on the cell phone. He wondered why she hadn't picked up, and new worries assaulted him. What if she'd accidentally left the phone off? What if she and Todd had gone someplace and forgotten it? What if—?

He had to stop this right now, he realized, because he was starting to panic, and that wouldn't do them any good whatsoever. He had to think. Yet what could he do to help them from here, thousands of miles away?

Now he wished he had never seen that cursed emerald.

CHAPTER TWENTY-THREE

In the backseat of the big Bentley, Allegra and Todd held hands. The chauffeur, Marcel, had told them that the drive to Monsieur Tadjer's was only a few minutes. Allegra wanted to ask him if he'd known Gérard, the driver who'd been shot, but she thought it best not to ask any questions. At least not yet. In her left hand, she held a small black satin clutch bag with a snap closure decorated with tiny rhinestones. She was glad she'd brought it. The pistol she'd stolen from Paul fit perfectly inside.

"We are here," Marcel said, pulling off the street and onto a cobblestone drive. He braked, then picked up a remote control device and pressed a button. Huge gates slowly swung open, and Allegra and Todd leaned down for a better view of what lay ahead.

"Whoa," Todd exclaimed. "Our host must sell a lot of jewelry."

"I'll say," Allegra replied. "And it looks like he knows how to spend the money."

The car pulled to a stop in the courtyard in front of the enormous limestone *hôtel particulier*. In the courtyard's center was a circle planted with trimmed boxwood, in the center of which was a neatly clipped boxwood standard of three spheres, the largest on the ground, the smallest at the top.

Marcel opened Allegra's door for her, and she stepped out. Todd slid across the seat and got out behind her. They both looked up at the imposing three-story mansion.

"It's breathtaking," Allegra said.

"It looks like late-sixteenth- or early-seventeenth-century," Todd responded.

The massive oak door at its entry opened, and Ramtane Tadjer stepped outside. "Welcome to my home," he said, smiling at them widely. He quickly shook Allegra's hand, then heartily shook Todd's. "Ramtane Tadjer, but please call me Ram. I'm so glad you could make it. It's a pleasure to meet you."

"Todd Hall, and it's a pleasure to meet you, too," Todd said. "Allegra's told me about your fantastic jewelry shop."

Ram looked at her. "How nice of you, Ms. Sheridan," he said.

"Please," she said. "Call me Allegra."

"Allegra, then," he said. "And Todd?"

Todd nodded. "Please."

"Come with me," Ram said, indicating the open door.

Allegra looked around, and saw that Marcel had disappeared as if the cobblestones had gobbled him up. Todd took her hand in his and gave it a gentle squeeze; then together they entered the imposing mansion. Allegra almost gasped aloud. "This is magnificent," she said in a voice of awe.

"It's home," Ram said in a humble voice.

An enormous chandelier with hundreds of rock crystal swags, balls, and pendants hung from the ceiling. The walls were hung with faded but still-colorful tapestries depicting pastoral scenes, and against them were exquisitely carved chests and consoles on which gilt candelabras and ormolu-mounted vases were displayed.

"I thought we would have a drink in the salon," Ram said.

Marcel appeared and helped Allegra out of her coat. Todd was wearing only his suit, but handed Marcel his gloves and the scarf he'd wrapped around his neck.

"It's this way, upstairs," Ram said, his hand extended toward the stairway with its ornamental metal railing.

She and Todd crossed the diagonally laid limestone floor to the staircase, with Ram at their side.

"Is this late-sixteenth- or early-seventeenth-century?" Todd asked him as they mounted the limestone, oak, and marble stairs.

"How observant you are," Ram replied. "It's early-seventeenth-century."

"Have you lived here long?" Allegra asked.

"For several years," he replied. "I inherited it from Jules Levant when he died."

"He was a very generous man," she said.

"Indeed," Ram said, "he was like a father to me. He and his wife took me in when I was a boy."

They reached the *premier étage,* and Ram indicated an archway to their left. "Here we are," he said.

Crossing into the enormous room, Allegra and Todd felt as if they had entered Ali Baba's cave. Two rock crystal chandeliers hung from the ceiling, and the walls were of heavily carved boiseries. The furnishings were all seventeenth- and eighteenth-century French antiques, and paintings and drawings from various periods decorated the walls. Small pools of light from lamps on tables bathed the room in a romantic light.

Ram seated them on a sumptuous suede-upholstered settee and sat across from them. Marcel appeared as if by magic, carrying a silver tray with three tulip-shaped glasses of champagne. He stopped at Allegra, then Todd, and finally Ram, then disappeared as silently as he had entered.

"I hope you don't mind my being presumptuous," Ram said, "but I thought champagne was called for."

"Not at all," Allegra said.

"It's very generous of you," Todd added.

Ram held his glass aloft slightly. "To . . . two young lovers," he said.

Allegra felt herself blush, and Todd looked at her and smiled. "I'll second that," he said.

They sipped the champagne, and Todd began a conversation dominated by talk of the magnificent house. He asked Ram many questions about its history and particular pieces of furniture and paintings, and the more he learned, the more impressed he became by the man's fine tastes and knowledge. It was difficult for him to imagine that this man could be engaged in anything shadowy.

After a half hour or so of drinking and talking, Ram led them to an equally grand dining room, which was softly lit by candles on the table. The walls were covered with masterful murals set in heavily carved boiserie. They depicted hunt scenes with expertly rendered horses, dogs, and huntsmen set in lush forests and meadows. Marcel appeared again and began serving a delicious meal of foie gras, grilled quail in a currant sauce with wild rice and asparagus, and then a perfect and calorie-laden crème brûlée. The conversation was light, centering on the wonders of the house and of French cuisine.

"I think this is the best crème brûlée I've ever eaten," Allegra said when she was finished.

"And I'll second that," Todd said with a laugh.

"I'm glad you like it," Ram said. "I'll tell the chef. So few people get it right, you know." His gaze touched Allegra and then Todd. "I thought that we could have an after-dinner drink at a little hideaway of mine," he said. "It's just around the corner, and the place where I'm at my creative best. I thought that perhaps we could discuss design possibilities there. That's why I asked you to join me tonight, Allegra, and I'm afraid we've neglected to talk about my ideas yet."

"That's awfully kind of you," Todd said, alarmed by the idea of going to some hideaway, "but we really ought to be getting back to the hotel soon. We're leaving for New York early in the morning, you know." They weren't leaving until Monday morning, but Ramtane Tadjer didn't need to know that. "What if you two talk about it on the phone after we're back in New York?"

Allegra glanced at him with irritation, a look Ram did not miss.

"Oh, surely this is something that should be discussed in person," Ram said. "Don't you agree, Allegra?"

"If it's that close by, then what's a little more time? We can sleep on the plane tomorrow, and I'd love to hear what you have to say about design possibilities." Her voice was determined, and the look she gave Todd was equally so.

Todd glanced from her to Ram. "So this place is around the corner, you say?"

"Yes," Ram said, nodding. "I have some things there I would like to show you. I think you would be particularly interested in them, Allegra."

"Oh?" Allegra said with curiosity.

"Some very special jewels," Ram said. He paused for dramatic effect, then added, "Emeralds." He looked from her to Todd. "What do you say?"

"I wouldn't miss it for the world," Allegra said.

"Well . . . ," Todd said, "I'm game." There was no way he would let Allegra go alone.

"Good," Ram said. "Marcel will drop us there. Shall we go?"

They were in the Bentley and on their way in a matter of minutes, chatting as the big car maneuvered through the narrow streets of the Marais. When they drew up to the building on rue des Rosiers, Allegra's breath caught in her throat. It was Monsieur Weiss's building. She wanted to tell Todd, but of course she didn't dare let on that she'd been snooping and had talked to Solomon Weiss about the emeralds.

"Here we are," Ram said. "My old studio."

Marcel was already opening Allegra's door, and she and Todd slid out. Ram came around and joined them on the sidewalk, and they entered the building together after Ram unlocked the door. They climbed the well-worn stairs to the fourth floor, where Ram unlocked a big steel door.

"I've kept this apartment since I was a kid. Jules Levant gave it to me," he explained. "It's always been a refuge for me. A home away from home."

The apartment consisted of one large room with a kitchenette and a separate bathroom. The room was furnished with a large, comfortable couch and chairs, several tables with lamps, and shelves filled with books. On the walls were inexpensive posters in frames, much like those a college student or a young couple starting out would hang.

The ceilings were high enough to accommodate a loft that was reached by a ladderlike set of stairs. The loft was surrounded by a metal railing, and from where she stood, Allegra could see that it held a large bed with side tables. A trunk sat at the foot of the bed. Under the loft area was a big built-in closet.

"This is charming," Allegra said, "and very comfortable looking."

"You can see why I escape to this occasionally," Ram said.

"It reminds me of my first apartment in New York," Todd said.

"Please have a seat," Ram said as he went around turning on lights. "Just put your coat and things anywhere."

Todd helped Allegra out of her coat and put it, along with his gloves and scarf, over the back of a chair. They sat together on the couch.

"We're going to have a very special Armagnac tonight," Ram said over his shoulder. He stood across the room in the still-darkened kitchen area with a bottle in hand. "It's quite old and very smooth. One of the best." He turned back around and busied himself getting glasses out of cabinets and pouring their drinks.

"I see that you have a lot of books about gemstones and jewelry design," Allegra said, gazing at the shelves from the couch.

"Yes," Ram said, his back to them. "Jules and Hannah Levant gave most of them to me. They put me through a regular course of study, you see, training me in every aspect of the business."

"So you never went to a gemological school or anything?" Todd asked.

"No," Ram said. "I learned on the job. The best training, I think. Of course, I was only fifteen when I began, so by the time I reached the appropriate age for studying in an institute I was already ahead of most of the students."

He finally turned around and faced them, holding two brandy snifters. "Here we are," he said. He crossed the wide room and handed them their drinks, then went back to the kitchen counter and returned with his. "Cheers," he said, lifting his snifter.

"Cheers," Allegra and Todd said in unison.

Ram took a swallow of his drink and watched as they sipped at theirs. Then he sat down in a chair facing them. "How do you like it?" he asked.

"It's wonderful," Allegra said, although she'd barely tasted it. She didn't like brandy of any sort because she'd found it gave her a terrible hangover, but she didn't want to tell him that.

"It's very smooth," Todd said diplomatically as he rolled the Armagnac around in the snifter. Actually, he thought, it tasted distinctly odd. Medicinal and not at all like the Armagnac his father occasionally drank.

"Yes, isn't it?" Ram said. He set his snifter down and looked over at them, placing his hands on his knees. "I suppose I might as well get to the point," he said. "I have some things to show you from the safe here. If you'll excuse me just a moment, I'll be right back."

"That's fine," Allegra said, suddenly feeling a little woozy. "Take . . . take your time."

Ram went to the closet under the loft and took a key from his pocket. The door had a large padlock on it that Allegra hadn't noticed before. He opened it, then pulled the door back and disappeared inside the dark closet.

Allegra looked at Todd questioningly, but he had a dazed expression on his face and didn't notice. "Todd," she whispered, reaching for his arm and squeezing it.

He turned and looked at her as if he was trying to comprehend what she was saying.

Oh, my God, she thought. *There's something in the drinks.*

She shook Todd's arm, but he only stared at her, his eyes slowly opening and closing. Grabbing his drink off the table, she pulled the back of the couch cushion toward her and poured its contents down into the couch. She set his empty glass on the table, then quickly repeated the process with hers. Adjusting a pillow against the cushion, she hoped that Ram wouldn't notice the drink stain when he returned.

Todd was now slumped back against the couch, his head falling to his chest. She shook him again, more vigorously this time.

"Wha—?" he mumbled.

"Todd," she hissed. "Todd, you can't go to sleep. You can't pass out."

"Wha—?" he mumbled again.

Ram came back out of the closet carrying an ordinary large black plastic garbage bag. "Here we are," he said, approaching the couch. He saw Todd and stopped. "Oh, dear," he said. "Did your friend have too much to drink?"

"I'm afraid so," Allegra said, forcing a laugh. "We're both lushes for good Armagnac." The woozy feeling came in waves, washing over her, receding, then washing in again. *I can't pass out, too. No. I can't let that happen.*

"Well, it's no problem," Ram said with a chuckle. "Marcel is quite capable of carrying him." He sat back down in the chair and placed the garbage bag on the table between them. "You've finished your drink, I see."

"Oh, I'd better not have another," Allegra said. "Or you'll have two sleepyheads on your hands."

Ram stood up. "I insist on pouring you another."

"No, no, really," Allegra protested. "I can't possibly drink more."

Ram picked up her empty snifter and returned to the kitchen counter. "I'll only be a moment," he said. "I think I'll have more, as well."

Allegra's body felt as if every muscle in it was becoming totally relaxed. *I can't panic,* she thought. *No, I've got to stay in control.* She began to shake her head, hands, and feet, to move her shoulders back and forth, to turn her torso side to side.

Ram returned from the kitchen counter and placed a drink in front of her, then sat back down. "Cheers again," he said, lifting his glass.

Allegra managed to lift hers, almost dropping it as she did so. "Ch-cheers," she said, making an effort to say the word. She put the glass to her lips but didn't take a drink.

"Now," Ram said, setting his glass down, "I'll show you what I have here. He untied the drawstrings on the garbage bag and opened the bag wide, sliding it down over several boxes inside it.

Allegra watched with interest, fighting to keep her eyes open.

He opened the first box and lifted out an object wrapped in several layers of once white tissue paper. Slowly he began unwrapping it, taking the tissue paper off several layers at a time. When he was finished, he held up a heavily carved gold necklace setting with an elaborate design.

The setting he held up was almost certainly nineteenth-century or a very good copy. Victorian or a little later. It had held many gemstones of the same huge size, and at its bottom was the setting for what had once been a hanging pendant.

"Do you know what this is?" Ram asked.

"It's—it's Victorian," she said, struggling for the words. "Or—or a little later."

"Yes," Ram said with a smile.

He quickly opened a procession of boxes and unwrapped their contents, all of them in many layers of tissue paper, as the necklace setting had been. When he finished, the settings were lined up on the table. What had once been a pair of earrings, a necklace, a brooch, and a bracelet were empty shells, artful in their own right, but forlorn to Allegra's eyes for their lack of stones. She struggled with all her might to make sense of them.

"There," Ram said after he'd lined up the settings. "Do you know what these are, Allegra?"

"Like—like the necklace," she muttered. "Vic-Victorian settings."

"That's all you see?" he asked, smiling.

She nodded, then was distracted by Todd. He shifted on the couch and let out a moan that was barely above a whisper.

"Then perhaps I should show you more," Ram said. He took another box, a long, flat one, from the bag and opened it. From it he withdrew a manila envelope.

He opened the manila envelope and removed small sheaves of paper from it. "These are photographs," Ram said, "and I think you will enjoy seeing them, Allegra." He offered them to her across the table.

Allegra put out a weak, leaden hand and took the photographs, but dropped them on the table. She scooped them up with both hands and looked down at the one on top. The lethargy that held her in its grip all but evaporated the instant she saw the photograph, her excitement overriding the effect of the drug.

The emeralds! she thought. *Of course.* The topmost picture was of the necklace with its stones intact, all of them of equal size and color, if the photograph could be believed. She shuffled through the others and saw what she expected to: the settings that were now lined up on the table were depicted with the emeralds. *The emeralds he has been purchasing for all these years after selling them through Jules Levant,* she thought.

She looked up and saw that Ram was staring at her, his eyes glittering, his mouth set in a smile.

"These are the emeralds you sold, then bought back, aren't they?"

"So you knew," he said mildly. "I thought as much. Would you like to see the emeralds?"

Allegra nodded. "You have them here?" she asked, surprised that he would keep millions of dollars' worth of emeralds here in this apartment.

"Yes," he said. "Right in front of you." He opened the last box that had been in the garbage bag and took out several cloth bags. As if they were nothing more than river rocks, he began emptying the shimmering emeralds out onto the table.

A gasp escaped Allegra's lips. She had seen many gemstones in her life—she owned many high-quality stones herself—but the sight of so many beautifully colored emeralds of the same size was truly dazzling. When he finished emptying the bags, she sat staring at them with wonder. There must have been a hundred or more.

"Impressive, no?" Ram said.

Allegra nodded. "They're unbelievable," she said. "Extraordinary."

"But there is one missing," Ram said.

She looked up at him. "Princess Karima's ring."

"Yes," Ram replied. "And I must have it."

Allegra saw a kind of self-righteous madness in his dark, glittering eyes. It was the look of a hungry maniac who would stop at nothing to possess what he did not have.

"But why?" she asked. "You have all of these." She indicated the piles of emeralds with a hand. "Why would you want her ring?"

"You really don't know?" he asked. "Or are you playing a game with me?"

Allegra shook her head. "No. I think I know where the emeralds came from," she replied honestly, "but I don't understand why you must have the ring, as well."

Ram studied her face for a moment. "The ring is the missing pendant from the necklace," he said.

"So?" Allegra said. "There are more than enough emeralds to substitute one."

"I can see that you need a bit of education," Ram said with smug satisfaction.

"I'm sure I do," she said tartly. "You might enlighten me about what you've put in Todd's drink, for example." She abruptly felt the effects of the drug wash over her body again, relaxing her muscles, making her eyelids heavy, and fogging over her brain. She sat upright and shook her limbs again, struggling to maintain control. "And mine, too, for that matter."

Ram smiled. "Just a little something to make you more receptive," he said, "and to keep your young man from interfering with our fun."

"You—you *bastard*," she said, her eyes now fiery with anger despite the heaviness of their lids.

"Such language doesn't become you, Allegra," he said, still smiling.

"And I don't think that inviting us here, then drugging us, becomes one of the world's top jewelers, either," she responded snappishly.

Ram laughed softly. "You are a challenging young woman," he said. "I like that."

"A lot of good it will do you," Allegra said, "because I think you are detestable."

His soft laugh came again and, with it, a smile. "We'll see what sort of firebrand you are later." He paused, looking at her, hoping to see fear in her eyes, but he was met with angry determination.

"You said that you thought you knew where the emeralds came from. You did say that, didn't you?"

"Yes," Allegra said, nodding.

"Why don't you tell me about it," Ram said. "I would like to hear your theory."

"It's my guess," she said, "that you, or more likely Jules Levant, bought the emeralds from Wallis Simpson, the Duchess of Windsor."

Ram lifted his snifter of brandy into the air as if toasting her. "Very good, Allegra," he said. "Indeed, they were purchased from the Duchess of Windsor many years ago. And by Jules Levant. Over the years he bought several pieces of jewelry from her. Some of it was jewelry that she had reported stolen to collect the insurance money. She and her husband, the duke, often overspent themselves, you see." He paused a moment, then added, "In fact, several of the pieces that were auctioned after her death had been reported stolen."

Although she had been fairly certain that her guess was an accurate one, Allegra still found its confirmation startling. *To think that the legendary lovers the Duke and Duchess of Windsor would have to sell jewelry to maintain their lifestyle,* she mused. *Not only that, but to file false insurance claims. He gave up a lot more than a crown when he married the woman he loved.*

"She could never be seen wearing these jewels," Ram continued. "Certainly not in their old settings."

"And I imagine she wouldn't even have taken a chance on wearing them if they were reset," Allegra said.

"Exactly," Ram said. "She might have created a huge scandal if she'd been seen in any one of these thirty-four-and-a-half-carat, dark green emeralds."

"Because the Duke and Duchess of Windsor stole them," Allegra said.

Ram applauded her. "You are exactly right again," he said. "I see you've put two and two together."

"And the British royal family would not be too happy about confirmation that the man who gave up the throne and his lover had taken off with the famous Windsor emeralds," Allegra said. "And if the duchess wore any of them, that would be confirmation for all the world to see."

"Yes," Ram said. "There were rumors, of course, but there was never any proof that they had stolen the emeralds."

"But you have it," she said.

He nodded. "Brava!" He took a sip of his brandy. "Jules Levant broke the set up, reset them, and sold everything separately over a period of years so no one would know anything."

"But you bought them all back so you would have your proof once again," Allegra said.

"Right again," Ram said. "Except that there is one little problem."

"The ring."

"Obviously," he said. "It is the key to everything."

"Because of its inclusion," Allegra guessed.

"Precisely," Ram said with a nod. "The ring, which was the necklace pendant, offers irrefutable proof that these are the Windsor emeralds. It is what those familiar with the royal family's jewels called the demon stone."

The demon stone. Allegra felt a chill run up her spine. It was the perfect name for the emerald's inclusion, she realized, because it described what appeared to be the head of a devil, complete with horns. The inclusion that should have made the emerald less valuable instead made it more so.

"So you have to have the ring to complete the set," she said.

"Of course," Ram said. "I must have them all for my plan to work."

"What plan?" she asked.

"I'm going to offer them back to the Windsors," Ram said. "Very discretely. Very quietly. For several hundred million dollars."

"Several hundred million dollars!" Allegra said.

"It's nothing to them," he said.

"What if they don't go for it?" she asked.

He smiled. "Oh, believe me, they will. Because I'm going to tell them that if they don't, then the whole world is going to know that their precious David Windsor and his lovely wife, the Duchess of Windsor, stole them. I'll create a huge scandal and I'm sure they wouldn't want another one of those."

"So what you're talking about is extorting money from them?" Allegra said.

"One might call it that, I suppose," he said, smiling again, "but I prefer to call it giving the British royal family the opportunity to repatriate some of their long-lost jewels."

"You don't need the money at all," Allegra said angrily. "You're really just a creep with no compunctions at all, aren't you?"

Ram shrugged. "Well, I haven't done it yet," he said, "and I won't until I have the demon stone." He paused and stared at her. "The stone you've got."

Allegra didn't respond to his remark.

"And if I don't get that emerald tonight," he said, "then you and your boyfriend will die. Here in this apartment. After I've given you a memorable night of sexual delight such as you've never experienced before. Too bad you won't have more than a few minutes to remember it before you die."

Allegra's stomach lurched, and she could feel a chill run up her spine again. She tried to keep her face blank, but she wanted to scream and cry at the same time. *What am I going to do?*

CHAPTER TWENTY-FOUR

Yamal entered the Ritz hotel dressed in a pin-striped, navy blue bespoke suit, a heavily starched custom-made white shirt, and a pearl gray tie from Charvet. His shoes were handmade by John Lobb. He was the picture of an international businessman with an enormous salary or the heir to a fortune. As the concierge knew, however, he was an exorbitantly expensive male hustler whose discreet services were sometimes required by the hotel's esteemed guests.

When Yamal approached him, the concierge nodded, and palmed the one-hundred-euro note that Yamal handed him. Yamal flashed his brilliant smile, then went to the elevators, boarded one that was waiting, and took it to the floor that the Sheridan woman and her boyfriend were staying on. When he reached their room, he checked to see that the hallway was empty in both directions before he removed his tools from his jacket pocket.

Yamal was inside the suite within two minutes and went straight to the closet in the bedroom where he knew the safe would be. Opening the door, he pushed aside the few garments hanging there and went down on one knee. From his other jacket pocket, he took out a small ring of keys. Looking at the lock, then at the keys, he got down on both knees and scooted closer to the safe inside the closet. He tried the key that appeared to be a fit, but after several tries he gave up with that one. Selecting another, he inserted it in the lock, but found that it didn't work, either.

So intent was he on his task that he didn't hear the door to the suite open. Nor did he hear the footsteps that quietly approached him from behind.

"Shit," he swore in English when he discovered that the third key wasn't a fit. He was selecting the next one when he felt a shift in the air behind him. The hairs on the back of his neck stood up, and he knew with certainty that someone was in the room. Jerking his head around, Yamal saw a tall, dark man holding a pistol, aimed down at him.

"*Laa!*" he whispered in Arabic. "*No!*"

He scrambled around to face the man, reaching inside his jacket for the revolver in its shoulder holster. At the same time he started to dive for the man's legs to throw him off his feet, but before he could move or say another word, the man pulled the trigger.

"*Laa!*" he cried plaintively. Yamal's dark eyes looked stunned as he heard the soft ping of the gun's report, and a small hole appeared in his forehead. His body jerked, and the back of his head blew out all over the closet and its contents. He fell forward onto the rug, soiling his bespoke suit as he lost control of his bodily functions.

Kadar shoved the body out of the way with his boot, then went to the bed and pulled the silk spread off it. He tossed it onto the closet floor, so as not to soil his clothes on the bits of bone, blood, and brain matter that had splattered over everything. He took a single key from a trouser pocket, then went down on his knees to reach the safe. He inserted the key, turned the lock, and opened the safe in a single swift movement.

He looked in, prepared to scoop out the box with the ring and anything else of value that had been put in the safe.

"Fuck!" he swore in English. "Fuck!"

The safe was empty.

Princess Karima poured herself another splash of Jack Daniel's over the ice in her glass. "Do you want another drink, darling?" she asked Marcus.

"Why not?" he replied with a smile. "I've already got a good buzz on. Might as well get good and sloshed."

Mimi shuffled into the room. "Madame," she said, looking at Karima. "You have a telephone call."

"Please take a message, Mimi," Princess Karima said. "I don't want to be bothered now."

Mimi cleared her throat. "You will not want to miss this call, madame," she said, her voice weighed with significance.

Princess Karima lifted an eyebrow and put her cigarette out in an ashtray. "Excuse me, Marcus," she said with annoyance. "I'll be right back."

Marcus watched her sweep out of the room toward the hallway that led to her office. Mimi shuffled off in the direction of the kitchen. He set his drink down and rose to his feet, steadied himself, then followed in Karima's steps, the copious amount of alcohol he'd consumed giving him reckless courage. When he approached her office, he saw that the door was ajar, and he sidled up to it.

"*As-salaam alaikum,*" he heard.

"*Hello*" *in Arabic. Whatever she's doing,* he thought, *it's naughty. No doubt about it. She wouldn't mix it up with any of them otherwise.*

As he eavesdropped, he didn't comprehend the conversation, but he easily determined that Princess Karima was extremely upset. Her voice rose in volume, and her tone became very agitated. Then suddenly, Marcus's efforts were rewarded. "He was murdered?" Princess Karima blurted out in English. Marcus tensed and felt giddy at the same time. He had hoped for some good gossip, but this? This was too much.

"*Maah as-salaama,*" he heard her say, and he knew that she was saying good-bye. He quickly backed up, then turned to dash back to the sitting room. Mimi, her tiny eyes blazing with intensity, stood down the hallway watching him.

Marcus barked a laugh. "Just checking on Karima," he said, "to see if she wanted her drink, but she's already hanging up."

Mimi did not respond to him, but watched as he walked back to the sitting room. Marcus sat down on the sofa where he'd been before and took a large swallow of his drink, then lit a cigarette.

Princess Karima slowly entered the room, her beautiful face wearing a troubled expression. She didn't look at Marcus at first, but went to the couch where she'd been lounging, sat down, took a drink, then lit a cigarette. Her silence was ominous.

"Everything all right, darling?" Marcus asked, trying to sound cheerful. "You look a bit worried."

Princess Karima looked at him with a haughty glare that she hoped concealed her fear. "I don't appreciate your listening in, Marcus," she said angrily.

"But Karima," he said apologetically, "I didn't mean to upset you, darling. Besides, I don't understand Arabic."

But you understand English very well, Princess Karima thought. She realized Marcus had become a liability.

"There has been a little family emergency," Karima said, her face relaxing and her tone softening.

"Nothing serious, I hope," Marcus said.

She shook her head. "No," Karima replied. She laughed, but it sounded false even to her own ears. "A little palace coup averted."

"Oh, my," Marcus said, relieved that she seemed to be recovering from his treacherous act. "How exciting."

"Actually, it's more the norm," Karima said. "Family feuds, you know."

Karima looked down into her drink, then took a sip. One of her contacts in Paris had informed her of the shooting at the Ritz. Yamal's death didn't bother her one way or the other—he was handsome and amusing but nothing more than a disposable hustler—but the loss of the ring saddened her. It was her last link with Stefano.

"I hope everything's okay now," Marcus said solicitously.

Princess Karima heaved a sigh. "Oh, I think so," she replied. "Another drink, darling?" she asked, suddenly more cheerful. "I'm having one. Attempted coups have that effect on one."

"Why not?" he replied.

"I'll get them," she offered, getting to her feet. "But I'd better get some more ice from the kitchen."

"Can I do anything to help?" he asked, anxious to please her.

"No," Karima said. "I'll do it." She picked up the silver ice bucket. "I'll only be a second." She glided out of the room.

Ram got to his feet. "Enough talk, Allegra," he said. "I think I've explained everything to you. A needy duchess sells jewels that don't belong to her. Jules Levant buys them. I buy them back after I've inherited his business, then—"

"I'm—I'm sure Jules Levant would be rolling over in his grave," Allegra broke in, the drug affecting her, making thought and speech an effort, "if he knew what you've done with his . . . with his legacy."

"Well, he doesn't know, does he?" Ram said. "He's dead, and I killed him, so I should know."

Allegra's eyes widened in horror. "You—you actually killed him?" she stuttered.

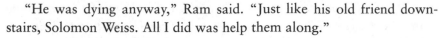

"He was dying anyway," Ram said. "Just like his old friend downstairs, Solomon Weiss. All I did was help them along."

"Mr. Weiss is dead?" She was stunned by the news. "But I only saw him—"

"I know you saw him," Ram said. "Why do you think I got rid of him?"

Allegra thought she would faint, but she fought back the urge. *I can't let him win,* she thought miserably. *If for no one else but Solomon Weiss, I have to fight back.*

Ram walked to a console and opened a large decorative box that sat on it. When he turned back around, a pair of handcuffs and something similar to them, only larger, dangled from his hands. He held them up for her to see clearly.

"Wh-what are you doing?" she gasped.

Ram approached the couch, and when she shrank away from him, he laughed softly. "These are for your boyfriend," he said, quickly encircling Todd's wrists with the handcuffs. He snapped first one side shut, then the other. Todd didn't react in any way, but continued breathing shallow, silent breaths.

When what he was doing registered in her foggy brain, Allegra cried out. "No! Don't you touch him!" She stood up on shaky legs and pushed at Ram with all her might, but she was so weak she succeeded only in falling down against the coffee table.

"Don't hurt yourself, Allegra," Ram said smoothly as he placed the leg irons around Todd's ankles, snapped them shut, and then locked them.

Allegra placed both hands on the coffee table and struggled to her feet.

"Now," Ram said, brushing his hands off, "your young man won't be going anywhere."

"Oh, Todd," she whimpered, sinking down onto the couch next to him. "Todd . . ."

Ram clenched one of her wrists in his left hand, then grabbed the other with his right. He pulled on her forcefully. "You're coming with me, Allegra," he said. "Into my closet. My little playroom."

Allegra felt herself being pulled off the couch, and since she didn't have the strength to fight him off, she let her body go completely limp, an easy task under the circumstances.

"You're not being cooperative, Allegra," Ram said impatiently, as if he were dealing with a recalcitrant child. "Stand up."

Allegra made no effort to get to her feet. *Let the son of a bitch do the work,* she thought. *Whatever his plans are for me, he's getting no help carrying them out.*

"Stand up now!" Ram said through gritted teeth.

Still she did not budge to aid him, but let him pull on her wrists with all his might. Her body slid off the couch and onto the floor, where she slumped as if she were a broken doll.

"Goddamn you!" Ram swore. He let go of her wrists, then slapped her face.

"You—you bastard!" Allegra cried, reaching up to touch her cheek.

Ram brought his hand back, prepared to strike her again, but his cell phone began ringing at that moment. "Fuck," he swore under his breath. He went to the console where he'd put down the cell phone when they'd first arrived. Picking it up, he flipped it open.

"Yes?" he said, staring across the room at Allegra as she struggled to get to her feet.

Princess Karima dropped ice cubes into Marcus's crystal old-fashioned glass, then splashed more Jack Daniel's over them. "Water, darling?"

"Not necessary," Marcus drawled drunkenly.

She took his drink to him, then made another for herself before sitting back down. "Cheers," she said, lifting her glass.

"Cheers," Marcus said before taking a sip from his. He set the glass down and then looked over at her. "My God, Karima," he said with a chortle, "we've put the booze away tonight. I think I'm actually drunk."

She laughed merrily. "Me, too," she said. "Perhaps we should take a moonlight walk in the garden to sober up a bit."

"A walk?" he said, looking at her. "You're serious?"

"Yes," she said gaily. "Let me get our coats. I'll be right back." She got up and floated out of the room, her silk caftan, this one turquoise with several rows of braided trim made from real gold, lifting like a cloud behind her.

Marcus lit a cigarette and inhaled deeply, happy that Karima was acting like her old self again. Not a care in the world.

She returned, wearing her floor-length Russian-sable greatcoat with its hood. Across one arm, she carried his cashmere overcoat. "Here, darling," she said. "Up, up. And off we'll go."

Marcus rose to his feet and took the coat from her, then put it on.

"Let's take our drinks," Karima said, picking hers up.

"The better to sober us up," he laughed, taking his from the table.

They went out through one of the French doors in the conservatory, crossed the stone terrace, and began walking down one of the garden paths, their breath visible in the night air.

"It's beautiful, isn't it, darling?" Princess Karima said.

"Gorgeous," Marcus replied.

"Let's go down to the pergola by the pond," she said, "and sit for a while."

"That's a lovely idea," Marcus said. He took a swallow of his drink. "You always have the best ideas, Karima."

They reached the columned pergola and sat down side by side on a bench. Huge, gnarled wisteria vines, not yet in leaf, crisscrossed the top of the pergola, casting bizarre shadows in the moonlight.

"It's so peaceful here," Marcus said. "So quiet and beautiful with the moonlight reflecting off the pond."

"Isn't it?" Karima said, swirling the drink around in her glass.

Behind them, a short, dark figure approached slowly on silent feet.

"Look, Marcus, darling," Karima said. "Is that one of the swans on the pond?"

"I don't see it," Marcus replied, squinting his eyes. Suddenly he felt something cold at the back of his head. "What—?" he began.

Karima quickly slid away from him and covered her ears with her hands.

Marcus started to turn to look at her, but his head froze, his mouth open in a question, his eyes wide with wonder. The bullet exploded in his brain, killing him instantly. He didn't even hear the soft thump of the silenced revolver before he slumped forward, then slid off the bench.

Princess Karima rose to her feet and backed away without looking at the body. Mimi came from behind the bench, sliding the revolver into the capacious pocket of the apron she wore.

"Go," she said to Princess Karima. "I'll take care of this."

Princess Karima didn't look into the old woman's tiny, close-set eyes, but nodded, her gaze averted. She turned and walked back to the millhouse, leaving the scent of Golconda in her wake.

"Laheen!" Ram swore in Arabic. "Damn you, Kadar!"

From where she sat on the couch, Allegra listened, certain that Ram was receiving the bad news that the emerald was not in the suite at the Ritz. The smartest thing she could have done, she decided, was take it to Monsieur Lenoir and have him send it in a diplomatic pouch to New York. He had contacts at the American embassy, so it had been an easy matter for him to handle.

Ram glared at her from across the room, alternately talking and listening, his voice quieter but his face purple with rage. He abruptly turned his back to her, and she was glad his hate-filled eyes were no longer upon her.

Todd emitted a barely audible moan, and Allegra ran her fingers through his raven hair with loving tenderness. When he moaned again, she gave his shoulders a shake, but he didn't respond. There was nothing she would like more than to curl up beside him and sleep off the effects of the drug, but that was out of the question. She had to fight the urge with every ounce of strength she had.

She wondered what would happen next, whether or not Ram would try to sexually assault her. A wave of panic swept over her, for she didn't think she could fight him off. But there was one thing she was sure of: he wouldn't kill her, at least not yet. She was the only person who knew where the emerald was. But if he found out it was already in New York, what then? What would he do if he knew the emerald was beyond his grasp?

"Maah as-salaama," she heard Ram say before he flipped shut his cell phone and turned back around to face her. His expression was at first solemn. Then abruptly his lips spread into a smile.

"You are very clever, Allegra," he said.

"Oh? How so?" she asked, feigning an expression of innocence.

"You have hidden the emerald somewhere," he replied, slowly crossing the room in her direction. "You haven't placed it in the safe or elsewhere in your suite at the Ritz. My man has turned your rooms upside down and inside out."

"I'm not a complete fool," she said defiantly.

"No," he said, now standing over her, "I'll give you credit for that." He paused, looking down at her upturned face. "But you're very foolish nevertheless." He reached over and grabbed her hair with a hand, pulling on it with fierce power.

Allegra cried out. "No! Stop it. You're hurting me."

"I've only begun to hurt you," he replied, giving the length of hair in his hand a jerk. "You don't yet know what pain is. But you're going to find out before I'm through with you."

Allegra's skull burned as if set on fire, but the pain signaled to her that her body was more capable of fighting back than she'd thought.

"Now, get up," Ram snapped. "You're coming with me, and if not willingly, then I'll drag you by your hair."

"If—if you'll let go, I'll—I'll get up," Allegra replied, barely able to get the words out with the pain streaking through her skull.

Ram loosened his grip, and Allegra pushed herself up off the couch. When she did so, her small beaded handbag slid off the couch and landed on the rug. She looked down at it, hesitated a moment, then bent to pick it up.

"I don't think you'll need your purse, Allegra," Ram said with a smile.

Allegra smiled brightly, holding the evening bag in one hand. "A lady never knows, does she, Ram?"

He took her free hand in one of his. "Come with me," he said. "We're going to have a little fun. Then you're going to tell me where you've hidden the emerald."

Allegra let him lead her toward the closet under the bedroom loft.

Ram stopped at the closet door, opened it, then reached around and switched on a light. He stepped back and propelled her forward into the room, and Allegra's gaze swept about it. For a moment, she thought she would be sick. Bile rose in her throat, its taste sour and bitter, but she fought it down. The bed, a twin-size covered in a black spread, was equipped with chains and ropes that were secured at both the head- and footboards. From the ceiling more chains dangled, at the ends of which were large, padded handcuffs. On the walls hung scary-looking belts, whips, cat-o'-nine-tails, and various masks and hoods.

The bile had receded, but Allegra felt her knees weaken and her stomach churn. A powerful chill ran up her spine and neck to the top of her skull, and she broke out into a cold sweat. She had never been as terrified in her life.

"It's soundproofed," Ram said from behind her, his breath on her neck, "so no one will hear us playing, Allegra." His powerful arms encircled her, and he squeezed her tightly.

She began to tremble, uncontrollably, and tears gathered in her eyes, threatening to spill down her cheeks, but she clutched her purse to her and pushed down her fear.

"Why, you're shaking, Allegra," Ram said in a mocking voice. "And I thought you were such a courageous young lady. Like all Americans. Fearless and brave."

Allegra turned in his arms to face Ram and pressed herself against him. "I was shaking with anticipation," she said in a whisper. "This room is so exciting, so . . . erotic."

Ram looked momentarily surprised, not certain whether he should believe her or not. "I'm glad you appreciate it," he said. "That will make everything so much easier for us both."

His breath was on her face, and she could smell the heat his body emanated. He shoved himself against her hard, and she could feel his engorged manhood. Ram's lips parted slightly, and he bent his face to hers, intent upon kissing her.

In one swift motion Allegra whipped her clutch bag upward and swung it as hard as she could against his skull. There was a resounding thud, and beads flew in all directions from the impact.

Ram suddenly released her, his hands flying to his head. *"Laheen!"* he cried out. "Damn you!"

Allegra quickly backed away from him, almost falling onto the bed when she did so. As she righted herself, her hands scrabbled to open the handbag. She pulled out the revolver and pointed it at Ram, whose hands still partially covered his face as he clutched his skull.

"You whore!" he spat venomously, finally removing his hands and glaring at her. Then he saw the revolver she held aimed at him.

Allegra's hand trembled, and she dropped her handbag in order to use both hands to hold the gun. It still shook in her grip, but she kept it leveled on him.

"You're not going to use that," Ram said nastily. "You don't have any idea what you're doing."

He lunged at her then, and Allegra pulled the trigger.

The roar of the explosion was so loud in the small room that her ears began ringing painfully. Time stood still, and she watched in horror as Ram stopped, seemingly frozen in place, his eyes wide, his arms outstretched toward her. Then a geyser of blood spurted from his neck, and she could hear a gurgle as he tried to speak.

He fell to the floor with a loud thump, and his entire body spasmed briefly before all movement abruptly ceased.

The room stank of cordite, and the only sound was that of Allegra's breathing. Her breath came in gasps, and her stomach lurched anew, the bile rising in her throat once again. She didn't move for long moments, staring down at the body, transfixed by what she'd done. Blood, what seemed like gallons of it, still poured from the wound in his throat.

He must be dead, she thought, *and I killed him.*

Finally, she leaned down and picked up her clutch bag, put the revolver in it, snapped it shut, then walked out of the closet. She turned and closed the door. Seeing the padlock that dangled on the wall, she closed the hasp, looped the padlock through it, and snapped it shut.

She looked around the room with fresh eyes, as if she had been gone from it for hours. Todd still lay slumped on the couch, breathing shallowly. She noticed Ram's cell phone on the console, and she calmly walked over and picked it up. She dialed 17, the number for the police, then told them to come to rue des Rosiers. She remembered the house number from her visit to Solomon Weiss. *Another death I'm responsible for,* she thought.

At last she noticed all the jewelry on the table. She gathered up the gold settings, the emeralds, and the photographs from the table and put them all back in the garbage bag where Ram had stored them. Then she searched for something to put the bag in. In the entry hall was a small closet, and in it she found a heavy nylon gym bag. After she managed to stuff the garbage bag and its contents into the bag, she zipped it shut.

CHAPTER TWENTY-FIVE

T he party was held a week later, so Allegra and Todd could attend. The American Hospital in Paris had treated her for shock, and Todd had been held for observation for two days. Then the hours of police interrogation began, which were carried out with a civility that surprised them both. At that point Hilton Whitehead and his powerful friends had intervened on their behalf.

Allegra and Todd had finally arrived in New York on Whitehead's private Gulfstream V. They had spent many hours closeted in discussion with Hilton since their return, and they found themselves in his private suite aboard his floating palace while the party he'd planned was in progress.

"I still hope that something can be done about Princess Karima," Allegra said. "You've all but proved that she's funneling money to terrorist cells in the Middle East."

Hilton nodded. "Without the names and numbers you found, the investigation would never have started," he said. "We still have no hard proof, but at least now Interpol is involved."

"It's outrageous," Todd said. "She's probably already sent hundreds of millions of dollars to Middle Eastern banks. I mean, Allegra saw the transfers."

"Yes," Hilton said with a nod, "but she can claim that the money was going to her family. I tell you the woman is virtually untouchable."

"There's no doubt that she was mixed up with Monsieur Lorrain at the auction house." Allegra said. "I think she may have wanted the ring for sentimental reasons, and like Ramtane Tadjer, she would stop at nothing to get it back. They linked her to the man they found dead in our hotel suite, didn't they?"

"The high-priced hustler? Her name was in his address book," Hilton said, "but they can't prove anything beyond that."

"And Marcus Penhurst's death?" Allegra said.

"His body was found in an alley in the Marais," Whitehead said. "The police say he was cruising for sex, and his family wants the case hushed up."

"I know she was involved somehow," Allegra said. "She and Marcus seemed thick as thieves to me when we visited."

"But nobody can prove anything," Todd said.

"Well, I think you'd both better try to forget about it," Hilton said. "You've nearly gotten yourselves killed and all because of me and that emerald."

"Did Kitty ever get to see the ring?" Allegra asked.

"Yes," he said. "I let her see it. Though I probably shouldn't have."

"Did you tell her that you'd bought it for her?" Todd asked.

"Yes," he said again. "And all hell broke loose when I told her I was going to return it to its rightful owner."

"She didn't want to give it up," Allegra said. She had met Kitty only briefly when they returned to New York, but she got the distinct feeling that Kitty was not the type of person to put much stock in concepts like rightful ownership.

"No way," Hilton said.

"You'll probably be made an honorary knight," Todd said.

"I doubt it," he said. "Nobody—and I mean nobody—is supposed to know that the emeralds were taken, much less that they were returned."

"It's a shame," Allegra said, "because you've really done a heroic thing."

"Thanks to you," he said, grinning. "You're the one who brought them all back in that little gym bag."

"So now that the engagement party's going on, what are you going to tell the guests?" Todd asked. "I mean, with Kitty gone."

"Well, I'm sure not going to announce my engagement," he said. "I'll probably never see her again."

"Do you miss her?" Allegra asked.

"Yes," he said, nodding. He shrugged. "You know, I always knew she was a kind of hustler. Hell, I am, too. Pulled myself up by my bootstraps like she did. Nothing wrong with that. But in the end she crossed a line. A kind of moral line as far as I'm concerned."

There was a knock on the door. "Who is it?" Hilton called out.

"Jason."

"Come on in, Jason," Hilton said.

The door opened, and Jason stepped into the suite. "Oh, I hope I'm not interrupting."

"No, I don't think so," Hilton said, indicating a chair. "Sit down."

Jason eased himself into the chair and took a sip of the drink he was carrying with him.

"I had a talk with Jason here," Hilton said. "He told me all about your business and, incidentally, about what he'd done while you were gone."

Jason's face reddened. "I hope that I can make it up to you, Ally."

"You already have," she said. She looked back at Hilton. "But what is it you've been discussing?"

"I know your business has been suffering, and I thought that I'd help you out. I really owe you."

Allegra began shaking her head vigorously. "No way," she said. "Stop right there. I appreciate your offer, but no thanks. Besides"—she looked at Todd and smiled—"I'm going to be opening a retail shop in a building that Todd's bought. He and I are going to be living there together."

"Well, that's good news," Hilton said. "Congratulations to both of you."

"Thanks," Todd and Allegra said in unison.

Hilton looked over at Jason. "It's exactly like you said it would be."

Jason nodded. "She's a hard case."

Todd laughed. "It's all I could do to get her to take up my offer of having a shop in the building."

"Then I would like to make this evening's festivities a publicity party for the opening of the Atelier Sheridan in Soho. The hot new jewelry shop in Manhattan," Hilton said. He held up his hands to stave off the protestations he could see that Allegra was about to make. "Give me just a minute. The press is here, and you'd get a lot of advance publicity that wouldn't cost you a dime. Come on, Allegra. Let me do this for you."

Allegra looked at him, then Todd, then Jason. "Well, I don't know," she said. "The shop isn't even open yet, and . . . I don't have a press kit or anything."

"Yes, you do," Jason said.

"What?" Allegra looked over at him.

"I hated to go behind your back again," Jason said, "but after Todd told me about your plans, I thought I would try to make things up to you. So I had a brochure printed and brought samples with me. Don't kill me, Ally. It's—"

"I'm not going to kill you," she said. She got up and went over and kissed him on the cheek. "Thank you," she said. "But you've got to promise to stop going behind my back."

"I will," Jason said with a laugh. "I promise."

"So," Whitehead said as Allegra went back to her seat beside Todd, "since you're going to be moving in together, maybe you'd like this to be your engagement party, too?"

Todd turned to Allegra, and she looked at him. He didn't say anything, but she knew what he wanted her to say. "I . . . well . . . I guess we could do that. That is, if you really want to, Todd."

He threw his arms around her. "You know I do, Ally, and so do you."

"Yes," she said. "I do."

Acknowledgments

If the first thing you did when you started this novel was flip to the back to check out the ending, I hope you'll reconsider if you've stumbled upon the acknowledgments and wait to read them. You'll have more fun that way. In any case, while this novel is entirely a work of fiction, its springboard was a bit of interesting history. Emeralds that purportedly had belonged to Queen Alexandra and were bequeathed to King Edward VIII, her grandson—who was later to become the Duke of Windsor when he gave up the throne to marry the American divorcée Wallis Simpson— were rumored for many years to have disappeared with the duke and duchess when they left England for a life in exile. Many people believed that the Duchess of Windsor had wheedled them out of the duke. More likely, some historians believe, Queen Alexandra's emeralds were distributed among female members of the family. Years later, the duchess's jewelry box was stolen while she and the duke were staying in the country with the Earl and Countess of Dudley, and rumors flew around London that Buckingham Palace was responsible for the robbery because they wanted Queen Alexandra's emeralds back. Whatever the case, at least thirty pieces of jewelry that had been reported stolen in the robbery—on which the insurance was collected by the Windsors—turned up at the sale of the duchess's jewels in Geneva in 1987 after her death. If the duke and duchess ever had the emeralds, which is doubtful, they never resurfaced, separately or collectively.

I owe a debt of gratitude to the late Lady Caroline Blackwood, whose fascinating book *The Last of the Duchess* (New York: Pantheon Books, 1995) first alerted me to the story of the missing jewels. She discussed them at some length in her study of the Duchess of Windsor's last days in Paris as a virtual prisoner of her powerful lawyer, Maître Blum. In addition, the missing jewels and the rumors surrounding them are among the startling revelations about the life of the Duchess of Windsor in Charles Higham's book *The Duchess of Windsor: The Secret Life* (New York: McGraw-Hill, 1988). The remainder of my story is total fiction.

I would also like to thank Laura Lapachin and Stefan Friedemann of Ornamentum Jewelry Studio and Gallery in Hudson, New York, for their invaluable tutelage on jewelry making and design. I hope your shop flourishes. My gratitude also extends to jeweler David Gourgourinis and Ivo Stoykov of Mykonos, Greece, and Boca Raton, Florida, whose stories about the jewelry trade, intelligence, hospitality, and, above all, wit have been an inspiration.